ROUGH LOVE

LAUREN LANDISH

Edited by
VALORIE CLIFTON
Edited by
STACI ETHERIDGE

ALSO BY LAUREN LANDISH

CHAPTER 1

BRUCE

"*F*uck, it's hot!" I bark to no one as the screen door slams behind me, blocking out at least a portion of the August heat. The sweat rag I'm using to wipe my face down is about as useless as tits on a bull, already soaked through, wrung out, and soaked again.

But as I open my eyes to the coolness of the kitchen, it's not the heat from outside that stops me in my tracks. It's the one raised eyebrow and glaring eyes on the face of the otherwise sweet woman in front of me. "Language, son."

Busted in my own damn house. How's that even happen? "Uh, hey there, Mama Louise. Didn't expect to see you over here."

There's a question in there somewhere, something along the lines of *'what the fuck are you doing in my kitchen?'* but I don't dare voice it out loud.

She ain't my mama, and I damn sure ain't her son, but as we've learned lately, sometimes, family is what you make of it, not what nature gives you. Mama Louise is the woman who has taken us Tannens on as fixer-upper projects. Me and my two brothers, Brody and Bobby, might as well be condemned buildings for all the work we need, but my little sister, Shayanne, seems to be doing okay with Mama Louise's motherly influence.

1

Regardless, everyone in town and out of town and the globe over calls this tiny blonde woman who could intimidate the sun itself to bend to her will 'Mama Louise'. She won't have it any other way, unless you feel fit to drop the Louise and just call her Mama, which makes her cheeks pink up in joy. So I don't do it. It doesn't feel right to do that to my own mom, may she rest in peace.

The other eyebrow raises to match its partner and I realize my misstep. "Sorry," I say simply, not really meaning it but willing to say it to keep her happy. It don't take much, and it's no skin off my back, so why not give her the little things? That way, she doesn't dig too hard for the big ones.

Shayanne grins from Mama Louise's side, enjoying seeing me put in my place, but she doesn't dare let those giggles that are shaking her shoulders free or Mama Louise will get after her too. Mama Louise dips her chin once in acknowledgement of my apology and then goes on as if I didn't just perform like some trained seal. Hell, if I'm doing tricks, where's my treat? Shouldn't I get a cookie or something?

I peek over Mama Louise's shoulder, hoping that maybe she *is* actually making cookies, even though I know she's neck deep in helping Shayanne. My sister is a force to be reckoned with, and one day, she's going to grow up to be just like Mama Louise, who keeps a household full of mannerless cowboys from going feral.

Of course, Shayanne helps with that, as do the other Bennett boys' wives. So maybe their work mostly consists of keeping us three Tannen boys in line. That's a full-time job that requires overtime on the regular, so Shay could probably use the backup because she's been doing it way too long on her own, even when she was barely a pipsqueak to us near-grown boys.

"What's next?" I say, giving up on my cookie dreams.

"Shayanne has one more round of deliveries for you today. Think you've got time before dinner?"

Mama Louise eyes the sun, which is sitting midway down the western sky. The ball of fire's position seems to light new urgency in her hands, and she pours the pink-tinted water through a strainer and into a big plastic jug.

They're working on Shayanne's latest creation . . . watermelon agua fresca. I'd teased her last spring that instead of people looking out for the milkman, they were going to be watching out their windows for the watermelon water woman. Which would be true, except that I swear I'm doing the bulk of her deliveries so she can keep up with the demand. At this point, I'm just glad she's making something of the watermelons we grew in one of the fields out back. It'd seemed like a lot when we started harvesting, but summer's not even two-thirds over and she's damn near used every last one of them in her special concoction of watermelon, lime, and sugar water.

"Yep, I've got time," I assure Mama Louise, starting to pick up the jugs for my first trip to the truck. Shayanne abandons her post to help me carry the load. She's got a spring to her step and as many jugs of pink drink in her tiny hands as I do in my big paws. Shay's a worker, down to the bone.

We step over Murphy, my old dog that doesn't even move as I grumble at him, "Git, Murph."

Instead, he rolls over like I'm going to set down the jugs in favor of belly scratches for him. I'm not a total asshole, though, so I do run my boot over his too-big gut a couple of times before pushing the door open with a hip and then holding it for Shay to come out too.

"Thanks, Bruce!" Shay's voice is bright and bubbly, happier than she's been in so long. Maybe ever. I guess I've got Luke Bennett to thank for that, not that I would ever thank him for fucking my sister's grumpiness out of her. But maybe for loving her, putting a ring on her finger, and showing her a world beyond our little pile of dirt . . .

Not that it's ours anymore.

Nope, thanks for that last knife in the back, Dad. He'd literally forced us to sell the farm when he died with his bad gambling debts, and we'd lucked out that our neighbors, the Bennetts, had wanted the land and had taken our motley crew on as ranch hands and pseudo-family.

The last seven months have been interesting, to say the least, but we're all settled into our roles for the most part. I've even seen

Brody smile a time or two, and that's like winning the Mega Power-ball Lotto for billions on a random, computer-drawn list of numbers . . . twice in two weeks. In other words, it doesn't happen. Ever.

But it did. I saw it with my own eyes, so maybe I'll pick up a dollar scratch-off while I'm in town and see if my odds are any better than usual. I snort at my own ridiculousness and Shay looks at me questioningly.

"Would you like to share with the class what's got you giggling?"

For the record, I don't giggle. Or chuckle. Or laugh. I smile on occasion, but it damn near cracks my face from lack of use. Well, maybe it's from turning that frown upside down. Hell, maybe Brody's smiled more than me lately. I'll have to consider that later.

"I'm fine, Shay, " I tell her, not answering her question in the slightest, but she lets me put her off. "Need to get going if I'm gonna get back by dinner. What're you and Mama Louise making? Maybe I should just grab a bite at Hank's instead?"

She stomps her booted foot. "You'd better not, Bruce Tannen. Family dinner tonight, no excuses." She purses her lips before tucking the bottom one behind her white teeth. "We've got some *special news*. You'll be there, right?"

I side-eye my little sister, dropping the not-that-heavy jugs onto my tailgate with a boom as if they weigh a ton. Her hair looks the same as always, brown with some streaks of blonde the sun puts there every summer. Her face is bare with a smattering of freckles across her nose and a bit too much sun on her cheeks from being outside every day. Her frayed shorts and watermelon-stained tank top are her usual work gear, and her boots are dusty and worn.

Nothing's out of place and nothing's unusual except for that glint in her eye.

"Are you fucking pregnant, Shayanne?" I grit out. I'm gonna kill Luke Bennett for sticking his dick in my sister. I mean, I know he does, and as much as it guts me, I guess she likes it, because she loves him and shit, but I don't need proof of their fucking walking around and calling me 'Uncle Bruce'. Or would a little Luke-Anne call me 'Uncle Brutal'?

Shit. Neither. Fucking neither is the correct answer.

Like the firecracker she is, Shay doesn't answer the damn question for two long seconds during which I figure out which field of dirt I can bury Luke's body in.

Not soon enough, she breaks and laughter rings out. Well, more like donkey guffaws because there ain't a thing prissy about my sister. But through the hee-haws, I gather that she's laughing at me.

"Oh, my cheesus and crackers, you should'a seen your face, Bruce! Priceless! Shoot, I wish I'd gotten a picture of that!"

I push closer to her, looming over her like only a threatening big brother can, but she's not the least bit scared of me. Probably the only person who isn't in this whole town.

"Shayanne Tannen, are you or are you not pregnant?"

She holds her hand up, admiring the way the sunlight catches her ring. "That's Shayanne Bennett, and you know it. You were there when Luke and I said our vows about loving and honoring and cherishing and obeying each other. Oh, yeah, especially that last one. You know I love when he tells me what to do."

She's being ornery and we both know it. There ain't a soul on this planet who tells my sister what to do. Hell, Luke's probably tried a time or two . . . again, not thinking of him railing my sister . . . and she'd probably still do whatever the fuck she wanted. I grind my teeth together, not sure if I want to strangle her neck or protect another generation of Tannens if she's got one in her belly.

"Shay," I say dangerously low and quiet. It's my line, letting her know that I've had enough.

"Fine, fine. No, party pooper. I'm not pregnant, though that honeymoon was something else. Some. Thing. Else. Whoo, boy. I didn't know reverse cowgirl was so much fun. Why didn't you tell me, big brother?"

I can't headbutt my truck, so I skip the words I can't handle and go for the important one. "You're not pregnant? Then what's the big news?" I say. Or growl. Same difference, mostly.

She boops me on the nose with zero fear for her own life, the only person on Earth who can do that. "Guess you'll have to show back up to find out."

And like that was an answer at all, she spins on her heel and skips, literally skips, back to the house, leaving me feeling like I just ran a marathon when all I did was walk from the kitchen to the driveway.

On second thought, good for Luke. If he can handle all that, good for him. Less for me and my brothers to have to deal with. I try to convince myself that's true and remind myself that I like Luke, that I was the one who knew Shay was sneaking out to go meet him long before anyone else did and even helped her cover her late-night proclivities. It works, a little bit.

I take two more trips back and forth from the kitchen to the truck, stepping over Murphy and listening to Shayanne and Mama Louise chattering away, though about what I have no idea, and for now, I don't care.

That's unlike me. I'm usually the silent sleeper who people somehow forget about, even though I'm the size of a barn and I listen intently to just about everything that goes on. I watch people, I listen to them, and I analyze them. I'm not particularly smart book-wise, but I'm observant, and sometimes, that's even more important.

But right now, I just want to check these deliveries off my to-do list, eat some dinner, and crash into bed.

"Bye, ladies. I'll be back for dinner," I tell them with my last load, and they both toss an easy smile my way.

Shay's happy, and that makes me happy. Way deep down in my heart, beneath all the mud and muck this farm boy is known for these days.

I SLAM THE DOOR OF MY TRUCK, DAMN NEAR PEELING OUT OF THE driveway of my last stop. Even though I'm ready to get the hell outta dodge, I glance up at Millicent Jenkinson, who's standing in her doorway waving at me. She's a nice old lady, but I really don't need another grandma trying to set me up with her granddaughter, and she was the third just today. I don't know why they think subjecting their beloved daughters and granddaughters to a bastard like me is a good idea. Maybe they're just desperate and figure beggars can't be choosers. Because nobody's choosing me willingly. Too big, too gruff, too quiet.

Little do they know, those are my best qualities.

But I'm not a complete asshole, so I toss a two-fingered wave to Mrs. Jenkinson from the steering wheel and drive away without revving my engine. Much.

The Chris Stapleton song on the radio is a good one, not as good as Bobby's, but it'll do for the drive back home. I'm in town but on the far west side from home, and with all the booming growth Great Falls has had the last few years, traffic will be piled up until I reach the city limits. We're still not big by any stretch, but the roads haven't quite caught up yet. This could take a while, but a look at the clock tells me I can still make dinner.

Music and dinner are all that's on my mind as I sit at the stoplight until I see a group of boys running around a field at the park beside me. In the three rounds of green, yellow, red, I haven't even made it to the light's white line, but my heart's already beating just a little too hard.

It looks like a football practice, or what's *supposed* to be one. There are probably twelve boys out there, around eight or nine years old, I'd guess, not that I'm good at judging kids' ages. But they're goofing around with a pigskin, playing more keep-away than running plays.

I remember being that small, just learning the ropes and enjoying every minute of it. Coaches yelling advice, Dad proudly clapping me on the back when I did well, and Mom cheering from the sidelines. We were so little, there weren't even bleachers, just foldable camping chairs the parents would set out to watch us play. It was picturesque and easy, and the bulk of my childhood centers around those happy memories.

I learned a lot on those fields in the early days, lessons that carried me through puberty and later, through high school in ways both good and bad. Football gave me a focus, a drive, and made me who I am. I hope for the same for those random boys.

A sentimental smile crosses my face, two in one day, which is probably a record for me. But it's premature because in the next instant, I see two of the bigger boys tackle one of the smaller guys. He goes down hard, and it was definitely not a clean hit or a good fall. To add insult to injury, I see one of the tackling boys, a blonde-haired lanky kid, dig a toe into the other kid's side.

Not just dirty but mean.

It shouldn't be like that. Not at that age, not ever. If you're not good enough to earn the win, take the L and do the work to deserve it next time.

I blink, and I'm pulling into the parking lot of the park, marching across the field. "Hey! You! What the hell are you doing?"

Who said that?

Well, *shit*. Guess that was my grumbling voice calling out Mr. Kicks-A-Lot. The kid looks like he's about to piss himself, which would serve him right.

I lean over and set the smaller kid back on his feet. He's got dark hair, which he shoves out of his face revealing big, frosty blue eyes that'll serve him well with the ladies later in life.

"You all right, kid?" His lower lip trembles, and I realize belatedly that it might be partially from the tackle and partially because I'm a scary looking motherfucker. Especially to someone his size.

I bend down, taking a knee and pulling my shoulders in to round them. It's as small and unimposing as I can get. I even smile to soften the fear factor I cause.

"It's okay, you ain't in trouble. But those shits might be."

I throw an arched eyebrow to the other kid, who's standing with his buddy-slash-partner in crime. While my attention was focused on the little guy, Kicks-A-Lot is digging down and finding his attitude, judging by the sneer on his face. He kinda reminds me of Brody in a four-foot-tall sort of way.

Little Guy sniffles once, but it turns into a sort of laugh. "You can't say that." I look at him questioningly. He shakes his head, the laughter blooming a little louder. "You can't say the S word."

I do honestly grin at that. Out of everything that just went down, getting tackled, kicked, and having some random guy step in to save his ass, he's worried about my language.

Mama Louise would like this kid, I think to myself.

"Uh, sorry. Just wanted to make sure you were all right. Saw what happened, and that's not all right." I say the last bit over my shoulder, accompanying it with a glare at Kicks-A-Lot.

Little Guy nods like a bobblehead. "I'm good. Johnathan's just mad that I can actually create a play, not just go where I'm told like a dog. Woof, woof!"

He smirks at Kicks-A-Lot, I mean Johnathan, like a badass. Little Guy's got big brass ones, I'll give him that. Something tells me it's not because he's got me for backup, either. If I had to guess, judging by the prepubescent testosterone floating through the air, Little Guy might've earned that tackle. Just a little bit.

And don't that just change the whole situation.

"I'm Bruce. What's your name?" I ask him, not sure what I plan to do with the information, but it seems like the proper thing to do.

"Cooper, but most folks call me Coop." He shrugs like he kinda wishes he hadn't said that part.

Johnathan's buddy pipes up, "Because you're a chicken, Coop. Bok, bok, bok." Several of the kids laugh at that and Coop flushes. No, not Coop, because that ain't right if they're nicknaming him to be cruel.

I turn my full attention to the gaggle of boys, stroking my beard like I'm thinking mighty hard about something. "Seems to me that the only chickens here are you bunch. Cooper," I say his full name with a bit of extra emphasis, "took a hit and got up swinging, verbally, at least. Took the whole lot of you to mob up on one little guy. That don't seem much like the chicken you're talking about."

They look suitably chastised, a couple of them even rubbing their toes in the dirt. But I'm not done. "Besides, you wanna know a secret?"

Twelve sets of eyes look at me with curiosity and I swear a couple of them lean in. I lower my voice like I'm imparting great knowledge, rumbling, "Chickens are mean as hell. They'll peck your hands even as you're feeding them. Yep, mean little things."

I nod sagely, pointing at some of the rough scars on my working hands. None of them are really from chickens, but these kids don't know that.

"My brother's got a whole flock of them, and a rooster too. He'll wake you up long before the sun even peeks over the horizon, and his girls lay enough eggs that she can feed our whole family breakfast every day. All the while pecking the sh-*stuffing* outta ya."

I correct my language at the last second, thinking Mama Louise would be proud.

Somewhere from my left, a voice cracks out, "How many eggs is that? You got a big family or a small one?"

I tap my temple, winking. "Smart question, kid. I guess it's a big family, but mostly because we're all big guys and big eaters. There's six of us like me, my sister, two other women, and one of them's got a baby but she don't eat much yet, and then Mama Louise. So we get enough eggs for ten people to eat breakfast, I reckon."

Rattling off the attendance roster of breakfast brings home just how much my life has changed in the last few months, because damned if it doesn't seem like those folks are something to me. Maybe not family, exactly, not really, but I'd do anything for Mama Louise and most things for the rest of the Bennett boys, which is a far cry from our previous pointless feud that was based on Dad's whims. I'm glad that's done and over with, even if it took his passing to make things right.

The same kid whistles. "That is a big family. You say you got brothers the same size as you?"

I can feel those same sets of eyes measuring me, so I go ahead and broaden my shoulders back out but keep my lower profile on my knee. "Well, let's be real, there's not a lot of folks as big as me. But my brothers are close enough."

They laugh like that was funny. I guess it might've been. "Hard to believe that once upon a time, I was as small as you guys." I hold my arms out wide, showing off my wingspan and the big paws attached to my wrists. "Eat your veggies, work hard, play right, and you can be a big motherfu— I mean, a big guy like me one day."

The boys start flexing, working their lungs more than their biceps as they hold their breath and try to show off to one another. And to me, I realize with a hint of humor.

From across the field, a voice calls out. "Hey, guys, I'm here."

I look up to see a thirty-something-looking guy hustling across the field, eyes locked on me. "Who's that?" I ask the kids.

Cooper says from beside me, "Coach Mike. He's Evan's dad."

There's the smallest, tiniest hitch beneath the words, something most folks probably wouldn't even hear. But I do.

When he gets close, I can see his eyes darting from me to the boys, like he's checking each one of them over and head counting his ducklings while never taking his attention off the interloper. He's a good dad, I'd bet.

He holds his hand out. "Mike Kauffman, Evan's dad. And you are?"

I take his hand, careful to walk the fine line of a solid handshake without breaking his hand accidentally. "Bruce Tannen. I was just happening by and saw some roughhousing. Thought a little intervention was warranted."

I purposefully don't say any names, feeling like I've handled what happened well enough and hoping it made an impression.

Mike looks behind him to the parking lot and then shakes his head. "There's literally six or seven moms sitting over there in their cars or at the playground with little brothers and sisters, and you're telling me that you just walked up to the boys and no one said a word to you? Stranger-danger mean nothing these days?"

Seems like he's asking that of the boys as much as the universe.

I hold my arms out wide, showing I'm no threat. "Look, man, didn't mean to cause problems. Just saw a dirty tackle, a bad fall, and some overzealous afterplay. Wanted to make sure everyone was all right because there didn't seem to be anyone overseeing practice. No worries, I'll leave you to it."

Mike's still watching me carefully, which I can appreciate. At least these kids have proper supervision, though he's got a point that I'm a scary looking bastard for not a single parent to have said a word. We live in a safe town, but nowhere's *that* safe.

I hold a meaty fist out to Cooper, giving the kid a tame half-strength glare. "Watch that mouth."

He bumps my hand with his own, a smirk curling his lips. "I will, but I can back it up, and that's what counts, right?"

He says it like someone's told him that before. I raise a brow, silently telling him to think again.

I offer my fist to Johnathan too, who returns the goodbye with a bit less cockiness. "Words first, then get it out on the field correctly. Head up, shoulders down, feet buzzing, drop into position, and shoot and rip."

He nods like he took a mental note of everything I just said.

I toss a two-finger wave to Mike. "Have a good practice, Coach."

I'm halfway across the field, almost home free to the parking lot to head home for dinner when I hear a voice behind me call out.

"Brutal?"

CHAPTER 2

BRUCE

$\mathscr{I}$ turn around automatically, more used to the nickname almost everyone calls me by than the name my mom gave me when I was born. "Yeah?"

Mike's eyebrows rise up to his hairline, or where it used to be, at least. His hair's buzzed down, and based on the slight dips above his temples, my bet is he's disguising an early receding hairline.

"You're Brutal Tannen?" he asks, and I nod once in confirmation. He claps his hands once before sticking his hand out for another shake like we didn't already introduce ourselves. "Why didn't you say so?"

I shake his hand again, though I'm not sure why, and lift and lower one shoulder. "I . . . did?"

He chuckles like I said something funny. "No, you said your name is Bruce, like you're not known around here for being one of the best football players to ever grace the grass in the whole city. Didn't you play for State too? Figured you were going pro!"

He recites my history like he has a clue. I thought I was going to get drafted too.

Plans changed.

"What happened?" he pries.

I grit my teeth. It's been years and I'm over it, but I don't think

13

it's ever easy to expose your greatest pain for public consumption, especially to someone you don't even know.

"Family stuff," I say coldly, not inviting further discussion.

Mike seems to realize that he's overstepped and retreats politely. "Yeah, I get it. Family's everything. Anyway, I was thinking . . . since you're here, you think you might hang out and help with practice? Like a guest coach or something?"

He looks hopeful, but I don't feed into it. "Nah, sorry. Gotta get home, got dinner waiting."

"Oh, uh . . . yeah. Of course," he stutters, like my refusal was not at all what he was expecting. "I was just hoping you might . . . I mean, you've got a lot more knowledge about football than I do. I'm more of an armchair quarterback, if you know what I mean, but Evan wants to play and I was the only dad who would do it. Kinda got *voluntold* by the wife."

He tapers off, not saying anything bad about his wife, and the smile on his face says he doesn't mind being voluntold for this gig at all. Past him, I can see those same sets of eyes watching our interaction. All except one pair of icy blue ones that are fastidiously studying the laces of the football in his hands. Something about that hits me. This smart-mouthy kid doesn't think for one second that I'm going to do this.

Has he been disappointed before and is protecting himself from useless hopes? Or can he see that I'm not cut out for helping kids figure out the game I know inside and out? Considering I said 'the s-word' within moments of walking up, it's likely the latter. But lack of a filter aside, I could probably help them with football and the most important part of the game, being a team.

I gnaw on that for a quick second, dissecting my reasons and remembering my youth on the field.

Football was everything to me for so long, truly saving me. Mostly from myself. Could one of these boys need that opportunity to? Could I help with that?

Though that's really bigger than what Mike's asking right now, he just wants a couple of hours of my time. That, I can do.

I sigh, testing the words on my tongue. "Yeah, I could hang out for a little bit, I guess. Let me just send a text home."

He smiles heartily. "Of course, thanks! I'll just tell the boys."

He steps away, and I fish my phone out of my back pocket. I remember a moment too late that I promised Shayanne I'd be home for dinner, but I feel like these boys need me more than she does today, especially for some special announcement she's making that's definitely not that she's pregnant.

Hell, she's probably just gonna tell us all that she and Luke are going on another trip. I don't begrudge her that excitement, but I don't need to be there to hear the blow-by-blow of their itinerary. Especially not the first time because she'll talk about nothing else for days if that's what her news is.

Still, even though I know she'll be fine when I explain why I'm skipping dinner, I decide to not incite Shayanne's wrath by texting her directly. I bypass her and text Brody instead.

Something came up, won't be home for dinner. Tell Shay sorry.

I get back a middle finger emoji so I check that off my responsibility list and head over to the boys, who are all sitting cross-legged and listening intently to Mike, who's singing the praises of my high school glory days.

"All right, Brutal . . . or, uh, Bruce. Which do you prefer? Or Coach B, even?" he asks. I can tell that in his mind, it stands for Brutal and that he really wants to call me that. Like I'm famous or some shit when all I did was crunch a few bodies damn near ten years ago.

"Coach B is fine," I tell him and the boys. Though everyone calls me Brutal, and I answer to it readily, I've never felt right introducing myself that way. The name brings up too many questions when you're a grown ass man who looks like I do. "I think first things first, I need to know everyone's name."

The boys start rattling off their names from their seated positions, and after three, I stop them. "Okay, hold up. Let's start with the proper way to introduce yourself, especially when you're looking to impress. Whether that's a coach, an employer, a girl's dad . . ." The boys giggle a bit and my lips quirk. "Or whoever. So, you stand up. Never introduce yourself to anyone sitting down. Offer a hand and shake firmly, but don't do that stupid squeezy thing where you're trying to break their hand. Look them in the eye and say your name clearly and loud enough to be heard. Like this."

I turn to Mike, dipping my chin to make sure he's on board with being an example for the boys. I hold my hand out and clasp his. "Bruce Tannen. Nice to meet you."

"Mike Kauffman. Good to meet you too."

We both turn back to the boys and I continue the lesson. "Your turn."

The first boy stands up. "Johnathan Williams. Nice to meet you." Seems Mr. Kicks-A-Lot is a fast learner, a plus in his column, especially given the good handshake and eye contact he offers me.

Down the row they go.

Evan Kauffman. Joshua Williams, apparently Johnathan's fraternal twin brother. Killian Bloomdale. Cooper Meyers. Anthony Mondela. Christopher White. Derek Simpson. Liam Holt. Julio Ruiz. Trey Thedwell. Marcus Stacy.

A better-behaved group of young men stands before me than were on this field just a few short minutes ago. "Nice to meet everyone. Great job, guys." I turn to Mike, moving on. "What did you have planned for practice?"

He shrugs, admitting, "It's only our second practice, our first active one because the last one was mostly going over rules and dates for the practices and games. I figured we'd run sprints and do a few drills today."

I nod. It's a good start. "Sounds good. Can I make a suggestion?"

Mike smiles warmly. "That's why I asked you to stay. Please do." He gestures toward the kids who are watching, waiting for any tidbit I can share.

I search my head for the words I'd heard from one of my favorite coaches. I've had many over the years, some great, some good, and some just okay.

I drop down to my knee again and address the kids. "What's the most important thing about a football team?"

"Touchdowns!" Derek shouts, his arms reaching over his head like a referee.

"Winning!" Killian corrects.

There's a few more suggestions, so I hold my hands up to stop their guesses and give the answer I was looking for. "Teamwork. Football is the only sport in the world where you need eleven people doing eleven different things, but all of them working toward a single goal. If even one of them is off, the whole thing falls apart. You might be the fastest sprinter, the fiercest linebacker, or be able to throw a perfect spiral and hit a target a whole field away, but without the whole team working together, you'll never win a game, regardless of what the scoreboard says."

Tiny bobbleheads all nod as if they're soaking up the words of wisdom. I say a silent thank you to Coach Stadler for saying them to me when I was not much older than this group and for then teaching me what they meant.

"Let's do what Coach Mike had planned and run. But with a small tweak. Instead of sprints, we're going to run as a team. I think three laps around the park should be a good start. This won't be like the races you do at school or even like the drills you'll do later where you can show Coach Mike what you've got individually. For this, we'll stay together at a pace slightly faster than the slowest and slightly slower than the fastest. We'll adjust as needed, but the important thing is . . . no man gets left behind. We cross the finish line together or we've already lost. Understood?"

"Yes, Coach B," they sound out as one.

I nod to Mike, all business. "You up for this?"

He looks surprised, his dad bod already flushing. "Us too?"

"Well, yeah. Team includes the coach. Lead by example." He looks at my boots and jeans pointedly, making it clear that I'm not dressed for running. I dig my heel into the turf, amused. "I wear boots and jeans in the fields all day, every day. I could run in these for miles if needed."

Any excuses gone, he shakes his head and chuckles, but he walks over to the gathered boys with me. "All right, this isn't a ready-set-go type of thing, so I'll just count us off. We'll practice this first bit and I'll call out which foot to run on so we stay together, but the goal is for you to not need me or Coach Mike to set your pace but rather for you to be in tune with the man next to you, on and on down the line. That's how you become a team. Got it?"

They seem ready to roll, so I call out, "One, two, three . . ." And we're off, not like speeding bullets but rather like slow-plodding sloths, each kid unwilling to go faster than the one next to him. The lesson is already sticking, but I speed them up a little bit. "Left, left, left, right, left." It's not quite military precision, and some of these boys probably aren't even sure which is right and which is left, but together, we make our way around the park.

The second lap is a bit faster, and I don't have to say a word to keep the boys together. They do it naturally and a warmth fills my chest. The third lap finds us slowing back down a bit, exhaustion starting to hit us. But we cross the fence post of the finish line together and all twelve boys cheer for themselves, high-fives given freely between all of them, even Johnathan and Cooper.

"Great job, guys," Mike says breathlessly. He's got his hands on his knees, not exactly gasping for air but damn close. "Take five, get water, and then we'll regroup for drills."

The boys all run toward their bags, newfound energy from their youth bursting forth.

Mike watches them and then turns one hairy eyeball at me. "Shit, man. I'm in decent shape, lift weights three times a week, but hitting the treadmill ain't nothing compared to running on uneven grass trying to keep up with those pipsqueaks." It's not an insult in the least. Instead, he seems pretty impressed with his team.

One side of my mouth quirks up. "I know. I work my ass off in the fields, but I don't think I've actually run flat-out in way too long. It was good, though, for all of us."

Mike nods his agreement as he puts his hands on his head. "So, drills next? What do you think?"

I squint at the boys. "First practice, you said? You know who's got an arm and who can catch yet?"

"Nah, most of these boys have played flag football before, but not all of them, so there might be a sleeper pro." He grins even as he says it.

"How about we do a couple of tossing drills then? See who can throw for distance, for accuracy, and with any form to speak of. And then reverse and see who can catch an easy toss."

For the next hour, as the sun races across the sky, we do just that. A line of boys throwing to Mike and me and then us throwing to them. After a while, we gather back up in a huddle and Mike tells the boys they did a great job. He gives them a parental look of expectancy and they turn to me as one. "Thanks, Coach B!"

"Thanks for letting me jump into your practice today, guys. It was a lot of fun. You're gonna have a great season," I say honestly. Being back on the field, even if it's just a bumpy field in a city park, brought back good memories, back when life was simpler, things were easier, and football was the solution to all my nonexistent problems. I don't mention the behavior that warranted my stopping in the first place, the incident forgiven but not forgotten.

Unprompted, the boys all line up to give me another handshake and do the same with Mike, which makes me feel like my earlier lesson did some good. And then they're off like the rambunctious kids they are, bags flying onto shoulders, loud shouts, and tumbling feet.

I watch them go, Mike at my side. "You did good today, Brutal. Those boys might not know what a treat they got, but I certainly do. You're something else."

I feel heat on my face, and I shake my head. "Once upon a time, maybe."

Mike scoffs. "And today. Not many would've stopped to help Cooper, and even fewer would've helped with practice the way you did."

"That kid's got a mouth. He might've earned a little bit of that. But just a little." I hold my thumb and finger up an inch apart. "The rest was uncalled for."

"Agreed. So, about that . . . about practice . . ." Mike pauses, looking at me curiously. "Like I said, I'm here for Evan, but I'm just the best they got out of a nonexistent pile of options. A couple of the

19

boys don't have dads for various reasons. Killian lives with his grandparents, and the ones with two parents didn't have anyone else step up to coach." He chuckles. "Not sure if that says Jamie's got me whipped or what because here I am."

He holds his hands out wide and then places them on his hips. "What I'm trying to say is . . . you interested in being an assistant coach? I could sure use the help, and the boys could use the expertise."

I shake my head no on autopilot, without even thinking it over for a second. "I don't think so. That ain't me. I'm no coach."

Mike's grin and bark of laughter are ones of disbelief. "Pretty sure there are twelve boys who'd disagree with you on that. Think it over. You don't have to answer now. Here's my number." He reaches down to his bag, pulling out a piece of paper and scribbling his information down. I take it, slipping it into my back pocket. It feels heavy with possibility.

Could I? Should I?

"You'd have to pass the background check and be listed on the roster or they won't let you on the sidelines at the games, but we can do that quickly. Plenty of time before the first game. Practices are here on Tuesdays and Thursdays at seven, Saturday mornings at ten, and the first game is several weeks away. We could use you, man. For all of it, any of it, whatever you're willing to volunteer for." He holds his hand out once more and I shake it firmly.

"Thank you, Mike. Truly. I'll think about it."

And I do. All the way home, down the paved asphalt of town, to the dirt of our driveway. I sit in the truck, not getting out and thinking.

I don't hear him coming, but the air is disturbed for a moment before the passenger door opens and Brody climbs in, slamming the door behind him.

"What are we doing?" he says casually. We both know there's nothing casual about his question.

"Thinking," I answer drolly. His quirked eyebrow says that's not enough, not nearly enough. I drum my fingers on the steering wheel. "Helped with a kids' football practice tonight. Coach asked me to come back and help again."

I don't think I could've surprised him more if I'd said I found a goose laying golden eggs and a giant beanstalk in town. "How the fuck did *that* happen?"

I relate the story of seeing the boys getting after Cooper and finish with Mike asking me to help.

Brody rubs at his bottom lip with his thumb, humming to himself. "You're thinking about doing it."

It's not a question. I see a lot, am observant to a fault, but Brody knows us all better than we know ourselves. He knows that football was always mine, my way of dealing with anything and everything. "You'd be good at it," he adds.

It's a rousing stamp of approval from my stoic brother. He might as well be waving pom-poms around and cheering like some shit-bad cheerleader.

"I'm thinking about it," I concede. It's all I can give for now. Changing the subject, I tease out how much trouble I'm in. "What was Shay's big news, and how mad is she that I didn't show?"

Brody takes his hat off, rolling the brim in his hands and sighing. "Another trip. Fuck, you know I love our sister dearly, would kill for her, but I really don't need to hear about every single pin she's sticking on her map. It's not even a big one! They're going to south Texas, for fuck's sake. As for you, she'll make you pay. No mistaking that."

He's right, but I don't mind. Tonight was interesting and different, and I can take Shay's punishment with one hand tied behind my back.

CHAPTER 3

ALLYSON

"*A*nd then Coach B and Coach Mike had us doing fast feet drills up and down the field," Cooper says excitedly, demonstrating by tap-dancing his feet across the wood floor of our rental house in town.

I smile. At least I think I do, but truthfully, I've only had one sip of coffee so far and I'm not firing on all cylinders yet. I wish Cooper would sleep in just a little later on the weekends, but I try to remind myself that too soon, he'll be a teenager who sleeps all day and I should enjoy his early morning energy. Maybe even suck a little bit of it up for myself.

Lord knows I could use it after the week I've had. Work has been weighing me down, long hours in the office poring over legal briefs and research, bringing folders of case information home to work on after Cooper goes to bed, and preparing for an important mediation meeting in a couple of weeks.

On top of those responsibilities, Cooper started football practice and has talked non-stop about it ever since. He's only had two practices, so I'm dreading, just a tiny bit, how much more football this boy can verbally throw at me.

"Footwork looks good, honey," I tell him, not really knowing if that's true or not but wanting to support his interest and hard work.

He does it again, forward and then backward, from the kitchen to the front door and back.

"Light and quick like a ballerina," Cooper says, surprising me.

"A ballerina?" I question.

He nods wisely, his eyes wide as he obviously recites, "How do you think ballerinas can move so fast?" He swishes his arms on top of each other, switching them in an imitation of a ballerina's feet. "They gotta be light on their feet so they can be quick. If not, they'd miss every play before they could get to the ball. Light and quick." Changing from his recitation, he asks, "Hey, Mom, did you know ballerinas dance until their feet bleed?"

My brows pull together. "Uh, yeah? Why so much talk about ballet all of a sudden?" The possibilities are already swirling around in my mind—do I make him finish the season since he made the commitment? Do I let him move on to what's apparently a new interest? What made him so interested?

Cooper shrugs his little shoulder. "Coach B was telling us about them being so fast, and Trey said he wanted to be a tough football player, not a prissy dancer. Coach Mike cringed like this—" He pulls his face, mimicking an unhappy Coach Mike. "But Coach B said ballerinas are some of the toughest athletes and showed us a video of their mangled up feets after a show."

He crumples his fingers into claws, showing me what their feet were like. "Like bloody claws with toes on 'em."

"Okay . . . first off, eww. Secondly, it's feet, not feets. Feet is the plural of the singular foot, honey. So, you don't want to do ballet?" I'm trying really hard to keep up with this kid's mental gymnastics, so I take a good long pull of coffee to corral the few brain cells that are awake and alert and encourage a few more to join the party.

It's Cooper's turn to pull his eyebrows together in confusion. "What? No, I love football. Coach B was just talking about ballet because of the footwork." He does his little tap-dancing routine across the room and back.

I shake my head, feeling like I just went on a trip that wasn't even needed. But I'm doing my best to do anything I can for Cooper and to do it all right. That's what single moms do, be everything in one. And I do it gratefully . . . for him.

"Well, now that's settled, how about some breakfast before we leave for practice? What do you want this morning?" I open the fridge, peering inside like inspiration will strike me.

"Eggs and bacon, and biscuits and gravy if you got any," my tiny, barely eats anything kid answers.

I lean back to catch his eye, one brow quirked and my lips tilted up. "That's a mighty big breakfast. Think you can handle all that?"

He nods so fast I think his head might fall off. "Coach Mike says growing athletes need fuel. Food is fuel, and occasionally fun. Like cake and donuts. But everyday stuff should be protein, fat, and complex carbs. One gram of protein per two pounds of body weight!"

I have to bite my lip to keep from giggling. This kid is eight years old and schooling me on nutritional facts like he's an expert. "Is that so?" I pull out the eggs, checking the date, and then dig around. I don't have any bacon, but I've got frozen sausage patties and a popping roll of biscuits. "And just how big is a gram? Tell you what . . . how about a biscuit, egg, and sausage sandwich?"

He seems to think about it and then decides it'll do. "Can you put jelly on it? I know that's sugary, but a little's probably okay, right?"

I set the jar of grape jelly on the table. "You can do it yourself . . . carefully."

While I make us breakfast sandwiches, Cooper tells me all about his two whole football practices. I think it takes him longer to tell me about them than it did for him to actually go. But I love listening to him ramble happily about his coaches, his teammates, what he's learned. He sounds good, happy, and carefree, which is all I ever wanted for him.

Giving this life to him is why I left our previous one. He's why I finally found the courage. Because this right here, breakfast sandwiches and football practices and silly stories, is what he deserves.

"So, tell me again, Coach Mike is Derek's dad? And whose dad is Coach B?" I'm trying to keep it all straight, but it's a lot for people

I haven't even met yet. My friend Michelle did carpool duty for me Tuesday and Thursday this week. Her son, Liam, is on the team with Cooper, and she's an absolute godsend to us. Though she'd probably say the same thing about me and Cooper.

Michelle's married, but her husband travels for work a lot, though I don't know what exactly he does. She always describes it as 'something with sales and robotic medical devices' like she doesn't know either, but with her being a pseudo-single mom sometimes and me being an actual single mom, we became fast friends when the boys started kindergarten. We'd bonded pretty hilariously over *not* wanting to be room mom while the other women were literally racing over each other to sign up.

Cooper's mouth is full, but he shakes his head. After swallowing, he corrects me. "No, Coach Mike is Evan's dad. Coach B is just one of Coach Mike's friends."

Something about that seems strange. I mean, most of the teams are fighting to get one person to step up and coach. So for this guy to help out and not even have a kid seems . . . odd? Maybe I'm jumping the gun, but I'm protective of Cooper, maybe even bordering on helicopter-y, not that I'd admit that freely. I'll definitely have to meet this Coach B today and get a feel for him. I'll make it a point to ask Mike about his qualifications and background check too. Due diligence to check the guy is the least I can do.

THERE ISN'T A CHANCE TO ASK MIKE ABOUT HIS FRIEND BEFORE practice starts because almost as soon as we arrive, they start running laps around the park. They look like a well-oiled machine, albeit one that occasionally misses a step or two. But if their line gets out of whack, they quickly correct it themselves. Pretty impressive for a bunch of eight- and nine-year-olds, I think.

I'm sitting on the makeshift 'sideline' of the boys' practice field with Michelle, fresh cups of to-go coffees in our hands even though it's hot as balls out here. "So, what do you know about this Coach B character?"

She laughs. "Let me guess, you're getting 'Coach Mike says' and 'Coach B said' as much as I am?"

I nod, sipping my bean nectar and not saying anything else.

"I saw him at practice this week when I was waiting for the boys." She lowers her voice, looking around and making sure none of the other nearby moms are paying us any attention, but still talking behind her cup like someone might read her lips. "Huge guy that I would happily climb like a tree. My ovaries damn near exploded from across the field. And that was before he started helping the kids. Pretty sure I was soaked down to my knees at that point."

I can't hold back the snort of laughter. "Oh, my God, Michelle. You are so hard up! When's Michael coming home?"

"Girl, it ain't about being horny," she says with a throaty chuckle. "Wait till you see him. You'll be dreaming about that beard scratching your thighs all night, too. That cowboy could wear his dirty boots to bed and I wouldn't complain a bit, especially if that was all he was wearing."

Her words bring up imagery I'd rather not have. It's not that I'm asexual. I have a sex drive and a battery-operated boyfriend like most red-blooded women, but it's been so long since I've had actual two-person sex that I've probably forgotten how to even do it. Is it still tab A and slot B? Or is there some newfangled way of doing things these days?

"I don't think that's my thought pattern," I correct her, shoving any lack-of-sex thoughts out of my head. "I'm more worried about Mike's random friend hanging out with a bunch of kids. Can you say *sketch-yyy*?" I singsong the last word under my breath, drawing it out.

Michelle shrugs, unconcerned. "Mike said he's some football pro or something that he wrangled into helping. The boys like him and they seem to be learning, and you know Mike appreciates the help. Getting those boys to play together is like herding squirrels, so if he got some backup that doesn't require me getting out there to catch a ball, I'm for it." She does little finger-quotes around the word 'catch', making it clear that she can't play any better than I can.

I turn back to watch the boys cross what appears to be their finish line, judging by the cheers and high-fives. "I'm still going to keep an eye out and talk to Mike."

Michelle makes a serious face, mean mugging at me as she points her V-ed fingers at her eyes and then the boys. "On it, Helicopter Mom Extraordinaire."

Okay, so maybe I'm a bit more transparent about my overprotectiveness than I thought. But she's got no room to talk. I had to convince her to let Liam play.

The boys' cheers renew and I hear them call out, "Coach B! You're here!"

The sun's blocking my sight a bit, throwing the newcomer into a bright halo so that all I can see is a black silhouette. A very large silhouette. And then a deep voice gruffly says, "Sorry I'm late, guys. Had to finish chores before I could leave, but I brought snacks for after practice."

"Yeah!" they cheer, not even knowing what he's brought. If I were a betting woman, I'd lay odds he could bring them tuna fish in a can, tell them it was good protein, and they'd scarf it down. At least that's what Cooper made it sound like when he was going all nutritionist on me this morning.

I grin slightly at the thought, and then the broad shape shifts and my stomach plummets. Not just to my toes but to the middle of the Earth beneath them. It can't be. Please don't let it be.

My past.

My dream.

My shoulda, coulda, woulda.

My . . . Bruce.

"Oh, fuck," I whisper and I feel the heat of the other moms' eyes glaring at me for daring to cuss in front of their snowflakes, even though there are no kids within twenty feet of us.

Michelle knocks my shoulder with her own. "Told you. Climb him like a *damn* tree." She leans forward and glares at the mom on the other side of me, and distantly, I realize she said that loudly this time on purpose in solidarity with me.

"No, I . . . Michelle, I know him." Her jaw drops a little at my lost expression. I pull myself together and grab her arm, hissing, "Michelle . . . I *know* him. That's Bruce Tannen. My first boyfriend, my first love, my first *everything*."

Delight makes her eyes sparkle. "Like in the biblical sense? That's a story I have got to hear!"

I shake my head, trying to stand up. "I have to get out of here. I can't see him. He can't see me. I have to go." Michelle arm-bars me across the waist, forcing me back into my folding camp chair.

"Nope, nu-uh, no way, just NO. Sit your ass down." She's using her mom voice on me, but since I'm a mom too, it should have zero effect on me. But because she's my best friend and I'm weak and feeling like the whole world just got yanked out from under my feet, I somehow do as she says, settling dumbly back into my seat.

"I'm going to get that story, but not right now while we have other ears," she whispers, smiling sweetly, but we all know it's saccharin-coated venom. She's got no problem with the other team moms, and neither do I considering I just met them, but we're a team of two inside a team of many, and they are all listening intently as they pretend to watch their sons on the field.

And Bruce. They're all watching Bruce, which makes possessive jealousy ignite in my belly like hot, sour lava. I swallow thickly, forcing it back down.

No, I don't have the right to be possessive or jealous. He could be married for all I know, or sleeping with the whole team of moms sitting down the sideline, or the whole town. I don't know, and I shouldn't care.

But I do.

I'm stuck. I can't leave, Michelle won't let me, but I can't stay because he'll see me, want to talk to me, and I've got nothing good to say.

Oh, you know . . . been here and there, fucked up my whole life but got Cooper, who is my sun and moon and every star out of the deal, so there's that. Makes the rest of the nightmare no big deal, you know? And besides, I'm mad as a damn hornet at you, so you can fuck off, asshole.

Or worse, maybe he wouldn't even recognize me, wouldn't even care. Maybe I'm just some girl he used to know way back when.

I consider getting up again and making a run for it, but Michelle hums under her breath. "Don't even think about it."

Shit. Is this woman psychic?

Helpless, I resort to the bad habits I worked and fought to lose and shrink myself, curling into my body and ducking my chin into my chest as I pull my knees up, resting my feet on the chair. I let the curtain of my hair fall forward, obscuring my face, and will my presence to be unnoticed and unobtrusive. All moves I'm way too familiar with.

Through a stroke of karmic good luck, it works for a while. I sit and watch the practice, my eyes jumping from Cooper to Bruce and back again. The team is running a few plays, and the other moms cheer for their boys when they catch the ball, but I keep my mouth closed, not wanting to draw any attention.

Luckily, Cooper looks over once and I give him a thumbs-up and a smile, and he seems happy with that. He's so easygoing some-times, has no idea that I'm freaking the fuck out, and he never will. I'll protect him from that at any cost.

As the practice winds down, my luck runs out. The boys give Coach Mike and Bruce handshakes, which is admittedly adorable, and then the boys all get fist-sized peaches from Bruce. "Thanks, Coach B!" they all say graciously.

I'm already standing, my back to the wild gaggle of sweaty boys as I try to fold my chair and forcefully shove it into its handy carrying bag so that I can get the hell out of here. Usually, this is a task that's quick and easy, but right now it's ridiculously hard.

From right behind me, I hear a deep voice that sends shock-waves through my every nerve ending, making them buzz with memories. "Thanks again, everyone. Good hustle out there today."

My shoulders climb to my ears and my cheeks heat as they stain pink. I know the other moms are looking at me, waiting for the show, but I'm determined to not give them one.

Choice one: play it cool, fake it until you make it, which is easier said than done. Choice two: make a controlled-pace run for it, which is crazy but preferable under the circumstances. If I toss back a breezy 'gotta go' over my shoulder, it'll just seem like I'm a busy mom, which I am, but not so busy that I'm rude to the men volunteering to help my son.

Rock, meet hard place.

Hard place, fuck you very much.

Choice three and the one I most don't want to pick: turn around like a damn adult and take my lumps, praying that he doesn't hate, remember, or even care about me. That's the best option, though the preferable outcome, I'm not sure which of those I'm hoping for.

I steel my features, willing my shoulders down and back like I've practiced. It's the reverse of the bad habit I used to have. Instead of making myself invisible, I choose visibility, choose the image I want to project. Strong, confident, capable. And when I force power into my every cell, only then do I turn around.

"Hey, Bruce." My voice doesn't waver even one iota, and I'm strangely proud of that fact, given the way my knees are shaking.

His eyes follow the sound of his name on my lips, and I see the moment recognition lights his eyes before they go dark. So dark and deep . . . and empty. Like the ocean at midnight on a moonless night, pitch black and hard, a bit scary, even, but not in a way I'm used to.

His jaw clenches once, twice, three times before he takes an audible inhale. I almost think it's in preparation to yell at me, but then he rumbles, "Allyson."

It's not a question or even a greeting, just a statement of fact, my name through his rough vocal cords, but it does something to me.

Something terrifying, something unwanted, something that makes my heart and my pussy clench. Because damn it all, after all these years, all the pain and the heartache and everything that's happened because and not because of him . . . *I want him.*

"Small world, huh?" I'm stupid, as stupid as that saying, considering we live in what used to be a small town but has grown so much while I was gone. Grown enough that I didn't even consider that this blast from my past would rise up at pee-wee football practice, of all places.

Bruce grunts, which I take as agreement. That I'm stupid? That it's a small world?

I find my tongue, managing to speak normally. "Guess you're

the Coach B I've been hearing so much about all week? You and Mike are all Cooper has talked about."

"Cooper your boy?" Bruce asks as he looks down to my side where my munchkin is happily slurping on a peach. If I'd given him that, he would've asked for candy peach rings instead, but Coach B gives it to him and he's chowing down so fast his chin's already dripping.

"Yeah, he's mine." There's so much tied up in the simple statement. More than anyone even knows. But it's the damned truth. Cooper is mine and no one else's. Especially not his father's. *Never* his.

Bruce's lip tilts up as he talks to me but looks at Cooper. "He's a good kid. Got a big mouth on him, but he's a good egg."

Something seems to pass between them, and I wonder what Cooper said that got him in trouble, because sure as I know my son, that's what Bruce is alluding to. Saying kind things and putting good into the world is one of the things I try so hard to instill in Cooper, but it's hard to put a filter on an unfiltered kid who lives big and bold with little regard for civilized society.

"Thanks." I don't know what else to say. So many things dance on the tip of my tongue, but none of them want to take that risky leap into the air between us. So I stick with stating the obvious. "Still here in Great Falls? I didn't know that."

His face turns to stone before my very eyes and the temperature drops ten degrees. With the August heat blasting down on us, it should be a welcome reprieve but instead feels painfully frosty.

"Yep, still here."

He turns to the boys, clearly dismissing me, which stings. Even Michelle raises a brow in question at the cold shoulder. "Okay, boys, practice on Tuesday. Let's go for the team yell we worked on."

All the boys crowd together, one hand to the middle in a messy stack of sweat, dirt, peach juice, and germs. "On three . . . one, two, three . . ."

"GO WILDCATS!" they scream as one.

Well, mostly together, at least.

They start to disperse, practice over. A few of the moms tell me goodbye, probing eyes still flicking between me and Bruce like they don't want to leave too soon and miss anything. I help their cause and gather Cooper up, along with my chair that never did go back in the bag, but I can do that at home.

"Let's go, honey."

Not looking over my shoulder feels like a major accomplishment, but getting in my car and pulling out of the parking lot feels like a reminder that I lost something. Something I didn't even know I still wanted.

Cooper is doing a play-by-play of practice for me from his point of view, his small voice filling the car as I mutter the occasional 'uh-huh' and 'hmm', and my mind wanders.

To the past.

To the last time I saw Bruce.

To the last time I loved him.

CHAPTER 4

BRUCE

*O*ur panting breaths fog up the already steamy windows of my old truck. There's even a handprint smashing what's left of the felt cushion of my headliner where Allyson used it as leverage to impale herself harder, deeper on my cock as she cried out my name, making me feel like a fucking god.

It's not the first time we've fucked or made love. We've done both dozens of times, at every available opportunity we can find. But this will be the last time for a while, and I want to enjoy the afterglow of the moment— her still straddling my lap, my softening cock still inside her warm, slippery pussy, and the floral perfume of her filling my nose where I have it buried against her neck in the mess my hands have made of her hair. I wrap my arms around her a little tighter, squeezing her to me and wishing we could stay like this a little longer. She's under my skin, on my skin, in my very veins.

God, I love this girl. And not in some high-school kid puppy-love way, though we're in that sweet spot between our birthdays that put us both at eighteen. I love her with everything I am.

Honestly, that isn't much, but she's never seemed to care that I'm just a dumb jock with plans of either playing ball or farming. That's the only two options for a guy like me, but not my Allyson. She's fucking brilliant and *can do anything she puts her mind to. I'm proud of her already, and she hasn't even left for college yet to start her pre-law studies.*

"You leaving in the morning?" I murmur against the soft skin of her neck between kisses. I'm sorely tempted to mark her, leave a big, glaring hickey on her milky skin to fend off any assholes at her new school, but I hold back . . . barely. Her dad would kick my ass, or well, he'd try and I'd be obligated to let him get a good shot in because I mostly deserve it for defiling his daughter. But I really don't have time for that because football practice starts this week. Two-a-days for all of August in preparation for my senior year of high school, starting on the varsity team.

It'll be the distraction I need because Allyson will be far away at State for her freshman year. Not there to cheer for me on Friday nights. But I know she'll be cheering from her dorm. We've already made plans for Friday night calls so I can give her the play-by-play of the game, not that she cares about football or even understands it, but she cares about me. It's the same reason I watch court shows with her and listen to her talk about legal this and legal that when I don't understand even a quarter of what she's saying.

She nods. "Yeah. I'm going to miss you, miss this."

Her voice is quiet and sad, and I don't want her to leave like that. She deserves to step into this new phase with all the excitement in the world. She's earned it. She deserves it. So I lighten the mood intentionally for her sake, even as it pains me to do it. I thrust up into her, pulling her down tight and grinding her hips against mine. "You gonna miss this dick, baby? He's definitely gonna miss you too."

I soften the crudeness with a low laugh and a sexy wag of my eyebrows.

She giggles, and I can feel her inner muscles squeezing me. I groan at how good she feels and wonder if we have time for another round before curfew. It's not as if her parents can ground her, anyway. She'll be gone.

She'll be gone.

Her palm smacks against my bare chest, teasing, "You're awful, you know that? I'm trying to have a moment here and you're making light of it." She's smiling, or trying to, but I can see the worry beneath.

I can always read her like a book, have been since before we even talked in Speech class my sophomore year. She'd been a junior and stunning. The quintessential blonde, blue-eyed cheerleader, but instead of being a mean

34

girl, she was kind and good-hearted. She gave a speech about baby ducks once and I'd been done for.

Okay, it wasn't actually about ducks but about pollution and its effects on the environment, but all I'd seen were the fluffy little yellow ducks she'd been flashing slides of. Her impassioned plea for us to do something had stirred something in me beyond just my dick, which she'd already been starring in fantasies for since day one of the school year.

"I'm not, Al," I tell her soberly, stroking her cheek. "I swear. Tomorrow, I'm gonna be bawling like a fucking baby that you're gone. But I want you to go start our life together. I'll be there soon, and we'll make good on all those plans we have. I promise. I love you, baby."

She wiggles, my flaccid cock sliding out of her, and I almost mourn the loss, but she turns, sitting sideways on my lap. I can feel the warm mess of our combined juices leaking out of her onto the denim covering my thigh, and I like the way she's marking me. I wrap my arms around her, cradling her as she lays her head on my shoulder.

"You promise-promise?" she asks.

I nod, touching my chin to the top of her head. The words pour out of her in one big run. "I'm just scared, you know? School's this big, new thing, and I'm not going to know anyone. I'm probably going to get lost and never find my way to classes or back to the dorm. I'll end up sleeping in the quad under a tree and flunking out. And you're going to be back here, the literal big man on campus. Rock of the defense, and so fucking sexy that every girl is going to try to hop on your dick. And I won't be here to fight them off. Don't forget about me, okay?"

I lift her chin with my thick finger and then cup her cheeks in my big, meaty paws. I'm not known for my grace and gentleness on or off the field, but for this girl, I could brush a butterfly's wings and not hurt it. That's how gentle I am with her. I meet her eyes, blue on near-black.

"Listen to me, Al. You're going to take that campus by storm and make it your bitch." So I'm not exactly a romantic poet or a good pep-talker, but I'm trying. "As for us, it's you and me forever, baby. There ain't a girl here who can touch what you give me." I see the flare in her eyes and clarify. "Not my dick . . . my heart. And there ain't a single guy at that school who's gonna love you like I do."

She presses her lips to mine, and it feels like a promise, a vow, sealing my words between us as truth. She tastes like love, like the future, like the sweet dreams only two stupid kids can have.

When she lays her head back on my shoulder, I just hold her, running my thumb up and down her arm and memorizing the moment. It's a turning point for us. Tomorrow, Allyson's going to school, and it'll be the beginning of a whole new phase for us. The first step in the rest of our lives. I can't wait.

I WALK THE FIELDS AT HOME FOR ACRES, WATCHING THE AFTERNOON SUN make its trek across the sky as I check on the crops. Some more peaches are looking good on the trees, probably ready for Bobby and me to pick this week. I need to check in with Shayanne to see if she wants them for one of her fancy recipes or if I should give them to Brody for the farmers' market.

But mostly, my mind wanders to the past, flipping through memories like scrapbook pages in my mind. Allyson Meyers—the girl I loved, the girl I thought I was gonna marry, the girl who dumped me as soon as she caught sight of the fancy, smart city boys at State.

The girl who broke my heart.

Anger burns hot and bright in my chest, and I rub at the hard muscles there, even though I know it won't do anything for the pain. The anger is the dark, bitter chocolate syrup on a shit sundae of hurt, disappointment, and disillusionment. Big words for a stupid cowboy, but there ya go.

I hear a guitar playing up ahead and almost turn back, knowing Bobby's been working on a song lately and it's giving him fits. Farming's always been this way. There's a lot of hard work, sure, but when you get a break, time stretches out and you can get a little too deep with your thoughts. I offered to find some rhymes and help, but like the asshole he is, he'd said he already knew how to rhyme cat and hat, as if that's the extent of my capabilities.

Love that fucker, though I'd never tell him in those words because that's not our way. Nah, I'd told him by sweeping his legs out from underneath him and holding him down while cater-wauling my dirty version of a 'cat in the hat' song. Though it was probably more of an unofficial naughty limerick.

There once was a man so hick,
That he thought his leg was his dick.
So he swung it this and that way,
Everywhere, every day,
Proud when people said, 'Look at that prick!'

So I decide interrupting him is all right and a fair shot at annoying him some more. "Incoming," I shout.

As I round the last row of trees, Bobby's poised with his guitar on his lap, leaning back against a tree. He's got half a smile on his face, shaking his head. "Incoming? You dropping bombs? There are easier ways to fertilize the trees, you know."

"Maybe," I deadpan. "Though I wanted to be sure you weren't serenading a *friend*. A naked one."

I look around pointedly, seeing that he's definitely alone, as usual. He's a hard worker, not much for screwing around with his life, with his music, or with girls. "Want me to sing for ya again? Give you a little inspiration? I could be your muse." I frame my face with my hands like I'm posing for a picture, mean mugging the whole time.

"Fuck no, asshole! I had to listen to two solid hours of Hank Williams and Johnny Cash after the other day to get my balls back where they belong. I don't think I've ever cringed that hard."

"You're welcome," I say, choosing to take it as a compliment. More seriously, I ask, "Song still giving you a hard time?"

He picks at a couple of strings, finding the melody he's been playing on repeat for weeks. "Yeah, it'll get there, though. Some-times, the hardest ones are the best ones."

I can't help it. He's being all profound, but c'mon, I can't skip a soft ball like that. "That's what she said."

"Dipshit," he says, kicking at my shins but grinning. "You know what I mean."

I nod, sitting down beside him in the shade. "You'll get it. You always do. Just let it marinate like Shayanne's roast."

It's a bit of a running joke in our family. When Shayanne has shit she wants to do that doesn't involve cooking us fuckers dinner, she throws a roast in the crockpot and calls it a day. She used to think she was being tricky, like we'd be fooled by the aroma of cooking meat, but we all knew that a roast meant she'd been up to something, usually something sketchy. It's become a bit of a euphemism to not work too hard on one thing and to let yourself branch out a bit.

We sit in silence for a few minutes, the only sounds the strums of Bobby's playing. He gets into a loop and pauses. "What's up?" he says, his fingers working chords on the neck of his guitar but his other hand resting on the body of the instrument.

I scoot down, laying against the tree more than leaning, and pull the brim of my cap down low so he can't see my eyes. "Nothing."

Drop it, I silently order.

But he does no such thing, making that annoying noise like I gave the wrong answer on a game show. "*Ehnnt*, try again. What's up?"

I stay silent, stewing in my head, and he doesn't push anymore. His patience is one of his strongest traits, and I know he'll wait me out with ease. One of his greatest weaknesses, though, is his big mouth. Boy can't keep a secret for a hot minute.

As I mull that over, I decide that maybe that can be an advantage this time. Brody and Shay are going to find out about Allyson being back, but I don't want to have this conversation three separate times. If I tell Bobby, I can probably get away with one telling and then a few grunts to Brody and Shay. Winner, winner, chicken dinner.

I sigh, pretending like I'm put out by his fussing even though he's just looking at me. "Allyson's back. Her kid's on the football team I'm helping coach. It's weird."

Boom. Mic drop. Full story and no drama on my part. I should win a damn award.

Bobby sits up, delicately putting Betty the Guitar in her case before turning to me and punching me in the bicep. "What the fuck? Lead with that next time!"

I push him over and we tussle a bit. We should've probably outgrown this by now, but somehow, we never did. I've had more bruised ribs from roughhousing with my brothers than from fighting anyone else. Well, except for being on the football field.

After a few go's, we push off each other and settle. It felt good to get that out, and I tell him so. "Thanks. I think I needed that."

He lifts his chin in recognition but doesn't leave it alone. "Good. Now spill."

"That's it," I admit with a single lift of a shoulder. "She was at practice. It was weird. She didn't know I was 'still in Great Falls', I guess." I do the finger quote thing around the words because I don't believe one single second that she thought I'd magically up and moved away.

"More," Bobby demands hungrily like a damn gossipy woman talking behind her program after church on Sunday. "What's she look like? She married? Her kid a demon spawn from hell?"

I press my lips together but tell him anyway. "She looked . . . good. Still blonde and blue-eyed and beautiful. She had on denim shorts and a tank top, and her tits looked like fucking peaches." I glance up at the tree above us, thinking the fruits don't do justice to Allyson's rack. "No wedding ring, but she did have on other jewelry. Not sure if that means she's single or if I give a fuck. Cooper's a good kid. Mouthy as hell, but good."

I can tell he's weighing all that, considering his next words. "You thinking 'bout hitting that again?"

He doesn't mean fucking her, or at least not *just* fucking her. Once upon a time, Allyson Meyers was my drug of choice. I became a willing addict and loved every second lost in her until she took it all away. I crashed . . . hard. Bobby was the one to pick up the pieces and put Humpty Dumpty back together again.

I lick my lips. "I don't think I can. I'm not strong enough for another round with her. She'd cut me to pieces. Hell, I'd carve out my own heart and hand it to her on a silver platter."

Bobby's the only person I'd be this frank with because while he'll share the basics with anyone and everyone, he keeps the emotional shit to himself. I'd do the same for him.

"And you know she'd say thank you like the well-mannered girl her momma taught her to be and then throw my heart in the trash. Or run over it with her car."

Bobby snorts. "Roadkill. Good imagery, and pretty accurate for back then. You were gone, man. For a long while."

He doesn't say it aloud, but we're both thinking it. Some people were happy about it, because it was my senior year that I really earned the nickname Brutal . . . and I sent a lot of kids home sore. A few I even sent to the hospital. I shared my pain with the world in the only way I knew how.

Right when I started to get my feet back under me, finishing high school and going to State myself to play ball, was when everything went to shit again. And that time, it was so much worse. That was when Mom died and I'd come home for good, taking to the fields of our farm and never stepping foot on a football field again.

"You still mad at her?" he says quietly.

At first, I think he's talking about Mom. I think we were all a little mad at Mom for leaving, even though she damn sure didn't want to. She fought tooth and nail, cussed every cancer cell to hell, but it still won and took her from us. But I realize he's staying on topic and means Allyson.

Am I mad at her?

"Maybe a little," I concede. "Angry, sad, hurt, and a whole host of other emotions all tied up in a messy knot."

"What are you gonna do then? You committed to those boys," Bobby reminds me, but I wouldn't dream of backing out on them or Mike now. My word's good, even if not everyone ascribes to that sentiment.

"Coach football. Avoid Allyson." I nod, having decided as the words came out. It even sounds like somewhat of a plan, tangible goals I can check off like one of Shay's lists in her ever-present notebook.

Bobby scans my face, looking for something but finally shaking his head. "Easier said than done, but I agree that it's what you should do, one hundred percent. Good luck with that. Just let me know when she gets her claws into you again so I can prepare for you to start beating shit up when it goes catawampus." It's a warning as much as a prediction, him begging me not to do this again.

Done with the conversation, I give him a middle-finger salute. "Do your song. Let me see if I can help."

He blinks a few times but then picks Betty back up. Before he plays, he adds one last piece of advice. "Fuck Allyson Meyers, but *not* literally. You hear me, Brutal? You're an asshole, but even you deserve better than her."

Having said his piece, he begins to play and sing. His voice is honeyed whiskey over gravel, and he gets pussy thrown at him left and right from just speaking, much less singing. He rarely takes advantage, though, which I don't get, but there are worse things than being picky.

Like being a fucking liar.

CHAPTER 5

ALLYSON

I am an adult. I can handle this. I can do this. Because I am a grown ass woman in charge of her own destiny, her own life, her own choices. I am doing this.

The pep talk's better today, my inner voice mostly chanting, 'I am woman, hear me roar.' That's a good thing, because as I approach the field to pick up Cooper and Liam, I know I'm going to need every bit of strength I can muster. I feel like myself, and I'm proud of that *and* the decision I made this weekend after seeing Bruce.

He's going to be spending a lot of time with Cooper, which means we're going to see each other regularly, and I do not want it to be weird. For us, for the kids, for the team. So I'm going to stand tall and have an awkward conversation about our past to make sure that it's all put to rest and won't affect the season.

See? Adulting 101. Communication is key.

The boys are on a knee, looking up to Coach Mike as he talks. Bruce stands off to the side, feet spread wide, arms crossed, old ball cap pulled down low. He looks like a bouncer at a country bar, like a bodyguard for the young kids at his feet. But, though I can't see his eyes under the brim, I get the distinct impression that he's looking at me, and my belly does a flip-flop it hasn't done in a long time.

Fuck, I missed him. I didn't even realize it, hadn't thought about him in so long with my own shit to handle. But seeing him brings back so many good memories—lazy days alone in the barn, talking about everything and nothing, making love in the back of his truck under the stars up at Make-out Point, knowing that the world was ours for the taking if we just worked hard enough. He reminds me of who I once was, the light, carefree, innocent girl without a worry in her head. He makes me remember when things were easy. Before they got so hard.

I lick my lips, remembering his taste. Not the one time he tried his dad's cigarettes and I'd yelled at him, spitting out the gross taste into the dirt, but the cinnamon-y heat of his kisses from the gum and mints he used to eat all the time. I never realized it, but I quit eating anything cinnamon flavored years ago. Not a single Red Hot has passed my lips in almost a decade.

I wonder if he still tastes like that?

Movement catches my eye, and I see the boys standing and putting a hand in for a cheer. "GO WILDCATS!" Then they all scatter this way and that, beelining for their moms.

Cooper and Liam come up to me, sweaty and bright-eyed. "Mom, did you see me? I caught the ball two times when Coach Mike threw it!" He holds his hand up and Liam smacks it.

"He did, Ms. Allyson! And I threw for thirty whole yards!" Liam boasts, not wanting to be outdone. The boys high-five again. I'm glad they celebrate and support each other and offer them each a high-five myself for good measure.

"Great job, guys!" I say with a big smile. I can see Mike and Bruce packing everything up to leave and know I need to act fast. "Hey, boys, do you mind playing for a few minutes before we go? I need to talk to Coach B for a second." The name sounds awkward on my tongue, but it's the most likely way to refer to Bruce and not get Cooper's interest piqued.

Cooper and Liam look at each other in excitement. "Let's go before she changes her mind!" They're off for the expanse of grass, a football appearing from one of their bags.

I don't give myself even a moment to second-guess this. I walk straight over to Mike and Bruce. "Hey, guys. Thanks for practice. Seems like the boys had fun."

Mike looks at Cooper and Liam, who are running some sort of zig-zag pattern and tossing the ball between them. He shakes his head with a grin. "I don't know where they get the energy. I'm beat. Did you need something, Allyson?"

My eyes meet Bruce's and hold. "Oh, no, I just wanted to talk to Bruce for a minute."

Mike clears his throat, but Bruce and I don't break eye contact. I feel like there are so many words churning below the surface but neither of us speaks.

Not yet.

He used to say my eyes were blue oceans he'd drown in, but right now his are raging rivers with currents that'll pull me under, batter me senseless, and leave me on the shore not knowing what the hell just happened.

"Sure thing, Jamie's waiting on Evan and me for dinner. See you Thursday." He hoists his bag onto his shoulder. "Hey, Brutal? Remember what we talked about."

Bruce breaks our staredown to nod at Mike. "I'm good."

Mike turns to go, whistling for Evan as he heads to the parking lot. Something about Mike's parting words pushes my buttons. "You talked to Mike about me, about us?"

Bruce's entire presence goes dark and cold as he huffs out a humorless laugh. "Conceited much?" He resumes his bouncer pose, defensive and walled off as he explains. "No, we didn't talk about you at all, actually. But he did warn me that every single mom would be looking for me to be their new daddy figure and that sometimes, it's not just the single ones. He told me to be careful."

I blush furiously, knowing Mike's right. It's not that the other moms are bad or slutty at all. But Bruce is walking sex, from his hat to his boots and everywhere in between, and I wouldn't blame any woman for taking her shot with him. Except for me. That ship has sailed and crashed to pieces.

"Well, that's not what I wanted to talk to you about," I say, trying to justify this little chat. He grunts like he doesn't believe me, so I roll into my practiced speech. "Look, what I wanted to say is that I know we have history and this could be really weird. But I hope that we can put aside the past for the boys. Maybe even be friends?"

He lowers his arms to his sides and steps incrementally closer, and I smile, trying to hide my nerves. "History? Is that what you're calling it?" Something flashes across his face too fast for me to decode it. His voice is a growl, low and powerful, hitting right where he aims. "I'd call it you ripping my guts out, Al."

His eyes pin me in place like a bug, and I freeze, not finding a response amid the warning sirens going off in my head. Always able to read me like an open book, he must see the fear, scent its bitterness on my skin, because he steps back the smallest inch but keeps his voice quiet, between us.

"Bruce—" I try again.

"No. I can't do friends with people who I know what they taste like when they come while screaming my name."

Memories flood me. I remember doing that.

"I'm not friends with people who bail on everything they've ever known and disappear for new and shiny shit."

Ouch . . . and the betrayal burns hot in his voice, searing at my heart.

"So no, we ain't gonna be friends, Allyson."

His venom pours over me, but I've withstood so much more for so much less. Even so, the verbal lashing from him strikes deep.

I'm not the girl he used to know, and for the first time, I consider that he's not the boy I once knew, either. This Bruce is cruel and hard. Though he seems warm and friendly with the boys. Which means this treatment is special, just for me.

He hates me.

I don't know why that hurts so much. Before last week, I hadn't even thought of Bruce in years, not really. He was this abstract warm, fuzzy feeling from my misspent youth that ended in a painful blaze of glory. No, what's the opposite of blaze of glory? Because there were no fireworks, no angry fights, nothing like that.

We just drifted and my predictions came true, and we were snuffed out like the cherry of a burnt-up cigarette.

A phantom echo stabs at my heart even now at how badly I wanted to be wrong, just that one time. It hadn't been a sharp ending, but it'd been cruel in its quiet loss.

Standing in front of me, he's so much *more* than I remember. Larger and sexier, but stonier and colder. It's messing with me, my head and my body at odds in their responses, and I don't know which to listen to.

The confused uncertainty breeds anger, and I don't give a thought to the words that spout forth from my mouth. The unfiltered rain feels cleansing, even as snarled and ugly as it is.

"Seriously? It was almost ten years ago, Bruce. Something tells me you haven't been locked away, pining for some girl you used to know." I let my eyes drop heavily over every inch of him. "No, you've probably been just fine without me." It's an accusation that I know more than I'm letting on—not about now but about back then.

His upper lip curls. "Jealousy looks good on you. See something you like, *baby?*"

He poses, holding his arms wide to let me get an unobstructed view of his body in all its glory. But the sarcastic endearment stabs my heart so painfully and suddenly that I can't stop the gasp before it passes my lips. I cross my arms over myself protectively.

"Don't do that."

I mean the nickname he used to call me by, but deep inside, I know I don't want to answer his question because I do see something I like.

A lot of somethings I like.

Six feet, three inches of tanned and tattooed muscle, maybe a bit bigger than the 240 he used to be, but even harder, if possible. Dark hair curling from underneath his cap and a dusting of stubble across his cheeks and sharp jawline. Full lips that, even though they're not smiling, look kissable and soft. Large hands that could span my waist or lift me into his arms with ease. And I know that behind that zipper is a thick cock that stretched me the very first time.

Even as what he's grown into registers in my mind, I can feel his dark eyes licking over me. Does he like what he sees now? In some ways, I'm the same blonde and blue-eyed girl he once knew every inch of. In other ways, I've changed so much. I've got curves I didn't used to have, my hair is shorter and more practical, and I'm already battling the faint lines trying to appear on my forehead. And that's just the stuff on the surface. More has changed inside me than outside. But his gaze sears me, rooting me in place as he leisurely looks his fill.

I'm definitely hot and bothered, and it's not anger now. But I wasn't enough once, and that was when I was whole. The woman I am now, with shatters throughout my soul that have been repaired with determination and grit, is definitely not enough.

I can't do this, especially not with him when he's got the clear advantage. Flirting or even playing at it in antagonism has stakes that are simply way too high.

I take a steadying breath, willing my shoulders to drop and my eyes to lift to meet his. This is just like a negotiation at work. Stay cool and calm, and never let the other guy see you sweat.

"Bruce, you don't know me anymore." I can see his mouth opening to interrupt me, and I hold up a staying hand. "And I don't know you. It's been a long time, and we have months of practices and games coming up. I don't want things to be uncomfortable . . . for *Cooper*. You and I are adults. We can handle it, but I need this to be okay for my son. He wants to play football and I want to give him that."

It's all I have. Blunt honesty laid bare at his feet with only a shred of hope that he won't destroy Cooper's dream because of our past.

He looks across the field, and I follow his sightline, watching Cooper and Liam. They've worn themselves out and are lying sprawled out in the grass, pointing at the streaks of clouds painting the sky as the sun sets.

"Where's his Dad, Allyson? *Who's* his dad?" The questions are gritted from behind clenched teeth, and the muscle in his jaw pops out beneath the shadow of his beard. His arms resume their position across his chest, and I wonder if it's a defense mechanism, like he's preparing himself for my answer. But there's no way he cares, not after all these years.

I blink against the sting in my eyes, not looking at Bruce but keeping my attention on Cooper. "I shouldn't answer that, but I will. He doesn't have one. I'm all he's got. All he's ever had. All that mattered, anyway."

Furious at the tears escaping, I swipe at my eyes with the back of my hands as I walk across the field, leaving Bruce behind me. I'm not crying for the loss of my ex-husband and Cooper's father. He can rot in hell for all I care. The tears are for my son who will never have more than me.

I'm a good mother . . . hell, I'm a fucking great mother, if I say so myself, but I'm not a father. Though I try my best, I can't be everything Cooper needs. But I'll be damned if I won't get it for him.

I don't want to know Bruce's response, can't handle his smug smile as he takes away the one thing I want desperately . . . again. So I focus on the task at hand.

"Come on, boys. Time to head home for dinner before Michelle gets done at the gym. You two are in luck. I'm making my famous mac-and-cheese with chicken nuggets."

They don't know that what makes the macaroni and cheese recipe so special is the squash puree I hide in it. Sometimes, a mom needs tricks, and I've become a pro at disguising vegetables in all sorts of ways.

They cheer, running for the car.

I hold my chin high as I pass Bruce, not risking a glance his way, but I can feel him watching me, analyzing me, judging me.

"I'll see you at practice on Thursday."

The good-bye should be simple, but I can feel the agreement to put aside our past and work together for the boys. For Cooper.

He could so easily take this away from him, but somewhere underneath the snarling beast he is to me is still the kind heart he always had. My gaze dips to my toes. "Thank you."

I virtually run for the car before he can change his mind.

THAT NIGHT, AFTER TUCKING COOPER INTO BED AND HAVING A GLASS OF wine, I tumble into bed without so much as opening a single file for work. I dream of Bruce, a superimposed double image of the boy I used to know and the man he is today.

I'm laid back in a fluffy bed of white sheets, a place we never had sex before. In the barn, in his truck, on blankets in fields, and once, even against the wall behind the old bowling alley, but never in a bed, so I know this is a dream.

His stubble scratches along the sensitive skin of my neck as his hot breath reaches my ears. "You want this cock, baby? Tell me."

I moan and writhe, in my actual and dream beds. "Yes," I purr.

His chuckle vibrates against my belly as he moves lower. "Just need a taste first." His tongue flicks over my clit, and I surge upward, chasing him, and he growls in approval.

"More," I demand, and he obliges. He sucks at my lips and then seals his mouth over my clit, battering it with the tip of his tongue. One thick finger teases along my entrance, and I push into it, inviting him inside me.

I want to be filled by him, marked by him, owned by him.

Something about that niggles at the periphery of my awareness, but I wave it away like an annoying insect, focusing on the pleasure he's giving me.

He slides in, immediately curling his finger up to that rough patch along my front wall that we'd experimented to find. He strokes it, tapping every once in a while in a pattern I can't anticipate, which drives me wild.

"Fuck, Bruce. Please . . ." I beg.

He covers me, pressing his naked body to mine and aligning his cock right where I want him. "Slow or fast?" he asks.

He's a considerate lover, always preps me to take him. He told me from the first time that he's big, though I had nothing to compare to. But I grew to love that initial shock of pinched pain when he thrust into me all at once, instantly stretching me to accommodate him. That edging on the line of pain and pleasure makes me feel alive.

"Fast!" I dig my nails into his back, spurring him on.

He slams into me and I . . .

Wake up. Panting and disoriented, I look around my dark room, not remembering where I am. Or when I am.

I'm drenched with sweat and my pussy is throbbing as my knees knock together and my thighs squeeze, looking for relief. My fingers brush over my clit through my soaked panties and I consider finishing myself off. I'm already so on edge, it won't take much, and he'll never have to know.

But *I* will, and that's dangerous.

Too dangerous.

I sit up instead, reaching over to grab the glass of water I always keep on the bedside table and drinking greedily, wishing it would cool off my arousal as it quenches my thirst.

I close my eyes, forcing myself to remember Bruce's cold words today, his sneer and hatefulness toward me. Not his flexing biceps, not his easy grin for everyone else, and definitely not the bulge in his dirty jeans.

I set the glass down and flop onto my back. Something tells me I'm not going to get any sleep tonight.

CHAPTER 6

BRUCE

"Good job, guys," I yell across the field as I loudly clap my hands together. "Keep it going!"

I'm aiming for motivation, but even to my ears, it sounds more like a barked order. I can feel Mike eyeballing me instead of the boys, who are running their laps. They've got the hang of running as a team now, and we let them go on their own, keeping watch.

They're rounding their third lap and going for the extension of the fourth, and their initial excitement is wearing off as tiredness sets in. That's where the motivation is supposed to come in, to cheer them on for that final push to success. I predict a dozen kids falling into their beds without a single complaint tonight.

A quick flash later, the boys cross the finish line and lay out in the grass. I look down at my watch as I walk toward them.

"Fellas, your best run time on three laps has been six-thirty. Today, you added another lap and your total time was eight-fifteen." They groan, too tired to do math, but luckily, I've already done it for them. "Want the good news or the bad?"

I see a few sweaty heads perk up and lift from the grass to look at me.

"Good news is, you maintained your speed even with the additional lap, and no man was left behind. That's amazing and shows that you pushed for it, judging by how you look right now. I like that hard work and dedication, gentlemen."

"Bad news?" one of them asks, but I'm not sure who since it was mumbled into the ground.

"That was a good warm-up. Now let's get to practice," I say with a hint of evil glee. There's a chorus of groans and I clap again. "Got two minutes for water and whining, boys, and then we're playing some football."

They rally, movement returning to their limbs as they seek out their water bottles and chug down some liquid refreshment. Hopefully, it reignites their fire because we've got forty-five minutes to go and some hard work to do.

We gather back up, and Mike gives us the breakdown of plays we're going to run. I see Evan flinch a bit when Anthony gets quarterback, because Evan wants that spot badly, but he does as he's told and takes the line. Good kid. He's going to be a hell of a player one day if he keeps working hard.

They run the drill over and over again, Mike and me giving feedback and constructive criticism each time. Finally, we switch to another play and then another. We're still in baby steps, dive right, sweep left, simple pass routes . . . but the kids are picking it up.

By the last twenty minutes of practice, my eyes are darting toward the parking lot every few seconds. Even if I won't admit it to myself, I know I'm looking for Allyson. I'm damn near holding my breath as I wait for her sensible grey sedan to pull in, for her to walk over to the field, for her eyes to meet mine.

I wonder what I'll see there. Hell, I can't wait to find out, and isn't that a fucking pisser?

On Tuesday, she'd come up all mouthy and strong, but I saw her crumbling when I pushed back and threw barbs at her. I almost felt bad until she'd spewed some shots back. We never fought like that when we were dating, but I always loved her fire, that she spoke her mind. Even about the damn baby ducks nobody else in our town gave a shit about.

And there'd been that moment of heat when I felt her eyes

tracing every inch of me. I'd wanted to puff up like a damn lion, show her what she'd lost and that I've been just fine without her. But I'd also taken advantage of her distraction to do a little perusal of my own.

I told Bobby she's still hot. But there's so much more that I didn't share. She filled out good, curves and swerves where there used to be hard angles. Her hair is shorter than it was when we were kids, but the waves still lick her shoulders, tempting me to fist them as I kiss her, fuck her mouth, pound into her pussy.

Not that I'll be doing that ever again.

As sexy as she always has been and still is, there's something else about her that drew my attention. She used to be so perky, the literal cliché of a cheerleader bee-bopping down the halls of our high school. She's an adult and understandably grown out of that, of course, but what's left seems . . . darker somehow? Like there's a storm cloud hovering on the horizon of her very being, and I wonder what brought that on.

She'd cried when I'd asked about Cooper's dad, though she'd tried to hide the tears from me with her bravado. I wonder if something happened to him, something that might explain the shadow over Allyson and why Cooper doesn't have a dad.

She feels like a new version of a puzzle I once could do from memory.

But whatever questions I might have about the girl I used to know and who she's grown into, one thing's for sure. I have got to stop watching for her and pay attention to practice.

"Good footwork, Cooper. Light and fast, I can tell you've been practicing. Make sure you keep your eyes looking for defenders as you run, Derek. Holes will open and close quick."

It's the smallest addition to what Mike already told them, almost a verbatim repeat of his critique. Mike raises one brow in question, but I smile to let him know I'm fine and hope he thinks I just wanted to emphasize it for Derek.

They run the play again, but I don't see a bit of it because she's here.

Allyson walks down the sidewalk of the park, keeping her

distance from practice. I automatically think it's to stay away from me, and a thread of anger starts to burn, but I realize a second later that she can't walk in the grass in her heels.

She looks like she's come straight from work in high heels, a slim black skirt that hits just above her knees, and a sleeveless blue blouse the color of her eyes. Her waves are pulled back in some sort of twisted knot on top of her head, and there are glasses perched in front of the bun.

She's got some sort of sexy librarian thing going on that I wouldn't have expected to do a damn thing for a rough cowboy like me, but suddenly, bookish nerds are looking mighty fine. Or at least this one is.

She doesn't smile, and even from here, I can see that she's biting her lip uncertainly. Her arms cross protectively over her middle as her eyes meet mine.

We just stare, words and thoughts and emotions crossing between us like Wonka Vision, but whatever it is she's trying to tell me, it's coming through all wrong and I can't decipher it. I used to know what she was going to say before she even thought it and took delight in finishing her sentences for her. Now, I couldn't tell you if she wants to kill me or fuck me.

Or both.

I hate it.

I want to stride across the field, cage her in, and ask her to just be straight with me. At least then, I'd know where I stand and could adjust accordingly. Because this confusion irritates the fuck out of me.

If she wants to be enemies, fine. I'll get on board with glaring at her and leaving her the fuck alone. I'm damn near angry enough to demand we do that myself. But if she wants to fuck, maybe I'll bend her over the nearest flat surface and make her scream my name again.

I'm just not sure which she wants.

Hell, I'm not sure which *I* want.

Coach football. Avoid Allyson.

My own words echo through my head. To hell with her. She

doesn't get to decide this. I do, and I'm not going back for more promises and sweet nothings only to be thrown away like yesterday's trash.

I turn around to the boys, dismissing her. I pull my cap down tight, curling the edges a little more, and then cross my arms over my chest.

"You good?" Mike says quietly from beside me.

Shit. Hadn't really considered that the silent staredown at fifty paces was a second act for Mike and the team moms who I now realize are watching raptly.

Instead of answering, I grunt.

"Might need to bring popcorn for the moms if you're going to keep the Showcase Showdown action going. I'm Bob Barker. Please spay and neuter your pets." He's trying to joke, but I'm not in the mood for it.

I let out a whistle, making everyone flinch with the volume, but it gets their attention. "Circle up, boys. Last push for practice." They form a loose circle that includes Mike and me. "We're going to do something new. Starting person" —I point at myself— "will call out an exercise, like burpees. Everyone does five."

I drop to the grass, do a push-up, and then jump up, repeating it four more times. Finishing, I wait for the last kid to complete his fifth and then point to Mike who's standing next to me.

"Jumping jacks," he says, catching on. Everyone does their five.

We keep going . . . squats, toe touches, windmills, tuck jumps, and then things start to get sillier. "Hop on one foot," Cooper says, and we do. "Hop on the other foot," Liam adds, and we do that too.

By the time we make it around the circle three times, we're exhausted and the kids are laughing. Mostly because the last exercise Joshua called out was for everyone to do the chicken dance. We'd sung and danced along, even shaking our tail feathers. I might've intentionally wiggled my ass Allyson's way a little bit too, rubbing her nose in what she can't have . . . me.

"I think that's a good point to call it a night," Mike interrupts. "I'm nervous what Johnathan would have us do as a follow-up, and I'm already not gonna live down that I did the chicken dance in the park." He looks around like there might be someone watching him make a fool of himself, but he grins, letting everyone know that he's not really embarrassed in the least.

Their eyes jump to me and I scoff. "I ain't embarrassed. I can cut a rug and teach ya how to Dougie."

The boys look to each other in confusion and then back to me. "What's a Dougie?"

I hang my head in faux shame, a hand pressed to my chest. "You wound me, making an old man feel even older." They giggle and I look back up. "I'll show you another day. For now, everyone under six feet tall had best be getting home for a shower, a healthy dinner, and early bedtime. Bring it in one time."

We do our pile of hands in the middle, cheer loud and proud, and then they scatter.

"Hey, Evan, why don't you go look at the ducks for a second? We've got a coach meeting really quick," Mike says, and though he's talking to his kid, he's really telling me to sit tight. Evan runs off for the water, shouting something that sounds like 'here, ducky, ducky,' and Mike turns to me, his hands on his hips. "Can I talk to you about something?"

I dip my chin in permission and he goes right for the jugular.

"What's the deal with you and Cooper's mom? You dating, fucking, one-night standing, she stalking you, you stalking her?"

My eyes narrow and I rumble menacingly. "Those the only options?"

His shit-eating grin tells me he wants the story, no matter what. I growl but give in. "Fine. Though you're worse than the gossipy moms."

He shrugs and interrupts, "Jamie's waiting on the good gossip when I get home."

"To use Allyson's word, we've got *history*." I even do the air quote thing with my fingers. "We were high school sweethearts, serious. Even thought she was The One. Then she went to college and shit changed. That's it."

He looks surprised. "That's it? Are you fucking kidding me, man? That woman was about to eat you with a damn spoon and I thought you were going to throw her over your shoulder and run out of here like a caveman. Hell yeah, I'd say there's history, but there's some present too."

I look across the field, immediately picking Allyson's curvy figure out in the group of mothers and sons heading to the parking lot.

She's avoiding me. None of the other moms talked to me tonight either, and I don't think that about them in the least. But Allyson? Yeah, I know she purposefully didn't say one word to me, which pisses me off and makes me hungry for her all at once.

I huff a laugh. "Less than you'd think. She yelled up one side of me and down the other. I think she decided we're going to 'be adults' and play nice for the kids' sake."

"You agreeing with that plan of action?" Mike asks hesitantly. "Don't let her run you off. I need you, man. The boys need you."

I meet his eyes. "I'm not letting her run me off. I'm the damn assistant coach of the Wildcats and that's what I'll be as long as you let me or until the season's over. My word's good."

"Thank fuck. I was scared I was gonna lose you. Actually, I was afraid it was some one-night stand thing that was going to make everything really awkward. If you start doling out dick, every mom is gonna line up and I'll have a roster of dads wanting to take a sucker punch at my assistant coach."

He's joking, and I laugh deep in my belly, which feels foreign but good. "I ain't dicking the moms." At his questioning look, I add, "*Or* the dads."

He laughs too but puffs up a bit. "By the way, have I mentioned my *wife*, Jamie? The one I love with my whole heart. Have I mentioned that I would kill anyone who so much as looked at her sideways, much less touched her?"

I hold up my hands. "I've got no interest in your wife, Coach." I grin wolfishly. "Wait, what's she look like?"

He lobs a solid punch at my shoulder, but his fist pings off the hard muscle. "It's a good damn thing I like you. But for real, fuck your way through the moms *and* dads, for all I care, but not mine."

"You're the one who asked me. I ain't dicking the moms or

dads," I repeat. "Just here for the kids and the football, though I'm second-guessing that right this minute."

He points a finger at me like he's going to hold me to it, and that's just fine.

Coach football. Avoid Allyson.

Done and done for another day.

CHAPTER 7

ALLYSON

I quadruple-check my notes one more time before the meeting. This is going to be the decision-maker for our client. Either mediation will work and we can all avoid the mess of court, or it won't.

One last glance, one more big breath, and I adjust my posture from sitting at my desk all day. Once upon a time, I'd dreamed of becoming a big-shot courtroom lawyer. Actually, more than dreamed. I had every step planned out.

College, law school, marriage, kids, my own firm. I plotted every step of my life the way only youth can, with zero regard for the possibility of anything other than my dreams becoming reality.

Back then, it was Bruce at my side when I walked down the aisle of my dreams. We'd discussed having two children, a boy and a girl. He was going to be a professional football player and I was going to be a lawyer, no ifs, ands, or buts about it.

College was a rude awakening. Harder than I'd imagined, lonelier than I'd anticipated, and my plans started to disintegrate in my hands, no matter how hard I tried to hold on to them.

Losing Bruce broke me inside and left me vulnerable for Jeremy. It wasn't until much later that I could see that though. At the time, he'd felt like a lifeline pulling me to shore as I drowned in my sorrow. And I'd been happy, slowly becoming more and more willing to adjust my plans to include him. Jeremy was pre-law too, and I changed the sign outside my imaginary firm to include both of us . . . Silverton and Silverton, attorneys at law.

Getting pregnant my second year of college changed everything for both of us. My redirection to becoming a paralegal was initially a huge disappointment to me, to my parents, and to Jeremy. But he'd adjusted quickly, holding my hand and promising me that we could still work together, and made everything I'd dreamed of still seem possible.

Now, with years of experience under my belt, I can honestly say that I love my job and wouldn't change it even if I could. Being a paralegal lets me be home with Cooper more, and it means I don't have to worry about the bottom line the way I would if it was my name on the door.

"Hey, Rick?" I say, poking my head into my boss' office. "I'm heading into the conference room to prep for Gloria's mediation. Anything you need before I'm locked in a room with her soon-to-be ex?"

I cross my fingers on both hands, waving them around even though luck will have nothing to do with this. It's all about my preparation and skills, both of which are beyond reproach. But no matter what, I just want this to go well for Gloria. She's a sweet lady who stood by her husband for decades while he built a decent-sized empire, but now that he's replacing her with a younger, perkier version, she's ready to move on.

Luckily, she's not out to slash and burn her husband's world, or Rick would be helping her because that's his specialty. Instead, she just wants what's fair, and that's where I come in.

"Nope, all good. Let me know if I need to step in, though. Use me as a threat," he advises, throwing a few air punches. He's not a scary-looking man, honestly, a little old, a little round, a lot bald. But he's a pit bull, and his intimidation factor isn't in those weak-ass non-punches but in the power of his sharp-witted and cunning mind.

I've worked for Rick long enough now that we've developed a

shorthand for the best way to handle our client roster. He takes the heavy hitters when he needs to play the 'good old boys' card or go aggressive for negotiations, and I handle the less dramatic cases or the ones where a soft touch is better. I won't say I get the easy ones, but compared to his clients, I get the easy ones. It's worked well for us both.

"Debra? Will you show Gloria in when she gets here? But when Mr. Jacobs and his counsel arrive, call before bringing them back."

Our shared receptionist nods and gets up to start fresh coffee for our incoming guests. Debra is about as old-school as you get with her perfectly curled silvery gray hair, sweater sets, and sensible shoes. But damn if she doesn't do a stellar job at keeping up with every task Rick and I throw her way. She's a dynamite with briefs and spends her free time reading legal journals for fun. In another era, she would've been a lawyer herself, and a damn fine one, but being our receptionist is her second career after her three kids grew up and flew the nest.

In the conference room, I adjust the chairs, removing the one at the head of the table. I want this to be as hospitable as possible without creating an unneeded power differential. Most importantly because I don't want Mr. Jacobs to feel that he has any undue dominance here.

"Allyson? Ms. Jacobs is here," Debra says from the doorway.

Gloria comes in, her back ramrod straight and her hands clasped in front of her. Her bottom lip looks a little raw where she's chewing it. "Gloria, relax," I say kindly, welcoming her in. "Today's going to be the first step in the next phase of your life."

She follows my guidance and comes around to the far side of the table, perching on the edge of the chair. "I know. I just never thought this would be my retirement plan. Hell, I thought we'd be going on that trip to Greece we'd always talked about." Her laugh is sour, verging on bitter, as she shakes her head.

She's still shell-shocked by the course her life has taken, but that's understandable. The important thing is that she finds some joy in her newfound freedom. "Was Greece your idea or David's?"

Her eyes, which had drifted off, most likely to Greece, refocus on me. "Oh, well, both of ours, I guess, or at least it has been for years, but initially? It was David's, I think."

"Well, then you get to pick. Do you go to Greece or do you go to Spain? Or Italy? Or anywhere in the world you'd like to go. It's your choice now. Research and plan or throw a dart at a map. Take a friend or go alone and make some." I inject as much excitement as I can into the idea, hoping she feels the infinite possibilities.

She smiles and it almost reaches her eyes. "You sound like you've made that speech before. To other clients or to yourself? If you don't mind my asking?" She looks at my bare finger curiously.

I shrug one shoulder, not wanting to divulge too much about my own personal life. "Both, maybe?"

Truth be told, I did have the same pep talk with myself once upon a time. I'd chosen to come home to Great Falls, even knowing that it wasn't really home anymore. The town grew, I'd changed, and my parents had moved, but the familiarity that remained was comfortable and it felt like the right place to raise Cooper. So Great Falls was where my dart landed.

Gloria pats my hand comfortingly, though I'm supposed to be doing that for her. "Okay, let's do this."

We go over the plans, what she's asking for and what she wants, what's negotiable and what's a deal breaker. When Debra calls back to announce Mr. Jacobs's arrival with his lawyer, we're ready.

The conversation goes on for hours, just as we expected. Gloria and David are pretty close to agreement on virtually every point, but there's a lifetime of items to divide. We've split the household items fifty-fifty, with only a minor sticking point about a vase they bought at a charity art gala.

"Doesn't Denice have children? It'd be a shame for such a beautiful piece to get broken accidentally. It's irreplaceable." Gloria's scalpel-precise bomb is a direct hit, though she delivered it so eloquently and with such deft concern, you'd think she was actually worried about the vase. David agrees with a sigh and a wave of his hand.

I'm impressed with Gloria, who looks clear-eyed without a trace of the uncertainty from before. It's a front, it always is, but she's pulling it off with spectacular believability.

We're making excellent progress until we get to the company ownership. Gloria wants half and it's a deal breaker, but David wants a seventy-thirty split.

"Are you actually serious right now?" Gloria asks him incredulously.

David leans forward, digging a thick finger into the tabletop. "It's my company. I worked morning, noon, and night to grow it. I've made every business decision since day one and it's mine. You should be thankful I'm considering giving you any of it." At that, the lawyer places a strong hand over David's, forcing his palm to the tabletop. He opens his mouth in an attempt to mitigate whatever damage his client might've done, but Gloria's fired up now.

"*You* worked morning, noon, and night? And who was taking care of the house and kids so you could be absent all those times? Who was right there next to you when you took out that first business loan and told you we'd make good on it? Who was beside you in those early days, working just as damn hard as you were? Who listened to you discuss 'should we do this or that' over dinner and again at night, when you couldn't sleep?"

She pauses, letting all that sink in. I keep my mouth shut this time because she's doing a better job of stating her case than I ever could and David looks to be responding to her. He's slouching in his chair, defeated. "To be clear, you're not *giving* me anything. I earned fifty percent of that company the same way you did—with hard work, faith in what we were doing, and the balls to take some big risks."

David's turning a bit red, so I add the cherry to the top of Gloria's sundae. "If we aren't successful in mediation, we'll have to go to court. We'll get the fifty-fifty split almost guaranteed, but this process will be drawn out a few more months. It's your call, Mr. Jacobs."

He whispers with his lawyer and then sits back. "Fine. But we're not running it together. How is this going to work?"

It takes us two more hours to figure out a plan for David to pay

Gloria for her share of the business. She doesn't want to work with him—or Denice, the secretary-slash-new woman—so it's a perfect way out, if a particularly difficult one to navigate a resolution to.

By the time we're done, I'm exhausted, but I still shake Gloria's hand as she preps to leave. "That's really it? It's over?"

I put a gentle hand on her shoulder, reading her face. Some clients are overjoyed that whatever they've been through is finally done, ready to throw a divorce party, even. Others are shocked and saddened that what had started with so many hopes and dreams is truly over with the swish of a pen.

"It's over. I'll file the paperwork, but barring something going awry, it's done," I say carefully. Gloria nods numbly, all pretense of her bravado and fight sapped out of her. As she walks out the door, I tell her once more, "It's all your choice, Gloria. You can go anywhere and do anything. Think about something you've always wanted to do and go do it. Skydive, travel, curl up with a good book and glass of wine. Big or small, celebrate the birth of the next phase of you."

She smiles weakly and disappears down the hall. A moment later, Debra appears in the doorway. "Sorry we kept you so late. I didn't think it'd go that long."

Debra shakes her head. "No worries, Allyson. But you got a call a little bit ago. Guy said he's Cooper's football coach?"

My head snaps up, on guard. "What's wrong?" A thousand scary thoughts run through my mind at once. Broken bones, concussion, car accident, even though Cooper shouldn't be riding in a car while at practice.

"He said that neither you nor Michelle showed up to pick up the boys after practice? I told him it's Michelle's day, but she didn't answer the phone when he called her. I tried too and no answer. I offered to come get them myself, but he said they're fine. He didn't want to drive them over without permission but said he'd stay at the park with them until you or Michelle could come. He said to tell you, 'No rush, we're just feeding the ducks.' I think he meant literally, but it kind of sounded like he was kidding when he said it?"

My emotions, which have been on a roller coaster, take another loop-de-loop . . .

Michelle didn't show up or answer her phone, but she's a nurse at the local hospital and sometimes gets stuck in the middle of a case and can't step out. Usually, it's no big deal and I can readily pick up the slack, but not when I'm in closed-door negotiations.

But Bruce is taking care of the boys, something he didn't have to do.

And last but not least, I'm a little bit giddy at his pointed mention of ducks. He must remember that's how we met, so is he trying to tell me something by bringing them up again? Or am I reading too much into it? It's definitely that, for sure. Because he could probably care less about some silly stuffed duck he won for me at the fair as a memento of a dumb school speech.

And why do I even care? I mean, not being arch enemies with him would be nice since he's coaching Cooper, but I don't need to go reminiscing about the good old days. Consciously, it only makes me mad about things that happened long ago, but unconsciously, if I do start to think about the past, I'm afraid I'll wake up from another one of those sexy dreams that I cannot have. Not about Bruce, at least.

"Shit! I'll go right now. Can you send Michelle a message not to worry, that I'm on my way for the boys, and she should do whatever she needs to at the hospital? I'll feed Liam dinner and he can spend the night if he needs to. And then put Gloria's mediation agreement in the safe for the night. I'll file it at the courthouse tomorrow morning."

Debra grabs the stack of papers from my hands. "Go on, I've got all this. Do what you need to do to, Allyson."

"You're the best!" I call out, running for the door.

CHAPTER 8

BRUCE

"Sorry you have to wait with us," Cooper says morosely. He's a mess of sweat and dirt, and I had to search my truck to find him and Liam a couple of granola bar snacks to feed their post-practice hunger. Even then, they gave half of the crumbly bars to the ducks that swarmed up on the edge of the pond as soon as we walked over. The ducks didn't seem to mind the stale snack in the least.

But all laid out in the grass with the darkness getting blacker, their bellies are starting to growl again. So's mine, and one of the guys at home probably already snuck into the kitchen and ate the plate Mama Louise leaves for me on football practice nights. Looks like a drive-thru is in my future before I head out to the farm tonight.

I mess up his hair, trying to stay casual. "No worries, kid." Realizing my mistake, I make an exaggerated face of disgust and then wipe my sweat-soaked hand on my jeans. "So, how does this carpool run for you two?"

Cooper raises his hand like he's in school, and I lift my chin his way, giving him unspoken permission to speak. Coach's rules still apply, I guess. "Our moms make this big official schedule. There's a calendar meeting once a month and everything, though it's mostly just our moms with pens, highlighters, and glasses of wine. They work on it together and then stick a copy up on both our refrigerators and keep another copy on their phones. We sneak out as soon as dinner's done." Liam and Cooper roll their eyes at each other, laughing at the antics of adults.

"The after-school babysitter dropped us off today, but it's supposed to be my mom picking us up," Liam explains. "Since she didn't answer the phone, though, I'm guessing she's stuck at work." Unconcerned, he plucks another blade of grass to add to the pile he's already accumulated beside his thigh.

When practice had ended and all the other parents had left with their kids, Cooper and Liam were the last men standing. I volunteered to stay with them so Mike and Evan could get home. After a few minutes waiting to see if she was just running late, we'd called Michelle and got sent straight to voicemail. Then we'd tried Allyson, both her cell and her work line, where I talked to a lady named Debra who'd worriedly said that Allyson was in a closed-door meeting. After reassurances that I was fine hanging out with the boys until someone got here, her appreciation had bordered on overwhelming.

I bump Liam's shoulder, having learned my lesson to keep my hands off their sweaty grossness. "What's your mom do again?"

"She's a nurse at the hospital. She works twelve-hour shifts a few days a week in the operating room so she can be home with me most of the time. When she's not, that's where Ms. Allyson tags in." Liam holds his hand up and Cooper slaps a high-five to his palm, not giving a single shit about the dirt they're smearing between them.

"Tag!" Cooper says a little too loudly in the quiet evening air. "Mom works days at Mr. Rick's law firm, so Liam gets to stay with us when his mom's working overnight or when his dad's home. They call it 'village parenting'." Cooper's voice says he's heard that saying more than a time or two.

Liam picks back up. "My dad does sales and travels all the time, so it's usually just me and Mom. And then we he comes home, they take a night to 'date' and then we all hang out as a family."

Even in the dark, I can see the flash of the boys' white-toothed grins, and they giggle as they make kissy noises and both say, "Date! Ewww!"

I chuckle along, acting offended. "What? Old people can date."

Cooper groans. "We know that means sex, Coach B. Gross."

"Oh, uh . . ." I stammer, not sure what to say to that. I mean, he's not wrong, at least about 'date' being code for sex, but it's definitely not gross. Knowing this is definitely not my place to add any details to their discussion, I stick with as little as I can say as possible. "You might feel differently about that when you're older."

Liam gives Cooper's shoulder a friendly shove. "At least your parents aren't having s-e-x every time they see each other while you go on sleepovers at my house." They giggle again, wrestling around a bit.

"So, what about your dad, Cooper?" The words blurt out before I can stop them. Part of me is desperate to hear his answer. The other part wants to shove my big paws over his mouth to stop him from saying a word. I don't want to cause him pain if it's a hard story, but my curiosity overrides my reticence when he doesn't burst into tears or show any real emotion.

"I don't remember him. And Mom doesn't talk about him. Ever." His complete lack of emotion is suddenly more telling than if he were upset. He's swallowing a lot, keeping it bottled way down deep. It takes one to recognize one, and I've definitely been accused of being a stoic robot a time or two.

Problem with that is, it's gonna come out one way or another eventually.

I grind my teeth together as I try to figure out what to say. A boy and his father is a special bond, one Cooper's missing. Allyson can do, and is doing, so much for this adorable pipsqueak, but he needs someone to show him how to be a man. Silently, I vow to do as much as I can over the course of the season as his coach.

I lean my elbows on my bent knees. "My dad was different from both of yours, but I guess that's true of everyone. No mom, no dad, no girl, and no boy is exactly the same. That's what makes the world go 'round."

I hope I sound wise and sage, not like I'm pulling shit outta my ass, which is closer to the truth.

Cooper looks over at me, eyes wide with curiosity. "What was your dad like? And your mom?"

So many answers to such simple questions. I swallow thickly, knowing that I can't tell them the whole truth. No kid needs those seeds planted in their heads. "When I was about the age you two are, my parents were pretty great. I have two brothers and a sister too, and my family owned a farm. We all worked together, and it was pretty awesome. I'd get up in the morning and do chores—"

They groan. "Ugh, chores are the worst!"

"They were the worst, or at least I thought so at the time," I agree. "Looking back, though, it wasn't so bad. I took care of some of the animals and did a whole lotta work in the fields. Less when I was younger." I hold my hand up, palm down, measuring about how tall I was back then. "And then more as I got older." I move my palm to the top of my head, measuring myself now. "That's my non-coaching job still. Work in the fields every day, just like my dad taught me."

Liam puts one and one together. "Is that how you got the peaches for practice?"

Smart kid. "Yep, picked them myself for the team. Guess I like you guys a little bit." I hold my finger and thumb up an inch apart but move them further and further until my hand is stretched wide.

Cooper laughs, bubbly and light, and I feel like he needs that. Especially as he says, "A mom and dad, brothers and sister, and a farm? It sounds like a Disney movie!" There's a brightness to the words, but I'm pretty sure there's a hint of jealousy hiding underneath.

I can't stop the bitter laugh that barks its way past my lips. "It definitely was not that picturesque. My mom and dad loved each other a lot, and I've got some great memories from when I was a kid. Later was a different story."

Any reasonable adult would hear the silent request to leave the topic alone, but eight-year-old boys have basically zero social skills.

"You don't like them now?" Cooper asks with his eyes narrowed like he can't imagine not liking Allyson.

"Well, they're gone now. Both of them passed away, and we sold our farm to the neighbors. But now, it's like I've got an even bigger family of brothers and sisters." I'm trying to make it sound like one of their big sleepover parties, but the truth is, it's been a hard adjustment for us all. But we're doing better now, with minimal authentic threats of loss of life and limb over the evening dinner table.

I keep a close eye on Cooper, gauging his reaction as I say my parents have passed. I'm still not sure what exactly is going on there, and even though it's really none of my business, I have a burning need deep inside to know everything there is to know about Allyson. And this seems like it's a big piece of what's turned her into the she-devil she seems to be now.

Cooper blinks a couple of times, long, dark lashes covering his pale blue eyes, and I'm afraid he's about to cry, but mostly, he seems to be processing what I just shared. He doesn't seem upset or sad, like he's having feelings about his own dad at all.

Before I can ask any follow-up questions, a car pulls into the parking lot going too fast. The headlights flash over us, blinding us for a moment. "Bet that's one of your moms." As the words leave my mouth, another car comes peeling into the lot. From here and half-blind, I can't tell what kind of cars they are.

I hear doors slam and feminine voices apologizing. "Oh, my God, I am so sorry!"

"No, I'm sorry! I was stuck in a meeting."

"I was stuck in the OR!"

I grin at the boys. "Double-shot of mom. Come on, guys." We all get up and start to walk across the field. I can see Michelle in scrubs and a messy ponytail and Allyson in another skirt and heels combo, both running this way looking harried.

Cooper puts a hand on Liam's arm and looks back at me. "Hey, Coach B?"

"Yeah?"

"Don't get mad, but you gotta take advantage when you can,

'kay?" Cooper's teeth flash again, and Liam chuckles but covers his mouth with his hands.

"Huh?" I say, confused and having no idea what Cooper's talking about until he starts blubbering.

"Mom? Mom! I thought you weren't coming back!" He's suddenly totally hysterical, and I have a heart-stopping moment where I think he was putting on a brave face for me.

Liam joins in the chorus. "Yeah, Mom. I thought you forgot me." He sounds on the verge of tears.

Allyson and Michelle coo and pet the stinky boys, promising dinner with cookies and apologies.

I realize what these monsters are up to. They are absolutely, one hundred percent playing their mothers for treats. The laughter bursts forth in a tidal wave and both women shoot glares at me.

"Thank you for staying with them," Allyson says coldly, though her eyes could burn me to ash where I stand.

I cross my arms over my chest, leveling a gaze at Cooper and Liam. They shrink under the weight of my deep frown.

"Boys, why don't you tell your mothers what we've been up to while they were working so hard and worrying so much that they rushed over here to get you?" My tone broaches no argument, and their tears dry instantly, their fake drama dissipating like cotton candy in water.

"We fed the ducks," Liam says, his eyes on the grass.

"We sat around and talked," Cooper says.

"No muss, no fuss," I add. "They were fine until they saw an opportunity for cookies and took advantage."

Cooper and Liam, suitably chastised, look to their mothers with real tears in their eyes now. "Sorry, Mom. Sorry, Mrs. Michelle," Cooper says, and Liam echoes the sentiment to his mom and Allyson.

I glance back to Allyson, not expecting an apology for her obviously frosty appreciation when she arrived, but she offers one anyway. It's with her eyes, not her mouth, but I understand it just the same.

In the lengthening moment, the air between us thickens, heating with possibility even though there's an undercurrent of distrust.

She looks good, the skirt hugging her hips and her shapely legs tapering down to the sexy heels that would feel great digging into my ass as I buried myself in her. But it's the swirling confusion I can see in her eyes that calls to me the most. She sets me off-kilter, but I do the same to her. And damned if I don't want to explore that, delve deeper into it and know what's running through that mind of hers.

Which makes me furious . . . at myself, at her.

Michelle's eyes bounce between Allyson and me. "Look, I know you two have some stuff to talk about. Let me take the boys home and feed them dinner . . . *with no cookies.*" She raises a brow at Liam before looking back to me pointedly. "Go to dinner. I hear Hank's even has two-dollar drafts tonight. Talk about old times, talk about life and love and whatever else comes up."

"Michelle!" Allyson hisses. "No, I'll just take Cooper home."

Michelle's scowl deepens, her eyes screaming at me to man up and take advantage of the opportunity she's presenting on a golden platter. I'm not sure I want it, but I can't pass it by, either.

"I need to eat before heading home anyway," I grumble. "I missed Mama Louise's dinner waiting around with these guys." I hold up a fist and Cooper pounds it, then Liam follows. They're smiling now, though it's cautious. "So, what do you say, Al?"

The nickname slips out again, but it feels comfortable on my tongue so I don't correct myself. I can hear her breath pause, though, and I know it hit her too.

Her mouth opens and closes a couple of times as she looks between me and Michelle and then down to Cooper. Finally, her spine straightens and she says tightly, "That sounds great, I guess. Let's get a beer and some dinner."

One side of my mouth quirks up in what passes as a triumphant smile. I know I probably look like a cocky shit, but I don't give a fuck. Dinner, a beer, and Allyson. Once upon a time, it was all I ever wanted.

Somewhere, I hear a little voice reminding me to avoid her, but I squash it down forcibly. It's just food, nothing more. Or maybe I'll figure out what the fuck's up with her so we can 'be adults' as she wants? Or maybe I'll fuck her in the parking lot? The possibilities are endless and unexpected, something I usually hate. I like knowing what people are going to say and do even before they do, but I can't get a read on Allyson. Damn infuriating is what she is.

I guide her toward the parking lot, my hand grazing along the small of her back. She heads to her car, looking over her shoulder. "I'll meet you at Hank's?"

I nod, not sure what I've gotten myself into.

In the quiet parking lot, Cooper's voice sounds as loud as gunfire as he asks a question that makes my heart stop. "Coach B? Are you taking my mom on a *date*?"

Allyson's jaw drops, and I shake my head subtly at her, telling her I've got this because she does not know the minefield she's walking in to.

"No, buddy. Just dinner between old friends. No dating or *dating*." Michelle and Allyson both look confused, but Cooper and Liam giggle before running for Michelle's sedan.

"I'll get the boys to school in the morning. Have a good night," Michelle virtually sing-songs, making me wonder just how much Allyson has told her about our past. Or if she's in the habit of pawning her friend off for God knows what with random guys. Not that I think Allyson's into that.

Hell, I have no idea what Allyson's into now. But I sure as fuck want to find out.

Michelle gets the boys loaded and pulls out, leaving Allyson and me alone in the now-dark parking lot. The moon shines down on us, and I can't decide if she's going to back out or go through with the dinner plans.

This is the opposite of what I want, I try to tell myself, willing ice through my veins. But it sounds like a distant echo through the thrumming of my racing heartbeat.

Drawn to her even as I fight it, I brush a lock of her soft blonde hair back, slipping it behind her ear. It feels natural but oddly unfamiliar at the same time. My voice is gravelly as I give her an out I'm only half-praying she doesn't take. "We can just skip it if you're not up to it."

She licks her lips, and I steel myself, not allowing myself to imagine chasing her tongue the way I'd love to. I grind my teeth, awaiting her verdict.

"No, dinner sounds . . ." she says, her voice a bit breathy. She shakes her head and my stomach drops, knowing she's going to bail. "It sounds good. Let's do it."

Well, shit. I wasn't expecting that.

Coach football. Avoid Allyson.

Fuck that. Or maybe fuck her?

Shit, I'm in so much damn trouble here, mad at the old Allyson and intrigued by the new one.

CHAPTER 9

BRUCE

*C*hewing up the last bits of the post-practice cinnamon mint I popped on the way over, I look around. Hank's is hopping for a Thursday night. It's mostly a hole in the wall dive bar, but for locals, there's nothing better than its worn pleather, greasy food, and overpoured drinks. There's a whole bunch of people in the back, hovering around the three pool tables, more than a few folks on the wood floor dancing around to the twang of a Luke Bryan tune, and another group crowded around the bar.

"Uh, do you see a table?" Allyson asks. It sounds like she's hoping there's not one and we can just call this a bust and cut the night short.

But now that we're here, I want to be. I have so many questions, so many answers I need, so much I want to know about everything that's happened since I last saw Allyson.

Something tells me that's a long story that would answer so much about who she is, and I want every little juicy morsel of it. Not to revel in whatever has turned her into this shadow self that runs hot and cold, but because once upon a time, she was the person I knew best, and it stings that maybe I don't know her at all now.

I grab her hand, tiny in my huge paw, ignoring the tingles that shoot up my arm to drag her through the crowd. In the back corner, there's a table that no one likes because it's a little too close to the kitchen. It's empty, just as I hoped. I hold an arm out, gesturing for her to sit. I'm an asshole, but I'm a gentleman too. She sits and I follow, plopping down across from her. But the table's a bit small and my knees bump Allyson's.

"Ow!" she cries out.

"Shit, sorry," I mumble, moving my chair a bit, which puts me closer to her side.

Her smile is small. "I forgot how big you are." Her cheeks flush hot instantly as she hears her own words and filthy, dirty thoughts run through my mind. Dozens of ideas of ways to make that pink tint spread over her entire body as I remind her just how large I am . . . everywhere.

"Ouch, you know how to hurt a guy's feelings," I joke instead, keeping it light.

She bites her lip, looking down and fidgeting with the edge of the paper placemat that proclaims Hank's as *The Best Honkytonk In Town*. Nobody is willing to remind Hank that he's the *only* honky-tonk in town.

She doesn't respond to my teasing and I think maybe I over-stepped, but I'm not sure how to handle this clusterfuck.

The waitress stops by, and we order two beers and two specials. When she leaves with a promise of being 'back in a jiffy with the beers', silence descends.

It was always easy with Allyson. Words flowed and even quiet times were comfortable. I remember spending hours in the bed of my truck, staring at the stars in relaxed silence, and listening to her talk non-stop about anything and everything. Her after-school chatter session was the favorite part of my day.

"Oh, my God, Mrs. Finley is such a bitch! She knows it's championship weekend, but she still gave us a huge project that's due on Monday! Monday! Like we're going to have any time this weekend at all. She's basically anti-school spirit."

I watch her mouth, mesmerized by the way her lips form the sounds that are washing over me. This girl could read the damn phonebook and I'd happily listen.

"Bruce! Are you even listening to me?" Fire fills her eyes as she calls me out for what she thinks is my dismissal of her rant.

I run my thumb across her cheekbone and she melts into my hand. "Yeah, Al. I'm listening. Finley's a bitch . . . blah, blah, blah. Honestly, though, I got a little lost thinking about kissing those sexy lips."

I did hear every word, but kissing her so she forgets what's bothering her is what she really wants right now. It's what I want too.

This weekend is a big deal for both of us. Al is a varsity cheerleader and this is her last championship game to cheer at. I'm the rock of the defense, the leader of the team even though I'm a junior. I need to prove myself. She wants to go out on top.

She licks her lips in preparation, and I lean in, covering her mouth with mine. She tastes like cherries, a new ChapStick she started wearing a while back. We lose ourselves in each other, forgetting about the pressures of our teenage life, letting go of the expectations and responsibilities that rest on us, not worrying about the future as we meld together. I wish there were time for more, but reality sets in.

"Come on, let's go start on your project now because after the game, you're mine." I take her hand, pulling her toward the library.

"I'm always yours." The promise is quiet, under her breath almost, but I hear it. I feel it.

Now at Hank's, it's not the comfortable connection we used to have. No, that's nothing like right now.

Allyson looks over at the pool tables as a cheer breaks out. "Looks like they've got a winner," she says uselessly, just filling the silence.

I revert back to the Neanderthal ways that have served me so well over the years and grunt. I guess she's not the only one running hot and cold.

Allyson rolls her eyes, huffing just a little. "What was that? Is that what passes as conversation these days?"

I raise a brow, challenging her little bark of displeasure with my continued silence.

She pulls her napkin from her lap, throwing it on the placemat. "This was a mistake. If you didn't want to go to dinner with me, you should've just said so."

As she stands, I put a firm hand on her arm, holding her back. "I just . . . I don't know what to say."

That takes the wind out of her sails, and she collapses back to her seat as she confesses, "I don't know what to say to you either."

It's quiet again, but thankfully, the waitress saves us by dropping the beers off. I watch Allyson's lips pucker around the bottle, zero in on her tongue licking the liquid residue off her bottom lip. I force myself to take a sip myself in an attempt to wash that image away.

"I remember the first beer you ever drank. Made a face like it was watered-down piss," I say, my lips quirking at the memory.

She does make a face at that. "Johnny Jackson's back field party, right?"

I hold up my bottle in celebration, impressed that she remembers, and we clink. "I'm guessing you've had a few more since then. Fuck knows, I have."

Even I can hear the bitterness.

Her nose crinkles cutely, but she seems sad as she asks the million-dollar question. "What happened to us?"

I damn near choke on the celebratory drink I took, sputtering roughly. "So much."

It's harsh, and I know I'm being an asshole, but I can't stop it. I'm so angry at her still, and I'm angry at myself for still being attracted to her. Because I am.

As much as I want to know what she's been up to, what's been happening in her heart and mind and life, I want to shove her up against the wall and fuck her raw and hard. Not the sweet way we used to when we were in love, but there's something to be said for hate fucking. Maybe that would get her out of my system? Because as much as I want her, I don't *want* to want her.

"Tell me about your life now," she commands. "How're your mom and dad?" She smiles as she says it and I know she has no idea. No concept of how crazy my whole life went after high school. I'd need a damn 4x4 truck with mud tires to show her just how off-path everything went.

"Small talk? That's what we're doing?" I say bitterly, tilting my head. Allyson blinks those baby blues that used to own me, waiting patiently, and I press my lips together, trying to decide whether I want to attempt to explain what my family's gone through in the last few years.

I sigh, planting my laced hands on the table. "Fine. Shortly after I graduated, Mom got sick. It was fast, it was hard. Cancer's a bitch."

Allyson's jaw drops open in horror and she shakes her head. "Bruce! I had no idea." Her hands reach across the table to cover mine. "I am so sorry. Mrs. Martha was such a great woman. She always welcomed me with open arms, and I have so many happy memories about her."

My eyes are locked on her hands on mine, the searing heat of her flesh touching me. I can't stop my thumb from brushing over her finger, feeling the softness of her skin, and she retreats, pulling back sharply.

"Me too. She was a great woman, a great mom," I say, picking up my bottle for another drink because I'm not sure what to do with my hands now that they're not touching hers. "Dad took it real hard, basically disappeared on us, but Brody and Shay took over running the farm. Bobby and I work the fields, and we did okay for a long while."

It's weird to put so much into so few words, but honestly, it's not something I've ever talked about with anyone. And it doesn't seem like the time to get verbose.

"And now?" Allyson asks, mirroring my action and taking a drink. Does she even know that she's doing that or is it unconscious?

The waitress interrupts, setting our plates down. The pork chop and cinnamon apples smell delicious, but I don't know if I'll be able to taste a thing with how badly I want to taste Allyson. Even with the uncomfortable conversation and simmering resentment low in my gut.

I pull my hat off and run my hand through my hair as I sigh. "Look, you want the short story? Fine . . ." I slam my hat back down and my mouth gets away from me. "Mom died. Dad died. We lost the farm because Dad gambled it away, had to sell to the Bennetts. And now we're like the bass-ackward, country redneck version of the Brady Bunch with Louise Bennett as the leader of our twisted motley crew of a family. The Bennett boys all have women, one of which is my fucking sister. And us Tannens are just trying to keep our heads down and work because that's all we've got."

I pick up my fork and knife and slice a big chunk of pork chop, shoving it in my mouth and chewing pointedly so she doesn't ask more questions.

The truth is a jagged pill to swallow. I've adjusted to not owning our family farm anymore and have sent enough curses to the sky hoping that Dad can hear them. And I appreciate the Bennetts' hospitality and problem solving by letting us stay on as workers so we didn't lose everything at once. But though my day in, day out life hasn't changed much and I still work in the same fields I have since I was a kid, I know the bottom line.

I'm unsettled. No wife. No kids. No land. No prospects. No future. I'm just doing what I've always done, one foot in front of the other, and one day, I'm afraid I'm going to look up and find that I've never gone anywhere or done anything permanent. Crops are transient. My life's work is disposable.

It wasn't supposed to be like this, and I thought I'd made my peace years ago with the direction my life had taken, but seeing Allyson brings back all the dreams of what it was supposed to be.

I force the too-big bite down and flip the tables on her, barking out, "You? What's your story?"

Her eyes drop first, then her chin, and though I can't see her hands, I get the distinct impression that she's twisting her napkin in her lap. "Uhm, got married, had Cooper, got divorced. Moved back to Great Falls a few years ago."

She sounds haunted. There's a lot more than the Cliff-Notes version she's telling. Like me. And there's a thread of anger too that mirrors mine.

How the fuck did we end up here like this?

But I know. And she knows. The past might be long gone, but it's not forgotten.

At least now I know her ex is out there somewhere, not dead.

Not to be crass, but there's no competing with the perfect memories of a ghost.

Though how someone could divorce Allyson, I have no idea. She's perfect. Except for the leaving me part.

"And your parents? How are they? I remember dinners at your house," I say, memories assailing me. "I washed my hands three times just to sit at your mom's table and made sure to wear my best jeans, the only pair that didn't have a hole in them."

Allyson looks up through her lashes, not meeting my eyes as she shrugs. "I . . . I haven't talked to them in a long time. I don't know how they're doing."

I set my fork down a little too loudly and it clatters on the plate. "What? What happened? You were always so close." It's more accusatory than I intended, but seriously, what the hell? Allyson's parents were picture-perfect nice in a Mayberry way that tended to make me feel that much dirtier and rougher.

Her shoulders tense, a sure sign the truth is buried deeper than what we're sharing tonight. That's okay. I'm not going to push her if I'm not willing to share either.

"Never mind. It's okay, Al. We don't have to talk about that."

She looks back to me gratefully, both of us not knowing what to say again. Taking the easy way out, I stand up. "Come on, let's dance."

"*What*?" she screeches as I grab her hand.

She doesn't fight me on it, but I wouldn't have let her off that easy, anyway. Conversation's hard. We need the action of spinning around the floor. I think it'll do us both some good.

I pull her to me, keeping space between us as I lead her around the floor. It's friendly but not *friendly*. It actually reminds me of the school dances we went to a few times where chaperones around the edges of the floor would keep everything PG-rated.

But though our bodies don't touch, I'm drinking her in with my eyes. We sway together, and I spin her slowly in deference to her heels, my hand teasing along her lower back until we're back front to front. This time, we're a little closer as the music transitions into the next song, a slow and sultry one.

Cody Johnson's *Nothin' On You* washes over the floor, over us, creating heat all around us as everyone feels the music flow through them. I put Allyson's hand on my chest and don't bother with any fancy spins or tricks. We just move together, shifting back and forth.

Her fingers dance across my chest, searing me through my shirt. Even in her heels, I look down at her, watching her eyes trace her fingers' movements. Her gaze moves left and right, measuring my chest, and my arms flex, drawing her attention. The pad of her thumb slips over the lines of black tattoo ink peeking out of my shirt sleeve.

"When did you get this?" she whispers into the space between us.

"A few years ago," I tell her. "I've got others too. If you want to see some time." Need rumbles through my voice, and though I'm shit for flirting, she knows exactly what I'm saying.

A tiny gasp passes her lips, and she looks up to meet my eyes in slow motion. "Bruce . . ."

I can't hear whatever she's about to say. I don't want to hear her say she wants me, really don't want to hear her say she doesn't. So I do the one thing that will shut her up and take her breath away.

I kiss her, right there on the dance floor at Hank's in front of the whole damn town, hard and sure. Not that I'm giving a single thought to them as I take her lips. She freezes for a single heartbeat, and then she's kissing me back with a heat echoing what's roaring through my blood. We stop any pretense of dancing, our tongues tangling and tasting, our bodies remembering and wanting.

"Fuck, Al."

I wrap my arms around her tighter, pulling her against me, and I feel her lift to her toes, giving me more of her weight as she leans into me willingly. She moans, a vibration I feel more than hear, and I slip one hand up to cup the side of her throat, wanting to make her do it again against my palm.

"Whoooo, Brutal! Yeah, man . . . getcha sum!" a voice calls out from over by the pool table.

A few chuckles sound out around the room, but the spell

between us is broken. She drops down to her feet, stepping back from me. A single step has never seemed so far.

I see the shock, the confusion in the blue of her wide eyes before she drops them, shutting me out.

"Al—" I try to say, but her hand twists my shirt over my chest and she shakes her head, refusing to meet my gaze.

"No, we can't." I'm not sure if she's telling me or asking me, so I answer as though it's a question.

"Yes, the fuck we can. We're adults and can do whatever we want. And make no mistake." I tilt her chin up, forcing her eyes to mine. "Allyson, I want you."

Heart, meet silver platter. Okay, maybe it's not quite like Bobby predicted because I'm not offering my heart. But I'm damn sure willing to give her my cock, even knowing it's stupid as fuck.

She closes her eyes like that hurts her to hear. "I know. I'm sorry, Bruce. I just . . . I can't." She takes another step back, virtually running for the door.

When it comes to fight or flight, Allyson was always a fighter, but damned if she's not flying away right now. Which pisses me off . . . at her, at me, at the fuckwit who interrupted us. As the door swings shut behind her, I whirl toward the pool tables. I'm definitely not a flight-er.

"Who the fuck is making my business their business? Because now, your business is mine," I roar so loudly the rafters rattle.

The crowd quiets and scatters, leaving behind a couple of skinny farm boys who are already a few sheets to the wind. They're both holding their hands up, and one says, "Sorry, man. Didn't mean to scare her away. Just . . . you know . . . WHOO!"

He pumps a fist in the air like he was trying to celebrate my possibly getting laid, like we're friends. I don't know this asshole from Adam, though.

I take slow, measured steps toward him, nothing fast or Hank, the bartender and owner, will pull out the Louisville Slugger he keeps beneath the bar. There's no need to do that because Hank's a good guy and I don't want him getting hurt. I grab the asshole's shirt, twisting the collar up so it's nice and tight around his throat and he has to stand on unsteady tiptoes. His buddy has already stepped off into the circle of the crowd.

"What's your name?" I snarl low, right up in his face. His breath reeks of beer.

"Bloomdale, Kyle Bloomdale. You're my boy's football coach." He's stammering, slurring words, but there's a thread of pride running through them.

I don't show my surprise, but I do set Kyle down on his feet. "You're Killian's dad?" He nods too fast and I sneer at what I see before me. "I didn't know he even had a dad, seeing as he never mentioned you. Seems like he's lucky to have his grandparents raising him. He's a good boy. Thanks to *them*."

The dig is knife-point sharp, taking the bluster out of whatever kinship he thought we'd have. He gapes like a fish and I hold his eyes as I yell over my shoulder,

"Hey, Hank? Kyle here is gonna be paying for my dinner, Allyson's too, plus a tip."

He whines and I stare him down. "Consider yourself lucky I'm in a good mood."

I'm not really, or at least not anymore. But I was there for a minute with Allyson in my arms, her taste on my tongue, her body writhing against mine.

From the other side of the crowd, I hear Hank's voice, smoker rough from the packs-a-day habit he broke years ago. "Sure thing, Brutal. You boys have a nice night, you hear?"

The threat of violence at Hank's hand is woven through the nicety with the subtlety of a crowbar to the head. I chuckle darkly and turn, walking away and heading toward the door. The crowd parts for me like the Red Sea.

Once upon a time, I would've busted Kyle's nose and walked out of here with his blood on my fists. I'd like to think I've grown up a bit since my misspent youth.

Some days that's true, some days not as much.

CHAPTER 10

ALLYSON

ing dong!

The doorbell chimes happily, and I set down the rag I've been working across the kitchen counter for the past ten minutes. It's already spotless, but Sunday is my day to reset for the week ahead, a little something I call 'bless this house'.

I've got laundry going, the bathrooms sparkle, and Cooper's been dusting every flat surface for the last hour. He's not the best at it, but I think it's important for him to have chores so he develops a sense of pride and ownership. A sense of home.

"Coming!" I call out, my steps quick toward the door.

I peek through the peephole and I'm left breathless. What's he doing here?

I put a hand up to my mess of hair, piled haphazardly on my head. I've got my glasses on, which make me look owlish and nerdy. But worst of all, I'm wearing a pair of ratty cotton shorts that are way too short for company and a tank top with a built-in bra that only mostly keeps everything locked and loaded. In short, I look like shit that slept on the ground outside overnight and then lucked into a roof over its head for the day.

And I smell like Pine-Sol.

I blink, wondering again what he's doing here. But I open the door anyway. "Bruce?"

I see the genuine surprise on his face, his brows jumping up and crinkling his forehead. But then his eyes sweep lower over me and something more animalistic takes over his expression. "Al?"

My skin tingles and there's a tiny piece of me that preens under his heated perusal. Maybe I'm at least a *hot* mess?

"What are you doing here?" I say, knowing I sound ridiculously breathless for the situation.

He holds his hands up, each one clasping a gallon jug of pink liquid. "Watermelon water delivery. This is the address Shay gave me?" He answers his own question, leaning back to look at the metal numbers affixed over the mailbox beside the door.

"Oh, uh . . . yeah. Debra said she was going to order me some fancy juice she had at brunch the other day. I guess that's you?"

Of course, it's him, Allyson. He's literally standing on the front porch with the juice Debra raved about. But I can't help it that my brain cells are misfiring when he's at my house, looking good enough to eat in worn boots, dirty jeans slung low on his hips, and a black T-shirt with the sleeves and most of the sides cut off like redneck air conditioning. I can see the sides of his torso, ridges and bumps that are new and tempt me to explore with my hands and my tongue.

Dear God, are you trying to torture me? Haven't I earned some good favor by now?

Apparently not, because Bruce looks at me questioningly. "Where do you want it?"

It takes me a full three seconds to realize he's talking about the watermelon water and not the other liquids my body is craving. His sweat on my skin, his hot mouth on mine, his thick cum filling me.

No. Get ahold of yourself, girl. No.

I remind myself to think about Cooper, my son, and how much football means to him. Fucking his coach would ruin all that. Not to mention, Bruce and me together is a supremely bad idea of epic proportions. Even though we still have chemistry between us—that kiss at Hank's sure as shit proved that true—there's been too much time and way too much has changed.

"Right in here." I finally answer his question with something resembling a brain. I hold the door open and he steps into the living room. It's always seemed like a perfectly respectably sized house, especially for just Cooper and me, but with Bruce in here, it feels absurdly tiny. Vaguely, I wonder if he stretched out his arms if he could touch wall to wall.

Deep inside, there's a seed of niggling worry, but I'm easily able to hush it. Bruce would never hurt me, at least not physically. With the barest tease through my psyche, I realize that despite his overwhelming size, I actually feel safe with Bruce. I take that seriously, listening to my instincts.

I give him my back, a respectful sign he likely doesn't even recognize the importance of, and lead him to the kitchen. "Here, let's put them in here so they stay cold."

I can see the condensation coming off the bottles, and Bruce tugs at the bandana knotted to his belt loop to wipe them down before setting them on the table. "One for them, one for me," he explains, dropping the damp bandana to his side before pulling one out of his back pocket like a magician. He lifts his cap and swipes the fabric across his forehead before setting his hat back down and shoving the bandana in his pocket again.

I open the fridge, setting one jug inside, and then realize the proper thing to do here. "Would you like a glass? I haven't had it before, but I hear great things about it." I'm already pulling two glasses from the cabinet.

"Yeah, that'd be great. Thanks." His voice is flat, cautious like I might spook at the slightest provocation, which is understandable, I guess, after I ran out on him.

We drink, and I'm surprised at how good it tastes, even after Debra's rousing endorsement. Bright, light, and refreshing. "Wow! So you make this?"

He snorts, almost choking. "No, I grow the watermelons or whatever Shayanne tells me to. She's the genius in the kitchen. Has her own business now, a couple of them, actually. She makes goat milk soap with the supply from her herd and then has about a dozen recipes she makes seasonally. She sells all over town, to the resort, to folks in Great Falls, and she's even shipping the non-perishable things out on special request. I'm just the delivery guy when she gets too busy to do it herself, which is damn near all the time."

I scan my memories, finding an image of Shayanne. She must be around eleven or so, dirt-smudged on her freckled face as she hangs upside down in a tree by her knees, teasing Bruce and me. We were out on a walk on his family farm and she'd tagged along, not under-standing our teenaged desire to be alone. "Guess Shayanne's all grown up now, huh . . . guess *we're* all grown up too."

His mouth opens like he's got something to say about that, and I'm already flinching as if it's going to be a biting response, but Cooper comes sliding into the kitchen, saving me. "Coach B! I thought I heard voices! What are you doing here?" He's excited and every word is a bit too loud.

Bruce smiles an actual teeth-flashing grin at my son, who doesn't realize in the least what a gift that is. "Hey, Cooper! Just making farm deliveries, brought you some watermelon water."

Cooper runs for the cabinet, grabbing a glass, and I hold myself back from helping as I watch him carefully pour himself some. He takes a big slug of it, not a care given to whether he might like the never-had-it-before flavor or not. He wipes his mouth with the back of his hand. "That's pretty good! Where does this fall on the whoa-slow-go scale?"

I have zero idea what he's talking about, but Bruce goes into coach mode before my very eyes. It's a sight to behold as his stiff harshness with me melts into kindness. "Definitely a slow. The fruit's good, but Shay adds a big dose of sugar syrup to it. And don't drink your mom's. Grown-ups sometimes like to add *extra* to theirs, and that's a definite no for you." He winks at Cooper, who's eating this up as he bounces around like he just drank a Red Bull instead of one sip of sweet juice.

"Got it." Cooper nods, taking mental notes on every word Bruce says. "Hey, you wanna stay for lunch? Mom's making sandwiches, and you can have my strawberries if you want." Cooper loves strawberries, so for him to offer them up is suspicious as hell. I eye my son, who looks innocent as a newborn angel. But I'm well aware of his scheming and genius-level gymnastics to get his way.

"Cooper, Bruce probably has other deliveries to make," I say, trying to give Bruce an out. Or if I'm honest, myself an out. I don't know if I can sit here with him in my kitchen like everything's fine when it's most definitely not fine at all.

I want to hate him. I want to love him. I want to kill him. I want to fuck him.

It's too much. I shut down with the overwhelming litany rushing though my brain on a loop.

Bruce's barest hint of a smirk dares me, though, a silent 'challenge accepted' passing between us. "Actually, a sandwich would be great. Mama Louise packed me a lunch, but I'm a growing boy, so an extra sandwich would be just right." He rubs his hand over his flat stomach, making the cotton hug his rippling abs.

Is he doing that on purpose? Is he flirting or trying to drive me mad? My mouth feels like I just swallowed cotton, but it's definitely the only thing *dry* around here.

My legs squirm, and I chug a solid drink of watermelon water, hoping it'll cool me off a bit. But the smug satisfaction I see in Bruce's expression tells me he knows exactly what he's doing to me.

Asshole.

"Fine. Let me get everything together while you boys wash your hands."

Cooper drags Bruce down the hall to the bathroom, and I wash my own hands in the sparkling clean kitchen sink before pulling out bread, chicken, cheese, mayo, and lettuce.

I can hear their voices down the hallway but can't make out what they're saying. Even the rumble of Bruce's voice partnered with Cooper's high-pitched, excited one makes me yearn for something I can't define. It feels homey? *Or like home,* I realize with a shudder.

Nope, not doing that. Not even going to allow myself to pretend or play the 'what if' game because there's no going back. There's no 'what if we hadn't broken up?' or 'what if this was our life?' or most painfully, 'what if Cooper was Bruce's son?'

Bruce and I screwed that up way too long ago for anything like this happy little family life to have been a possibility.

When they return, I've got sandwiches arranged on plates around the table and every wall I can construct up and fortified.

Cooper, in his glorious obliviousness, asks, "Coach B, you said you and Mom are old friends?"

My eyes meet Bruce's across the table, and I'm damn near scorched by the heat I see there.

It's not orange flames of fresh fire but rather black coal embers that have been burning below the surface for so long. A single poke is all it'd take to bring them back to a flashpoint, though.

I answer, wanting to set my own narrative for Cooper. "Yes, honey. Bruce and I went to high school together. We were good friends back then."

Bruce's teeth grit for a second as he swallows whatever it is he wants to say, and then he takes a big bite of sandwich. With his mouth still full, he tells Cooper, "Yeah, we were *best* friends, used to hang out *all* the time. Your mom ever tell you about the time she went muddin' in Mr. Sampson's back field and almost got arrested?"

He grins around the food, taking evil delight in throwing me under the bus.

"Mom, you did not!" Cooper yells, indignant that I might have been a bit of a rebellious hellion in my younger days. Little does he know, I was mostly a good girl until I met the man across the table. With him, I was bad—sneaking out, going to parties, having beer, and later, having sex. All the things a wayward teen isn't supposed to experience, but I'm thankful for those experiences because otherwise, my high school days would've been stuck in the boring rut of schoolwork and cheer practice, the same routine on repeat that life was before Bruce.

I glare at Bruce, wishing he hadn't chosen that particular story to tell my kid. "Bruce might be exaggerating a little bit, but I did go mudding. And there might've been a very friendly conversation with one of Great Falls' finest officers. But there was no 'almost arrest'. He just told us to leave."

Cooper looks skeptical as his eyes jump from Bruce to me, trying to decide which version of events to believe. "Just one question. What's mudding?"

Bruce drops his sandwich to his plate. "What the hell are you teaching this kid, Al?" His voice booms, and I jump but laugh at my overreaction, feeling silly. I see Bruce catalogue the response before explaining to Cooper, "First off, it's muddin', not mudd-*ing*. Second, muddin' is when you take a big truck with special tires and drive through mud. It's messy, slippery, crazy fun." He makes a few growling sounds that mimic an engine working its way through the mud, and the shock of his joking around with Cooper surprises me.

Cooper's eyes are as big as saucers. "I wanna do that! Mom, can we do that?"

"Probably not, honey. We don't know anyone with a mudding truck, and it's not exactly the safest thing to do." I'm trying to let him down easy, but his face falls anyway.

Bruce clears his throat, and I glance over to see him silently asking permission to take Cooper. I look over my shoulder toward the front windows but can't see his truck in the driveway. I wonder if it's still the big green monster of a diesel truck he drove in high school. Good Lord, the things we did in that truck.

I correct myself. "Well, I take that back, I guess. Looks like Bruce might be willing to take you out. As long as you don't go in Mr. Sampson's field."

"I'll take you both," Bruce declares.

I look at him, and something electric passes between us, sending an unwelcome jolt through my body.

"Oh yeah, going muddin', that's right!" Cooper's oblivious to anything between Bruce and me, instead doing some crazy version of a celebration dance with his knees knocking together as he twirls an invisible rally towel over his head. I notice that he's changed his pronunciation to match Bruce's twangier version too.

Cooper's wild joyfulness is the break for Bruce and me, anger dissipating and heat cooling. It's not a truce, more like a momentary lull in a war that we agree to with a searching look in each other's wary eyes.

Bruce high-fives Cooper and throws a smile my way that makes my belly flutter. It's so similar to what he used to look like, happy and fun, but in a masculine, grown-up way that his younger self promised to be. My breath catches in my throat at the cruelness of the world. This is who he was meant to be, but somehow, it all went wrong.

For both of us.

I want to disappear to when things were simpler, easier, and surer. "Are you so surprised that I might've actually been cool once upon a time, Cooper?" I pinch at his cheek, grinning when he pulls away and scrubs at his cheek as if he can wipe away the affection. "I'll have you know that your mother" —I tick off on my fingers— "went mudding, was the top of the pyramid, which means I had to jump down like nine feet, went swimming in the no-swimming-allowed river, won a teddy bear as big as I am at the fair by throwing softballs at a milk can, and did all sorts of crazy things."

I want to add more to the list, but I can't exactly tell my son about skipping school to go to the movies, or the pasture parties with big bonfires, or any other things I did that might just give him ideas for his own teen years. I'm willing to spill a little in the interest of being cool to my kid, but I don't want to give him ammunition to throw in my face later.

Bruce has no such reservations.

"Listen to your mom, Cooper. She was the coolest person I knew in high school. Did she tell you about the time she made an actual one hundred on a huge science test on the same day she led the pep rally for the whole school?" Cooper listens raptly, eyes glued to Bruce. Honestly, I'm listening just as closely, not remembering the day he's talking about but somehow not surprised that he does. "And then after we won the game, she led what had to be almost the entire school in a rousing rendition of the school song. Everyone was singing along." He sways a bit in his chair, humming under his breath, and I remember.

What he's leaving out is that all that happened at one of those back-pasture bonfires and that we were all a little tipsy, some on beer we shouldn't have had, but mostly on the excitement of the win and the buzz of possibilities. He's leaving out that he picked me up by my waist and helped me stand on the roof of someone's truck, keeping his big, rough hands circled around my bare thighs so I wouldn't fall as I conducted everyone's off-key singing like a choir director. He's leaving out that after we all sang our fool hearts out, he'd helped me back down and my whole body had run the length of his as my feet met the grass. He's leaving out that we'd made out in the bed of his truck that night, going further than we ever had before.

I don't recall the test or the pep rally, but I remember the feeling of his hands on my breasts through my sweater that night and the way he'd moaned the school song against my neck while the bonfire burned out. I remember that part like it was yesterday.

One look at Bruce, though, puts a damper on those memories. He's smiling lightly, like none of that has even occurred to him. It's just a silly story to tell to a kid about some high school fun.

I take a breath, forcing my mind into the past with an open heart. I can do this too.

"What Bruce is forgetting to tell you is that he won the game for us that night," I say brightly, smirking at Bruce, who shakes his head at me in warning. Oh, two can play this game. "He might not've scored any touchdowns, but he literally stopped the other team from gaining a single yard all night."

Cooper's excitement bubbles up. "Tell me *everything*," he says dreamily, hands tucked below his chin and elbows resting on the table.

We do.

Somehow, Bruce and I manage to talk for over an hour, telling Cooper stories or at least the child-safe versions of them.

Homecoming dance. School carnival. Parties. Movie dates. Stargazing. Sandwich picnics. Walking the fields at Tannen farm. Dancing in the church parking lot after fast-food dinners in town because we were broke. Football games.

As soon as I let one memory out, they all rush back at once, overwhelming me. But it's in a good way. The happier times remind me of who I was, maybe of who I can be again. Not fully, but maybe just a little drop of that innocent girl could grow again inside me? Like a seed or sapling? Or hell, more like a weed that refuses to let the ugly concrete keep it down and searches out any crack to grow through until it finds its own sunlight. That's me . . . Dandelion Allyson.

Bruce seems to be feeling it too. His gruff grunts and monosyllabic answers toward me have turned into drawn-out stories, amped up for dramatic effect, much to Cooper's delight.

Best of all, we don't feel like enemies. Not like friends exactly, either, but the progress feels important.

Too soon, he says he has to go.

"Oh, man, just one more story?" Cooper begs, and Bruce looks at his watch.

"Sorry, kid. Gotta get the rest of my deliveries out and get home for dinner." But he says no with kindness and a smile Cooper soaks up happily.

I intervene, hoping for a redirection of Cooper's attention. "Are you telling me that your bedroom and bathroom are clean? Are they worthy of a visit from the queen?" I eye him speculatively.

Cooper's grin is so wide it shows off the gap on the back side where a baby tooth has come out but the permanent one hasn't made it all the way down yet. "Why, yes, Milady. 'Tis spotless, I proclaim."

"Even the ring of soap residue under your bubble bath?" He always misses that, sometimes accidentally, sometimes intentionally.

"*Mom!* Don't tell Coach B I use bubble bath!" he whines in a hushed whisper.

Bruce chuckles. "Ain't nothing wrong with bubble bath, buddy. Hell, I've been known to take a bubble bath myself on occasion. It's relaxing and fun to blow the bubbles around."

I know for damn sure that this man has not taken a bubble bath since he was a kid. For one, the only tub he can use is a swimming pool. And two, it doesn't seem like it'd be his thing. I imagine he's a shower in five minutes kinda guy.

But he scoops up some imaginary bubbles and blows them toward Cooper, easing the embarrassment I didn't mean to cause.

"Clean, mister," I order, and Cooper scoots out after pounding Bruce's fist once. "Thanks. Didn't realize bubble bath was a cardinal slight to his manhood."

Bruce's lip tilts upward, but it's nothing like the smile he flashed Cooper. Without that buffer, we're falling back into uncertain territory.

"Thanks for lunch, Al. I had fun, hadn't thought about those days in a long time." His voice washes over me, perking up goose-bumps over every inch of my skin. I know he can see them, considering the little amount of clothing I'm wearing, but he doesn't mention it.

"Me either." I should say something about last night, apologize again, maybe, but the words don't come.

He turns to go, his long strides getting him to the front door quickly. "See ya at practice."

And he's gone. The door stands open where he left it, but I watch silently as he gets in his truck, not the green one from high school I remember but a newer, black, jacked-up Ford with a dent along the side of the bed.

I like it. It's a little like him . . . functional, but a little banged up. He pulls out of the driveway, and it growls loudly down the street as he accelerates just a bit too fast. Yep, just like him.

"What the fuck just happened?" I wonder aloud, but as I'm alone, no one answers.

I certainly have no idea.

CHAPTER 11

BRUCE

"*H*oly fuck, I think you could fry eggs and bacon on the hood out here! A whole damn country breakfast." Bobby scowls at the sky like the sun's personally insulting him by shining.

"What crawled up your ass?" I ask but still send a bottle of water arcing his way. Bobby snatches it out of the air, tilting it toward me in thanks before draining it dry. "It's August and we've got zero cloud cover, so it's not exactly a newsflash that it's hotter'n balls."

I chug a bottle myself to rehydrate as I scan how far we've made it today. We've got a mixture of fields, some that are harvested with big machines where you might as well be sitting in a luxury sedan with air conditioning and satellite radio and other areas that are strictly hand-harvested. That's where we're working today.

Shayanne asked us to plant some fancy heirloom tomatoes for this summer, which are now as big as softballs and ripe for the picking, and then there's a whole row of cherry tomatoes too. They're all gorgeous and red but fragile and have to be gathered one at a time.

We get back to work, filling another crateful in easy silence now that our hourly bitch fest is done.

"What the hell's wrong with you?" Bobby bites after a bit.

My brow furrows. "Whaddya mean? Nothing's wrong." I keep

working, setting a particularly big Brandywine tomato on the top of another full crate.

Bobby sets his crate in the bed of the truck and rests his arms over the edge, squinting as he looks me over. "You don't even know it, do ya?"

"Know what?" I ask, stopping work to give him my full attention.

"We're working, it's hotter than Hades, we've got a good couple of hours till dinner, and you . . . you're smiling." It's an accusation, like he's incredulous because it's never happened. Although, maybe it hasn't?

I shove at his shoulder after I set my own crate in the truck. "Fucker, so what if I'm smiling? That should mean nothing's wrong. Maybe I'm just happy today. Shouldn't my brother want me to be happy?" I give him my back, heading for the next plant to pluck a few more fruits.

I once heard a saying . . . *Intelligence is knowing a tomato is a fruit, wisdom is not putting it in a fruit salad.* I'm guessing whoever said that had never enjoyed Shay's cherry tomatoes with watermelon and basil. Fancy looking, but it tastes damn good and probably qualifies as a fruit salad with tomatoes, so take that, chefs of the world.

Shay's recipes aside, I wish Bobby had some intelligence or wisdom and would leave shit alone, but I'm not that lucky.

"I do want you to be happy, but I'm curious what's prompted it right now." He already knows the answer so I don't bother telling him. He smacks the truck with his palms. "Damn it, Brutal! You said you were gonna avoid her, but she went and got her claws in you again, didn't she?"

I whirl. "Her *claws*? What do you think she is? A damn bear?"

"Cougar, maybe?" he snipes.

"That's a low fucking blow, Bobby. She's only a year older than me, same as always. And no, she doesn't have her claws in me." The denial is sour on my tongue, even though it's mostly the truth. After yesterday, I don't know what to think.

"So just being around her, in her orbit, that's enough to make you giddy as a schoolgirl? You gonna bust out in giggles next? If so, give me a warning so I can put my waders on first." Bobby's digging in on this and not gonna let go.

I growl in frustration, hopping up onto the tailgate. "What do you want me to say?"

He leans a hip against the truck, thinking. I appreciate that, at least. He's not talking off the cuff but considering his words. Or at least I do until he speaks. "I want you to say you hate her, that you're still mad at her, that you don't want to see her ever again. But none of that's true, is it?"

I think just as hard as he did and quietly confess. "We had lunch yesterday."

"A date?" Bobby barks.

I shake my head. "No, not a date. I was doing deliveries and one of them was to Al. Cooper invited me to stay for lunch and one thing led to another." He raises a stern brow at me, and I clarify. "I didn't sleep with her. I meant that we talked, mostly about the old days. Just the good stuff, happy and silly memories."

"There," he says, pointing at me. "You're doing it again. Smiling like a damn fool."

"That's probably because I'm thinking about the kiss at Hank's on Saturday night," I bait him.

He closes his eyes, huffing and puffing as he talks to the sky like anyone's listening to him. "What the hell? He says he's going to avoid her, so what does he do? Take her to Hank's, kiss her, have lunch with her . . ." His eyes jump to me as he stops ranting abruptly. "So what does this all mean?"

"Nothing, not really," I admit. I scrub at my hands, bits of dirt falling to the ground.

I go through all of it, from the electricity shooting between Allyson and me to the kiss and her running out. I tell him about the awkward weirdness, the light-hearted memories, and the anger still simmering in my gut. And I tell him about how Allyson seems different, which stops his questions short.

"I want to be happy for you, I do, man. Maybe if this was all stars-aligning easy or some Hallmark movie shit, I'd make my peace with it, but it's not." He shakes his head vehemently. "I don't trust it, don't trust *her*. Especially if she's got baggage she's dragging you into and has already got you on a string, tugging you in and then letting you out like you're a damn yo-yo. You're already hooked and you don't even know it. And that pisses me off, for you and at you. At her," he spits out.

He brings up some good points, which I hate to concede, so I brush him off. "Well, shit, man, I didn't know you cared so much." I chuckle as I say it, pushing his hat off his head. It's guy-speak for 'Thanks, I love you too,' which he'll get clearly.

He growls as he bends down to pick the dirty camouflage cap up, slapping it across his thigh like that'd get the dust off it. "Such a dumb fucker."

He mutters it, but I hear it anyway. He's right, usually, but about this, I don't think I'm wrong.

I see Allyson, and even though she ripped me to shreds when we were younger, I don't know that she did it intentionally. That doesn't mean she's not responsible for hurting me, doesn't mean I'm not still mad at her for it, but she's not cruelly twisting me up like he says. If anything, I think she's more lost now than I ever was.

"Maybe our best wasn't good enough back then. Maybe you're right and it's still not good enough now, either. I don't know." I hop off the tailgate, heading back toward the rows.

Bobby's eyes track me, confusion in the lines on his forehead. "So, what are you going to do?"

"Pick some more tomatoes." I know he's asking what I'm going to do about Allyson, but I don't have the answer to that question so I sidestep for now. "Thanks for looking out for me, though."

"Guess I'll go ahead and stock up on the Jim Beam just in case. Hell, maybe it'll be to toast with." He's answering right back, letting me know that whether this goes right or totally fucked ten ways from Sunday, he'll be here for me, celebration or consolation.

"Get the good stuff just in case." I'm not sure if it's just in case I need to drown my sorrows or lift it in a toast, but good whiskey is always the right option.

"Pass me the fried okra, will ya?" Luke begs.

Mama Louise ain't having it. "You'll wait your turn and it'll get around to you soon enough."

He whines about it being his favorite, but he's just mouthing. We ignore him and continue passing tonight's dinner platters around the table family-style, everyone taking what they want because there's always plenty.

At least now there is. At first, when we all started eating dinner together, Mama Louise wasn't sure how much to make to feed the additional mouths around her table. Some nights, we had mass quantities of leftovers, and others, we were fighting for the last roll.

Somewhere along the way, she figured it out and now it's just right. Enough seats around the new table on the back porch under the fans with room to grow, as she calls it, and enough food on the table for folks to eat their fill.

Mama Louise outdid herself tonight with roast chicken, fried okra, and scalloped potatoes. When everyone's got their plate, we dig in.

"Sure is good, Mama," James says as he shovels his food in his mouth. If you didn't know any better, you'd think he's afraid someone's going to steal his plate right off the table with how fast he's inhaling his chicken, swallowing with barely a second to chew. Truth is, he and Sophie have to eat in shifts, one eating while the other feeds their little girl, Cindy Lou, and then trading so they all get a chance to eat.

The sentiment is echoed around the table, and as hungers begin to get fed, conversation starts back up.

"And I'll be able to bring back organic dried lavender from the farm we're going to. I think I'm going to do a line of sleepy time products, soap and lotion. Maybe that'll help with Cindy Lou?"

Shayanne's been giving her daily plan for her trip just like I knew she would, so my missing her 'big news' was actually no big deal. She was over the moon to discover there's a small family-owned lavender farm near the horse Luke's going to see.

Sophie looks at Shay gratefully. "That'd be great. Can you put a rush order on that?"

Cindy Lou is the cutest baby ever, I reckon, but she's never been a good sleeper. And with James having to get up early to drive out to the ranch and Sophie being on call all the time for Doc Jones's vet practice and finishing up school, they need their sleep and have resorted to trying any and everything. Desperate times call for desperate measures, I guess.

But as they switch roles and James takes over feeding Cindy Lou her pureed baby food, he coos at the blonde little thing whose hair sticks straight up no matter what they do. "It's a good thing you're cute, isn't it? Isn't it? Or Daddy'd have to put you in the back yard so he could get some shut eye." His threat is delivered with the sweetest smile in high-pitched baby-talk, so I'm pretty sure he's kidding.

"She'll sleep eventually," Mama Louise predicts. "Nobody goes through life on a few hours here and a few hours there."

Sophie mutters, "I am."

I can see the tiredness settled on her shoulders and the faint blue tint under her eyes. But even so, she laughs at her own joke, her smile genuine.

James puts his arm around Sophie's shoulders and pulls her in to lay a sweet kiss to her forehead. She closes her eyes, melting into him for the quick moment. When she opens them again, his eyes lock on her though he talks to his mother. "Mama, you think you might be up for babysitting tonight? Or tomorrow? Or anytime soon?"

Katelyn answers first. "We can! We'd be happy to have her over tonight and get those baby snuggles." Her husband, Mark, seems to have a different definition of 'happy' because there's a rumbling in his chest that sounds like an actual growl. But Katelyn bats her eyes at him and he quiets. She's a full-on magician, I think.

I grew up with Brody and am therefore inordinately used to grunts and glares as a form of top-notch communication, but Mark Bennett is a whole 'nother level of Neanderthal. If I were a betting man, I'd wager that Katelyn has a tattoo somewhere that says *Property of Mark Bennett—Touch & Die.*

Not that I'd ever gamble after Dad's shitstorm with that particular vice. Or see Katelyn naked to know what marks she might have. But Mark, for all his gruffness, is transformed by the slightest look or softest touch from Katelyn.

Katelyn blows Cindy Lou a kiss with a big "Mwah! You wanna stay with Auntie Katelyn tonight, sweet girl?"

Cindy Lou smiles, kicking her pink-striped sock-covered feet, and then returns the kiss. Except it's more like she blows a raspberry, and orange baby food goes everywhere, getting all over James and dribbling down Cindy Lou's chin.

"Sum of a bifch!" he shouts in shock, disgust wrinkling his brow. "Oh gawd, it's in ma mouf! I 'eed a 'apkin!"

We're all fighting back laughter as Sophie, who hasn't missed a beat of her own dinner, hands him a paper towel. To his credit, he wipes his daughter down first then scrubs at his own face.

"Language," Mama Louise corrects.

You'd think she'd give up on that by now. We're all pretty rough around the edges, even though we have some decent manners. The language rule just doesn't seem to be one that stuck . . . to any of us. Hell, I've even heard the girls go off worse than any of us boys before, depending on the topic and their level of excitement or fury. Mama Louise's fighting a losing battle on a sinking ship, but she combats every instance in her presence and says what we do when she's not around is something we'll have to make our own peace with.

"I think it was warranted, Mama. Do you know how gross those carrots are? Blech," he argues his case, but Mama Louise isn't swayed in the least as she purses her lips at him.

"Bet you'll feel differently about your language, and everyone else's" —she doesn't look around the table, but we all hear the admonishment— "when that little girl starts repeating every word you say like a magpie." She reaches over with a bare finger and wipes a bit of orange gunk out of the babe's hair, smearing it on the paper towel James laid on the table. "And I'm happy to babysit. Not to be too crass, but I'm happy to get those baby snuggles myself so that maybe I can get another grandbaby soon. Cindy Lou wants a sibling or a cousin."

She looks around the table this time, measuring each of us.

Mark steps up to the plate first. "Mama, you know we're not ready so quit pestering us. You make Katelyn feel pressured." I glance at Katelyn, whose eyes are deceptively steady. I don't think she's the one feeling pressured.

Mama Louise tsks. "Don't be pawning your own nerves off on your sweet girl. We all know you're too much of a stubborn mule to share her with a baby just yet. But I have hopes that one day, you won't be such a selfish boy."

I can't help but crack the smallest of smiles at Mama Louise calling Mark a boy. He's not as big as me, but he cuts an intimidating figure at over six feet of 'I'd rather kill you than talk to you' attitude.

But Mama Louise is right. I don't know the dynamic Katelyn and Mark have, but they are deeply wrapped up in one another. It'd be cute if it weren't so sickening.

Of course, then there's James and Sophie, who are playful and sweet and so in love, it'll make your teeth hurt from sugar overload. James takes the wind out of Mama Louise's sails too. "Mama, one day . . . maybe. But right now, if you'll take Cindy Lou tonight, I have grand plans of taking my wife to bed, curling up under the sheets, and sleeping for eight hours straight."

Nobody thought that was where that sentence was going to go, but Sophie looks at James like he just promised her a trip to the moon or a night filled with orgasms.

Mama Louise looks at Luke but then winks at Shayanne. Mama Louise is a good mother figure for Shay, one I don't think any of us really knew she needed. She was so young when Mom died, but Shay has always been one to tackle the world so we all thought she was fine. Really, she was, but she's gotten close with Mama Louise and it's done her good. I know they talk a lot about Shay's businesses and her plans and dreams. So whatever Mama Louise already knows must answer her question about Shay and Luke.

Which leaves her with us Tannen boys as options.

Technically, any kids we may or may not have wouldn't really be her grandchildren. But I don't think she's ever met someone she didn't instantly take under her wing, whether they want it or not. As evidenced by the three tall, dark, and handsome assholes perched around her dinner table, she's pretty much adopted us. She isn't Mom, but I suspect that the next generation of Tannens will call her Grandma . . . and that won't be a bad thing.

I don't even see it coming, but Bobby throws me under the bus like he planned the schedule and route himself. "I guess you could call the Wildcats your latest additions, if you want? Those boys would probably love for you to fuss over them and cheer them on. You know what they need? Zucchini bread with chocolate chips." He nods like he solved all my problems, even though the asshole knows he just created one.

I cut my eyes to him, killing him a thousand times with the daggers I'm throwing and warning him to sleep with one eye open. One of the benefits of still living at home, in our childhood house, is that I know where all the squeaky boards are and can sneak into his room silent as a ninja to exact my revenge.

Mama Louise claps. "Oh, that would be fun. I won't bother you for practices, but I can make zucchini bread for snack on Tuesday. And we'll all be at the games, of course." She glances around the table to make sure everyone heard her decree, and I see heads bobbing in agreement.

"You don't have to do that. Any of you. It's not a big deal. Just Peewee Football." I shrug, downplaying it. I don't want them all there to see me fail, to see how soft I am with the boys, to see me not knowing what the hell to do about Allyson.

Bobby scoffs. "You're not kidding anyone, Brutal. You're all 'Mike . . . blah, blah, blah . . . the boys . . . blah, blah, blah . . . Allyson . . . blah, blah, blah . . .' Oops!" He slaps his hand over his mouth dramatically like he misspoke, but I know damn well he said exactly what he meant to say.

Fuck ninja. I'm going in like a Spartan, straight kick to the chest.

"Who's Allyson?" Luke asks, and I see Shay's hand leave the table to rest on his thigh. I strongly suspect she's silently telling him to shut up and that she'll explain later. I don't even know if she knows anything. She was so young when Al was around. But the question is out there and eyes are on me.

"One of the boys' moms. We went to school together."

I intend for it to sound casual, but my reluctance is more of an answer than my words. It's probably moot anyway, because Luke and I are close enough in age that he and I were at Great Falls High together, though we ran in different circles. He would have known about Al. But I just can't imagine talking about her like this.

Mama Louise is a wise woman indeed because she changes the subject with a knowing look. "How many loaves of zucchini bread do you want? I'm happy to make however much you think they'll eat."

I do quick math in my head of how hungry each kid is after practice. "Four or five would be great. Thank you."

I give her a smile of appreciation and then deadface glare at Bobby, promising death and dismemberment.

CHAPTER 12

ALLYSON

*P*ractice ended ten minutes ago, and I should be halfway home by now, mentally preparing for an evening of spaghetti and frozen meatballs. I know it's not the best option, but Cooper said the carb loading of just spaghetti was an overindulgence and we needed protein to balance it out. I'd blinked in surprise but finally agreed that adding some meat would be fine.

But that's not where I am and not what I'm doing at all.

Nope, I'm standing off to the side, trying really hard to *not* look like a stalker. But I guess that exactly what I am, considering I'm waiting for Bruce to finish talking to Mike.

My eyes roam over the park, finding Cooper, Liam, and Evan happily sharing their homemade zucchini bread with the ducks. Though sharing might be an exaggeration because they're taking huge mouthfuls for themselves with each bite and tossing tiny pinches of the bread for the birds.

I don't mean to eavesdrop, but I can't help but tune in when I see Bruce put his hand on Mike's shoulder and rumble, "I'm so sorry, man. That shit sucks."

My ears perk up. I'm not usually gossipy, but I've got enough small-town experience to recognize when there's something to know.

He shakes Bruce's hand off. "It could be worse. I could be one of the guys they laid off. A shift change isn't so bad when you look at it like that," Mike says glumly, like he doesn't believe his own words.

Mike told us at the first meeting that he's a machinist in a factory two towns over. I'm not sure what exactly he builds or even what he does, but he seemed to like his work.

"What's that mean for you and Jamie? And Evan?"

Mike scrubs a hand across his head, the shaved-short hairs making a scratching sound I can hear even from a few feet away. The park's gone quiet, kids all headed home for dinner, and now only the occasional scream of a cicada sounds out.

I try to step away to give them a bit of privacy, but I feel Bruce's eyes telling me to stay, to wait for him. I want to talk to him, though I have no idea what I want to say. It just seemed like the prudent and polite thing to do after the weekend of weird ups and downs.

I'm going for Adulting 201 now, I guess.

"It'll be fine. Jamie understands, and we'll make whatever adjustments we need to at home. I'll be there in the mornings more, so I can do breakfast with Evan and take him to school. And sleep in the afternoon until I have to go in." He nods, trying to convince himself as he repeats, "It'll be fine."

Bruce nods. "What's that mean for the team? You won't be able to come to practices at all if you're working third shift, and you'll be sleeping when we have games."

And suddenly, I'm selfishly upset. I feel for Mike and Jamie and the changes their family is apparently going through, but if Mike can't coach, does that mean the team is no more? Cooper is going to be devastated. I'm going to fail at giving him this thing he wanted so badly.

Mike's grin is feral. "You remember telling me that your word is good and you were the Wildcats coach until the end of the season, no matter what?" His eyes look over to me, letting me know he's aware of my presence in the darkening evening.

"Yeah . . ." Bruce says slowly.

Mike points a finger at Bruce. "Good, 'cause I'm holding you to your word. I want you to coach the boys, run the practices, and lead the games. You up for that?"

Bruce's chuckle is huffed from deep in his gut. "Fuck no. I ain't ready for that shit and you damn well know it."

"Too bad, Coach. You're the new leader of the Wildcats. Don't let me down." Mike acts like Bruce didn't even speak, certainly not like he said no to the proposal that he be the only coach. He even holds his hand out for a shake on it like they agreed to the sales price on a used car.

"Need to clean your ears out, man. I said no."

Mike lets his hand fall and steels his eyes. "Didn't take you for a quitter, Brutal. You told me your word was good, so are you saying that was a lie?"

Bruce sniffs, not swayed. "Don't try to play a player, asshole. This ain't what we talked about and you know it."

Mike sags under the pushback. "Fine, here's the whole deal," he starts but then pauses and looks at me. It's so sudden and unexpected that I don't have a chance to pretend I wasn't listening to every word. "Allyson? You wanna come on over and be a part of this conversation instead of eavesdropping? It involves you too, so you might as well."

I step over slowly, glad the heat of the night gives me an excuse for the flush on my cheeks at being caught so blatantly. "Sure, Mike. Uh, sorry for what you and Jamie are going through. It sounds like a pretty major adjustment." Acknowledging that I was eavesdropping seems like the least dishonest way to join in.

"Thanks," he says reflexively, but I can tell his mind is already focusing on how to say what he wants to.

"Here's the deal . . . the Wildcats need a parent on roster as the head coach. Now, what that coach does or doesn't do can vary. Most teams just have the one, so he—or *she*—does it all. Coaching, scheduling, emails, snacks, uniforms, practices and games, handling parents, and whatever other shit comes up. I don't know for sure since I've never done this either."

He shrugs as he lists out all the things on his plate before settling heavily on Bruce. "But we have Brutal, and let's be honest, there's not a single parent in the city who can coach these boys like you can. Unfortunately, you can't be the 'Head Coach'." He pauses to do air quotes with his fingers. "Or at least, not on paper. So here's what I propose . . ."

He lets a dramatic silence stretch out, and Bruce and I chance a glance each other's way. Why do I feel like we already know what Mike is going to say?

"Brutal, you'll be the coach in action. You'll run practices and handle the sidelines at the game. And Allyson, you'll be the coach on paper. You handle emails, snacks, and parents. It's the best of both worlds."

Yep, that's where I thought Mike was going and I'm already shaking my head. Out of the corner of my eye, I see Bruce doing the same thing.

"I can't, Mike. I'm sorry. I'll be there for the games, but I've got work during the week. That's why Michelle and I rotate. Surely, there's someone else you can put down as head coach if it's only on paper," I argue.

Mike's eyes narrow, not checking me out but sizing me up as an adversary. I square my shoulders and stand straighter.

His voice is hard as he tells me the truth. "There are no dads who come to practices. You know that. Maybe Killian's grandparents, but they can't even walk to the sidelines every practice. You know they're not the youngest or the healthiest. As for the moms, yeah . . . there are at least three who come to every practice and will be at every game. And you know as well as I do, they're only half here for their kid, so if you think for one second that their husbands are going to be onboard with their working elbow to elbow with Brutal, you're delusional."

He looks to Bruce. "No offense, man. We talked about this."

Bruce spreads his hands like 'whatcha gonna do?' I can't help but roll my eyes. I mean, he's not wrong, but does he have to be so damn arrogant about it?

Mike zeroes back in on me. "You don't want those women working with him, either."

He says it so quietly I tell myself that it was my own consciousness speaking and not him saying that out loud in front of Bruce, but the lift of Mike's eyebrow daring me to disagree says it was him.

He's right. I don't want that, but I don't want to admit it. So I bite my tongue, refusing to give in either way.

"You want football for your boy? You want this team for him?" Mike asks, driving his point home. "This is how that happens. Brutal handles X's and O's, and you do the organizing and be the face of the team."

"Damn, that's some serious guilt-tripping. What else you wanna throw at her? Got some shit about football being a metaphor for life too?" Bruce comes to my defense, but the damage is done. I know Mike's right.

This is going to suck. And be so ridiculously awkward. And lead to so many sleepless nights and ruined panties.

But I told Cooper he would get to play. And I told Bruce we could be adults about this. One kiss and a trip down sunny memory lane doesn't change that.

I take a deep breath, willing my words to be a prophecy. "It's fine. I'll be okay as head coach. On paper." I look to Bruce, fearful that he's going to desert me right as the shit is hitting the fan.

I might be willing to fight for this, but he doesn't have any skin in this game. Not really. These aren't his kids. He's only here for the love of the game and because he said he would. But the situation has changed drastically and I wouldn't blame him for walking away.

Well, I would. I'd blame him a lot and be pissed, but deep down, I'd understand.

Bruce's eyes search mine, his hands clenched like he's holding them back. "Are you sure?" he asks gently. So kindly and sweet that it almost brings a hot burn to my eyes, but I nod. "Okay, if Al's in, I'm in. What do we need to do?"

Mike's mouth hangs open in surprise. He didn't expect that to work. Guess he doesn't know the strength of his own arguments.

Or maybe he underestimated me and Bruce?

"I'll take care of it as my last official head coach duty. But starting Thursday, it's you two. Good luck," Mike says, almost like he's ready to see some fireworks start any second. "I'm going to get on home. But holler if you need anything. I'll get back with you during the day when I'm not at work."

He whistles loudly, and Evan perks up, used to the sound. He runs toward us, throwing back a goodbye over this shoulder to his teammates, and then he shakes Bruce's hand. "Bye, Coach B! See you Thursday!"

And we're alone. Mike and Evan are gone, and Cooper and Liam are down at the pond. They're not far, but they can't hear us.

"Are you sure about this?" I hedge.

"Are you?" he counters.

Our eyes lock, so much unsaid between us. But I can feel the commitment we both have to see this through.

"Give me your number so we can talk about practices and stuff," I say, using my business mode as a shield.

Bruce pulls his phone out of the bag at his feet and rattles off his number. I text it, and the ding sounds like possibility, like opportunity, like a really bad idea when I'm hot and bothered at three in the morning from dreaming of him.

"You gonna be available for practices? I know how busy you are," Bruce says quietly. I feel like he's asking so much more.

I nod, not a single thought on my schedule at the office. "I'll make it work. I want—"

He cuts me off, stepping closer and moving into my space. Every cell in my body is aware of how little air separates us as each inch of my skin yearns for his touch. He folds his shoulders in, cocooning me against the August night, and his lips softly brush over the shell of my ear.

"Tell me, Al. Tell me what you want and I'll make it happen. I'll do it." His breath shudders, and though he dwarfs me, I feel powerful and in charge with him. My eyes slip shut and my palms find his chest, feeling the hushed rise and fall that belie his outward calm.

He's waiting for a signal from me. One I contemplate giving.

It would be okay. Nobody would blame me. There's so much fire between us, and I know firsthand how amazing he is. I bet he's only gotten better with time.

But even as I know that in the moment, it would be so good, devastatingly good, later, I'd feel conflicted about it.

The pause drags out long enough that Bruce reads my messed-up, confused mind. His fingers weave into my hair, holding me still as he lays a butterfly soft kiss to my cheek. "Goodnight, Al."

He steps away, leaving me cold even though it's still humid and hot tonight. I don't find my tongue to say anything before he disappears into the parking lot. His truck is loud, breaking my trance as he pulls out.

What have I done?

CHAPTER 13

BRUCE

I don't have time for this, but I don't have time to not do it, either. I need to leave for practice in exactly thirteen minutes, but if I go without relieving some of this pressure, my cock is going to explode as soon as Allyson walks up.

Once again, I'm stuck in that strange combination of pissed off and turned on that seems to be my new normal where she's concerned.

I shuck my jeans, dirty from the day's work in the field, and swipe a fresh towel out of the linen closet before hitting the shower. The hot water runs over my body, but instead of the quick efficiency of my usual five-minute wash and rinse, I grab the soap to get to work.

I try to fight the images of her, bringing up material from my own personal mental spank bank. But her face keeps super-imposing with a little sassy smirk that says she knows what I really want.

"Fuck it," I say to the tile wall, knowing I need to just get this shit over with.

My hand morphs into hers as I imagine her kneeling in front of me.

"Fuck my mouth, Bruce," Allyson says.

With a groan, I close my eyes and tighten my fist, imagining slipping into her wet mouth.

I hold her head, fingers woven into her blonde hair, and thrust deep. She chokes for a split second, but then her throat opens, letting me in. Her blue eyes look up at me, glossy as she eye-fucks me, begging for more.

She slurps messily, cheeks hollowed as she moans against my cock. I fuck her mouth just like she demanded, hard and fast. Her fingers slide down my thighs, nails raking the muscled skin, making my cock even harder.

Her knees spread, and she slips her palm over her clit, down to her pussy. She gathers her own juices, holding her hand up to show me how wet she is from sucking me down. "Play with that pussy, baby. Touch yourself and come for me."

She nods, the pressure causing me to pull her hair, but she doesn't seem to mind in the least. In fact, it seems to rile her up even more. She swallows my cock, her fingers a blur against her clit where I'm watching. If I lean just right, I can see both at the same time, and that's sexy as hell.

"Take me, take all of me, Al. I'm gonna come down your pretty little throat. You want that?" I growl.

She whimpers hungrily.

And that does it. She comes, bucking against her fingers, and my balls pull up tight as I blow, jets of cum filling her mouth. I hold her against me, nose buried to my skin as I make little thrusts into her throat that drive us both mad. I stream cum down her throat as she gulps me down, but it's too much and some runs down her chin, where she scoops it up with one of her honey-coated fingers, sucking it clean of both of our juices.

"Fuck," I sigh, returning to the shower from my fantasy. A shudder works its way through my body, muscles tensing and relaxing in order from my shoulders to my calves. "What the fuck was that?"

I haven't come that hard in forever. I know that it's because I was fantasizing about Allyson, something I haven't let myself do in years. It feels important that I wasn't picturing my high-school-era girlfriend, a blast from the past, so to speak, but rather, the Allyson I see now. I'm not sure if that's a good thing or a bad thing, which knots my stomach up.

Quick as I can, I soap up the rest of me and then rinse my body and the shower wall, where my cum runs down the tile like an accusation.

Yeah, I'm an asshole, a filthy, crude motherfucker who probably never deserved a nice girl like her, but at least now, I'll be able to handle being around Allyson at practice without needing to fuck her right there on the grass.

KIDS ARE SO FUCKING RESILIENT. THEY TAKE THE NEWS ABOUT MIKE'S schedule change in stride, mostly just giving Allyson curious looks when I explain that she's the new Head Coach.

Johnathan raises his hand. "But you're still our *real* coach, right?" He blushes a bit as he says it, eyes darting to Al like he doesn't want to hurt her feelings, but he's asking what all the other boys want to know too.

"Yep, you're stuck with me. You just get her too." I point at Allyson with a thumb. "So, let's get to work."

After my little session in the shower, I dressed in workout gear on purpose. I have no intention of standing around for ten minutes with Al while the boys run their warm-up laps. Nope. Today, I planned to run with them.

When Allyson arrived in athletic gear too, tiny little shorts that show off the creamy skin of her thighs and round ass plus a tank top that hugs her full tits before brushing down her belly, a new idea planted itself into my mind.

"All right, line up for warm-up." The boys hustle to the imaginary line in the grass. "You too, Coach."

Al's eyes jump to me in surprise. "Me? I wasn't planning on running. Mike never did."

I whisper but keep my voice loud enough that the boys can hear me. I want the façade of being nice even as I throw her to the wolves of pre-pubescent kids, letting peer pressure work for me. "Gotta prove yourself, Coach. Mike and I ran with the boys the first few practices. It's good for teamwork."

She must see the glint of a dare in my eyes because I can see her baby blues go steely. She straightens her back and lines up. "Okay, so what's the deal? Fastest wins?"

She smirks, and I know she's well aware that's not how this goes. She's giving the boys a chance to 'teach' her too. Good methodology, but I guess I shouldn't be surprised. She's got Cooper, after all, and is probably a pro at working the system in her favor because a parent's gotta have a lot of tools in their bag of tricks.

"*No!*" the boys cry out in unison. "No man left behind!"

But Cooper interrupts their chanting. "Uh, guys? My mom's not a man. So maybe we should go with 'No Wildcat left behind' instead?"

Pairs of eyes jerk to me for approval. "Sounds good to me. Good for you, Coach?"

Allyson nods with a smile. "No Wildcat left behind, it is. On three . . ." She counts us down and we're off.

The boys are so much better at this now. They instinctively stay together, but they're watching Allyson and me, adjusting as they need to so we all stay together. I push the pace a bit, wanting them to progress, and then pull back as Allyson starts panting.

"Don't forget to breathe," I tell everyone, though I'm really just talking to Al. She darts a dirty look my way, but her breathing stabilizes.

A few minutes later, we cross the finish line and she high-fives every boy. "Great job," she tells them, and they tell her the same thing, a degree of respect earned in their eyes.

I clap my hands, getting everyone's attention. "We're going to start with tackling again today. On the dummies!"

The boys' excitement is palpable. Every kid loves tackle day. It feels so raw and balls to the wall to run at something with the express intent of destroying it.

But first, we review the angles of a hit, where their knees and shoulders should be, how to hold their head, and driving through with form. It almost sounds more like a geometry lesson, but it's important so the boys are safe with each and every tackle. Even one bad hit can be catastrophic, so it's all about muscle memory.

Allyson and I work with the boys, sometimes giving correction and sometimes doing the drill right along with them.

After a few minutes, I grab a big foam pad. "Okay, now let's take it up a notch. Same drill, same form, but you're going faster . . . and you gotta hit *me*."

A chorus of *oohs* goes through the boys and I chuckle.

"Don't get too excited. Ain't none of you pipsqueaks gonna take me down. But that's the point. You hit with all you've got, even when the target's bigger and badder than you and you have no shot. You still give it your all."

Allyson's been standing off to the side while I gave my rah-rah speech, but I have what's probably the worst-slash-best idea ever. "Al, tackle me," I order.

She startles. "What?"

"Tackle me. Show them how it's done," I repeat.

She laughs nervously. "I don't think that's a good idea."

She's looking at the boys like they're going to agree with her, but they're on my side. "Get him, Coach. Take him down!"

The power of positive peer pressure is on my side once again as she nods slowly, agreeing. She lines up and I coach her through it.

"Step one, most important . . . wait until I say go. You don't want to hurt me or hurt yourself because you're rushing." I drop into position myself, holding the thick pad up and setting my feet apart for stability. I don't think Al's really going to come at me with all she has, but the boys will so this is a good practice round for me too.

"Head up, shoulders down," I say, and Allyson obliges. "Feet buzzing." She shuffles her feet, dancing on her toes. "Shoot 'n rip," I say and clench my teeth, preparing for the hit.

Allyson runs dead at me, fiery challenge in her eyes. *She thinks she's taking me down*, I think in the half-second before she gets to me.

The slam is nothing to me, a mosquito on a horse's flank, more annoyance than anything else. But I push back, holding my position as she drives into the padded dummy between us.

Suddenly, my foot slips on the grass beneath me and she has me teetering. Her momentum and my loss of balance send us careening backward and she tackles me to the grass. My breath whooshes out and Allyson yells in surprise, "Whoo!"

Time utterly freezes. With her on top of me, our bare legs tangled, and our faces so close together, I can see the freckles I used to count with kisses over the bridge of her nose and across her cheeks. There used to be twenty-two, but this close, I can see there are definitely more from the years of sun upon her face. Our eyes lock in shock, her mouth opening like she's trying to say something. An apology, maybe? An insult, more likely.

"You okay?" I ask even though I'm the one sprawled out on the grass. I can smell her, a sweet blend of perfume and sweat, and then she wiggles, trying to get up.

"Oh, my God! I'm sorry! I don't know what happened," she rambles. It's cute how freaked out she is, but the squirming is not doing me any favors when she's this close and smells like sweat and flowers, which reminds me of sex with her.

"It's fine. Let me help you up," I grumble.

"Oh, I've got it," she argues.

"Al, quit wiggling or this is gonna be a different kinda show," I say under my breath.

She gasps and finds the adrenaline to pop to her feet, leaving me on the ground with just the big pad to cover my hard on.

"*Shit.*" I keep my voice down because of the boys, but the curse comes out unbidden at her reaction. It's only natural, not like it's my fault my cock stood right up at attention when she was writhing around all over me with her sexy body.

I roll to my side, coming up into a squat to give my cock some breathing room as I hide behind the dummy. "You good, Coach?"

Allyson's nod is a bit too fast, but I return my attention to the boys, who are watching slack jawed.

"And this is why you give it your all every single time. Would you have thought Coach had a chance in hell at taking me down?" They all shake their heads, and I agree with them. "Me neither. But she came in full-throttle, and I wasn't as ready as I thought."

Why does this sound like a bigger metaphor than the tackle she just got on me?

"My foot slipped, but that's an excuse. Truth is, she took me down, fair and square. And if we'd been playing a game, it'd be a fair tackle. So even when you think you've got zero chance, you've still got a shot. Remember that next time you have to line up against someone bigger than you. Remember tiny Coach" —I hold my finger and thumb up, an inch apart— "taking out 'Brutal' Tannen." I hold my arms out wide, making myself as big as possible in comparison.

Little do they know, their coach did more than take me out. Once upon a time, she utterly destroyed me. But that wasn't on the football field, so I try to keep my mind where it belongs.

"All right, who's up first?"

With Allyson's unexpected success, all the boys are chomping at the bit to get a shot at me. None of them are successful, but they have a damn good time trying. They find success in counting the number of steps back they can push me, and I fight harder to hold my line, making them work for each and every inch.

They're gonna be a great team come game time.

Too quickly, our first practice with the new coaching lineup is over. It went better than I expected, honestly. I was afraid we'd resort to snarky biting remarks or thinly-veiled insults. The not-quite grind was definitely preferable, though embarrassing.

We gather up, rallying around for our cheer. Allyson's hand lays on mine and all I can think of is taking her soft palm in my rough, callused one. But then the rest of the team's sweaty hands pile in and we count down. "Three, two, one . . . GO WILDCATS!" The dogpile of hands dissipates instantly, but I feel Allyson's hand leave mine in slow motion.

The kids all make a run for the parking lot, parents trailing behind.

"You got the boys tonight or is Michelle coming?" I ask without playing the words in my head. I realize a heartbeat too late that they sound rather damning. "I mean, I figured we should talk through some of the team stuff."

Her face relaxes slightly, though she still looks wary of me. "Yeah, that's fine. I'm taking the boys home, but they can hang for a few." She looks over to Cooper and Liam, giving them permission to play. "Just stay close so you can hear me when it's time to go."

They run off toward the duck pond, their laughter echoing back to us in the wind.

CHAPTER 14

ALLYSON

"*T*hat went pretty well," I say with certainty, but then I hedge. "I think."

Bruce grunts but is making progress with actual words. "Mostly. Except for the part where you tackled me."

He's teasing me and has an actual smile breaking across his face when it's just the two of us. It's breathtaking, especially when it reaches his eyes. They sparkle like I haven't seen in way too long, though the once-familiar light is surrounded by new crinkles at the corners of his eyes.

I push at his shoulder playfully, wanting the easiness to continue. "You told me to."

Oh, shit. I'm flirting.

Am I flirting? I didn't mean to, but it just happened. When was the last time I actually did this?

A quick flashback of the handful of dates I went on after my divorce plays across my mind like a flickering movie. It seemed like the thing to do at the time, a 'hop back up on that horse' mentality, and I'd wanted to show Jeremy, and myself, that I was fine. I think the ink was still wet on my divorce papers when I'd downloaded a popular dating app.

I quickly realized after a few dates that I wasn't fine or ready and just as quickly deleted the app, choosing instead to take the time to work on me, in particular undoing all the mental shit Jeremy did to me.

I've been happy for a while now, but somehow, it never seemed like riding that horse again was in my cards. Too busy, too focused on Cooper, too proud of being on my own.

But here in this moment, flirting with Bruce feels easy and natural.

"That's true, but I wasn't expecting to slip and end up in the grass. You got me good." The smallest chuckle makes his chest shake, making me feel victorious that I've made this beast Bruce has become smile and laugh.

Maybe this is going to be okay? This has got to be a good sign that we can work together for the kids and no one will go ballistic or get their feelings hurt. Realistically, I know Bruce would be the explosive one, and I'm the one with the most potential of having my heart stomped on. I don't want to want Bruce, but the magnetic pull he has on me is strong, which means I have to be even stronger to fight it.

"That's what you're going with?" I banter back. "The old 'I slipped' excuse? You said it yourself. I took the infamous Brutal Tannen down fair and square."

"You're something else, Allyson Meyers." It sounds like high praise, maybe even an admission he didn't intend to make, as he shakes his head and eyes me thoughtfully. I can feel his eyes sweeping along my skin like a palpable touch. "You okay from the tackle? Sorry I didn't even ask. I was a little caught up."

I nod slowly, my lip disappearing behind my teeth in an attempt to keep words back. I'm not even sure what I want to say, what I want to ask, but I know it's not about the tackle. No, it's all there, fighting to get free from the deep, dark hole I've shoved those thoughts into. And letting those birds fly sounds like a dangerous idea.

Bruce's thumb reaches up to brush the edge of my mouth, and I don't stop the poutiness of my lower lip as it pops from my teeth to chase his touch.

The light moment's gone in a poof, replaced by the heated thought of our bodies pressed against each other, even though the pad had been between us. I don't mean to, but my attention drops to his crotch, remembering his earlier warning about his erection.

"I'm okay. Are you? That was a pretty hard hit."

Fire. Dynamite. Nuclear fuckin' bombs. I'm playing with them all at once, daring them to consume me, but I can't stop, even as my mind screams at me to back away slowly and run the other way. As loud as my brain is, my body is louder, hungrier, needier, and its growls of desire are deep and hot. And undeniable.

He steps closer, and I can feel myself leaning in as he pulls me into his orbit. Sexy, big, growly man with eyes I want to fall into, swimming in their dark depths until I gasp for air. Suddenly, riding that horse sounds like something I could do. I've never been a real cowgirl, but I'm sure as hell that I could ride the fuck out of Bruce Tannen right now.

"You're always a hard hit. To my body . . ."

Yessss. His words are vibrations against my skin, though his lips don't touch me. I tilt my head, giving him better access to my neck, but he doesn't kiss me. Instead, I can just feel the heat of his breath.

"To my mind . . ."

Mmmm.

"To my heart . . ."

Errrk. Record scratch on that one.

"What?" I ask in confusion. "I didn't break your heart. You broke mine." It's a bitter accusation that reminds me why this is such a bad idea.

Bruce's brows jump together and his face goes stony cold. "You said yourself that we have history. Don't try to rewrite it now because you need dicking."

Crass, crude motherfucker.

Wait, no . . . not that last one because I'm not playing into his game. He's trying to distract me, throwing up walls and flashbangs to spin me around. I don't play games . . . not anymore. So I call his bullshit right out, no holds barred as I step back to get some space between us.

123

"I don't need dicking. If I wanted to get fucked, I could get fucked ten ways to Sunday by any number of guys on several different websites." His jaw clenches, and I take that as acknowledgement that I'm right and keep diving deeper. "And I'm not rewriting shit. What happened, happened. It was a long time ago, and neither of us can change it now. Nor am I willing to hop on your guilt-trip train. It's over. Done."

With that, I turn to walk away, not giving a shit that my damp ponytail probably flicks him in the face. He deserves it after his little digs.

His rough hand wraps around my forearm, stopping me, and I instinctively jerk it out of his grip. "Don't touch me."

Bruce holds his hands up, fingers spread wide and showing me his palms. He's acting like I'm a skittish animal that might go into a biting-foamy-mouth-rabid-attack mode any second. "What did you mean?"

"About what?" I bite. But not with my mouth, just my tone. Besides, I don't have rabies or any other diseases. I know because I got tested after Jeremy.

Bruce speaks quietly. "You said I broke your heart, not the other way around. I remember that conversation, Allyson. *You* broke up with *me*."

Sometimes, emotions and the way we express them get a little haywire in our brains. That's why people laugh at funerals or cry happy tears. Like it's all just so much to process that the little emotional characters at the helm just start pulling levers and flipping switches, and paradoxical emotions pour forth without sense.

That's the only reason I can imagine for what happens next.

I laugh. And not some dainty, sweet bell-tinkling laughter. Oh, no, big belly laughs erupt from me like I just heard the best joke ever told. But the truth is, what Bruce just said isn't a joke.

He's looking at me like I've lost every marble I ever had, and maybe I have because I take the time to actually explain myself. My therapist would be proud. I am.

"I might've been the one to say the words 'it's over', but *we both know* it was over long before that." I emphasize the words, wanting him to hear them specifically. Because surely, he knows that I was well aware of what was happening here at home while I was away at school. We never discussed it then, but I knew.

I knew so much it cut me to the bone and destroyed me. I knew that things would never be the same between Bruce and me and that I'd never love like that again, innocent and naïve, giving my whole heart without reservation.

Bruce leans down, putting his face in mine. "What. The. Fuck. Are. You. Talking. About?"

If he did that to anyone else, they'd melt under the sheer weight of his demand to speak. That I can withstand it gives me a twisted delight at how far I've come.

Or maybe it's a sign of how much you trust him.

Well, shit. That's true too, and probably the larger contributing factor that lets me hold my position without giving Bruce an inch.

"I knew you were always in a hurry to get off the phone with me, didn't want to hear about my classes or what was going on with me. I knew . . ." I pause, taking a fortifying breath as I delve into the most painful betrayal of my young life. "About the parties after the football games, about walking Naomi Wilcox to classes and carrying her books, about giving her rides home. I knew you were cheating on me."

His eyes are wide as saucers and dark as ink, but pure fury radiates off him. "Are you fuckin' serious right now, Allyson? Is that what you think? Who filled your head with all that shit?"

So many questions, but I've got some of my own. As mad as he is, as scared as I should be by that, this conversation has been a long time coming and I'm not backing down. I shouldn't have given up so easily back then, should've told him off and gotten it all of my chest no matter how hard it was. But I'd been young and hurt, inexperienced with how to talk about my feelings. Now, I think finally getting all this out in the open might even be therapeutic. Finally, a closure to a chapter that defined me.

"How could you? Nikki and Naomi were thick as thieves, and when Nikki called me and told me what was happening, I couldn't believe it. But she knew. You even talked about Naomi once, some-

LAUREN LANDISH

thing about a test coming up and you both studying hard. Do you know how much that hurt me? You talked about your side bitch with me like it was nothing. Like *I* was nothing."

The anger is giving way to sadness, the tears coming fast and hard. I let them run down my cheeks, not bothering to even wipe them away. I'm not one of those pretty girl criers either. Nope, I can feel my eyes puffing up, my nose getting snotty, and my face turning red.

"Holy fuck, Al." Bruce curses and yanks his bandana from the bag at his feet. *Guess there's no place in his workout shorts for one,* I think randomly. He scrubs at my cheeks, and for some unknown reason, I let him take care of me even though he's the one who destroyed me so long ago and this is an echo reaction to those old hurts.

"Are you talking about Nikki Rigston?" I snort and nod. "If she weren't already dead, may she rest in peace, I'd kill her myself."

I look up from beneath the bandana, where I've taken over wiping my own face. "What? Nikki's dead?"

Bruce sighs and looks at the sky like he could rip a hole in it, rummage around to find Nikki, and then yell at her good and loud. "Car accident, years ago."

I silently say a prayer for the girl who saved me from being a fool, nothing more than small-town gossip fodder.

"Let's sit down so I can get this straight." Bruce has his hands on his hips, preparing for battle, but I think I need this, so I sit willingly. He follows me to the ground, stretching out beside me with his arms resting on his bent knees. I cross my legs and mindlessly play with the grass beneath my fingers.

"So, back then, Nikki called you and told you I was hanging out with Naomi? She told you I was cheating on you? And you believed her? Is that what you're telling me?" he grits out like even the words pain him. But he's the one who did it. He had to know I would eventually find out.

"She told me everything. Or well, at least as much as I wanted to hear. I didn't want to believe her, even told her that she had to be mistaken and that there was a good explanation. But then I started

126

thinking about it, and I knew. I knew that as soon as I was gone and you were the big man on campus, girls were going to be all over you. It was inevitable. We were just kids." All the things I've told myself over the years, especially back then, come out of my mouth robotically.

"That fucking bitch," he spits out, not giving me any clues about who he's talking about. Nikki? Naomi? I'm ninety-nine percent sure he doesn't mean me, but my brows drift up anyway. "Nikki knew that Naomi was tutoring me. Yeah, Naomi had a crush on me, but I shut that shit down fast. We never dated, never did anything other than talk. But I needed a tutor because I was going to do anything to get into State. To be with you."

Confusion swirls through my brain, seeds of hope wanting what he's saying to be true. But there's no way. Nikki said, and Bruce even admitted, that he was studying with her.

Studying?

Oh, my God. Could I have been this stupid?

"Tutoring. Not dating? Not going to parties with her? Not kissing her, fucking her, falling in love with her?" I need clarity, a big dose of it, from Bruce right the fuck now.

"Tutoring. That's it. She might've been at some of the parties, I don't know. We weren't even friends, didn't run in the same circles. I never kissed her, certainly sure as hell never fucked her, and I've only loved three women in my life. Mom, Shay, and you. Naomi? Just tutoring."

The foundational axis of my world shifts helter-skelter, making me nauseous. I press my hands to my belly, trying to stop the rolling. "What the fuck? Why would Nikki . . .? Why didn't you tell me all that? I would've believed you!"

He stands up, pacing and running his fingers through his dark hair, making it stand up wildly. "Because I was fucking embarrassed, Al. You were so damn smart, with all these big dreams. Meanwhile, for all I could do on the football field, I was barely making it in the classroom. And I didn't want to hold you back, didn't want to be the dumb jock who couldn't even carry on a conversation with your smart-ass friends. I didn't want you to know that I was failing English so badly, I had to get a tutor just so I could pass and play. Because football was my only way out, my only way to become something besides a farmer, my only way to keep you."

I stand up too, pointing at him accusingly. "You are a stupid son of a bitch, you know that?" His lips curl. "Not because of some damn English class but because I was never embarrassed by you. Damn it, I loved you!"

I push at his chest, but he doesn't move in the slightest.

"I would've loved you as a football player, as a farmer, as a fucking frog in a swampy pond. Don't put your own insecurities on me. You pushed me away, made me doubt you. And you have no idea how much that hurt me . . . no idea what you did."

It was a pivotal moment for me.

The loss of everything I thought I was going to have, going to do, with Bruce by my side. Breaking up with him had been an attempt at self-preservation, but it'd been a one-eighty turn that sent things on a roller coaster ride that routinely went off track. It had utterly destroyed me, and I wasn't the one who picked up my shattered pieces. No, that'd been Jeremy. He'd picked up the Humpty Dumpty mess of me and glued me together in a Frankenstein I couldn't even recognize anymore.

Hateful indignation makes him sneer at me, hostile and ugly. "Yeah, you seemed really torn up about it when I came to see you." He dismisses me with a wave of his thick-fingered hand.

"You didn't come to see me!" I argue, working to keep my voice down. We're getting louder the madder we get, our hurt and pain amping up our heart rates and volume. But I don't want the boys to hear any of this. I glance toward the pond where they're playing, happily oblivious to the turmoil going on so nearby.

Bruce follows my gaze and steps closer to me, keeping his voice low and gravelly. "I came to see you at school, thought maybe I could do some stupid grand gesture to get you back. It was Bobby's idea, but when I got there, you were sitting with another guy, Allyson. Pressed up against him from knee to hip, his arm around you playing with your hair, and you were holding his hand. You looked at him like you looked at me back then, like he was your everything."

"Jeremy," I breathe out, the name sticking in my throat. "Why didn't you say something?"

"I knew what I was seeing, Allyson. You broke up with me and you were falling in love with him. I didn't want to get in your way, never wanted to hold you back. I wanted you to be happy, even if it wasn't me, even if it was some asshole in fucking . . . *khakis*."

He says khakis like it's the world's worst curse, his breathing jagged and rough. It killed him to feel that way back then and still hurt him to say it even now.

"I wish you had said something—" I start, but he interrupts me.

"So you could cut me down in front of your fancy-schmancy new guy? Fuck *that*."

He turns away, grabbing his bag. I want to stop him. I want to tell him everything. But he's not listening, too caught up in his feelings and what he thinks he saw so long ago. Just like I was when Nikki told me all that stuff. All those *lies*.

Goddamn it, how did things get so fucked up?

"Boys! Let's go," I yell across the field. In the faint light, I can see them scramble up and start running this way. Running . . . that's what I want to do too.

But I won't. Not yet.

I throw one last nuclear bomb at Bruce. "I wish you'd said something because one word from you—hell, even just seeing you there and explaining all of this—would've saved me. Saved me from a hell you have no idea about. But don't worry, Brutal. I saved myself."

I rarely call him by his nickname, never did. He was always Bruce to me because I could see the man behind the football field monster. But I need that distance right now. Because what he did, going home with his tail between his legs, was brutal . . . to us both.

The boys fly past, beelining for the car, and I take the cover of their presence, following them.

I hear Bruce call out from behind me. "Save you from what, Al?"

I shake my head, glancing over my shoulder. His back is to the moon, so he's in silhouette and I can't see his face, but I can imagine the feral look. He's the predator, I'm the prey. But not anymore.

"It doesn't matter now."

It's the truth. Too much time, too much heartache, too many misunderstandings . . . it's all too much. I want a happy, healthy life on an even keel, not drama and tension. Not this standoff with Bruce where I'm always waiting for him to flip . . . hot or cold today? I lived like that for far too long, excused it away, but I'm not willing to do that again.

Not even for Bruce Tannen.

CHAPTER 15

BRUCE

*E*veryone pushes back from the table with full and happy bellies after another one of Mama Louise's delicious dinners. I'm not sure how she does it, but she feeds us all three times every day and does it with a smile.

I couldn't do it, that's for damn sure. Without Shay to feed us before and Mama Louise to feed us now, I'd probably subsist on piled high sandwiches and vegetables raw from the field. Hell, even now, some days I think I'd prefer that because it'd be easier and put me in the safe zone.

Because I'm definitely not safe tonight.

Mama Louise has been eyeballing me the whole meal, and I know there's something coming, I'm just not sure what. She's keen and perceptive and wants to be all up in our Tannen business where she's not wanted. But when she shoves her way in, Brody, my brother who lost the most with this transition, melts and damn near invites her on in. I know it's a reprieve for him to not be the leader all the time, and I'm sure he thinks that sometimes Mama Louise's unique perspective is needed. But it still makes me want to walk away from all of this.

But I don't.

I sit right here at the table and help with cleanup when we're done, just like every night. We all, except for Sophie, who's holding Cindy Lou, do a dance around the kitchen—trash in the can, leftovers in containers for the fridge, edibles for the goats, and dishes in the sink. It couldn't be quicker if we choreographed it.

I try to make a run for it, not because I'm scared of the pint-sized woman watching me like a hawk but because I don't have any need for her to pick around in the messed-up maze of my mind.

"Brutal?"

I freeze with my hand on the screen door, so close to freedom. So close to escape. I don't even turn around, eyeing the black night just beyond my reach and wishing I could disappear into it. "Yeah?"

"Can you help me for a second?" Mama Louise asks, but she's not, if you know her.

Mark grabs Katelyn's hand and shoves by me with a grunt while Luke and Shayanne quickly say their good nights and follow. Sophie and James take a second to gather up Cindy Lou's things and then they disappear out the front door. Brody and Bobby give me careful, guarded looks—Bobby's asking if I'm okay, Brody's telling me not to fuck this good thing up. All told, they scatter like damn roaches, leaving me alone with Mama Louise in a matter of seconds.

Mama Louise smiles like she's already gotten her way. I guess she has.

"Whatcha need?" I ask warily.

"Dishes first, and then, I might have made a batch of my special sweet tea," she replies with a devious tilt to her smile. I've had her special sweet tea, and it's definitely evil. So syrupy sweet you could drink it by the gallons, but the sugar hides the bottle of bourbon she adds. It'll sneak up on you faster than a one-legged man in a butt-kicking competition.

Stuck, I dutifully go over to the sink. Next to me, she sticks her hands in the soapy water, scrubbing a plate in silence before handing it to me for rinsing and drying. Neither of us says a word for several long minutes, though I can hear her humming softly under her breath. The tune sounds vaguely familiar, but it takes me a while to figure it out.

"Are you humming Bobby's song?"

She smiles, the kind sweetness as obvious as the lines on her face. "Yes sir, he played it for me the other day. That boy is touched by God, working miracles with his hands and his mouth."

I snort, not remotely interested in doing the 'that's what she said' joke Mama Louise just unintentionally set me up for, but it runs through my mind anyway. I clear my throat instead. "Bobby's good, for sure."

The demon in my head still giggles like a twelve-year-old boy.

"How about you? You doing as well as he is?" She says it lazily, like I didn't just mosey right into the trap she set for me.

I lift a brow in warning, glaring at her so she knows that I'm well aware she's trying to figure me out. Thing is, I'm simple as fuck. I don't need much, don't want much, either. Just my family all together and maybe a little slice of happiness for myself.

"I'm fine, Mama Louise." It should be the end of it. Not many people stand up to a big motherfucker like me when I make declarations. Hell, I could walk into Hank's on any given day and proclaim it two-dollar draft night, and even Hank would probably go along with me. He might threaten me with his Louisville Slugger at the end of the night, but he wouldn't be too quick at arguing with me.

Mama Louise has no such compunction. She's a pro at this game from years with her own boys. She touched the boundary line, I defended, so she backs up and comes from another angle. "I'm glad to hear it. How about those boys on your team? Are they all fine?"

Halle-fucking-lujah! A safe zone. I can talk about the kids all day.

So I do, telling her about the plays they're running, the progress they're making, and the fun we're all having. She's got a mind like a steel trap, and I predict she'll know each and every boy by name and by story within moments of meeting them. "You still planning to come to the games?"

She bumps me with her shoulder, but it hits somewhere barely north of my elbow. "High winds and rainstorms couldn't keep me away!" She chuckles. "Well, I guess the game would be cancelled in that case, but you know what I mean."

I do. She's solid for the games, gonna be sitting right there on the sidelines with the rest of the crew cheering the Wildcats on. Cheering *me* on.

"Thanks, I appreciate that." It's the polite and proper thing to say, but I actually mean it, and she nods like she knows it.

We finish with the dishes, and though it's on the tip of my tongue to decline her offer of sweet tea, it's not an often-extended invitation and I can't be rude to the woman who's taken us in. We're not exactly orphans since we're all full-grown, but even big guys like Brody, Bobby, and I can use a mother's love every once in a while, even if we don't admit it. And Shay is blooming like a damn sunflower under Mama Louise's watchful care. I don't want to fuck that up.

So I grab two glasses from the cabinet and she smiles like I just gave her a gift. She pulls the pitcher of tea from the refrigerator and pours us each a healthy dose of the brown liquid. "Let's go on the back porch. I've been cooped up inside all day."

I lead the way, opening the back door for her, and we settle in the wooden chairs on the porch. I think they're called Adirondack chairs, and they usually make me think of the beach. Tonight, they feel comfortable and perfect, though, and I relax into my drink, my chair, and the night.

And pray that the team was all she wanted to talk about.

"So, what's got you irritated as a racoon with no trash?" she asks conversationally and then takes a sip of tea. No such luck, I guess.

I sputter on my own drink, even though the bourbon is smooth as honey. "Nothing. I ain't riled up over anything, ain't irritated in the least."

Her face says 'doubt it' loud and clear. "How's Mike?"

I swear to God, butter would not melt in this woman's mouth and a pit bull would lose his bone to her determination.

"Fine. Working third shift and can't coach anymore, which you apparently already know. One of the moms took over as head coach." My voice gives nothing away, and my hand is steady as I take another sip.

"How's your Allyson handling that? How're you doing with it?" She's looking at the sky so hard she could probably count the stars, but I feel like her real attention is all on me.

How does she even know Allyson's name? I sure as shit didn't tell her. It's then I remember Bobby's dinner 'oops'. That boy couldn't keep his mouth shut even with duct tape. I'm guessing he's the one who told her Allyson is my co-coach too.

"First off, she ain't *my* Allyson, not my anything," I spit out with more venom than I intend. "And we're doing just fine."

Even I don't believe that, not after yesterday.

Practice went so well, or mostly so, other than the hiccup with the tackle, and even afterward, we'd flirted and talked like . . . old friends. It'd been comfortable. I liked her giving me shit, loved her body so close to mine that I could smell the blend of her floral perfume and sweet sweat. And then that'd all gone to hell in a handbasket again.

Cheat on her? Goddamn, that girl had me spun around her finger so tight I didn't know my ass from my elbow. I never would've cheated on her. I was doing everything I could to be worthy of her.

I realize too late that I've been silent too long. Mama Louise can see right through me or maybe even hear my thoughts with how loudly I'm thinking them.

"You can talk to me, you know?" she says quietly and then waits.

Maybe she's magic, maybe this tea is stronger than I think, or maybe I just needed this right now, but I do talk to her. Like a cork popped off the champagne bottle of my emotions, I spill everything.

I tell her about Allyson and me in high school and all our plans and dreams. I tell her about how much I loved her and wanted to do right by her. I explain that there was some misunderstanding, but we were too stubborn and stupid to just talk it through. I tell her about going to see Al at school and seeing her with that fucking khakis guy who married her and gave her the baby I always wanted to have with her. And finally, I tell her that I think something went wrong with Allyson's marriage, that she'd said she'd had to save herself.

I dump it all out, purging the poison from my soul. Mama Louise sits there, sipping her tea and listening. Even as I rage and admit that I want to find this fuckwit, Jeremy, and peel him open with my bare hands for hurting Allyson.

Through the whole thing, Mama Louise doesn't say one word, not even about my coarse language or desire for violence. She just lets me vent.

Finally, I sag, empty of words and full of confusion and anger. "Feel better?" she inquires like I didn't just spill my guts to her for the first time ever.

I'm not upset at her calm reaction, though. In fact, I think I prefer it. If she started spouting off advice or asking more questions, I'd probably bail and head home. But it seems this wasn't about my giving her information. Instead, she knew I needed to get every-thing out and gave me a safe space to do it.

I nod. "What the hell did you put in this tea? Truth serum?" Even as I question it, I take one more gulp of the sweet, delicious liquid, finishing my glass.

"A mother never tells all her secrets," she says innocently, taking a tiny sip of her own drink. "So, what are you going to do now?"

I shrug sullenly.

"Okay, so maybe you don't have to know what you want to do about the whole Allyson situation just yet. Let that simmer like chili and figure it out slowly. You two have time enough, and I suspect you don't know your own heart just yet, so don't be mucking around with hers. But what about the boys?" I can feel the careful-ness with which she asks. This is a defining moment.

"I want to coach them, but why am I even doing this? They're not my kids, not my responsibility. I could just walk away. It would be so easy . . . to just walk away." My voice trails off as I imagine the Wildcats having practice without me. It leaves a hollow, gnawing hole in my gut that feels like shit.

How did this happen?

Just a few weeks ago, I didn't even know these kids, but now, I feel an obligation to them. I need to see them play, to see them grow, both on the field and off. I pulled up on a fighting group of kids who insulted and hurt each other. Now, they're a team that looks out for each other, celebrates each other, and supports one another.

I did that, I think proudly.

Not alone, but I played a major part in it. I changed those boys' lives for the good the same way so many coaches did for me. Not by waving a magic wand and making whatever good, bad, or ugly shit they have to go through disappear, but by giving them a place where none of it mattered and they could be themselves.

But she'll be there now, and that changes everything.

"You gave your word." Mama Louise looks at me, her blue eyes boring into mine in the dark. "Some of those kids have happy homes, never known a day of difficulty, and would bounce right back with no problem. Some of them have had people let them down over and over again. Don't be one more person to lie to them. They need a strong example, a man who gives his word, follows through even when it's hard, and doesn't give up on them. They need you to be Brutal Tannen, football star, and they need you to be Bruce, role model."

"It's so hard to see her and not take her in my arms," I confess, my head dropping back to rest against the chair. "Whatever shit went down before, I still love her. I think I always have. And coaching is going to be damn near impossible with her right there but so out of my reach. She was always out of my reach."

It's the most honest thing I've ever said to Mama Louise, all my fears and hopes and insecurities laid bare. She presses her lips together, and I get the feeling she's holding herself back from hugging my neck like one of her boys.

"Fight for the boys first. They're the priority for the next few weeks." She nods her head, emphasizing the important truth of her statement.

I think she's done at first, but after a long beat, she adds. "And along the way, fight for yourself a little too. You said she was in an unhappy marriage and is a single mom now? Get to know her again. Don't be in love with the girl you knew. Fall in love with the woman she is now. No pedestal, no better than or less than, just two people with a whole lot to build on."

That's a lot to swallow and even more to think on. I tell her honestly, "Thank you. I didn't know I needed this."

She smiles, all the heaviness of our conversation gone. "You're not the only observant one around these parts, mister. I've got eyes in the back of my head, and you can ask the boys, I know everything that goes on around here."

"I actually believe that." She preens under the praise, straightening in her chair and stretching out her denim-clad legs. "You heading in? Want me to close up the kitchen?"

Her gaze ticks back up to the sky. "Nah, I'm gonna finish my drink and talk to John a bit. I'll take care of the glasses." She gestures to the empty one in my hand, and I set it on the table next to her for her to clean up.

I step off the porch, walking toward our family homestead a few acres away. Bobby took the truck, so I'm hoofing it. But the quiet night surrounds me like a soothing blanket and I don't mind the walk. I could use the time to process everything Mama Louise said, and hell, everything I said too.

From the darkness behind me, I hear Mama Louise's soft voice whisper into the night. "Hey, honey, how was your day?"

I'd been overwhelmingly confused when we first started hanging out with the Bennetts. They all talk about John Bennett in the present tense, like he went to the grocery store and will be right back. But he's been dead for years now. I'd even worried that Mama Louise might be a little bit bonkers or have a touch of early-onset dementia that her boys were ignoring.

But over the last few months, I've realized it's nothing like that.

Mama Louise is well aware of the fact that John is gone, but her faith that he's waiting on her in heaven is unshakable. Even in his absence, she loves him with all her heart.

That's admirable. That's a love we should all aspire to have, one that transcends time, space, and every obstacle life and death puts in our way.

So if she wants to talk to the night a little, I say let her. I even whisper myself, "Thanks for letting me borrow your girl tonight, Mr. Bennett. She helped this old motherfucker out a lot."

I swear a star winks back at me, but that's not possible. Right?

CHAPTER 16

ALLYSON

I can't help but look toward the parking lot for the fifth time in as many minutes.

The boys started their warm-up easily, lining up for their run, and I'd even tacked on one bonus lap while I got my shit straight. Because I am tits-up fucked over.

Bruce isn't here.

Our fight Thursday night had been near-nuclear, but I never dreamed he'd just bail without a word. I thought he at least had the balls to send me a text saying he was out if he was going to quit after our argument.

I've played it over in my head more times than I can count. If the scene had been an old-school VHS tape, I would've worn it out. But my brain cues it up easily, ready to play it across the screen in my mind again, fresh and bright like it was the first time. I grit my teeth and blink hard, forcing the mental image to change to a set of X's and O's, a play that we worked on previously.

Another glare at my phone tells me that nothing from Bruce has come through, nor has any other divine intervention come my way. This is on me. I need to rally and handle this on my own. It's fine. I've done harder stuff before.

I laugh at myself. Because running a football practice on the fly for twelve pre-pubescent boys might actually be the hardest thing I've ever done. Not because the rest of my life has been rainbows and unicorn shit but because these kids are vicious and I know they already smell blood in the water. My blood.

And I have an audience. It's Saturday morning, so more of the parents are available to sit on the sidelines, not that they'll help me, but they'll definitely be watching me flounder in my new role.

The team crosses the finish line with customary high-fives and then they crowd around me. "Where's Coach B?" someone asks. I'm not sure who, but we're all thinking it so it doesn't matter.

"Honestly, I'm not sure, guys. Something super important must've come up, though, because I know he wouldn't miss out on a practice unless he really had to." I'm trying to convince myself as much as them, but no one's believing the meaningless crap I'm serving up. I can see their faces fall, resolute that they've been let down again.

But I won't let them down.

"Let's get to practicing. Coach B won't want to hear about your slacking off just because he wasn't here to push you. This is a chance to step up and push yourself, show him and each other how far you've come as a team."

As far as rally speeches go, it's not half bad. Maybe a little rah-rah, but I was a cheerleader. And I'm absolutely willing to make Bruce out to be the scary bad guy who'll be disappointed in them if it gets me through the next hour without a revolt.

"Set up to run the play from Tuesday. It was looking good, but it could be better. You guys are better. Let's do it!" I inject enthusiasm into my voice, but they grumble as they get set.

We run it several times, and each time it seems to get worse instead of better. I don't know enough football to correct them and resort to calling on them to dissect their own mistakes.

Johnathan smirks. "I know what we did wrong. We got a girl as a coach. Girls don't know football."

Ouch. Little shit.

He's been the hardest kid to reach, for both Mike and Bruce, and now me and Bruce. He'll be solid gold sometimes, even show true leadership potential, and then a minute later, I want to choke him. I'm not sure what's up with him yet, so I'm not sure how best to handle his bratty mouthiness. Especially when his brother is the most laid-back, follow-along-with-whatever kid on the team.

Cooper rears up in my defense. "Shut your mouth, Johnathan! It's not like your mom or dad is even here to watch you practice. At least my mom is helping." His pride that I'm here burns bright white in my heart, and I have to fight back the urge to scoop him up in a hug because he'd die if I did that right now in front of his friends on the football field.

But Johnathan isn't done either. "Yeah, but where's your dad, Chicken Coop?"

It's a low blow, uncalled for and cruel.

I stick my fingers in my mouth and whistle loudly, glad that my own dad taught me that trick when I was a little girl. I'd lost the ability when I was missing teeth as a kid, but it came in handy again as a cheerleader.

The boys jerk and twelve pairs of eyes turn to me. Not a single one blinks, and quite a few look guilty even though they didn't do anything.

"Is this how a team behaves, gentlemen?" I ask harshly.

There's a grumble of nos.

"I asked you a question. Is this how a team behaves?" I get down in Johnathan's face, letting loose the full powerful strength of my mom glare.

"No, ma'am." They answer together this time, as militarily precise as eight- and nine-year-olds can be.

"Do you want to be a team, Wildcats?"

"Yes, ma'am," they say, getting better with each response. Backs are straightening, shoulders dropping, and eyes locking on me.

"Good. Because you are a team. Good or bad, you're in this together. With me." I raise one eyebrow at Johnathan again, who's looking considerably less cocky. "Line up and take a knee."

They hustle to follow the order, and I pace the line back and forth once, meeting each little boy's eyes. I try to filter through the military movies in my mind, or even a football jock romcom, something to help me out here. Finally, I decide speaking from the heart is my best bet.

"I am a woman. And I don't know a lot about football. Which, to be clear, is not true of all women. There are female team owners, coaches, reporters, and even players. Just because I'm not doesn't mean you can disrespect them. Or me."

I can see the quiver of Johnathan's lower lip and decide maybe he's had enough . . . for now. "But I have been part of a team before, and how you behave when things are tough is what makes you or breaks you. So maybe we don't work on that play anymore. Maybe we don't do the throwing drill I had planned next." They groan at the loss of their favorite activity. "I think what we need is some good old-fashioned team building. Wouldn't you agree?"

"Yes, ma'am?" they say uncertainly.

"Circle up, but make it a big one. Get some room between each of you." They stand and move to make a loose circle around me. "Drop and give me ten push-ups."

Several of the stronger boys do so instantly until I stop them. "On my count. Together."

I can hear the groan work its way through them, but they hold a plank with me and I count us off. I don't make it too slow, nor too fast. They're just kids, after all, but this is an important lesson.

We move on to high knees, jumping jacks, air squats, lunges, and every single body weight exercise I've seen on infomercials late at night when I'm working at home after Cooper's gone to bed. We're all sweaty and tired, and my breath is coming in hard pants.

"Last but not least, we're pulling one from my cheerleading days. Are you ready for this?" Not a single soul makes a peep. They're too exhausted and probably too nervous to argue at this point.

"Here's the drill. You turn to your left, double high-fives, drop for a pushup, pop up, and everyone yells 'WILDCATS!' Then you double high-five the teammate to your right, tagging them for their turn. Pay attention and don't miss the team yell," I warn them. "We have to make it all the way around with everyone cheering together every single time or we start over."

I point at Johnathan, letting him start. He high-fives Anthony, drops and pops back up, as everyone watches raptly. They yell together, and then Johnathan turns to high five . . . Cooper.

I didn't set them up that way, but it seems serendipitous, and their high-five seems filled with meaning. Maybe I don't suck at this, after all. At least the team part. The football part . . . definite suckage.

And talking to Bruce? *I'm even worse at that,* I think painfully. I still can't believe he didn't come, but there's no sign of him. I haven't checked my phone in a bit, but there's really no excuse barring an emergency.

My heart stutters. Maybe something really is wrong? Maybe I'm being a bit self-absorbed to think this has anything to do with our fight the other night. He could've had an accident on the way to practice, be lying dead in a ditch somewhere, all while I curse him for no-showing. I nibble at my lip, suddenly nervous.

The boys continue their way around the circle, picking up momentum like they're racing the clock. My heart speeds up to meet their frantic pace, but where they're smiling and having fun with what's become game-like, I'm freaking out a bit.

Anthony is the last kid, and when he high-fives Johnathan, completing the circle, they all cheer wildly. Wildcats seems like a rather appropriate name right now.

"Great finish, guys!" I praise them, having achieved what I'd hoped to with the game. I even saw Johnathan apologize to Cooper while Killian was doing his push-up. It'd been fast, but Cooper had nodded his forgiveness, so I'm taking that as a win.

Hell, I'm taking the whole damn practice as a win . . . for me! I have no idea what I'm doing, but it wasn't that bad in the end.

"Bring it in." I hold my hand out and their sweaty ones cover mine. "On three . . ."

"WILDCATS!"

They grab apple slices and peanut butter from the bag where I left the snacks and run for their parents. I see some questioning eyes from the adults too, but I hold my thumb up in silent assurance that everything's fine. *Just fine.*

Except it's not.

Now that practice is over, I'm flipflopping between fury at Bruce for no-showing and terror that he didn't come because something's wrong.

Michelle comes over. "Uh, so that was God-awful. What the hell, Allyson?"

I called her Thursday night after Cooper went to sleep to give her the whole sordid story of my conversation with Bruce, so she knows how bad it got.

I shake my head. "You know everything I do. Bruce was supposed to be here, but he no-showed and he didn't call." I pause to check my phone but hold it up to show her that I have zero missed calls and no text messages. "We had that argument on Thursday, but I didn't think he'd take our shit out on the boys. What if something's wrong, like really wrong? Like a car accident or a farm mishap?"

Okay, so maybe I sound a bit hysterical because she tilts her head, a bemused smirk on her face. "Is this the part where I get to smack you and tell you 'get ahold of yourself, woman'? Because I could be in for that."

I mean-mug at her. "No."

She fans herself with her hand, holding her hair off her neck. "Look, I'ma be straight with you. Practice? It sucked ass and those boys nearly did you in. We need him. Go get him, beg him if you have to, Allyson. Hell, beg him on your knees if you have to." Her eyes glint with mirth. "Or just drop to your knees and get dicked for shits and giggles if you want to."

"Michelle!" I hiss, "We just had a fight, he left me high and dry, and I am not doing that with him, anyway. We're not going there. I'm not going there."

"No shame in it, Ally," she says with a shrug. "I told you, climb that man like a damn tree. Whether you kiss him or smack him when you get there is up to you. But go see him, find out if he's quitting or if something happened. Don't go in blazing double barrels, but don't let him keep you on a chain either. You're too good for that, even for a specimen like him."

God, she is hung up on him. Not really. I know she's ass over teakettle for Michael, but every time she says something flirty or sexy about Bruce, I wanna claim him.

I licked him, he's mine!

And doesn't *that* bring up images that Michelle's trying to plant in my head.

Me on my knees in front of Bruce, his cock tracing my lips before he tells me to open my mouth. And when I do, he feeds me every inch until my tongue touches his heavy balls. I'd close my mouth, hollow my cheeks, and suck him down.

No. No, I wouldn't. No, I'm not.

But checking on him sounds like a good plan. Reasonable and safe. Logical, even.

She must be able to see that I agree with her, at least about going to see him, because she asks, "Want me to keep Cooper? We're going to visit my mother-in-law this afternoon, but I can take him if you need some privacy for this visit."

Michelle's mother-in-law has Alzheimer's and lives in a memory care facility. It stresses her out to take Liam there, always worrying that he'll confuse his grandmother because she's thought he was Michael more than once. Another kid tagging along is a recipe for disaster.

"No, it's fine. I'll take Cooper with me. A drive to the country will be good for us both." Even I don't sound like I believe that.

"And he can be a buffer so you don't bend over and present your dried up, unused lady bits to Bruce and beg him to go easy on you." Michelle jumps out of reach, knowing that I was about to slap my hand over her mouth.

"Girl, the shit you say! Do you use that mouth with Michael?" My cheeks are pink, flushed with embarrassment.

She laughs heartily. "Honey, that's me *with* a filter. You should hear the things we say when it's just the two of us in bed and Liam's at your place. Dirty, filthy, sexy things that'd make a porn star blush and cause a sweet, innocent thing to have a heart attack." She steps closer and flicks my ear, leaving me in no doubt that I'm the innocent she's talking about.

I'm not. It's just been a while. A long while. Like since those post-divorce dates kinda while. But that's *not* changing anytime soon.

———

Cooper's excited to go for a drive, even though I don't tell him where we're going. I want to hedge my bets.

What if we drive by the farm and he's just sitting on the porch sipping lemonade like missing practice was nothing? Or what if we see his truck, upside down with wheels spinning in the air, along the way?

No, I don't say a word to Cooper.

But I head toward the Tannen farm by memory, not needing a map or directions even though it's been so long since I made this drive. I feel like I'm heading straight toward the lion's den.

There's been quite a few changes, landmarks I remember gone. Like old man Sampson's field, the site of our infamous mudding. It's a pharmacy now, the rough turf replaced by the growth of Great Falls. It stings more than I let on, and I wonder if Bruce realizes.

Bruce. If he's okay, I'm walking right into a trap, admitting that I need him, that the team needs him. Will he hold it over my head? Take delight in leaving me to fail?

I don't want to think he's that cruel, but I'm not sure.

The moment of truth arrives too soon, and I pull into the open gate at the Tannen farm. Except the metal arch says *Bennett Ranch* now. It tugs at something deep in me I didn't even know existed. A bit of nostalgic sentimentality, a touch of sadness at the way things change.

I pull up to the house, and the front door opens.

A tall, dark-haired guy steps out cautiously. He could probably be described as handsome, but there's something cold and scary about him, like without even knowing who's come onto the property, he's already half-planned your burial site on the back forty.

A thin, honey-brown-haired woman dips under his crossed arms, smiling at the car and waving like she was expecting us.

The two welcomes couldn't be any more diametrically different.

I blink and realize who they are. Brody and Shayanne. Older versions of the people I used to know, but I can see it now.

"Uh, stay in the car for a second, baby. Let me talk to these folks real quick." I unbuckle my seatbelt, eyes locked on Brody.

"Who are they?" Cooper asks from the backseat, trying to lift up to see over the edge of the door.

"Old friends," I say, praying that's true.

I get out slowly, approaching cautiously like they might attack me. I hate moving like this, willing myself invisible and non-threatening, but it seems to settle Brody a bit.

"What do you want?" he barks from the porch.

Shay smacks his chest with the back of her hand. "Ignore my rude brother. He's Brody, I'm Shayanne, and you are . . . ?" She trails off, waiting for me to finish the introductions. She was so young the last time I saw her. I guess she doesn't remember me.

"I know who you are," Brody growls. Apparently, that's a family trait, as is the 'fuck you' stare that makes me shrink from several yards away. "What are you doing here, Allyson?"

I swallow, my throat constricted tight with nerves. Absently, my fingers do a trick my therapist taught me to use when I feel anxious. I tap my thumb with each finger . . . 1, 2, 3, 4 . . . and then in repeating patterns . . . index, ring, middle, pinky, and then reverse the whole thing. It's a little thing, but it helps focus me, helps me feel in control of something.

"Bruce didn't come to practice this morning. We were . . ." I breathe deeply and try again. "I was worried because I didn't hear from him."

Shayanne's smile is huge and bright. "Oh, you're the mom coach! Dumb ass probably forgot to text you. He's been helping me this morning, you see. I had a bit of a goat milk soap emergency and it was all hands on deck." She talks fast, one word on top of the last, and the energy coming off her is more than I could get from a double espresso. But I still have no idea what's going on or why Bruce no-showed.

"Goat milk soap . . . emergency?" I ask in confusion.

She nods and taps her nose. "You got it."

I don't have it. Goats can have emergencies? Or was it the milk that was the emergency? Or the soap? And what would be a soap emergency, anyway?

I am so lost, so I stick to what I do know.

"Could you point me toward Bruce? I thought I'd better touch base with him before Tuesday's practice."

You know, to see if he's even going to come or if this so-called 'soap emergency' is going to keep him tied up? The least he could do is come up with something believable.

Brody grunts again, his dark eyes narrowed as they scan me. "I'll take you to him. On one condition."

I nod, because what am I gonna do . . . say no?

"Don't fucking hurt him again. We got more than enough shit on our plate and don't need to add your fucking him over to it." His thick finger points at me threateningly, his lips curled.

Familiar. So fucking familiar.

My jaw drops in shock as a shiver of recognition runs through me, but I straighten my spine and talk back just as forcefully. "It seems that was a bit of a misunderstanding. We hurt each other."

He scoffs, and Shay's eyes are ping-ponging between us like we're a tennis match, a grin spreading on her energetic face.

"Damn, girl. Not many folks bite back at Brody. I like you already." She hooks her elbow through mine, pulling me along with her, and I follow even though I have no idea where she's taking me. She's preferable to Brody, at least. "What'd you say your name is again?"

"Allyson. Allyson Meyers. We met several times when you were little, used to have dinner with your family," I explain.

Shay's eyes flicker. "That was a long time ago then, wasn't it?" I can see that she still feels the loss of her mom and dad, and I hate that I carelessly brought it up. I'm just distracted . . . by Bruce's MIA routine, by Brody's glare, by my own heart's racing.

I call out to Cooper, and he steps out of the car, looking at me for guidance. "Honey, this is Brody Tannen and Shayanne Tannen. They're Bruce's brother and sister."

Brody's eyes go downright black as coal, burning me with questions. I hadn't considered that he might be confused by Cooper's appearance and jump to the wrong conclusion. "Brody, Shayanne, this is my son, Cooper Meyers." As Brody shakes Cooper's hand, I give the slightest shake of my head and Brody visibly relaxes, the coiled tension in his muscles dissipating the tiniest bit.

Shayanne's all smiles, though. "Well, hey there, Cooper! Wanna see some goats?"

He looks to me for permission, and when I smile, his excitement bubbles up. "Yes, ma'am!"

So I guess we're going to see goats, and hopefully, Bruce.

CHAPTER 17

BRUCE

"Come here, you little fucker," I snap at the monster that's trying to escape the reach of my outstretched arms. As rough and mean as my words are, my hands are sure and gentle. Shay loves each of these beasts, and they're the bread and butter of her soap operation. Well, maybe not bread and butter, but they're the milk of it, at least.

Baaarbara the goat bleats at me, which I swear sounds like 'neener, neener, you can't catch me' and darts off again. I give chase, cussing a blue streak the whole time as I slide around the dirt and she escapes again. It's then I hear giggles coming from over by the gate.

I look up and see Shayanne first, her cheeks puffed up by the big grin she's wearing. I flip her off before I realize why she's so amused. It registers a heartbeat later that right next to her are Allyson and Cooper, who just saw my utter failure at catching the tiny critter. Shit, I must look like a damned fool.

"Uh, hey, guys. Didn't expect to see you out here. How was practice?" I say, wiping my brow with a bandana and glaring at the black and white fluffball that's making me look bad.

"Seriously?" Allyson snaps.

I recognize that fire. She's not just pissed. She's furious on the

151

edge of volcanic rupture. Her eyes are narrowed, she's damn near bull-snorting through her nose, and her jaw is clenched like she's holding back a whole litany of curse words. Probably because of Cooper, because I get the feeling she'd love nothing more than to light into me.

"I take it practice didn't go so well, then?" I don't dare smile as I say it, even though seeing her hot and bothered does something to me. I hate to see her upset, but damned if she's not adorable when she's ready to give me what-for.

"How could you?" she hisses. "They were counting on you. I was counting on you. And you're just out here playing with goats. I'm disappointed in you, Bruce Tannen."

She whirls on her toe, grabbing at Cooper's hand. His eyes are wide, and I'm betting it's likely he's never heard his mom go nuclear on someone. She might not have gone off in a big, spectacular fashion of yelling and foot stomping, but make no mistake, her disappointment cuts deep and wide.

She's already making headway back toward the house, and her car, I'm guessing, when Shayanne snaps her fingers, breaking me out of my trance. "Holy shit, man! What did you do? Whatever it is, you'd better go fix it. Now!"

I stumble toward the gate, the same fucker that was running from me before now chasing after my feet and getting me tangled up. "Al! What the fuck, woman! Wait a damned minute!"

She glares at me over her shoulder, and I realize that might not've been the right thing to say. Or appropriate language in front of Cooper. "Please, wait. What happened?"

I finally just hop over the fence and stride over quickly. I step in front of her and she makes a move like she's going to go around me, but I'm a defensive lineman and I block her left, and then right, before she stops and huffs heavily. "Let me go. I'll just do it on my own."

I look to Cooper for some guidance here because I have no damn idea what's wrong with his mother. He's no help, though, just shrugging his bony shoulder.

I put a hand on each of Allyson's shoulders and bend down to get in her face. From inches away, I keep my voice steady and steely, quietly demanding. "Tell me what's wrong. What happened?"

The flints of anger in her eyes are as sharp as knives. But before she can answer, Shayanne interrupts.

"Hey, Cooper! Wanna come see my pig so the grown-ups can talk? Her name's Bacon Seed." She might as well be playing a flute like the Pied Piper because Cooper's full attention goes to Shay.

"Did you say you have a pig named *Bacon Seed*?" He sounds pretty sure my sister is one card short of a deck. He might not be wrong.

"Yep," Shay answers, examining the tip of her ponytail for split ends like she doesn't have a care in the world. "Wanna see?"

I raise one brow at Allyson, asking permission. She softens under my hands, looking at her son. "It's fine, honey. Go with Shayanne for a minute so I can talk to Coach B."

Not Bruce but Coach B. I'm so fucked. If only I knew why.

Cooper all but runs for Shayanne, already asking questions about Bacon Seed. Though my eyes stay locked on Allyson, I hear him say something about holding the pig and Shayanne's promise that he can.

Once they're several yards away, I ask again. "What happened?"

She scoffs, but the hard line of her spine stays softer. "You no-showed and you damn well know it. How could you throw me to the wolves like that? Practice was a total clusterfuck." She rolls her eyes, looking at the sky, and I swear I think she's fighting back tears. Just how bad was it?

"Al," I say, shifting my hand to her jawline. I'm playing with fire and I know it, but she looks so lost. "I'm so sorry. I sent you a text message that I had to miss today and included ideas for you to use for practice to keep the guys progressing. Hell, I even included a damn video of me with one of Shay's monsters for you to show them to explain my absence."

She goes stiff beneath my palms, jerking away. "No, you did not. I've been checking my phone all morning and nothing, nada, zip. Don't try to make me think you did something you didn't. I'm not that stupid."

She steps back, putting two feet between us. It feels like a cavernous ravine and I hate every single fucking inch. "Al . . ." I say, following her to close the gap.

"I know we left things ugly the other day, but I never dreamed you'd take out our history on those boys. You are not the man I thought you were, not then and not now." She somehow finds even more distance to put between us, switching to what I imagine is her professional voice. "We won't be needing your services at any future practices or games. I'll have your name removed from the roster. You're off the hook, Brutal."

I pull my phone out and shove it toward her, thinking it's the only way to stop this merry-go-round from hell. "Look at my damn phone, Allyson. You'll see the fucking messages."

She rips it from my hand and presses the home button, gloating like she knows she's going to trap me in a lie. There's no passcode, never needed one, so she can see everything right away. She clicks into my messages and it's right there like I said it was . . . her name at the top, a few messages in a row, and then a video.

She clicks play and my recorded voice fills the air.

"Hey, guys! Sorry I'm missing today's practice, but I've got some extra chores to do today for my sister. You know how sisters can be!"

My eyes brows waggle, and I grin at my own joke on the screen.

"But Coach Allyson has the plan, so do everything she says. I'll be checking for progress on Tuesday night. Oh, and one more thing . . . GOOOO WILDCATS!"

I finish the video off with a waving goat's hoof, like she's saying 'bye to the team too. I'd felt a little dorky doing it but had thought the boys would get a kick out of it.

Allyson looks up at me, stricken. "I . . . I didn't get these. Any of these. And I jumped to conclusions. I thought . . . I thought you abandoned me. I mean, abandoned *us*," she corrects. She takes a shuddering breath, her blue eyes meeting mine like she's staring down the executioner's firing squad. "I'm sorry."

"Me too," I say honestly. I don't know what happened to the messages because they show as sent on my end, but I believe her that she didn't get them. Technological Karma fucking me over, I guess. "Was it that bad?"

She laughs all the way down to her toes, but it seems to be covering horror. "Oh, my God, it was awful! There was back-talk and freak-outs and cardio punishments . . . and that was just me! The boys didn't do so hot either." She's shaking her head, and I can tell she's replaying her morning over in her mind. "At first, I was furious. Then I got scared that something had actually happened to you. I drove out here looking in every ditch for that truck of yours, terrified I was going to find it. And then you're just goofing off with goats! I might've overreacted a smidgen." She holds her finger and thumb up an inch apart.

I raise a brow and spread her fingers apart several more inches. "More like that size overreaction."

"Hmm, my memory must be going because I could've sworn it was bigger than that." Her eyes go wide and her hands slap over her mouth as she shakes her head. She says something, but it's muffled by her palms and I can't make it out.

I push her hands down, chuckling as her joke hits me. "What was that?"

"I didn't mean to say that! It just came out. I didn't mean that I was thinking about . . . well, you know . . . or back then . . . or now." She's stammering, cheeks flushing, which makes her freckles stand out in stark relief. She looks down like she can't meet my eyes, but I see her quick check of my midsection and can't help but tease her.

"It's all right, baby. You can tell me that you were thinking about my cock. We already discussed that you need dicking. You know I'm the man for the job." I'm flirting again, stepping through a minefield with no map and no clue where the IEDs are hidden. Last time didn't go so well, so I should be extra cautious this time. Careful ain't exactly my strong suit, though. I'm more a blow shit to smithereens and deal with the aftermath type.

So I step closer, invading her space. My throat goes tight at the thought of getting between her pretty thighs again. We might have all kinds of issues, past and present, but sex wasn't ever one of

LAUREN LANDISH

them. "Say the word, Al, and I'll take you in that barn right there. You know there's a spot up in the hayloft. We've been there before."

I pause, letting the memories wash through us both. Her laid out on a blanket on a backdrop of spun-gold hay. My jeans shoved down around my thighs and her shorts still hooked on one ankle because we were trying to hurry. Swallowing our moans of pleasure with kisses so we wouldn't get caught by my brothers or parents.

She bites her lip, desire written all over her face and her chest rising and falling rapidly. But I can see the doubt, the questions, the uncertainty. I don't want to take her like that. I want her sure when I slip into her heaven again. I want her begging for my cock. I want her crying out my name as she comes apart all over me.

And there's so much I don't know. She's leaving tiny breadcrumbs of hints at what her life has been like, and I'm gathering each and every one of them up like a fucking pigeon, wanting to figure out who she's become. I don't want to mess that up by going too fast, because she's a runner now and she'll bail on me sure as the sun's gonna rise tomorrow. It'll have to be a dance of my take-no-prisoners style tempered to meet her skittish-colt tendencies. I try to marry the Valkyrie who just came in screaming and giving me hell with the woman who quietly walked away the other day, and I just can't. It doesn't make any sense.

But I want it to.

So I'm going to figure this woman out, and I'm doing it proper. All fuckin' in.

"Let's go for a walk," I say, grabbing her hand.

"What?" she exclaims, but she doesn't pull away from me.

I take it as a win. Baby steps like Mama Louise advised, getting to know her again. I'm going to win her over, win her back. Because I should've never lost her in the first place.

I'm getting this train back on track, right now.

We walk past the barn, and Shayanne holds up her thumb, letting us know that Cooper's good. He doesn't even notice us, wiggling his nose against Bacon Seed's snout and smiling happily. I mean, Cooper is, not the pig. Though Bacon Seed would probably smile if she could. She's a bit of a spoiled diva, thanks to Shay.

156

I lead Al further, past our personal garden and into the crops we grow to support the farm. Well, and the Bennett ranch now, since it's all theirs. This feels both familiar and new, something we used to do all the time back in the day, but now it's different.

"So did you really have a 'goat soap emergency'?" I can hear the air quotes in her question.

I scratch at my lip, eyeing her from under my hat. "Is that what Shayanne said?" Allyson nods, still not believing it. I squeeze her hand in reassurance. "Well, yes and no. More like an emergency in the making . . ."

I explain how Sophie had gotten word about an entire herd needing what amounts to goat foster care because their owner went into the hospital unexpectedly. So the herd arrived in the middle of the night and we'd spent the better part of the early morning hours making sure the new herd and our existing animals got along without butting heads. Literally. And today, we had to milk twice as many nanny goats so it was all hands on teat.

It'd been back-breaking work, but it was the right thing to do . . . for the goats, for the poor owner, and even for Shayanne. The owner gladly told her she could keep the milk as bonus supply for her soaps. She'll put it to good use with the upcoming busy holiday season.

"An actual goat emergency," Allyson says with a laugh. "I never would've believed that."

I laugh with her, and the last bits of today's drama melt away, leaving just the two of us. Allyson smiles at me shyly. She breaks our eye lock first, looking down to our interwoven hands. I run my thumb along the soft skin of her hand.

"Come on, let me show you everything."

We walk for what seems like hours. I show her the large fields, telling her about how we rotate the crops to keep the soil fresh, and the specialized fields, where we mostly grow things for Shay's businesses and the farmer's market. She listens to every word, raptly paying attention as if farming is an exciting topic.

Eventually, we end up in the orchard toward the back of the

property. There are still peaches on lots of the trees, and as we walk beneath the green canopy, Allyson looks up.

"It's beautiful, Bruce. All of it."

She means it. Not everyone gets it, the farm life. Some people prefer the city, the hustle and bustle, sidewalks and neighbors, and a grocery store on every block. It's different out here. We're just as busy, but it's in a unique way, sunup to sundown and repeat with each new day.

"I didn't know if I could do this, you know?" I admit. "When we were kids, I wanted out. Not because I didn't appreciate what my family had but because I was a stupid kid who thought I needed to conquer the world. But I was wrong. This is where I was always supposed to be. I love this land, even if it's not ours anymore."

"I'm sorry. That's got to be hard, not at all what you planned." She sounds truly sad for my family at the loss.

I shrug and grunt. "It was at first, but we're doing a lot better now. Mama Louise isn't the kind of woman to pussyfoot around. She basically told us all to get our shit straight right-quick and we said, 'Yes, ma'am.' Especially with Shayanne on her side. She's married to Luke Bennett now."

Allyson's mouth drops like she just put some puzzle pieces together. "You said at Hank's that one of the Bennetts was fucking Shayanne. I wasn't sure which one or what the situation was there, and it didn't seem like the time to ask."

The reminder of the dinner at Hank's and how we'd started out so badly but ended somewhere else. With that kiss. If Kyle Bloomdale hadn't interrupted us, I don't know how far we would've taken it.

Would we have ended up in the parking lot? At her house?

At the time, I'd been furious, but maybe it was for the best. It gave us time to battle out some shit. There's still more to go. I know there's a whole lot more to her story from the last few years, but we're getting there little by little.

"C'mere." I pull her along with me, jogging slightly. I need to show her something before I lose my guts. I'm not a coward, but if this isn't as important to her as it is to me, I don't know what I'll do.

I pause when we get close. "Close your eyes," I order her, slipping my hands over her eyes from behind.

She tenses for the barest second and then laughs, reaching up to hold my wrists. "What are you doing?"

"This," I whisper hotly into her ear. I move my hands and her lashes flutter. I know the instant she sees it.

She gasps, her hands covering her mouth, but then she reaches out. One finger traces the lines in the big tree trunk.

B + A = 4EVR

We'd playfully discussed for over an hour if it should be alphabetical or if my initial should be first, not because I was the boy but because it was technically my tree. She'd won, and my initial was the first one I carved. But she'd been there with me for every scratching mark with my pocketknife. When I was done, she'd kissed the tree and then kissed me.

I remembered that kiss like it was yesterday, the taste of bark and cherry lipgloss.

She spins in my arms so that she can look me in the eye. "Is this what I think it is? Is that original?"

I nod, searching her face. It means something to her too. She licks her lips and my eyes track the movement hungrily.

"Bruce."

I think she's going to tell me to stop, tell me she can't do this again. Instead, she lifts to her toes and kisses me.

It takes me by surprise. I think it takes her by surprise too, actually. But in the span of a heartbeat, we go from standing beside one another to trying to occupy the same space. I need her, need to be inside her. If not her pretty pussy, at least her mouth. Holding her jaw gently in my big hands, I nip at her lower lip, and she opens for me without hesitation. I dive in, our teeth clacking in our rush to consume each other. I claim her mouth, tracing it with my tongue, wanting to know every nook and cranny of her again.

She's pressing into me, her whole body aligned with mine, but she's so much smaller than me that I have to bend over and she's still reaching for me on tiptoe. I slide my hands down her back, my thumbs brushing along the sides of her tits until I'm cupping her ass. I want to touch her everywhere at once, cover her body with mine. With the slightest squeeze, she hops up, wrapping her legs around my waist and her arms around my neck. Holy shit, that's even better . . . her covering me, choosing me.

"Oh, fuck, Al," I murmur as she kisses down my neck. I've been working all day and probably smell more like an animal than a man, but she doesn't seem to mind. Fuck, she even seems to like it as she lets out this cute growl of hunger against my skin.

I hitch her up a bit higher, ordering her to hang on as I drop to one knee and then the other before flipping over. I lean back against our tree with her sitting astride me.

She pulls back, her blue eyes flashing and bright. Her ponytail is floppy, falling to one side, and her cheeks are flushed with desire.

"So fucking beautiful."

"Thank you," she whispers, and I realize I said that part out loud.

She's thinking, I can feel the hamster spinning out in her mind, but I don't rush her. My cock has other ideas about our timeline and throbs painfully, wanting through the few scarce layers separating us, but that's not what this is. This is baby steps. This is getting her used to us again. This is making things right.

"Whatever you want, Al. Anything, nothing. Say the word and it's yours." My voice is too rough, my breath too jagged, my body too needy, but I'll stand by my word. Anything she wants from me, I'll give it.

She leans forward, delicately kissing up my jawline toward my ear, and I can't help but squeeze the fullness of her ass where I'm still holding her. Her breath is hot against my ear as she whispers, "Touch me."

I groan, loving even the faintest hint of dirty talk from her. She was never shy, but I always had a much filthier mouth, and she loved that, got off on it. I pray that hasn't changed because I want clarity here.

"Touch you where, baby? You want me to suck and lick on your sweet tits?" A tiny whimper answers that. "You want me to rub your hot pussy, circle your clit, and fuck you with my fingers until you coat me in your cum?" She shudders, and that seems like a damn good place to start, so I don't push her any further. This I can work with.

I pull at her tank top, and she rips it over her head, revealing her sports bra. There must be a God that still loves a dirty bastard like me because the bra zips in the front. I yank the zipper down and am greeted with the most beautiful set of tits I've ever seen in my life. I thought maybe I'd imagined them through rose-colored glasses over the years, but I don't think I remembered them as gorgeous as they actually are.

I hold her ribcage in my hands, almost touching all the way around her thin frame, and she arches, presenting herself to me. I lick one long line up her sternum because I know it drives her crazy and then feast on her. Al's nipples are bright red and puffy, stiff with desire against my tongue as I circle one and then the other. She holds my head to her, fingers fisting my hair. I have no idea where my hat went, nor do I give a shit when she's letting me touch her like this.

Her hips are moving, rubbing her heat up and down the hard ridge of my cock. If I don't stop her, I'm going to come in my damn jeans. I wrap a strong arm around her waist, forcing her to arch more so that her tits are in my face and her ass is lifted in the air. My free hand rubs over the globe of her ass, and she responds, lifting up even more for me.

Slipping my hand beneath the waistband of her running gear, I say another prayer of thanks to the person who invented lined shorts because Allyson Meyers isn't wearing any underwear.

"Jesus," I hiss as I feel the softness of her skin and the tautness of the muscles of her ass. I dip lower and then lower still, finding her soaked and ready for me.

"Yes," she says on along exhale. "More." I love her bossy tone telling me what she wants.

"Right here?" I tease, but my fingers aren't teasing. I'm going right for her honey pot, spreading her juices all over her lips and up to her clit. I want her messy and coated with her cream, both of us knowing that I'm the one who made her so wet.

LAUREN LANDISH

She cries out, and I swirl my finger over her clit in lazy circles, dipping into her pussy without rhyme or reason so she can't anticipate it. She's going wild in my arms, thrashing as she tries to fuck my hand. I meet her thrust for thrust, going faster and harder, pummeling her sweet pussy roughly, but she's mewling for more with every stroke.

"I'm gonna come, Bruce," she warns.

I want that orgasm, want her to fall apart for me once again. I want it so bad I can taste it in the air. "Do it, Al. Come for me, baby. Come all over my hand, let me feel that pussy clench on my fingers." She's already spasming, the orgasm overtaking her, but my words send her flying even higher. When she calls out my name, I feel ten feet tall and bulletproof.

I fill her pussy with my fingers over and over, slowly as she comes down, letting her catch her breath. She collapses against me, her head cradled on my shoulder. Too soon, I pull my fingers from her and bring them up, staring at the glistening proof of her pleasure. It's covering my hand, stretching between my spread fingers, and I suck them into my mouth one by one, savoring her cream as she watches. "Goddamn, you're so sweet. I forgot how good you taste. I want to drink you down, make you messy, and then clean you up with my tongue."

She turns her face to my shoulder, but I don't think she's embarrassed. I think she's pleased at the crude compliment.

Her hand tiptoes down my chest toward my waist and she says, "What about you?"

I put my hand over hers, stopping her from undoing the button of my jeans. "Not yet, Al. If you take my cock out, I'm going to fuck you right here in the dirt."

"You being all gentlemanly now? We had sex out here before." She's pouting a little and it's cute as hell, almost enough to make me waver in my resolve.

"I'll fuck that pussy anywhere and anytime you'll let me at you, but I don't want to mess this up. You're not a meaningless fuck, Allyson. You never were, and I won't start treating you like one now. When I get back inside you, I want it to be because we've

162

worked out all the old shit that never should've gotten in our way. When I fuck you, there won't be any going back. You'll be mine again, so you need to be prepared for that." I know I'm asking a lot, and doing it pretty gruffly, and that's before you get to the deep growl of my voice.

But she's mine. She's always been mine, and I'm going to make her realize it too. Because I've always been hers.

Her head is against my chest so I can't read her face's reaction to my declaration, not of war but of peace. Our peace, our piece of happiness. But I can feel her body's delight as goosebumps pop up along her arms, even in the August heat of the late afternoon.

Oh, yeah, this girl's gonna be mine again. And now I've put her on notice that it's happening. But I'll give her a minute to adjust to the idea because I know she wasn't looking for this, didn't plan on my swooping back into her life and demanding a place in her heart.

So I'll wait. But not long.

CHAPTER 18

ALLYSON

*T*here's a loud rumble of an engine coming closer, but the noise that draws my attention is the purring in Bruce's chest beneath my palm. "Should we . . . I don't know, get up? Sounds like someone's coming." I know it's one hundred percent what I should be doing, jumping up and righting my clothes, but I'm so floaty and dreamy in this post-orgasmic haze. *At least my bra's zipped and my tank is back on,* I think distantly.

Good Lord, it's been years since I've come like that, and I'm not exactly bad at using my favorite vibrator. But even with its ungodly amount of horsepower, it's got nothing on Bruce's fingers . . . or his tongue . . . or his cock, if I remember correctly. I wonder what new tricks he has up his sleeve these days and realize I am in so much trouble.

He's talking about making me 'his' again, and I heard that proud caveman grunt when he said 'mine.' That alone should send me running for the hills as fast as my legs can carry me. So why am I still sitting here?

He's bossy, that I know. But it's in an oddly respectful way that doesn't set off every alarm bell I have in my body. He sets off some sirens, but it's mostly the good ones, the really good ones.

"We've got about thirty more seconds until they're close enough to see us, and I'm using every one of them in case you go skittish on me again. I want as much of you as I can get." He grinds his still-rigid cock against my core, and I moan, forgetting to argue that I'm not skittish. Nervous maybe, wary definitely, but I'm not some jumpy, on-edge runner.

Or am I?

Deciding to do some self-analyzation on that at a time where I don't have Bruce underneath me, I smirk at him. Challenge accepted. "Count it down, then."

He blinks slowly in confusion, and I give him two heartbeats to start counting, even if he doesn't know why. "Thirty, twenty-nine . . . fuck, Al, what are you doing?" He groans as I move my hips, fucking him through our clothes.

My shorts are so soaked, I'm probably leaving traces of my juices on his jeans and I don't care in the slightest. He grips my thighs, not stopping me but not guiding me either, just letting me ride him however I want. I pick up the pace, and the numbers fly from his mind as he begins cursing instead.

"Uh-uh, keep counting," I admonish and continue my torture of us both.

I don't know who this wanton woman is. This playfulness, this forwardness isn't me, at least not anymore. But with Bruce, she comes out of her hidey hole, ready to be frisky and fun. I like it, even as it makes me sad that I haven't been like this in so long.

Since Bruce. Only with Bruce.

"Ten, nine . . ." He spits the words through clenched teeth. "Fuck, Allyson. You're gonna make me come."

I can't help but cry out, wanting that desperately. I'm close again too, and I want us to come together.

The engine sound quiets and I hear a voice call out instead, "Incoming!"

"Goddamn it." Bruce grabs my ass, fingers spread wide to squeeze all of me, and pulls me against him hard and tight, grinding against me for a second before letting me go. He rests his forehead against mine, panting as his eyes bore into mine.

"Wait a fucking second, Bobby!" he calls out into the air around us. "Fucker knows exactly where we are." His eyes are scanning the trees around us like he's expecting Bobby to sneak attack.

The tension of being on the edge fades away slowly, the adrenalin cooling, and a sense of normalcy returns to the moment. I start to laugh lightly, but everything I've done hits me at once.

Did I seriously just come barreling onto Bruce's farm to yell at him and fire him from the team? Only to end up apologizing when he talked me down because I did actually overreact? And then walk around all afternoon like old times and end up riding Bruce, trying to make him come in his jeans against a clock? Who the hell am I?

Yourself, a tiny voice says from a deep recess in my mind.

Is that true? Could I be this woman?

I've worked so hard to be even-keeled and analytical, safe and routine-oriented. But what if I'm also emotionally tumultuous, passionate, with just a dash of wild? Have I really shut myself off that much?

"Well, at least you're both dressed this time," Bobby drawls from behind me. There's an undercurrent of fury, though, one I've never heard from him before. Bobby was always our alibi, Bruce's best friend and brother who helped us sneak out as much as we could or sneak in whenever we had to.

I might be realizing I'm a bit wilder than I thought, but being caught astride Bruce still isn't exactly a comfortable position. Nor is this the first time Bobby's caught us, though the last time was a very long time ago.

My spine straightens, and I don't look over my shoulder, staring at the tree over Bruce's head in embarrassment instead. "Hey, Bobby, how're you doing?"

He snorts disapprovingly. "Not as good as you two, apparently."

Bruce looks over my shoulder, seemingly having a conversation with Bobby through dark-eyed angry scowls alone. Even I flinch, and they're not directed at me, so surely, Bobby is cowering. "Did you need something?"

Bobby hums for a second, and I imagine he's stroking his chin thoughtfully. "Dinner. Mama Louise invited Allyson and Cooper . . . good kid, by the way . . . to dinner. He's already snapping green beans at the kitchen table, so I was elected to come hunt you down to extend the invitation. Knew where you'd be."

It almost sounds like an accusation?

"Oh, that's so sweet," I say politely, my manners automatic even though something's off about the invite. I turn slightly to finally see Bobby. His eyes tick over me, but just as fast, return to Bruce, giving me a chance to do a quick scan of my own.

Bobby's grown up too. His lanky limbs have filled out into bulges of muscles—from working on the farm, I guess—and his previously round face is all angles and shadows. He looks like a model, and I bet he has women chasing him twenty-four seven. Ironically, his darkly Hollywood looks do nothing for me and actually trigger a small flinch in my gut. I don't like pretty guys. They can hide monsters beneath the attractive façade.

Guess I like my men a bit rougher around the edges, like Bruce, where what you see is what you get. Not that Bruce is my man. Definitely not that.

He's currently death glaring at Bobby, who's making a damned good attempt at returning the frown. I suddenly feel like a gazelle caught between two competing lions. I know it's the lionesses that hunt, but my mind doesn't care about *National Geographic* level accuracy right now.

I sense danger, and my gut reflex is to apologize even though I've done nothing wrong. But I check myself and instead go to my second instinct—mitigate this, mediate it, deescalate whatever the hell's going on.

"Or that's not sweet?" I say, trying to figure out what's wrong between the two boys who were the best of friends when I knew them. "We don't have to stay if you don't want us to."

"It's very kind," Bruce reassures me, squeezing my thigh. "Here, lemme help you up, and we'll go back to the house. You can check on Cooper while Bobby and I have a chat."

Why do I get the feeling that chat will be done with their fists and not their tongues?

"Uh, okay."

I move to stand and Bruce helps set me on my feet before rising from the ground himself. He adjusts his cock in his jeans with zero shame, somehow turning me on again but pissing Bobby off another degree or so.

Bobby spins on his booted foot and stomps back through the trees.

"Is everything okay?" I ask Bruce quietly. "Why's Bobby so mad?"

Bruce squeezes my hand and sighs softly. "He was there for me through the worst of it and it was ugly as fuck. He's got my best interests at heart and is mad at my utter lack of self-preservation."

It hits me hard. Bobby's not mad at Bruce. Well, maybe a little, but mostly, he's mad at . . . *me*. Upset at the past and scared that I'm going to hurt Bruce again, worried he'll have a repeat performance of propping him up through the heartache. Just like Brody said. *Bruce's brothers hate me*, I realize painfully.

"Don't worry, I'll talk to him. It'll be all right." The reassurance doesn't feel so comforting this time. I don't want to cause problems between them, and I don't want Bruce to tell Bobby that everything's fine because I'm not sure it is.

I'm not sure I am.

I climb in the Gator with Bobby and Bruce anyway and head for the house. Bobby's going too fast, getting airborne over every bump, and I have to hold on to the oh-shit handle to keep from flying out. He even skids just a little on the dry grass when he slams on the brakes at the back of the house.

"Head on in, Al. We'll be there in a second," Bruce tells me, his voice cold and his eyes on Bobby.

I climb out and walk in front of the vehicle. I pause, seeing their matching clenched teeth. I can't leave them like this. I have to try. "Hey, guys, can we just agree to not kill each other? Or even harm or maim each other? That'd be a great line in the proverbial sand. Agreed?"

There's a growl in the air, but I'm not sure which man it's coming from. "*Okay*, then. I'll take that as a no." And like a fucking coward, I skedaddle into the house.

It feels like I'm running for safety, right up until the second the screen door closes behind me and a whole bunch of eyes turn to me. Frozen bug, pinned to the pine floor . . . yep, that's me.

My hands clench and unfurl, tapping fingers to my thumb as I wilt under the weight of the stares, some curious and at least one unfriendly. Brody gets up in my face again.

"What's wrong." It should be a question. It's definitely not.

I look behind me, worried. "Bobby hates me. I think they're fighting it out?"

I can hear the waver in my own voice. The fear of violence so close by and that I might be the cause of it makes me feel guilty, even though on some level, I know it's not really my fault. But it's all so mixed-up in my head.

"Fuck," Brody hisses, shoving past me. Three other men do the same, harsh looks on their faces and blonde instead of the Tannens' dark hair, and I realize that these must be the grown-up versions of the Bennett boys. I knew of them in school, but I don't know if I would've recognized them on Main Street if I passed them now. But in this context, there's no way they're anyone else.

Suddenly, I'm alone with Shayanne, two other women I don't know, Mama Louise who everyone knows, and Cooper.

Mama Louise smiles serenely, like this is nothing more than a regular Saturday evening around here. Maybe it is? "No worries, dear. They'll get it sorted."

The other women are looking at me with deep interest. Thankfully, Cooper runs to me, hugging me around the waist. "Mom?"

There's a fear there I promised myself he would never know. I run my fingers across his head before patting his back. "It's fine, honey. Bruce and Bobby are just talking. Tell me about your day. Did you see the pig?"

He doesn't want the redirection, but Shayanne jumps in to save the day. "He sure did. He held Bacon Seed like a pro, supporting her round little body. He even fed her." Shayanne holds her hand up and Cooper hesitatingly slaps it with his own.

It's working, though. Cooper's shoulders are dropping back into place, and he steps back, quoting. "Only one cookie treat per day. And they're not really cookies like you and me eat. They're special pig formula cookies and taste gross. *So* gross." He sticks his tongue out and his nose crinkles.

"You ate a pig cookie?" I ask, horrified.

I marvel at how resilient he is and how he can jump focus as Shay and him giggle like they're sharing a special joke with zero thoughts about what's happening outside. "All natural, nontoxic, safe to eat. Just yucky, I promise," Shayanne says. "It's good to know what you're feeding your animals."

"Speaking of feeding our animals, there's work to be done," Mama Louise says, her meaning quite clear to everyone.

The two women I don't know move over to the counter, where it looks like they're making a salad, but their prying eyes still bore into me. Shayanne heads to the stove, Cooper trailing along after her. I look to Mama Louise for an assignment, and she nods, obviously pleased at my willingness to jump right in. "Allyson, dear, could you set the table, please? Plates, glasses, silverware," she says, pointing around the kitchen.

"Yes, ma'am," I answer, doing her bidding.

It occurs to me that she knows my name already. From Bruce? From Cooper? From high school? From Brody and Bobby telling them all about me today?

I feel like an interloper. They've accepted Cooper, but he's a kid and ridiculously adorable. But me? They're looking at me like a freak show, the woman who broke Bruce's heart and is setting him up to fall again, especially if they've been listening to Brody and Bobby.

I'm not, or at least I don't think I am, but I don't think for one second that they'd believe that.

"I'm Allyson, by the way," I tell the two salad-makers. They have the manners to look slightly chagrined.

"I'm Sophie," a pretty woman with a country air says, though she doesn't have that same drawl Shayanne does. "James's wife, and that butter ball over there is Cindy Lou, our daughter."

She points at the baby happily sitting in a highchair at the table. Her hair is standing up like she stuck her finger in a light socket and her socked feet kick out in a dance only she knows.

The blonde waves a wet hand and smiles welcomingly. "Katelyn. I'm Mark's."

We get to work, and it's not quiet in the kitchen—the stirring spoon against the metal pot, the rip of lettuce, and the clatter of the dishes—but somehow, the silence is suffocating. These women all have questions for me, want answers I don't have, and I want to escape to my own little kitchen. Just me and Cooper having dinner at the small four-seater table that's only ever held that many people when Michelle and Liam come over.

All of this—the people, the eyes, the unasked questions—weighs on me.

Most of all, I feel guilty that the guys are all outside fighting. Bruce and Bobby were always crazy-close, and I don't want to mess that up. Especially when I don't even know what the hell's going on between me and Bruce.

Today's been an utter rollercoaster.

He's serious, or at least I think he is. But I'm not looking for that. Not looking for another relationship, a marriage, a dad for Cooper. My heart begins to race and my mind starts whirling, anxiety coursing through me.

I set the table, but it takes me forever as I tap, tap, tap my fingers. I bend down to baby talk with Cindy Lou, mindlessly telling her how cute she is because she seems like the friendliest face in the room.

The back screen opens and a herd of elephants enters the kitchen, or well, a whole gaggle of cowboys, but it's about the same noise level, reminding me again of the uncomfortable silence with the women. The guys all look a bit heated, from the August evening sun and whatever drama they just went through. Each and every one of them looks at me with a stony gaze, though, hard ice coursing through the lot of them. Even Bruce, though his anger seems to be directed at the guys instead of me.

All in all, I'm adrift in a sea of people who are sending me drastically varying messages of welcome. Or flat-out unwelcome in some cases. Brody and Bobby, I'm looking at you.

"Dinner's ready if everyone's cleaned up?" Mama Louise says, and there's a grumbled chorus of 'Yes, ma'am.' before everyone sits.

I hang back, biting my lip and twisting my fingers, not knowing where to sit. Mama Louise guides Cooper to her side, and he goes happily, blissfully unaware of my impending freakout, thankfully.

"Al?" Bruce says quietly. I find him amid the sea of broad shoulders to see he's gesturing to the chair beside him. I sit stiffly, primly perched on the edge. He leans over and whispers in my ear. "You okay? You look ready to run for the hills."

I look sideways at him, hearing his earlier assessment that I'm skittish. Then, I wanted to argue that fact. Now, I'll admit to myself that he might be right. But it's for a damn *good* reason, the boy sitting at Mama Louise's side. Running saved me and saved him once, and I'll damn well do it again if it'd protect us from any more pain.

Or this awkward aggression that's assaulting me from every angle right now.

"I'm fine," I say quietly, not even believing the lie myself.

"Shit." He sighs heavily.

"Language," Mama Louise says, never taking her attention from filling Cooper's plate with more food than he'd eat in a week of suppers.

Bruce dips his chin in apology, and I resort to daintily stuffing my face so I don't have to say anything. Little bites so that I'm always feeding myself or chewing . . . *just ignore me*, I beg silently.

No such luck.

"How're practices going?" Bobby asks me directly. Why does it seem like he's accusing me of something with the barest small talk?

I swallow thickly, dabbing at my mouth with my napkin before laying it back in my lap. "Pretty good. Except for today," I admit, looking at Bruce. "But it worked out, I guess."

Cooper laughs, unaware that he's saving my bacon by interjecting. "Uh, yeah, Mom. You told Johnathan off, which he totally deserved. And my arms and legs are still limp noodles from all the drills you made us do as punishment." He holds up his arms in front of him, wiggling them loosely.

The group chuckles, and I realize he might be my only saving grace to get through this meal. Seems about right because he's easily the best thing I've ever done.

He goes on to tell them about the circle high-five-pushup drill we did to wrap up practice, and Bruce nods approvingly, pointing at Cooper with a fork. "Sounds like practice ended better than it started. We'll build on that." Cooper nods like a bobblehead, and I think he'd agree with anything Bruce said. Hell, any of the boys would.

So would you, that sex kitten voice purrs in my head. And though I was just wildly riding him this afternoon, it seems like that was ages ago already. It was a pocket of time and space where there were no rules, no consequences, no reality, a blip that blinked out, leaving this awkward uncomfortableness of eyes staring us down like we're specimens to be dissected.

"So, what's the deal with the two of you?" Mark demands of me with a lift of his chin. I only know he's Mark because Katelyn's by his side, and at his brusque pseudo-question, she lays her hand over his. "What?" he says to her, shrugging carelessly. "It's what we all want to know, the elephant in the room or whatever. We heard Brutal's version outside and wanna hear Allyson's too. Might as well get it out of the way so we can eat in peace, right?"

Well, shit. There's no hiding now, not with the big ass spotlight Mark just shone on me.

"Leave her alone, Mark." Bruce's voice is powerfully furious but quiet. A calm before another storm. With Cooper sitting right here with a front-row seat. No, I can't let that happen.

I steel my nerves, limiting my tapping to just one finger against my thigh under the table. I can do this. Short and to the point is key. Be firm so as not to invite further questions that might dive too deep. Just like I tell clients when they're preparing to testify, because this feels eerily similar.

I meet Mark's eyes, no small feat in itself, and recite the basics, being very intentional with my words because of Cooper's presence even though he's building some sort of green bean log cabin that keeps falling over. He's completely oblivious to the adult conversation and thread of tension going on around him.

It feels like I've said some version of this story so many times recently, to myself, to Bruce, even to Michelle. It's easier with each telling, but it still makes me feel like I've got a target on my back with the staredowns I'm getting. Like they're comparing whatever Bruce said to what I just said, and like it was some test, I'm dying to know if I passed. Or if he said something different.

But what would he have said? I just told the truth.

Mark hums in approval as I finish, and Bruce lays his arm around the back of my chair in what would be a casual move in any other situation. This one, as his rough fingers tease along the bare skin of my shoulders, is a bold claiming, telling everyone that's enough and to fuck off. I'm thankful for the backup, but my basking in his support is a flashing neon danger sign to me.

All of this is too much, too soon, too fast, too strong, too scary.

I'm having dinner with his family, for fuck's sake! He's throwing about words like 'mine' and talking about 'us' like there is such a thing.

I can feel myself rebuilding the walls that came down when it was just the two of us, slapping up brick by brick to give me a quick defense against it all. Cold settles in my veins, and I stay stoic and quiet.

The rest of dinner, no one says a word to me, no more questions, no more snarky remarks, nothing. It's exactly what I want, but it feels like I've already been dismissed as unworthy.

Not soon enough, dinner ends and I make my escape.

"Thank you so much for dinner, Mama Louise. And for hanging out with Cooper, Shayanne." The two women smile in response, a rare and appreciated kindness given the mood of the rest of dinner. "We need to get going with the drive back to town."

"Of course, dear. Drive safely, and you're welcome at my dinner table anytime," Mama Louise says with a smile that says she knows the gauntlet I just endured and is maybe a bit apologetic about it. Or is that pride glinting in her eyes? "You too, Mr. Cooper!"

She hugs him, and he hugs her right back without hesitation, making my heart stutter.

Bruce walks us out, using a flashlight from by the door to shine the way back to our car parked closer to the Tannen house. When I unlock the doors, Bruce holds up a fist and Cooper pounds it. "Your family is awesome, Coach B! Shayanne told me I can visit Bacon Seed anytime I want. Is that true?"

Bruce nods. "If Shayanne said it, she meant it. But only if your mom says it's okay too."

Cooper looks at me with puppy dog eyes, pleading his case over clasped hands. "Please, Mom?"

"We'll see." He hops around wildly like I agreed and then climbs in the car, still wiggling happily. I close the door behind him and then it's just Bruce and me in the dark night as he clicks off the flashlight.

"You okay, baby?" he murmurs. I know he sees the flinch the endearment triggers when he sighs. "Two steps forward, one step back is fine if that's where you're at, Allyson. I just need to know if we're still dancing."

I bite my lip, not sure how to answer that.

"Maybe?" It's all I can honestly give.

Bruce nods his head, and I wish I could see his eyes. "I can work with that." He bends down, his breath hot on my cheek, but he pauses, giving me time to stop him. The refusal doesn't come, and he presses his lips to my cheek.

I want them on mine. I want him to leave me alone.

I am such a clusterfuck of emotions . . . want, desire, and hope battling safety, routine, and fear.

"I'll see you at practice on Tuesday," I finally say.

I know he's disappointed in my reluctance, but he agrees. "Yeah, see you Tuesday. Call me if you need anything. Or text me. But if I don't respond, assume it's a glitch or bad cell service. I promise, I'll respond to you PDQ."

My brows knit together. "PDQ?"

Even in the moonlight, I can see the glint of his smile. "Pretty damn quick . . . for you."

I smile, ducking into my car. "Good night, Bruce."

"Good night, Al."

CHAPTER 19

BRUCE

$\mathcal{T}$uesday's practice is a tough one. I go hard on the boys, recementing the expectations and team building we did previously, even though Allyson already handled their behavior. Those bonds and boundaries shouldn't crumble so easily.

I pay special attention to Johnathan, who actually apologizes to Allyson unprompted. Guess he had a bout of conscience later. I'm glad because he's a good kid. He just lacks some impulse control and a filter. But didn't we all need some growth in those areas at this age? Fuck knows, I did. Hell, I probably still do.

When we're done, the team cheer dying in the wind, I try to talk to Allyson, but she's not having it. She's fighting me, fighting herself, fighting us and doing a damn good job of retreating in an attempt to hide away.

"Sorry, we have to hustle tonight. Cooper has a science project due in the morning for his STEMP summer camp and we've got a busy night of cutting and gluing ahead of us. He'll definitely be up past his bedtime." She sounds like it's a personal failure on her part that he's going to stay up late. She's even nibbling on her lip like she's second-guessing herself on her evening agenda.

"No problem. Raincheck?" I keep it casual, not wanting to scare her off, but I can see the hamster in her mind hitting that wheel like a speed demon. Even though I want to force the issue with every instinct I've got, I fight to use my brain instead and make a strategic retreat before she can say otherwise. "See you Thursday. Call me if you need anything."

I press a quick kiss to her forehead and she flinches. I have an echoing twinge of hurt in my gut until she presses her fingers to my lips, wiping the kiss off them. "Don't kiss me like that when I'm all sweaty and gross. Ew!"

I grin beneath her fingers. "I don't care if you're sweaty. Hell, I'll make you sweaty and then lick you head to toe just to taste your salty sweetness." I stick my tongue out against her fingers, demonstrating.

She blushes fiercely and the freckles on her nose stand out in stark relief. She might cringe away from serious talk, but she's all too willing to listen to my dirty talk.

If I have to win her back using my dick and some filthy words, so be it.

New plan—I'll get her pussy and then her heart. It's not bad as far as plans go and maybe won't scare her off so badly. My cock agrees with my brain for once, and I put the new plan into action immediately.

I lower my voice, letting that gravelly bedroom sound into my vocal cords. "Allyson, fresh from the shower with your soft skin smelling like flowers . . . I want you. Sweaty and wet with salty trails running down your body . . . I want you. Anytime and anywhere, I'll bend this body over and fuck you so raw and hard that you forget your own name. You won't give a single fuck about whether your hair is fixed or even clean because all you'll care about is the way I'm twisting it in my hand as I feed you my cock. I'll make you forget everything but how good I can make you feel. Because you know I can. I know you didn't forget that. I'll make you come so hard you fucking leave your body to float around in bliss while this pussy creams all over me. And even then . . ."

I'm on a roll, and she's panting, her tits rising and falling to brush against me because she's stepping closer, leaning into what

I'm promising her. I don't think she even realizes she's doing it, but I don't call attention to it. Not yet.

"Even then, after you're messy with juices from your clit to your asshole, I'll lick up every drop with my tongue. Happily, greedily, thirstily. So I don't give a rat's ass about a little sweat, baby."

I kiss her forehead once again.

This time, she leaves it. On my lips, on her skin.

She's breathy and weak, but still, she argues. My little spitfire. "Bruce. Science project. Cooper." I love that I've made her unable to string words together to form sentences. I actually feel damn proud and want to strut around like a peacock a bit. But I'll save that for when she's truly speechless.

"I know. Go take care of Cooper. Mom gig first and foremost, always." I get that and would never begrudge her need to spend time with him and help him. "But if you get a little time alone after he goes to bed and want to call me or send me some dirty pics, I'll be sleeping with my phone in my hand, praying to God that he'll bless me with some spank bank material."

It's irreverent and silly on purpose. I need her to leave feeling good about this. It's a long game, not just a quick ambush to get in her pants. Though I definitely want in there, it's a directed step toward more.

She giggles, slapping lightly at my chest. "I think that's blasphemy. It's definitely not how prayer works."

"To-may-to, to-mah-to. Agree to disagree. But you need to get home. Do some science or *something*." I tilt my voice, letting her know that I'm not nearly as invested in Cooper's project as I am in what she'll be doing after his bedtime.

Her smile is easy, which feels like a win, especially considering how ready to run she was a few minutes ago. This new plan is a fucking brilliant one, I decide. I'm making progress, a little bit at a time.

"I'll talk to you on Thursday," she says emphatically.

I hold my phone up, waving it back and forth. "If I don't hear from you sooner."

By Thursday, I'm desperate to see her. She never called, never texted, and I'm afraid I overplayed. Direct scared her off. Indirect might've scared her off too.

Shit.

I'm not a player by any stretch of the word's definition, but I should have better game than this. Especially with her. She's the one person I know almost as well as I know myself. Or at least I used to. Maybe that's how I should go at this? Not with promises, not with sexy talk, but with . . . a date to get to know each other again?

Or maybe everything at once? If I come at varying angles, she's got to see reason. See that this is happening, that we're meant to be. We would've been together all along if not for the stupid shit kids pull and our being too immature to use our words. I curse the silly little fucker I was, but I'm not that kid anymore.

Which is what I keep telling Bobby. He's been a bitch all week, saying 'remember when' and 'what about . . .' as he asks me questions to make me 'see the light', as he calls it. That's even after I explained what happened all those years ago.

He means well, I know that, but I'd rather have him on my side, helping me figure out how to get Allyson back, because talking it all through with him, even with his being pissy, has actually solidified things in my mind.

I want her, should've had her all along, but damned if she's not going to make me work for it, fight for her smiles, and earn her heart. But I'm man enough for the job, and she's worth it, no matter the obstacles she throws in my path.

Practice is a bubble where we focus on the kids. Drills, coaching, throw the ball, catch the ball, run for TDs.

But there's also tension. I can feel Allyson shyly watching me when she thinks I'm not looking, can feel her arousal like it's a palpable thing in the air between us. By the time we do the team cheer, I've decided on my move.

"So, what's for dinner? I'm starving," I say, throwing my arm over Cooper's shoulders. Yep, I'm using the kid as an in. But I like Cooper, so I don't think I'm too damned by it.

He grins excitedly. "Mom made lasagna. It's in the oven at home already."

I pat my belly and groan. "Sounds delicious. I can't wait."

His brows climb up his little forehead. "Are you coming to dinner?"

"Why, thank you for the invite, Cooper. I'd be delighted." Kid doesn't even realize he just got played, but it's for a good cause so I don't feel too guilty.

Allyson walks up at the perfect moment. "Mom, Coach B is coming over for lasagna! Woo-hoo, I'm gonna go tell Liam!"

He runs off and Allyson gives me a hell of a mom look, but it doesn't have near the impact on me that it would on Cooper. "Can I pick up some wine or bread or something? It's not far to your house, and I pass by a grocery store on the way."

"I know what you're doing." She makes it sound like I'm hiding shit, but my intentions are crystal clear so I just shrug. My smirk's answer enough. There's a pregnant pause where there's a very real chance she's going to tell me no. But she sighs and rolls her eyes. "Fine. You can come to dinner. I've already got bread and beer. But you can get wine if you'd rather have it?"

I chuckle, scratching at my lip with my thumb. "Hell naw. I'd rather have a beer any day, but I was trying to be fancy for you."

She laughs and teases, "Do you even know what fancy is?"

I love the brightness of her eyes, the relaxed slope of her shoulders, the flush on her cheeks. I realize all at once that the haunted look is fading, the shadows are receding, and her smiles are more frequent. She's less rushed and rigid, more chill and relaxed. Does she realize that too?

Is it because of me, the football team, or something else? I'm not saving her like some prince in shining armor, but I want it to be because of me. I want that because making her happy makes *me* happy. I'm such a sappy shit for this woman.

"Yeah, I know what fancy is. It's when I wear clean jeans without holes and a shirt straight from the laundry. Not just one from the floor that passed the sniff test." I turn my head, taking a big whiff of myself, and make a face. "So we're definitely not doing fancy today."

Her repeated laughter bolsters me, as does her confirmation of the invitation. "See ya at my house in a few."

Hell yes.

I drive around the block once, chomping three cinnamon mints nervously before pulling into her driveway to give her an extra minute to prep for company she wasn't expecting. I considered stopping for flowers but decided they might spook her, so I'm saving that idea for another time.

I knock on the door, and it opens quickly, like she was waiting for me. The thought that she might be excited to see me sends a warm buzzing though my entire body, making me feel drunk.

"Hey," she says. I think she's aiming for casual, but she fails spectacularly, leaning against the door with her hip popped out and her hair falling around her shoulders when minutes ago at practice, it was up in some messy pile of a bun.

Oh, yeah, we're *dancing* and dinner tonight is a good two steps forward.

I just need to watch out for the backslide.

"Hey yourself," I reply, keeping my tone the casual she tried for. I step inside and she shuts the door behind me. I'm officially in.

"Coach B!" Cooper yells, beelining toward me from down the hall. He stops short in front of me, holding up a fist. I pound it, liking that he initiated the greeting this time.

"Wash up. Dinner's ready."

Cooper and I disappear down the hall to wash up as ordered and hit the kitchen. I wait to see where they sit and take one of the remaining seats, choosing the one that puts me across from Al. I think she expected me to sit beside her, but I want to see her face, read her reactions, and make sure I'm not fucking up, so this angle is better.

We dig in, moaning in ecstasy at the pasta goodness. "This is delicious. Did you make the sauce yourself?" I ask Allyson. "Shay might need this recipe."

She laughs, her smile bright and her eyes crinkled. "No, I didn't make it. I bought it jarred . . . from your sister. Well, Debra did. She's a big fan of Shayanne's goodies and is basically my dealer for all things homemade by Shayanne now. Apparently, there's some pumpkin concoction she makes? Debra has the first sale date on her calendar already, says she wants to make sure she can get the hookup before Shay sells out."

"Mmm," I hum in blissed-out carb heaven, and Allyson looks pleased at my positive reaction to her food as I shovel another bite into my mouth. "Yeah, she makes smashed pumpkin. Jarred and whole pies. She'll start running around like a chicken with her head cut off here shortly. My watermelon water delivery route has nothing on her pumpkin season orders." I shudder violently and dramatically. "I'm exhausted just thinking about it."

"Will you still coach us if you're that busy?" Cooper asks. I can see the concern swirling in his blue eyes, several shades lighter but so much like his mother's.

"Of course. With me coming into town three times a week, I can do deliveries then or people can pick up their orders at the park. Might even be easier if we offer that option." I purse my lips, thinking and praying that's true. "Actually, I should see if we can offer that for the last of the watermelon water too. A bit of a trial run." I wink at Cooper, thanking him for the inspiration for an idea that might give me some time back, time I'll happily spend getting to Allyson.

We talk about everything and nothing, letting conversation drift here and there. It feels good, homey with the three of us around the table chatting about our day, and I have an image of what could've been. Maybe even what could still be.

"I had an idea I wanted to run by you . . ." Allyson's voice fades like she's unsure of herself. She's fidgeting with the placemat in front of her, and I take a leap of faith, reaching across the table to cover her hand with mine. Her eyes meet mine, a tiny gasp escaping. I know she's freaking a bit. I can see her pulse racing in her neck, but she doesn't pull away. I'm acutely aware of Cooper's gaze too and hope he's okay with this. I wouldn't ever disrespect his feelings about the situation.

But the situation is . . . I'm trying to make Allyson give me a shot. A real one.

And risks must be taken.

Eventually, after what seems like an eon, she settles and relaxes without moving her hand. It feels like a great fucking victory, and I gently rub my thumb over hers in celebration.

She licks her lips and starts again. "I thought it would be fun to do a sleepover with all the boys before the first game. Not the night before, because I don't have a death wish. But maybe the weekend before? A team-building thing and a celebration of how great they've been doing with practices. What do you think?"

If ever there were a moment to agree with anything she says, it's this one. But I don't agree because I want her. No, I nod my head because it truly is a great idea. "I like it. But one tweak . . ." Her brows rise, and I can see a slight clenching of her teeth like she thinks I'm about to shit all over her seed of an idea and call it fertilizer. "What if we did it at the farm? S'mores, a bit of muddin' in the Gator maybe. Campfire stories, stuff like that."

"Mom! Yes! Say yes, please." Cooper interrupts loudly and with more enthusiasm than his little body can hold. "Never mind, I'll answer for her. Yes, Coach B! The boys would love that!"

He points at his own chest when he says 'the boys', apparently electing himself their spokesperson. I laugh but keep one eye on Allyson to gauge her reaction. She looks at Cooper and then back to me with a laugh of her own. "Guess we're in."

"YES!" Cooper goes off with excitement, hopping from the table and doing a weird dance that kinda reminds me of that chicken dance Johnathan had us do.

"Looks like you're done with dinner, mister. Why don't you go hop in the shower so you can hit the hay on time tonight? I think you're still a bit worn out from The Science Project night." The way she says it, I can hear the capitals, like it was An Incident. Cooper pulls a face, his lips wincing, and salutes before running down the hall.

A moment later, I hear the water start and my eyes lock on Allyson, my gaze heavy with intention. "Alone at last. I love that kid, but he's fucking with my dating life." I mean it to be funny and flirty, because I obviously love the little guy, but it bombs flat.

Allyson sighs. "Bruce. We're a package deal. You need to know that."

My brows knit in confusion. "I'm well aware, Allyson. I like the kid. He's pretty fucking cool. But that doesn't mean that I can't enjoy a moment alone with you and want to take advantage."

She tilts her head like she's considering that. "That's true, I guess. I just haven't done this—any of this—since I had him, so I don't know the proper thing to do."

"Fuck proper. Do what *you* want. He's your number-one, so you're not going to do anything to fuck that up. But you deserve happiness too." She looks unconvinced. "Hell, Cooper would want that for you too. He doesn't need a martyr who doesn't live and uses him as a buffer against the world. He wants a mom who shows him how a beautiful, strong, smart woman goes after every single thing she wants and creates the life she deserves."

I mean it to sound persuasive, but something in my words hurts her. I replay them to figure out what it was, but I'm not exactly sure.

"But only if that thing I want is you, right?" There's venom in her tone, accusing me of something, but I don't know what it is, though I've obviously misstepped.

Damn, I suck at this. I'm more than a little lost and wishing I had a GPS for these uncharted waters because something really important is happening here. But she's the only one who knows what it is. She goes back to fidgeting and I can feel her pulling away from me.

I push out from the table and come around to kneel at her feet. It puts my face even with hers, and I take her hands in mine, holding them on her thighs. I duck down, getting my face in hers where she's looking down, not letting her away from me, from this.

I'm going into dangerous territory, approaching a wounded animal with nothing but the good intentions I hope she can read. Because I might not know what Allyson's deal is, but any fool can tell that beneath her hard shell, her soft heart has been hurt. Badly.

"You're different from before. I get that. This woman you are now? I want to know her, fall in love with her and that kid down the hall too. But only if that's what you want." I pause, trying to make the next words come as I cup her jaw in my big hands.

"I'm not here to make it harder for you, Al. If you don't want me, if you'd rather I just coach the kids and disappear when the season's over, I will. It'll kill me, and Bobby will throw some big 'told ya so' shit my way, but all I want is for you to be happy. Fuck yeah, I want it to be with me, but if not, just . . ." I lick my lips, hating the catch in my throat. *"Just be happy, Al."*

I don't know where these words are coming from. I'm not a pretty poetry sort, but it's the damn truth. I've gone from wanting her, to wanting to possess her, to wanting to watch her shuck the shackles holding her back. I want her to fly because fuck, is she stunning when she soars, and hopefully, she'll come back to me after feeling the wind through her wings.

She blinks several times and I think she might be about to cry. But her voice is steady as she speaks. "It's funny you say I'm different from before. These last few weeks, especially these last few days, I've felt more like my old self than I have in years. And I like it." The very corners of her mouth tilt up in the smallest smile, and she whispers confidentially, "I don't know how to do this, Bruce. I don't date, haven't wanted to, not since . . ."

It's on the tip of her tongue to say his name, but I don't want him and whatever shit he did to her to intrude on this moment. I might not know what happened, but he did this to her. He turned the fiery, mouthy girl who shone so brightly and lived life wide open into this fearful, rigid woman who dully lives well within the confines of safety. It's not that she's an adult now. It's that her true self is buried under years of grime from him.

And yet, she's so close to letting her inner wild-child free to choose me, the rough, gruff cowboy she once knew who doesn't deserve a sweet thing like her, the man who'll do anything for her. Her eyes dip to my mouth, and I take the initiative, kissing her softly. But though it's sweet, there's deep meaning to our every caress.

I pull back, meeting her eyes directly and swimming in the blue I see there. "Allyson, we can go as slow as you need or as fast as you want. Just try this . . . for you. I think you need this, need *me*, and that's not arrogance talking. It's okay if you use me up and throw me away when you're done. If it's what you need to get right with yourself, I'll do it."

I know what I'm offering is pure and utter stupidity on my part. She's not ready, might not ever be ready for what I want with her, but I'll take what I can get for as long as I can get it and pray that along the way, she will fall in love with me.

I can hear Bobby calling me a dumb shit already, but I don't care. A moment of happiness with her is better than a lifetime of nothingness without her. I know that she's why I never found someone, not in all the years after high school. Somewhere, deep inside, I knew I gave my heart away to this girl, and though she left me, she left with my heart in her hands. It's always been hers, whether she wanted it or not.

Her face is written in pain, past and present, and fear for more in the future. "I don't want to hurt you or get hurt, not again. I just don't know what to do."

A single tear tracks down her cheek, and I catch it with my thumb, wiping it away. I wish I could wipe whatever's hurt her away as easily.

"Go on a date with me Saturday." It's not a question. It's a solution to her confusion. "Just to prove to yourself that you can."

"Bruce, I don't want to hurt you," she argues again weakly.

I thump my chest with my palm. "Let me worry about that. You just enjoy figuring out Allyson Meyers again. From what I recall, she's a hell of a woman, a spitfire rebel who danced on the roof of my truck, lived without fear, and was willing to try just about anything once. Maybe twice just to be sure," I say with a shit-eating grin, memories racing through my mind in flashes of our past.

She nibbles her lip uncertainly, but after what feels like a lifetime but truthfully is only a few seconds, she smiles. "Okay. A date."

She's probably gonna freak about this later, but I'm absolutely going to hold her to her word. In the meantime, I kiss her lips once more, hard and rough to build up her need. She might not know her heart, but I know her body. I want her to think of this later when she panics and when she touches herself.

The water turns off down the hall, calling our moment of alone time to a halt.

"Tell Cooper good night for me. I'll see you on Saturday for practice, and then I'll pick you up at seven for our date." I scan her face, looking for any sign of an impending freakout I need to address before I leave, but I find none. She looks . . . hopeful?

One last quick peck and I'm out the door.

I think I did the right thing. I hope I did. I'm going to help her find herself if it's the last thing I do, even if my heart breaks again in the process. But maybe I can help put hers back together instead?

CHAPTER 20

ALLYSON

"*I* can't do this." My reflection looks back at me with fear-filled eyes as I shake my head.

From the bed behind me, Michelle's bored voice repeats the same thing she's been telling me for the last twenty minutes. "Yes, you can. Yes, you are."

"I shouldn't do this." Maybe a different argument will get her to see reason?

"Yes, you should."

No dice, apparently. I plop down on the bed beside her, blowing a loose curl of hair out of my eyes. "Michelle, I'm serious. This is such a bad idea. I'm going to hurt Bruce, or I'm going to get my heart broken, or we're both going to end up mad again."

Michelle flops back on the bed and closes her eyes. "Tell me again."

I've already told her all about my conversation with Bruce, and I mindlessly repeat it again, focusing mostly on what he said. I don't know how he ever thought himself only a 'dumb jock' because he's one of the most perceptive people I've ever known.

I've been thinking about everything he said, turning it over in my mind time and time again, evaluating and analyzing from every angle.

I've worked hard to let the past go, but I won't argue that it's shaped my thoughts, reactions, hopes. And Bruce's learning all that, the down and dirty of my last ten years, is inevitable with the way he notices every single thing about me. I don't want to be lessened in his eyes when he finds out.

That's my real fear, I guess.

What if I don't date anymore, not because of Cooper like I've been telling myself but because I'm broken, unsalvageable? I'm a walking, talking FUBAR—Fucked Up Beyond All Repair despite all the work I've put into being better. And I am better, so much better that I want to grab up the me of years ago and shake the ever lovin' shit outta her.

But the scars and the shame run deep. Even so, I don't want to be FUBARed anymore. And Bruce makes me hope that maybe I won't always be.

"Whatever roller coaster you just went on, that's the real shit you need to dig out and deal with." Michelle's voice breaks into my train of thought, and I peek over to find her watching me closely through narrowed eyes. "With yourself, with him, or hell, with me, if you want."

I shrug, not sure whether I want to share all that with her. She knows a little about my marriage but respectfully tiptoed around my boundaries when I clammed up about the details and has never toed the line again. She's a great friend.

Unfortunately, she tells me the truth even when I don't want to hear it.

"Let's recap. He wants to fuck you and he was the best dick of your life." It's not a question, so I don't answer, but I tilt my head, looking at her with exasperation because she always gets stuck on the sex part.

"So, that's a yes. He wants to date you. He wants to get to know you. He wants to fall in love with you. He wants to make you fall in love with him. And barring all that, he's willing to just fuck you senseless because you need some good dick. I'm not seeing any downside here, girl. Get out of your own way and live a little." The last part is an order if ever I've heard one.

"Yes, ma'am, Boss Bitch!" I bark it out with a salute, ending with a middle finger that's not one hundred percent a joke, but maybe ninety-five-ish, so that's not too bad.

Michelle laughs and pushes my finger down, her tone turning serious. "Allyson, give him a shot. Give yourself a shot. Be a little reckless, do date-y things and get to know each other again. See what comes of it. Just make sure it's you. At least three times." She holds three fingers up, wiggling them emphatically.

I laugh. "You have such a one-track mind." Standing up, I spin. "How do I look?"

Bruce didn't say what we're doing or where we're going, so I'm trying to cover all the bases. My floaty sundress seems perfect. It hits below my knees, but the deep crisscross V neckline is flattering to my breasts, and the small blue flowers are the same color as my eyes. It feels fresh and light, making me feel the same.

Michelle traces a circle in the air, and I spin, the dress swirling out around me a bit. When I face her again, she's smiling. Actually, it's more of a devious grin. "He's not going to know what hit him, Allyson."

"Who are you hitting, Mom?" Cooper's voice squeaks out from the door. "Ooh, you look pretty. Where are we going?"

Shit.

I was hoping to avoid this until a conversation became necessary, like if this thing with Bruce actually goes somewhere other than just sex. But I won't lie to Cooper.

I sit on the bed, patting it so Cooper will come over. Once he's settled, his blue eyes looking at me, I take a breath for strength. "Honey, you know I love you so much, but sometimes, adults like to hang out with other adults. That's what I'm doing tonight, having dinner with Bruce."

The words should be casual, but they're definitely not, and Cooper's such a smart kid, he knows it. "Mom, are you talking about a *date?*"

I mess with his hair, combing my fingers through the tangles. "Yes. I'm going on a *date* with Bruce."

"Are you gonna have sex with him?"

I choke on my own spit. "What? Where did you hear that?"

His eyes dart to Michelle and he shrugs. "Liam says that's what his parents do when his dad comes home and they send him over here for the night. Go on a date and have sex."

I glare at Michelle, but even on her olive skin, I can tell that she's blushing big time so I let her off the hook. To Cooper, I say, "That's between Bruce and me, and Michelle and Michael. We'll have a bigger discussion about sex later, but for now, I just want to make sure you're okay with my going out to dinner with Bruce."

My tongue feels too big in my mouth. I'm very open and honest with Cooper, but I'm not prepared to have the birds and the bees talk right this second, moments before I leave on my first date in years.

Thankfully, his smile is mega-watt bright and his words ridiculously casual for how important this is. "Yeah, Coach B is cool."

I feel like I just ran an obstacle course over Legos blindfolded, barefoot, and with one hand tied behind my back.

Michelle hops up. "On that note, let's get you boys loaded up. We've got pizzas to make, popcorn to pop, and movies to watch." As she ushers Cooper out of my bedroom, she mouths back, "Oh, my God!" Her eyes are filled with horror, and I expect she's going to have an awkward conversation with Liam too.

"HOLY FUCK, AL." IT'S NOT A FLOWERY COMPLIMENT, BUT IT SWIRLS through my veins like warm honey as Bruce's eyes appraise me from my curled hair, over my sundress, to my red-painted toes in high wedge-heeled sandals.

"Thank you," I say, giving a little curtsy.

"These are for you." He holds out a bundle of flowers tied with twine. They're not roses from a florist but a riot of colorful wildflowers. They're perfect.

"Thank you," I say again. Do I sound like a broken record? Am I already fucking this up?

But I force that voice to shut up, focusing on getting a vase down and filling it with water for the beautiful flowers. Once I set it on the kitchen table, Bruce clears his throat. "You ready?"

I glance up, realizing that he's nervous too. Somehow, that revelation puts me at ease, or at least in damn good company with my own nerves.

"You look nice too," I say, cringing a bit at the weak compliment compared to his when he saw me. But he preens anyway, letting me look my fill.

As if I'd ever reach that point.

He's got on brown boots without a speck of dirt of them, dark wash jeans slung low on his hips, and a button-up shirt tucked in behind his belt. His hair's grown out a bit over the last few weeks, dark hair that wants to curl at his neck even without his usual hat, and his beard's trimmed neatly. He looks like a fancy cowboy tonight. My fancy cowboy.

Once my eyes trace down and back up slowly, he offers an elbow to me, which I take delicately. Bruce leads me to the door, waiting while I lock up, but I can feel his eyes on me the whole time even as he helps me into his truck. I can tell it's had a fresh wash too.

I appreciate that he pulled out all the stops. It makes this feel more real. Thirty minutes ago, I would've said the exact opposite, thinking that casual bordering on lazy would be preferable. But that's because then I could've written the whole thing off as nothing more than a convenient re-visit to the past. But Bruce is putting in effort here. And that means something, especially to me.

As he pulls through town, Bruce gives me a sideways glance. "So, I have two options for you."

My brows rise as I look at him. It's dark, but I can see the tension working in his jaw. "Options?"

He nods. "I planned it out either way. I'm not putting that on you. I want you to know that." I hum in acknowledgement and he continues. "Option one, we go to the resort. They've got a nice restaurant where we can eat dinner, and the bar pours a decent drink and has a dance floor. It's no Hank's, but it's all right for something a bit more traditional. Option two, we have a picnic and stargaze and talk. More like old times, I guess."

"You packed a picnic?" I ask doubtfully.

"Yep, sandwiches, but they're pretty good ones. Made them myself. Plus, Shayanne's potato salad—it's Mom's recipe—strawberries with chocolate dip, and wine. But no pressure. It'll all go back in the fridge at home if you'd rather go to a sit-down dinner." He truly sounds okay with either option.

I was just thinking that the fancier start, with the amount of care Bruce gave, was better than casual. But he's managed to give me an option with both . . . the picnic. A nod to what we used to do, a return to our roots, so to speak, and an opportunity to actually talk, which terrifies me but is what Michelle advised that I do, mixed in with her jokes about sex. And it sounds like he put a lot of work into the picnic and I don't want that to go to waste.

I hope this is the right decision. I smile and offer my choice. "Let's do the picnic."

Bruce's smile is huge, so opposite to the grumpy asshole I met weeks ago. I like this version better, even though he's more of a danger to my heart. "It was the chocolate dip, wasn't it? I know you can't pass up sweets."

He does know that. He knows so much about me, but he's missing a big piece of the puzzle. I try to prepare myself because I know he's going to ask me some hard questions tonight, and I need to answer them. He's shared so much with me—his story, his newly expanded family, and his intentions. Meanwhile, I've run every chance I got.

"Bring on the chocolate!" I cheer, because I'm done running. It's silly, but it does the trick and he laughs. The engine roars a bit as we speed up, leaving city center for the outer edge of town.

I know where he's going. It was always our place, and that awareness sends tingles through me. It's where we would escape everything to focus on each other, it's where we said 'I love you' the first time, it's where we both lost our virginity to each other, and it's where we said goodbye. It's definitely symbolic for us to have our first date there again. I just hope it's a good sign.

We drive through a copse of green trees, the very tips of which are starting to hint at the yellow of fall that's coming quickly.

There's a climb, and then we pop out into a clearing that overlooks all of Great Falls. It's blessedly empty, other than us, and that sends a fresh round of tingles through me at the possibilities.

Not that I'm letting Michelle's craziness get to me. Nope, not in the least.

Nor am I thinking about how good Bruce looks all dressed up tonight, or how hot he looks all sweaty at practice in baggy athletic shorts, or how sexy he was when he delivered that watermelon water with his abs on display. And I'm definitely not thinking about how his kisses alone have led me to take matters into my own hands, even after he fingered me to that earth-shattering orgasm.

Nope, just a date. Dinner and talking. That's it.

I don't believe it, either. But a girl's gotta have goals. They've been my saving grace over the last few years and might keep me making good choices for the next few hours.

"Stay there," he instructs me as he gets out. He comes around, opening my door and helping me down. He's not doing it because this is a date. Bruce always did things like that. He might look like a big beast of a man, but Mrs. Martha taught him right and he's got manners and always treated me well. It's good to know that hasn't changed, especially since my appreciation for it has grown.

He leads me to the back of the truck and holds out a hand for me to wait while he gets to work. In minutes, he's turned the bed of the truck into a luxurious spread with a thick egg crate cushion covered with a soft blanket. He moves a cooler from the backseat into the bed and then examines his work. It looks pretty, nice and cozy.

Satisfied, he turns and offers me a hand. I take it, and he pulls me close, his hands going to my waist. "Hop up."

He helps me sit on the tailgate, and then his hands catch my right foot, where he unfastens the ankle strap of my sandal. It feels oddly intimate, and my breath catches. He notices, his thumb tracing along my arch before he slips the left one off too.

"Scoot back." He lifts his chin toward the cab, indicating for me to climb into the truck bed. He shucks his boots too and follows me. I notice that even his socks are pristine tonight, and it makes me all the more tingly inside.

Yes, I'm getting turned on by socks. I really do need help.

"Hungry?" he rumbles, and I don't think he's talking about those sandwiches, but my stomach answers anyway. "I'll take that as a yes."

He opens the cooler, handing me a thick foil square. He sets one down for himself too and then pours wine into plastic cups.

"Ooh, fancy," I tease, holding up the cup before taking a small sip. "Good, though."

"Katelyn told me what to buy," he admits. "She works at the resort and knows all about that stuff. But I have other talents."

He's flirting again. I make a quick call that I like it and play along. "You do have some big talents."

He seems pleased with my favorable response, which breaks the tension as we both grin and dive into the sandwiches.

Somehow, it all goes okay. I don't say anything weird, he doesn't press me, and we talk about everything and nothing, laughing and flirting, the thread of connection that had been snapped between us comfortably knitting itself back together strand by strand as the sun goes down and the sky turns indigo. Stars begin to twinkle, and the air gets the slightest chill, celebrating that fall is coming soon.

Having thought of everything, Bruce grabs a light blanket and lays it over our laps before pulling me to his side and wrapping an arm around me. He's a big furnace, warming me instantly. Though that might not be entirely because he runs so hot but rather because his body is hard to my softness, making me all too aware of him.

He seems unaffected, or at least is pretending to be, as he simply snuggles with me, eyes on the sky.

After a while, I can feel his arms tense around me, hugging me tight. "I missed this," he whispers into my hair, and goosebumps break out along my skin. It's a confession on his part, highlighting how amazing the evening has been. It was always comfortable and easy with Bruce, and tonight feels like we slipped right back into that groove together.

That time and space where there was an us. Or maybe where there *is* an us.

I owe him more than I've given so far. I know that, even as I loathe dipping into the past. I have fought those demons into boxes, their own personal prison cells. I wrapped them in layers of tape and shoved the stacks of them away into the recesses of my mind. But for him, maybe I can take off a single layer of tape, not on the biggest, ugliest monsters, but on the little ones? He deserves that.

"After we . . ." I don't finish the sentence. He knows what I mean. I go for the 'after' instead. "I was devastated, shattered. College was hard for me, Bruce. I was nervous, but I don't think I ever considered it would be what it was. I pictured going to class, studying in the quad under a tree like some stupid pamphlet picture. I thought my roommate and me would be best friends and it would all be so easy. It wasn't, not by a long shot."

He doesn't say anything, but I can feel his support, his strength. He's letting me do this at my own pace.

"My roommate hated me on sight, called me a Barbie Bitch just because I was a blonde cheerleader. She made my dorm life hell, turned a lot of the girls against me from the get-go. But I made a few friends in my pre-law classes. We were all so busy, though, and the competition is fierce, so even the people I called friends would bail when I did better on a test than they did. It was lonely, and I lived for those Friday phone calls."

"I'm sorry, Al." He sounds truly remorseful, but it's not on him. We both made mistakes and should've just talked to one another.

I duck down deeper into his side, my cheek against his chest as I confess. "After, I was vulnerable. I didn't realize it at the time, but Jeremy took advantage of that." He goes tense, and I can feel a slight vibration in his chest. He's growling at my statement. "No, no . . . not like *that*."

"He just . . ." I search for the words. "He liked me weak. It gave him a chance to save me, to be the hero." Such a simple statement, but it took me a long time to recognize that truth. "We were happy for a while. He did help me get over you, in a way. But it was because he seemed safe."

I laugh ironically at how not-safe Jeremy really was, but I'm not digging out that particular box, not tonight and maybe not ever.

"Safe?" Bruce asks. "Did you feel unsafe with me?" I know he's talking about his size, about the nickname he earned on the field, about how people expected him to be this monster off the field too.

I shake my head, sitting up to look in his eyes. It's dark, but this close, I can see the reflection of the moon in the blackness. He looks hurt. "No, I always felt safe with you. Jeremy, he was safe emotionally. I liked him, I even loved him for a while, but not like you. I wasn't in love with him like I was with you, and I think that was one of the things I liked about him. Jeremy and I just got stuck. Because of Cooper."

I settle back against him, and his hand caresses up and down my arm, soothing me so I can do this. "We got married because I was pregnant, and I changed my major so I could be a paralegal. It was all coming together, not exactly what I'd planned, but I could see that it had the potential to be a good life. Jeremy had very specific ideas about what our life was supposed to look like, though, and we fought about that a lot. It wasn't pretty, and sometimes, he didn't treat me well," I say carefully.

Bruce is a smart man, despite his fears to the contrary, and he's always been attuned to my every thought and reaction, so I need to walk this fine line carefully or I'm going to end up pulling out every demon-stuffed box and letting him peruse through my damage.

His voice is tight. "What do you mean, he 'didn't treat you well'?"

I have no doubt that Bruce would beat the ever-loving fuck out of Jeremy at my slightest word, and I don't want that. I've moved on, or at least I am moving on, day by day, minute by minute, consciously challenging the now-rare occasion when I hear Jeremy's voice in my mind spouting ugliness.

I shake my head, not wanting to get into that. "I'm good now, and that's all that matters. He's out of my life, out of Cooper's life. We got divorced when Cooper was two and half, so he barely remembers Jeremy. The papers are sealed and he gave up parental rights. He's gone, which is exactly what I want. I wouldn't change any of it, not even what happened between you and me, because whatever twisted path I went on, it got me that little boy, and he's my everything. We're happy, just the two of us."

But could there be more? a new voice whispers.

No, not a new voice. An old one . . . my own. I am happy with our little family of two, but maybe Bruce and Michelle and even my own quiet hopes are right and I could have more. I could have Bruce.

CHAPTER 21

BRUCE

J can hear the blood roaring through my veins, a dull constant in my ears at her saying her ex didn't treat her well. I can read between the lines, and I know she's making it seem like less than it was. I can hear it in the small way she said he liked her weak.

This is the shadow that haunts her, the thing that stole her easy smile. I suspected it was something to do with her ex, but not this, not that he took this beautiful woman and broke her. I want her to fly even more after hearing the little bit she shared. Because there's more, of that I'm sure.

She's right about one thing, though. "I'm glad you're happy, Al. That's all I want, all I ever wanted. I know we both thought it would be with each other from high school on, and our lives would look so different if that's how it'd played out, but this detour . . . I think we can get back on track, if you want that too."

I'm not trying to put pressure on her. I've already told her I'm willing to do anything she wants, from no-strings casual to as serious as a diamond ring on her pretty little finger. But she gets to decide our next step, especially after what she just divulged. I want her to know deep in her heart that I want her strong, that I want us to be partners.

I'm usually sort of an alpha caveman myself, but I like the fiery side Allyson always had. Al needs this power right now, and I know I need her strong too. It takes a strong woman to handle Brutal Tannen.

She's quiet for a long time, both of us staring up at the sky. I don't know about her, but I don't really see the stars. I'm seeing us, the years we missed, the sadness that haunted us both, the journey we went on without one another but still converged into this moment.

Like we're meant to be.

"Michelle told me something tonight. At the time, I thought she was crazy, but I think she might be right." She's rushing the words, but in the dark, I can't tell if she's excited or nervous without seeing her.

"What did she say?" I ask cautiously.

"This is a date, but not it's not really like it's our first date because of . . . everything." She's hemming and hawing, which only makes me that much more interested in what she's trying so hard to say. "So, if it's not really a first date, it wouldn't be bad for us to do . . . *not-first-date things.*"

Her tone is heavy with meaning that even a stupid fucker like me can decipher. I'm surprised that's where she's going, especially considering the deeper thoughts that'd been playing through my own mind, but I'm not going to look a gift horse in the mouth.

I move fast, pulling her across my lap so that we're face to face, her thighs straddling my hips. Like there's actually a god looking out for us, the moon comes out from behind a cloud and I can see her pretty clearly. She's nibbling at her bottom lip, and though it's too dark to tell for sure, I get the distinct impression that she's blushing.

"Say it, Al. Tell me exactly what you want. Be *real fucking sure* about what you say, though, because you know I'll give you anything." She means sex. I truly mean anything.

"I want you to . . ." Her spine straightens as she finds her spirit. "I want you to fuck me, Bruce. Hard and rough, like I'm not some fragile thing that's broken inside. I want to forget the years in between us then and us now. Fuck me, Bruce."

She gathered steam as she spoke, her voice steady and more confident, her needs and desires laid bare. It's sexy as fuck to hear her tell me to fuck her, but the thought that she feels fragile breaks my heart. She's one of the strongest people I've ever known. The urge to hunt her asshole ex down flashes though me again but is quickly washed away by the urgency of what she's asking.

This will be the first time we ever have sex without being *in love* and that's fucking with my head.

No, I correct myself. We're just not in love *yet.* But I do love her, or the idea of her, of us. And I promised her I could handle this, would let her lead and give her whatever she needs to find herself, especially after her story highlighted just how lost she's been. This is the dance of my life, two-stepping for *our* life, the one we could have together. But it starts here.

It's definitely not a bad gig, tasting her sweetness again, working her body until she's drunk on me the way I'm already drunk on her.

I want more, but I'll greedily take what she has to offer for now and hope she finds what she's looking for fast because I already have.

Her.

I shut down my heart and focus on what she's willing to do. I won't push her for more, not when I can give her what she wants.

I cup her jawline firmly and drop my voice down, letting the gravel wash over her and giving her the filthy words I know turn her on. "You want me to fuck you, baby? Kiss you . . ." I press my lips to hers. "Suck your tits . . ." I let one hand drop to squeeze her breast, my thumb stroking over the hard nipple I can feel through her dress. "Lick that clit . . . and stretch your tight little pussy with my cock? That what you want?"

I buck beneath her, letting her feel the already hard ridge of my cock against her molten core.

The air has gone steamy between us, the cool of the evening licking along our skin, and Allyson moans. Somewhere in the long syllable, I hear her yes, but I need to be clear.

"Look at me, Al." She blinks slowly, fighting through a haze of desire to focus. "Are you sure? I need you to be one hundred percent certain because I don't know if I'll be able to stop with how badly I want you. Fuck, I want inside your sexy body, that sweet pussy." I'm growling, but I can't help it. "Be sure, Allyson."

It's almost a beg, for her body, for her heart.

She surprises the absolute hell out of me, doing something that once upon a time I wouldn't have given a second thought, but I know how out-of-character it is for her now. She pulls her dress right over her head, baring herself to me in only a lacy blue bra and panty set.

"Fuck. Me."

She might not've planned for this to happen tonight, and I would've gladly looked my fill of her in granny panties and a plain bra, but like this? She's absolutely stunning. Breathtaking.

While I've been gobsmacked, she's been unhesitatingly working at the buttons of my shirt, letting me know that she's not having any second thoughts. Once she gets it open, I pull it off and yank her to me.

Her skin feels like silk against mine. I grip her hair, feeling the strands weave through my fingers as I direct her head back, exposing her neck. I lay a long line of wet kisses down the curve, tasting her racing pulse.

I murmur against her, "Take your bra off. Show me."

I might have let her be in charge of getting us here, but now, this is my show. It's the way we've always liked it. I'm bossy and foul-mouthed, and she gets off on it, knowing that I'm watching her every nuanced reaction to guide us somewhere amazing.

She reaches back, making quick work of the hooks, and then shrugs the lacy scrap off. I hold her ribs, arching her back and pressing her nipples toward my mouth. They're pearled up in need and probably from the chill a bit too, but I warm them up quickly. I suckle at her hard, drawing her deep into my mouth and then letting go with a *pop* to swirl my tongue in circles. She cries out, her hand going to her mouth to muffle the echoing sound.

"Nuh-uh, you don't have to be quiet out here. It's just us.

Nobody around for miles. Let the night hear what I'm doing to you, how good it feels. Let me hear you." She whimpers but lets her hand fall. "Good girl."

I lick along her sternum, teasing the sensitive skin between her tits as our hands explore each other. Her nails score along my skin, and I want her to mark me, show me how far gone she is.

"Stand up," I tell her, helping her to stand on the egg crate cushion beneath us. I reach up and slide the pretty blue panties down her legs as she lifts one foot, then the other to help me. Once she's nude, I guide her to step closer to me as I scoot down, leaning back against the cab of the truck. "Come here."

I look up at her, making sure she's still with me. Her mouth is open, small pants of need passing her lips as she presses her hips forward. So slowly, I lick along her lips, right then left, before flattening my tongue and tasting the honey coating her slit.

"Mmm, so fucking delicious," I moan as her juices coat my tongue.

"Oh, my God," Allyson gasps, her fingers diving into my hair to encourage me. "*Yes.*"

Her cry is music to my ears. I devour her, slipping my hands through her spread legs to grip her ass, serving her pussy to my hungry mouth. I lick her clit, swirling and sucking the nub into my mouth as her cries fill the night around us. She bucks against me, riding my tongue.

It's driving me wild with desire even as my heart fills with pride at her using me for her pleasure. I keep a tight grip on her ass with one hand but let the other wander, teasing her with a finger.

"More," she demands breathlessly.

"This what you want, baby? You want me to slide my fingers in your pussy even though you know what you really want is my cock?" My words are murmurs against her skin as I rest my cheek on her hip, enjoying the tease as much as she is.

Her whine spurs me on, and I press forward with one thick finger, filling her. "Damn, Al. You're so tight, I don't know if you're gonna be able to take me anymore. Relax and let me in, baby."

She shudders, and I finger-fuck her slowly, stretching her. I'm not just dirty talking her. She really is fucking tight, and I can't wait to feel her slick satin walls choking my cock, but I don't want to hurt her. But she's so wet that after a few seconds, I can add a second finger and she turns molten.

"Yes . . . oh, God . . . Bruce . . . please." She's basically chanting as she pleads with me to get her there. She's walking that edge so close, stunningly beautiful as she holds on.

"Come for me, Al. Fly for me," I growl, then suck hard on her clit, driving my fingers in deep with short, hard thrusts.

And she does. Her orgasm is loud and messy, a revelation in release as every bit of tension leaves her body at once. She spasms, and I hold on tight, making sure she doesn't collapse. After a moment, her pants slow and she looks down at me. I wish the moonlight would let me see the truth of her reaction, but it's too dark to read her eyes.

Her words are crystal clear, though. "More."

She steps back, bending at the waist to kiss me as her hands work at my belt. I growl and push her hands out of the way to make quicker work of it, shoving my jeans and underwear down my thighs. My cock springs up, slapping against my belly, hard and throbbing. I take myself in hand, meeting her eyes.

"Allyson?"

One more chance. To stop herself. To stop me. To stop this freight train that's not running off the tracks but rather is getting back on track. Right the fuck here and now.

She drops to her knees, aligning herself as I use a thumb to hold myself at the right angle. She kisses me wantonly and drops onto my cock, impaling herself and wrapping me in a slick velvet vice.

Her anguished cry scares me at first, but it quickly turns into a sound of pleasure as her body makes way for me. "Fuck, Al. So damn tight. Are you okay?"

I force myself to stay still, letting her adjust to me as I fight my orgasm off. I just got back inside her. I'm sure as hell not gonna come like some two-pump chump, no matter how good she feels.

She moves first, fucking me, and I let her take what she needs as I brush my thumb across her clit. But after a few thrusts, I can't hold back anymore and my hands find her hips. We slam into each other, powerful and rough, violently coming together like we can blot away the past years apart if we just go hard at each other. She said she didn't want me to treat her as though she's fragile, but that's the last thing she feels like right now. She feels fierce and wild, like my Allyson always has been.

Once, weeks ago, I'd had a passing thought that I could hate-fuck her out of my heart. Now, I want to fuck myself into hers—harder, deeper, brutally claiming her as she tattoos herself on my heart too.

"You feel too good," I manage to grunt out through my clenched teeth. "I can't stop."

"Don't stop, Bruce. Please. Fill me." Her beg is stilted as I thrust into her, but on the same page, we explode together.

The sky might be full of stars, but all I see are the flashes behind my eyelids as I come, filling her with my seed at the same time she spasms around me, milking me for more. Both of us cry out to the dark, mine deep and grunted and hers high-pitched and hitched, in a shared moment of absolute frozen bliss, and then we sag, spent and gasping for breath.

We stay tangled in each other. I feel like warm, fizzy champagne is buzzing through my veins, making my edges blurry, like I can't tell where I end and Allyson begins. She's languid against me, almost purring with an occasional hum in her throat.

There's no awkwardness now, something I didn't even realize I was nervous about. We just roll right back into talking, relaxed and easy like we used to, as I trace swirling lines along her back. The stars twinkle, the night chills, and we just curl up into each other.

Bobby writes songs about moments like this, I realize. This sense of hopefulness, of the start of something greater, of love.

But I bite back any words about that, not wanting to scare her. She asked me to fuck her. She didn't ask me to love her. I do, but she's not ready. Two steps forward, though, I'll take.

CHAPTER 22

ALLYSON

"I feel like when we were kids and I'd drop you off after a date, praying that your parents didn't answer the door. I knew if they saw my shit-eating grin, they'd know exactly what I'd been doing with their sweet little girl."

The nostalgia turns into something sexier as he does a slow perusal, hot and hungry, down my body before smirking like he can see right through to what's underneath.

"But now, instead of getting caught by your folks, I'm checking the windows to see if Cooper's looking out." Bruce chuckles but leans forward to look through the windshield, scanning every window. "No movement in the blinds. Looks like we're in the clear."

Tonight has been amazing. *More than amazing*, I correct myself. I knew I was going to go out with Bruce and we'd end up fighting or fucking. We definitely fucked, but it was something bigger than a cheap thrill and we both know that.

He patiently let me unpack one of my boxes of demons, listening thoughtfully and without judgement, and that meant more to me than he'll ever know. He made me feel not just okay, but . . . worthy. And letting me set the pace was something I hadn't even known I needed, but he did.

He's still watching me for the clues. He's been nothing but transparent about what he wants, but still, he lets me lead. To me, that shows just how strong and good Bruce is, all the way to his core, and how much faith he has in me to know my own heart and find my own way. I know he hopes I find my way back to him, but I think he'd understand if I truly wanted to go a different way. It'd hurt him, no doubt about that, but I think he was being brutally honest when he said he just wants me to be happy.

I want that too.

"Cooper's not home tonight. Michelle said he could sleep over at her house just in case . . . you know." I blush even though there's no reason to. I'm a grown woman who wants to have sex with a man who wants me. There's nothing wrong with that. I'm not sure if I'm telling myself or society at large that single mothers can be sexual creatures with wants, needs, and desires beyond their kids, and that it's not only okay, it's damn healthy. My old therapist and my currently throbbing pussy say so.

I don't examine my words, just let them come freely and wildly. "Want to come in?"

"Fuck yes," Bruce rumbles before getting out of the truck and damn near high-stepping to get around to my side. Instead of helping me down, he turns and gives me his back. "Get on."

I laugh, thinking he's kidding. "I am almost thirty years old and a mother. I do not do piggyback rides unless I'm the one giving them, and Cooper's been too big for that for years now. I'm also too big for you to carry me like that." I try to hop down from his stupidly jacked-up truck, but his broad back is blocking me.

He looks over his shoulder. "You ain't got your sandals on, and I could carry you one-armed. We can do that instead, if you'd rather? Want me to throw you over my shoulder, smack your ass on the way to the house? Might be harder to unlock the door if you're hanging upside down, though." He shrugs like he doesn't care because he's winning this battle of wills either way.

He paints a rather specific and sexy image. And while I might be all on-board with dating as a single parent, having Bruce carry me

LAUREN LANDISH

caveman style might be a little beyond the pale. I can only guess at the gossip if word got out about that.

Reading my face in the light coming from the porch, he grins like he won. "Piggyback it is. Hop on." Guess he is winning, because damned if I don't do it.

I push the truck door closed, and somehow, he beeps the alarm without my feeling wobbly at all. He's got me secure, his strong hands locked under my thighs, which are spread around his waist. I've got my heels in one hand and my key in the other, both arms resting over his shoulders.

It feels silly and childish but also fun. Something I think I forgot how to do unless it was related to Cooper.

You've been having a lot of fun with Bruce.

I can hear the voice in my head teasing, but it's right. I have had fun more fun in the last few weeks than in ages. Playing football, even though I suck at it, flirting, and just talking with him have all brought back this light inside me I hadn't even realized was dim, barely flickering and on the verge of being snuffed out.

At the door, he bends forward so I can unlock it, and then he kicks it shut behind us. The house is quiet, the living room lamp on so the house doesn't look deserted. Being alone behind a closed door suddenly feels full of possibility.

My sandals and the keys fall to the floor with a clunk, and I squeeze him tight between my thighs, wishing I were on his front instead of his back. I lean forward, my arms crossing over his chest, and whisper in his ear, "Down the hall."

He angles his head, looking at me carefully. I can't see myself, but I know my eyes are clear and bright. I'm sure. Of myself, of him, of this.

I point Bruce to the last door on the left, and he stops when he enters. I watch as his eyes scan my bedroom, and I wonder what he's gleaning about me that he didn't already know. I try to see it through his eyes—fluffy white comforter and enough pillows on the bed to give away my addiction to all things smooshy, a headboard I refinished myself with chalk paint and wax before deciding DIY was something I was never doing again, a white dresser with candles

208

and knick-knacks I thought were pretty, and a cozy chair where I sit and read, usually for work but occasionally for fun.

"Pretty. Comfortable." It's just two words, but it's my aesthetic to a T. It's stupid, but I like that he gets it.

"You like it?" I ask, but my fingers are tracing the line of his trimmed beard along his neck.

"Love it. My room's basically a place to crash. So I'm probably not the guy to ask for decorating advice." He's answering me, but at the same time, he's tilting his head, giving me access to kiss his neck as his hands knead my thighs.

It strikes me as sad that he lives so casually. Nothing about Bruce has ever been casual. He's always been full-throttle and had a plan —football, wife, farm, kids. Somewhere along the way, he got stuck too. I won't be so narcissistic as to think it was because of me. He's had enough other family drama going on, but we both petered out along the way, losing steam and settling into a rut neither of us saw coming.

Maybe he's right? Could we somehow put right what went wrong all those years ago? That sounds crazy, but it doesn't mean it's not possible. Stranger things have happened, right?

He spins, dropping me onto the bed unexpectedly, and I bounce, laughing. He turns back, leaning over me and caging me between his arms as his fists dent the fluffy bedding. I feel pinned beneath his gaze, his heat, his intentions. But there's not a bit of anxiety in my body. Instead, I feel safe . . . and needy.

"Cooper's gone all night?" His voice is pure grit and sex.

I nod, on autopilot as my body simply yearns for his. Every cell inside me wants him, wants to be marked by him, wants to be possessed by him. That should be scary as fuck, but with Bruce, it's not. Not at all.

Even that plan he always had, his expectations of what his life would be like, what *our life* would be like, should terrify me because that's exactly where things started to go wrong with Jeremy. But deep inside, I know it's different. Jeremy and Bruce are as different as night and day.

If you saw them side by side, you'd think big, rough Bruce

would be the night, with its scary darkness, and Jeremy, with his pretty looks, would be the bright promise of each new day.

You'd be wrong. So very wrong.

Bruce is the light-bringer, the one who helped me grow up, reach higher for dreams I thought might be beyond my grasp. Jeremy is the one who put me into hibernation, a dormancy that shunted my progress as he savored my fading glow.

But the sun is back, and he's looking at me with fiery need, daring me to reach for him again.

"Allyson, we've got all night, and as crazy as it sounds after everything we've been through, it's our first time in a bed. Do you know how many dreams and fantasies I had of this? Let me worship you, let me love you. Please." His voice is low and slow, so transparently hungry for me.

I can feel a hot burn stinging my eyes that he even recognizes this or feels like it's important. God, the people who look at him and only see the brutal monster he once was in football are missing the very best parts of this man. But I'm not. I see every bit of goodness, kindness, and gentleness in his heart.

"Probably as many dreams and fantasies as I had about it," I confess. It's the truth. So many of my teen imaginings were of this very thing. An entire night to revel in each other, to fall asleep in each other's arms, and to wake in the morning to a sleepy-soft Bruce was something I wanted desperately.

He falls over me, pressing me to the bed as his mouth covers mine. Softly, he kisses me, stoking the fire between us, not with lighter fluid and a quick flash of ignition but with a slow burn, taking time to build the flames, caring for the embers until we both need more.

We strip bare, and Bruce hauls me up, laying my back against the pile of pillows as he kneels between my spread legs. "God-damn, you look better than I ever imagined. So beautiful." His eyes slide over me, a palpable caress, and though some small part of me is nervous about my body not being the younger version of myself he used to stare at hungrily, that inner wanton woman he brings out preens proudly as he groans in appreciation. It helps that his hand is stroking his hard, proud cock slowly as he looks at me, like he could get off just seeing me laid out like a feast for his eyes.

My eyes are drawn to that up and down movement, but I trace his entire thick body with my eyes too, appreciating the broadness of his shoulders, the V lines of his waist, the bumps of his abs, and every dip and bulge of muscle. I study not only the tattoo on his arm but the black linework on his chest, including a small, script *MT*. My heart breaks that he lost his mother and that I wasn't here to love him through that, but I'm here now.

"Bruce —" I say, but he interrupts me.

"I'm going to take my time tonight." His voice is deep and dark with promise as he makes that vow. One I know he'll keep, one I want him to. I want to fall into this . . . whatever this is . . . with him.

It's too fast, too crazy, too stupid, but damned if I don't jump off the cliff anyway, trusting that he'll catch me before I crash-land. But first, I want to enjoy the freefall, the flight with the wind through my hair and the air rushing up to buoy me like I'm floating. That's what tonight is. The rest I can figure out later.

I'm going to luxuriate in him, let him indulge in me, bring that dream we both once had to reality because I think it'll be better than we ever thought possible.

The night outside fades away until it's only the two of us in existence—his lips on my skin, our fingers mapping each other's body, and him filling a void inside me I didn't even realize existed.

As we collapse, exhaustion overtakes us and one other piece of those younger dreams comes true as we fall asleep in each other's arms.

It's even better than I'd imagined.

———

I stir the eggs, adding a bit of pepper as they scramble. Bruce grabs two plates out of the cabinet, setting them next to me at the ready. The bacon's crisped and the bread's toasted golden brown, so I start making plates with those as Bruce grabs juice.

He's half in the fridge when the front door opens and Cooper comes running in. "Mom, guess what I got! *Mom!*"

Time stops, freezing in an instant.

Distantly, I'm glad I'm not naked. Bruce and I had put on the barest stiches of clothing to cook when he pointed out that bacon grease is a known boner killer. I'd laughed and let him slip his shirt over my shoulders, and he'd pulled on his boxer briefs. Now, I'm so ridiculously grateful for the risk of splattering hot oil because otherwise, I'd be naked when my son comes in.

Bruce unfreezes first. "Hey, Cooper! What'd you get?" His voice is casual, but as I look over, I can see that he's carefully examining both mine and Cooper's reactions from behind the refrigerator door.

This is bad. Unbelievably so.

Mitigate. Mediate. Deescalate.

"Hey, honey! Yeah, what'd you get?" I echo, knowing my voice is too high-pitched.

Cooper's looking from me to Bruce, though. He's a smart kid, which scares the bejesus out of me right about now, especially given the question he asked before my date. "Did you come over for breakfast, Coach B? Uh, why don't you guys have clothes on?"

Michelle comes in right then. "Oh! Shit! He's quick, got out of the car and was running before I even got it in park," she says apologetically. "Allyson, Cooper got you something . . ." She tilts her head, urgently pointing with her thumb like she's trying to give me a topic to address other than the near-naked state Bruce and I are in.

I give Michelle a 'duh' look because I obviously already tried that, but I try again. "What'd you get, Cooper?"

I guess the third time's the charm because he blinks and brings his hand out from behind his back to show me a teddy bear. It's pale blonde and fluffy with a heart on the white belly. "I won a bear for you."

"Oh, my gosh! It's adorable!" I squeal, dropping to my knees beside him. I hug him, turning him slightly so he's not waist-level with Bruce. "Thank you so much. Have you named him yet?"

Cooper smiles, giving me a slight reprieve from the horror of being busted. "Not yet. I thought we could name him together. I got the lightest one they had so he'd match your room."

Tears pop to my eyes. "That's . . . that's so sweet, honey. Thank you." I hug him again, but the moment's gone as far as he's concerned because he's doing that infamous kid shrug-cringe combo to let me know I'm overdoing it on the affection.

"Want me to put him on your bed?" Cooper asks innocently.

"NO!" My voice is too loud, too sharp, but I cannot have Cooper going in there when the bed is still mussed from Bruce and me having sex, last night and again this morning. I'll need to wash the sheets or at least make the bed before he goes in there. That's normal, right? I make a mental note to read up on that.

I adjust my voice to a more normal manner of speaking, correcting myself. "I mean, let's just set him right here on the counter while we eat breakfast, okay?" He nods and points to a place by the coffee pot.

Bruce clears his throat, his back going straight. "Uhm, if you'll excuse me, I'm gonna go take a leak."

I blink, not used to the crassness, but I guess it's better than saying he's going to go get dressed. I definitely don't want to call any more attention to our lack of clothing.

He steps toward the doorway, but Michelle doesn't move, instead daringly staying right in his way. Bruce looks down at her, one brow raised, and greets her with a cocky smirk. "G'morning, Michelle."

"It is a rather lovely morning, Coach B. Even with the chill from the fridge, a *quite lovely* morning indeed." She's fighting back laughter, and I swear Bruce turns the faintest shade of pink, but to his credit, he doesn't slink away down the hall.

No, he damn near struts like a peacock. He's got the right to because Michelle's not wrong. even with the cold of the fridge shrinking things, Bruce is well-endowed enough that those boxer briefs don't hide much.

Michelle's eyes follow him, even going so far as to lean back so she can catch one more glimpse. "Hey!" I snap.

She looks back at me, grinning like the Cheshire Cat as she mouths *Huuuuge*. Pervert.

Cooper's voice interrupts the talking to I want to give Michelle. He's trying to drop it down lower than his little boy tenor, quoting near-verbatim. "Excuse me, Mom. I'm gonna take a leak."

And with that, he runs off down the hall.

I freeze, and then slowly, my head turns to find Michelle's mouth hanging open too. Then we both burst into giggles.

"If he teaches Liam that, I'm blaming you," she says through her laughter. And then her eyes go wide and she grabs my shoulders, shaking me. "Oh, my God, Allyson! I texted you like thirty minutes ago so you'd be ready in case you had company. Guess you were too busy to see the message?"

I think I may have to get a new phone because I never heard it make a peep. No text message alert, not even a buzz. Once is a glitch. Twice is a problem.

"I never got it. This is bad, isn't it? I mean, Cooper's probably scarred for life and I'm going to get the Worst Mom award. I think the only thing worse than your kid walking in on your mostly-naked morning-after would be his walking in on your actually having sex."

I'm panicking, verging on hysterical. But I've never done this, never even thought about doing this, and have not read the hand-book on introducing your kid to a new guy. But I'm sure it recommends *not* doing it with the guy in his underwear and you in his shirt.

"He's fine, or he will be. Just talk to him. He didn't care at all that you were going on a date. Allyson, remember that he's got friends whose parents are married, divorced, and dating. Kids are flexible and accepting. If you don't treat it like a big deal, he won't either." She seems pretty sure of herself and it's helping me calm down.

I nod. "Okay, that sounds good. Kids are flexible," I parrot, engaging the fake it 'til you make it methodology. "Act like it's no big deal."

She nudges my elbow, asking the million-dollar question. "It is, though, isn't it? A big deal? Inquiring minds want to know." She looks so hopeful, her hands folded beneath her chin, begging for details.

I take a big breath, knowing that saying the words to her will make it so. It's the truth, but admitting it is major, especially when it's all so fresh and new. I'm not even sure what label I'm slapping on this, but it's more than I thought it'd be. "It's a big deal," I say on a blissed-out sigh. "And not just his dick, which I don't appreciate your staring at," I admonish her. Even to my ears, I sound possessive. I might as well be grunting 'don't look—mine, mine, mine.'

She doesn't look the least bit remorseful. "Like you wouldn't have looked." She leans back, checking down the hall. "Do you want me to take Cooper for a bit longer? I can if you need me to, but just for a little bit. I got called into work and Liam's already at the sitter's house."

I shake my head, wishing I could have a few more minutes in this fantasy with Bruce but knowing it's time to face reality. "It's fine. Go to work and I'll handle this . . ." I wave my hands around, indicating the now cold eggs and the two guys down the hall. "I have no idea how, but I'll manage."

She kisses my cheek, gleefully dancing around a bit with a silent squeal of delight, and then the door closes behind her. I turn to the stove, splitting the two servings of eggs into three and putting them in the microwave. It's not the best way to eat them, but I suspect breakfast is going to be awkward enough that I won't taste them anyway.

I set the three plates on the table and then realize it's presumptuous. Maybe Bruce won't want to stay? He might want to get the hell out of here after getting caught unaware this morning. Or maybe I should have him go so I can do this on my own? I don't know if that's the right thing, either.

The decision's made for me, though, when both Bruce and Cooper come back into the kitchen together, both in jeans. At least everyone's dressed now. Well, I'm not, but I can pretend this is a regular nightgown. It's certainly long enough, reaching halfway down my thighs. "Breakfast is served."

As they sit down, I look between them. Do I deal with Cooper or Bruce first? I mean, obviously, Cooper is my priority, my number-one always, but what do I even say to him when I don't have any real clarity from Bruce?

As my mind races, they both look cool as cucumbers, though. Dare I say zero fucks given? Well, about Bruce. I wouldn't cuss, not even in my head, about Cooper. But he does seem fine.

"Where'd you get the bear, Cooper?" Bruce asks, shoving an entire slice of bacon in his mouth.

Cooper grabs one too. "Ms. Michelle took Liam and me to the arcade and I played skee-ball. I got four 462 tickets. The bear was 450 so I had plenty." He sounds so proud of himself, which makes me inordinately happy too.

My mom mode kicks in, glad for the distraction from the elephant in the room. "So 462 tickets minus the 450 for the bear left you with how many?"

He quickly does the math in his head, his fingers not moving at all, and answers, "Twelve. Come on, Mom, that's too easy."

His sass is strong, letting me know how easy that was for him. He's getting so big. But is he mature enough to handle this thing between Bruce and me? Am I?

"Thank you again, honey. That really was so sweet." He smiles at me and then looks over to Bruce for approval too. Bruce smiles and even winks at him, so fast I think I imagined it. It's only the glow on Cooper's face that lets me know it was real.

Cooper looks up to Bruce so much, as a coach and as a role model. Admittedly, there's a tiny sliver of me that feels left out of that, but I know this is one of the reasons I signed Cooper up for football in the first place. He needs that positive male presence in his life, even as I try to be everything he needs.

And Bruce . . . a boy could do a lot worse, and not much better, in having him as a role model.

"So, are you two like boyfriend and girlfriend now?" Cooper asks as he carefully spreads jelly on his toast.

I'm glad Cooper's eyes are on his task so he doesn't see my gaze lock with Bruce's across the table. He smirks, popping his brows like he's interested in the answer to that question himself.

"Well . . . you know how I told you that Bruce and I were going on a date yesterday?" Cooper nods, licking sticky grapey goodness from his fingers. "We'd like to do that again, maybe have dinners and hang out together, all three of us too. How's that sound?"

Did I do that right?

Shit, I wish I'd had time to read this chapter in the parenting books. Not that I had time to read any of those. I've been winging this gig since day one, but so far, that's worked mostly okay.

Cooper finishes his jelly spreading and his head swivels left and right, from me to Bruce. I feel like I'm awaiting a judge's verdict on a major case, but this is way more important. He shrugs. "M'kay."

That's it.

It's a bit anticlimactic. No drama, no muss, no fuss, no tears. He's better about this than I am.

Bruce smiles and reaches across the table to take my hand, soothing my nerves with his touch and silently telling me that I did well. It feels like a major step . . . for me, for us, even for the three of us.

Holy shit. I'm dating Bruce Tannen.

The pleasant soreness between my thighs says I'm doing a hell of a lot more than that, but my decision to slap a label on it is even more important than what we did last night. This is me moving on . . . finally.

"So, what's the plan for today?" Bruce says, crunching another slice of bacon.

"It's Sunday, so it's 'bless this house' day. All cleaning and grocery shopping. Ugh." Cooper groans as he rolls his eyes.

I laugh, even though he's right. That is our routine so we can start the week fresh and prepared. "Maybe we could do something a little different today, just this once."

Bruce shakes his head. "No way. If that's what you do on Sundays, then point me to the vacuum. I can make some mean lines in the rug, just like driving a tractor through the fields."

I shouldn't be surprised that Bruce is willing to clean with us, but it warms me that he's comfortable doing such mundane things with us. It makes it feel more real, more like . . . family.

I search my body for those telltale signs of panic but find none. No tension in my muscles, no clenching in my jaw, no bees buzzing in my chest. I just feel . . . good. Such a bland word, but the feeling is powerful.

"Chore day it is," I tell them with a smile.

CHAPTER 23

BRUCE

*I*t's somehow been the longest and the shortest week of my life all at the same time.

As far as planning a campout, I could use another couple of days. We're not doing anything too fancy, but I want it to go well and have spent some time dragging logs up to a clearing so we'll have a place to sit around the campfire pit I dug up.

On the other hand, the week's dragged on because I haven't had a single real moment alone with Allyson.

By the time I got home on Sunday afternoon, Bobby was running at near-Brody levels of grunts, obviously mad at me because he knew my absence could only be because of one person. I ignored him for the most part, too happy to let him bring me down with his cynicism.

Happy? I'm *this close* to belting out in song, and my voice is worse than shit. Bobby got one hundred percent of that talent in our family, though I might beat that gift out of him if he doesn't quit glaring at me every chance he gets.

He kept up the pissy mood on Monday too, even as I smiled ear to ear while I worked, looking forward to every ding of my phone and praying that Allyson got every text I sent on her piece of shit phone. We've spent hours talking on the phone at night, about the past and present, and even carefully about the future, until we both have to hang up, knowing our morning alarms will go off early.

Tuesday, I'd called her on the way to the practice field to be sure she was coming. Not because I thought she'd gotten cold feet—she seems to be done dancing away from me now—but she'd had a busy day at work and I'd wanted to be sure something hadn't come up that'd keep her stuck there. She'd said I was being sweet while I felt like a possessive fucker who just needed to lay hands on her.

But she'd shown. With a smile for the boys and another more meaningful and private smile for me.

After Tuesday's practice, the three of us had gone to the grocery store because we never got around to it on Sunday. For such a mundane outing, we'd actually had fun, giggling as Cooper had tried to worm his way into something sweet on every single aisle, even in the produce section where he found some caramel dip he wanted for the apples he'd already agreed to. We'd escaped with minimal sweets when I reminded him to 'whoa' on the sugar while managing to buy hamburger buns and hot dogs fixings in preparation for the campout.

Allyson had left me at the back door that night, though, because Cooper needed to eat, bathe, and hit the hay. It'd been hard to leave, but I understood. Still, when she'd sent him to get cleaned up, I'd made the most of the few minutes we had alone and kissed every inch of her mouth right there in the doorway of her kitchen. If I'd gotten one step further in the house, I would've leaned her over the table and had her coming on my tongue before Cooper could get his hair washed, but she'd gently pushed me back, saying she didn't want him to walk in on us.

I respect that. She's responsible and caring, things I can appreciate. But fuck, do I want to sweep her away for a little bit.

Thursday, we'd at least gotten a family dinner in before Cooper's early bedtime had kicked in. Al said she's trying to start inching him back to his school-time bedtime from his later summer hours. All I knew was that it meant we had an extra half-hour alone before I needed to head home for the sunrise chores.

We'd made the most of it, waiting impatiently until Cooper had sufficient time to fall asleep and then escaping to the back deck. I'd hoped that once I was in her house again, I'd be inside her in no time, but it seemed the devil-may-care attitudes of our younger days had grown up slightly because I'd held back from taking her out in the open where the neighbors could see. That doesn't mean we didn't make out like high school kids again, kissing and grinding and squeezing each other, but our clothes had tragically stayed on.

I jacked off twice when I got home, once when I took a shower and then later, to my delight, on FaceTime with Allyson. She said she'd never done anything like that, and I could tell she was nervous, hiding out in her bathroom and biting her lip to be quiet even as she wanted me to talk to her. But she'd done it for me, for herself. She was so fucking beautiful coming on her own fingers. I just wished they'd been mine.

But somehow, we've made it to the big day. Campout day, just this morning's practice to go.

The boys deserve this for how hard they've been working. They're doing great, really coming together as a team, running plays like a well-oiled machine, and we're ready for our first game.

As the boys high-five after their successful play, my eyes are drawn to Allyson again. It's all I can do to root myself to the grass and not take her in my arms. Now that I've held her, tasted her, possessed her, I want to live inside her, learn her every nuance, and tease out every smile I possibly can.

Finally, we do our team cheer, and I make a waving motion to gather the parents over. I move the group closer to Killian's grand-parents so they don't have to walk too far onto the uneven grass, and we progress to the planning part of the practice.

Allyson addresses the gathered parents. "Thank you again for signing up to help with the campout. I know the boys are really looking forward to it." The boys find renewed energy, dancing around a bit beside their parents, and I hear one *oh, yeah* of agreement. Allyson smiles, looking down at Cooper.

I continue her speech, heading off an issue I know Mom would've had with me and my brothers. "Showers between practice and camping are required. We're gonna get messy and muddy and end up smelling like the animals at the farm, but we should all start *not* smelling like a locker room or one of my sister's goats."

I sniff my own pit, making a disgusted face, and wave the air in front of me. The boys all laugh as intended and a couple of the parents give me grateful looks.

Allyson pulls out her phone and taps around at the screen. "Okay, I emailed the address again so everyone can GPS out there. It's a good twenty-minute drive outside town. If anyone needs a ride, let me know because we've got several parents going as chaperones and a few not going, so carpooling is a great option. I also re-sent the sign-up list so everyone who volunteered to donate can confirm what you're bringing. We're planning a delicious dinner, some sweet treats, and lots of fun! Everybody ready?"

"YEAH!" twelve kids roar, not even in unison. It's more of a riot of excitement.

Everyone disperses, and I notice Michelle talking to Killian's grandparents. "They gonna be okay?"

Allyson follows my line of vision and nods. "Yeah, Michelle is going to bring Liam, Cooper, and Killian out to the farm. The Bloomdales can't camp anymore, of course, and Michelle offered to let Cooper hang out so that we can focus on getting everything set up. She's going to take him from practice so we can head right out."

She looks at me, her smirk giving away her flirty mood before she even speaks. "Though I won't have time to take a shower between practice and camping. Is that going to be a problem?"

There's a light in her eyes that I remember so well, and the faux-innocent seductive tone to her voice sends tingles through me. I step closer, tracing along the soft skin of her arm with the back of my hand, not wanting to be too obvious but needing to touch her.

"I already told you, Al. I'll take you fresh and clean or sweaty and filthy. Any way I can get you."

She shudders, and in her thin workout tank and sports bra, I can tell her nipples are diamond hard. "What's the plan for this afternoon?"

"Oh, I've got big plans for you. Big, filthy, hot ones . . ." I say quietly.

"You play dirty," she teases.

I act surprised. "I have no idea what you're talking about. I meant that we've got a lot of work to do to get everything ready on the farm. If you thought I was talking about something else, that's on you, dirty girl."

She blushes, but her smile tells me loud and clear that she likes it. "I wish we had time to detour on the way to the farm," she says, looking up at me through her lashes. "Even a quick one?"

"Fuck, Al. You're gonna kill me," I growl, stepping in front of her to block the few remaining people's view of our hushed conversation. "I would give just about anything to drive back to your house and fuck the shit out of you, slide inside your heaven and inside your heart." Her chest is rising and falling faster with my every word. "But we've got things to do, promises to fulfill. After that, I'm gonna fuck that pussy, though. I promise you that."

"You can't say stuff like that . . . the kids . . ." she whispers, looking around. But there's no one close enough to hear.

She licks her lips, inviting me to kiss her, her eyes telling me how much she wants me to. I take a big breath, willing my dick to settle down, and cup her cheeks. There's so much hope, so much possibility in the small space between us.

It's not what she expects, but it's what we need. I kiss her forehead instead of her lips like I want. "We need to go. The kids are counting on us."

———

"Remind me again how I ended up helping you with this shit?" Mark grunts, pushing at a log to get it lined up into the circle we're creating.

Wow, a whole sentence. Either he's doing better or I'm asking for so much he needs to rub my nose in it.

"It's for the kids, asshole." James answers before I do, kicking at the other end of the same log. "Get used to it, *Uncle* Mark."

We've got a pretty good handle on the preparations now. The guys, Bennetts and Tannens both, have been working side-by-side to do the heavy lifting, and Mama Louise and the girls swept Allyson off as soon as we got here.

I already said it once, and it's not really our style, but I tell the guys again, "Thanks a lot for letting us do the campout here and for helping set everything up."

"Not like you asked before planning the whole shindig." Mark's brow raises with the accusation, but he's not wrong.

"I know. It just seemed like the right thing to do at the time," I explain for what's got to be the tenth time. He's like a dog with a bone and won't let it go. The only reason I haven't bowed up at him over the whole thing is that I can see a tiny flicker in his eyes as he gives me shit. Almost like . . . he's teasing? But I don't know if Mark has a funny bone in his entire body. If so, it's gotta be just the very tip of his pinkie toe or . . . what's that tiny bone in your ear? That thing could probably hold more humor than he has in his whole body.

Bobby snorts. "He means Allyson had him by the dick and he would've agreed to anything she asked."

He sounds full of piss and vinegar and I've had more than enough. I drop the small log I'm moving with a thud, my hands going on my hips to keep from shoving him. "What's your problem, Bobby?"

I don't give him a chance to answer the rhetorical question, barreling in myself. "I get it, I was a pain in your ass when all that shit went down, but I'm the one who went through the hard shit. If I can forgive her, why the hell can't you stand down?"

He gets right up in my face, hissing, "She's dangling everything you ever wanted in front of your face. The whole deal—her, a kid, football." He ticks each thing off on his fingers. "Like a ready-fuck-ing-made family, but it's not *yours*. She's not yours, that kid ain't yours, and you'll have a few weeks of football and then what? She's gonna chew you up and spit you out . . . again. And I'm not gonna be the one to prop you up this time."

My fists are curling and unfurling with how bad I want to beat the shit out of him. He's my brother, but we've always been a family of fists over words. And right now, he's spoiling for a fight I'm more than willing to give him.

"You just can't stand that I'm happy, can you? I've been walking around like a damn ghost for almost ten years, your partner in every crime, but now that I'm getting what I want and have a real shot at being happy, you . . . you . . . you're jealous!"

It hits me like a branding iron, hot and painful.

The questions, the doubts, the eye rolls as I tried to tell him about Allyson, the way he found problem after problem with our getting back together.

He laughs, but it's sarcastic and twisted. "I ain't jealous, mother-fucker. I'm *scared*. I know how close to the edge you were after Allyson, after Mom, hell . . . I know just how furious you were with all that shit with Dad. And you ain't got football to take it out on this time. You ain't even got the Bennetts since they're family now.

"You've had a knot of anger inside your chest for so long that you didn't even feel it anymore because you'd gotten so used to it," Bobby says, "But it's gone now."

He pushes at my arm, and I let him, so stunned I don't even reply before he throws one more knife my way.

"You think you're the observant one around here, but it never occurs to you that we're watching you too, does it?"

I have no idea what he's talking about, but as he looks at the other guys, I follow his eyes around our tight circle. They look ready to step in if we throw down, but also like they agree with Bobby. "We've seen you look like you could chew nails and spit them out, beat the shit out of people, and literally growl like an animal. Your nickname is Brutal, for fuck's sake. And now you're all Mr. Sunshine and Rainbows. Your shoulders are down, you smile all the damn time, and I swear you're this close to skipping around. If I see you with a kid on your shoulders, I'm calling bullshit."

"What. The. Hell. Are. You. Talking. About?" I enunciate slowly and clearly.

Brody clears his throat. "Uh, Brutal? He's right, you know, though if a big fucker like you can skip, I'd pay good money to see it." He's trying to make a joke to defuse the situation, but Brody's not exactly a laugh-a-minute sort so it's a bit flat. "You've been different the last few weeks. Especially since whatever happened last week."

He lifts his brows pointedly. But I didn't tell Brody all the nitty-gritty of my night with Allyson after I tried to tell Bobby. He hadn't been particularly interested in listening. Maybe I picked the wrong brother to celebrate the breakthrough with Allyson with. Though looking at Brody's brooding glare, maybe I should've just told Shayanne. She'd have been happy for me.

I sigh, taking my hat off and running my hands through my hair. "Okay, so I'm smiling? Shouldn't my being happy make you happy? Isn't that like a family thing we're supposed to be doing? I mean, I know it's been a while, but it seems like that's a thing."

Brody dips his chin. "It is, not that I'm some expert on family shit, but yeah . . . we're happy for you or whatever." We're so great at talking about our feelings. "It's just fast, real fast."

My mouth gapes. "Fast? It's taken ten years, for fuck's sake!"

Bobby interjects then. "No, it's been like a month. And most of that, you were at each other's throat."

"Because of a misunderstanding!" I boom. Every man tenses his shoulders, ready for battle between Bobby and me. "Ugh, damn it, Bobby! It's not fast. It's like we had this all planned out and things went sideways for way too long. I lost her once, but I won't do it again. You're right about one thing—this is what it should've been. Her, me, a kid. A future. And I'm gonna grab on to this chance with both fucking hands and hold on tight because I love her."

"Fuck yeah," Luke cheers, giving a slow clap. I can't help but glare at him a little. He might be on my side but he's still with my baby sister. Mark and James nod along with him. Of course they do. They've got wives of their own. It's just Brody and Bobby who're looking like we've all lost our minds.

Fuck. I'm becoming a *Bennett.*

Brody relents, though, flashing an actual teeth-baring smile and reassuring me. "Well, okay then. Why didn't you just say so?"

I whirl on him. "What?"

He holds up his hands. "I'm just glad to see you growing up or whatever big brother shit I'm supposed to say here. Help me out," he says, looking at Mark. They've gotten to be better friends working the cows every day. It's weird and grunty, but they seem to understand each other somehow.

Mark makes one of those typical grunts and then adds, "I'm the last one to give relationship advice, so don't ask. But if she's the one, don't fuck it up."

He acts like that's some groundbreaking suggestion, and Luke and James nod along agreeably.

Brody shrugs. "Sounds about right to me."

Bobby shakes his head, not convinced. "Fine. Whatever. Just . . . good luck, I guess."

With that, he walks off. But at least he heads in the direction of the other logs, so while he's mad at me, he's still helping us get ready for the kids who'll be here any minute.

I sigh as he leaves. We've always been close, but I don't know how to fix this. I have to take this shot with Allyson. Hell, I'm already deep in it with her, so Bobby's just going to have to trust me on this one.

"If you don't mind finishing up the log circle, I think I'm going to go check on Allyson. See if she got the same interrogation I did."

They don't look the least bit upset at the dig, and I swear I see a couple of middle fingers fly out of the corner of my eye. I ignore them, too ready to lay eyes on Allyson.

At the house, I see Mama Louise and Allyson on the back porch peeling a huge pile of potatoes. I'm about to holler out a greeting when I hear something that stops me.

"Bruce told me a bit about the two of you." Mama Louise makes it sound casual, but it's anything but.

Allyson pauses her potato peeling. "He did?"

Mama Louise hums. "Seems like a second chance is something you both need. You planning on taking advantage of it?"

"Wow, that's very . . . direct." Allyson's resumed her potato peeling with a manic energy that belies her nerves at the question. Mama Louise is the queen of patience, so she waits Allyson out,

227

silent and expectant. Like a newbie, Allyson speaks, giving Mama Louise exactly what she wants. "If you'd told me a few weeks ago that I'd be doing any of this—football, camping, Bruce . . . I mean, not that I'm *doing* Bruce. Oh, God."

I can't help but grin at the blush creeping up Al's neck.

"I know quite what you mean, dear," Mama Louise says easily. "I'm old, not dead. And John and I had a *very* happy marriage."

Allyson's laugh is small and uncomfortable, but she tries again. "This whole thing with Bruce, I never expected it. I think it was something I wanted but I'd given up on a long time ago. Maybe that's why I was so scared?" She bites her lip, her voice quieter, and I have to strain to hear her. "But I like it. He's good with the boys, especially Cooper. And he's good with me, *to me*."

I hear the tiny hitch in her voice and remember how she'd said her ex 'wasn't nice' to her. It makes me want to spoil her, treat her so well that she never wants for anything.

It makes me want to show her what love is supposed to be like.

This is going to be the best damn campout these kids and Allyson have ever had.

CHAPTER 24

ALLYSON

J mentally check off that everyone's here, all the food contributions are in Mama Louise's kitchen, and with a look around, I can tell the fun has already started.

The boys are running wild like they've never had this much space and fresh air, their joyful shouts echoing across the land. "Look at all the trees!" Johnathan says, spinning in a circle so fast I'm surprised he stays vertical.

Oops, spoke too soon, I think as he tumbles to the ground. He doesn't seem any worse for wear, though, as he laughs it off before hopping up.

"All right, gather up," Bruce says, clapping his hands loudly.

The boys scramble to pile in around him, but the parents come over too, naturally drawn to Bruce's charisma. I can't blame them. I'm just as pulled into him, the fight I initially put up all but useless and utterly forgotten at this point.

He seems at home out here, completely in his element. It's a good look in dusty jeans, a T-shirt that lets the tattoo on his bicep peek out as he moves, well-worn work boots, and a ballcap that's currently turned backward as he squats down to rally the troops.

"Okay, so out here, we're in charge. Me, my brothers, and the Bennetts, and most of all, the scariest person you'll ever meet in your entire life . . . Mama Louise." Bruce gestures at each of the men standing back to offer mean mug glares and ends with the small blonde who looks like she wouldn't hurt a fly. Mama Louise gives a smile and a wave.

A few of the boys giggle like Bruce is joking, and Mama Louise's smile falls, turning into the best mom glare I've ever seen. I need her to teach me that because every boy and even a few of the adults straighten right up. I even hear Killian say "Sorry, ma'am." She flips a switch and smiles again, like all is forgiven.

"My sister, Shayanne" —Bruce points her out to everyone— "is in charge of every animal as far as you're concerned. You don't so much as let one sniff you without her saying it's okay. And remember, what's the meanest animal out here?"

He looks around the circle, and I expect the kids to answer with something like a bull or an old horse, but they laugh instead and Cooper shouts out, "Chickens! They'll peck your hands even as you feed them."

I have no idea what he's talking about, but all the boys seem to think it's hilarious.

"Okay, who's ready for a tour then?"

Twelve skinny arms shoot up, and a few parents raise their hands too. I wiggle my fingers in the air, wanting a tour even though Bruce took me on one not too long ago. How can that be? It seems like a lifetime ago, and so much has changed since the day I came stomping out here mad as a hornet, ready to rip Bruce a new one.

We walk, taking the same paths he took me on, through the smaller garden areas and then the larger fields with him telling the kids all about everything they see and life on a working farm. They listen raptly to his every word, following him like the Pied Piper. Eventually, we end up in the orchard, and Bruce plucks down a peach to show the boys how to tell when they're ripe.

"These are the last ones of the season. The late bloomers, the ones that took just a bit longer to ripen and be ready, but you know what?" He pauses, and every eye is on him. "Just because they didn't ripen first doesn't mean they're any less delicious. Each one is ready in its own time, and when that time's right, they're perfect—just as they are, when they are." He takes big chomp out of the peach in his hand, the juiciness dripping down his fingers as he smiles at the sweet flavor. "Just right."

Yes, he is.

Bruce Tannen is better with words than he thinks he is. He's better with kids than I think he expected himself to be, too. He was this beast on the football field, and I know people anticipate certain things from him off the field too. The reality of who he is is so much deeper. I feel lucky to be one of the few people who get to see that side of him because while he used to be an open book, I know he's been more the brooding type for quite some time. But still waters run deep when it comes to him.

A soft smile stretches my lips and Cooper takes my hand. He's quiet, talking only to me. "I don't think he's just talking about peaches, Mom. You think maybe I'll be ready one day too?"

I look down at my son, seeing the beautiful, happy boy he is to me. But I know he's struggled. He's smaller than the other boys and can't cash the checks his mouth writes just yet. I tell him honestly, "I think you're already perfect just the way you are now, honey. You'll still grow and ripen a bit more, just like those peaches, but you're doing so well. I love you."

He grins for just a flash and then cringes. "*Mom,* don't get mushy!" But despite his protests, I think he heard me loud and clear. The devil is in his eyes as he challenges me, "Besides, if you keep getting riper, eventually, you'll rot!"

He runs off, but he's dragging his left leg and his arms are outstretched in front of him like some waywardly drunk zombie. "Zombie touch!" he shouts, tagging Johnathan, who mimics the weird run.

Soon, all the boys are screaming, either to get away from the zombies or because they are one.

Kids are weird and great. The other parents seem to agree as we watch the spontaneous game of tag erupt. Eventually, we get pulled into it too when Evan tags Mike.

Mike acts offended. "Me? Your own father?" But still, he runs off with Evan to tag more people. I'm glad he was able to come today. I know it was hard for him to get the day off and not need to sleep, but he knew how much the boys would want to see their old coach.

After everyone's a zombie, we decide to take a break and head back to the barn. Shayanne allows a few boys at a time into the yard with her goats, and I pull out my new phone to take pictures of each boy holding Baaarbara. The ornery goat seems to enjoy all the attention, licking faces and bleating happily.

"She thinks she's a dog," Joshua says as he wipes away a bit of spit from his cheek. Johnathan laughs at his brother's grossly silly predicament until Baaarbara leans back and licks him too.

"You're probably just a bit salty from sweating in the sun," Shayanne explains, showing us how the goats like their salt lick. "Wanna know a goat fact to surprise your friends?" The boys nod, and Shayanne continues her lesson. "They don't eat everything, though I bet you've heard they do. But nope, not true. Their favorite food is hay, and they'll eat some fruits and veggies too."

With that, she brings out a bucket of raisins. "One handful each, sprinkle them around or just hold your hand out, and they'll eat them all." The boys' grubby hands fight to get into the bucket at once, but eventually, everyone has some fruit and is feeding the nearest goat.

"This is awesome," Liam exclaims, and all the boys agree loudly.

"Ready for something even more fun?" Luke drawls out. "A birdie told me that he promised some muddin' to one of you."

Cooper's eyes go as big as dinner plates and his hand waves through the air. "Me! Coach B said he'd take me muddin'!"

Bruce grins and runs his hand through Cooper's hair in a familiar move that makes my heart sing. "Cooper's first, and then we'll take turns. Sound good, guys?"

"YEAH!" they all yell, following Bruce as he opens the goat pen gate, careful to keep the animals inside as the boys escape.

Over a hill, we pass by a big pond. James tells everyone about how this piece of land is the most important of the entire property because it lets them have a constant water source. "We use it for swimming most of the time, but earlier today, we pumped some out for a very special reason. Just over there." He points to the other side of the ridge, and the boys run up so fast that I can't keep up, even with the practice warm-ups doing wonders for my mile time. But they freeze at the top of the hill.

"Whoa," Liam says.

Finally, I get there and see what's got the boys' attention. There's a small oval dug into the grass, just the top layer of grass scrubbed off, and with the addition of water from the pond, it's a mud track. There's a two-seater Gator sitting there, ready to roll.

Bruce loads Cooper in the passenger seat, buckling him up tight. He loans him a pair of goggles and a helmet and then double-checks the seatbelt again. He's so careful and attentive, and there's something so sexy about his being fatherly. I mean, coachlike. Yeah, that . . . that's for sure what I meant.

No, it's not.

I remember telling him that Cooper and I are a package deal. I fully expected him to bolt. Most guys would, I think, so I'd been spoiling for a fight as a means of self-preservation.

But Bruce doubled down, saying he wanted a chance to love me and Cooper. And he asked me out on a for-real, official date. He's more than I could ever hope to find mixed up with something I'd already found once.

My heart constricts tight in my chest and then unfurls, its racing pace making me want to run to Bruce and tell him that I'm sorry. For not having faith back then, for fighting us, for being scared, for being damaged, but *not* for being hopelessly, deeply in love with him.

Again.

But I can't, not yet. Not while Cooper is laughing wildly, screaming with excitement as they speed around the loop. They're not going very fast, but the loud engine roars, making it seem dangerous and rowdy. When they come to a stop, Bruce helps Cooper out and does the same safety checks for the next boy.

"Mom! Did you see me? I went muddin' and did so good! *Vroom, vroom.*" Cooper's voice is high-pitched and loud, full of excitement. I listen as he gives me the play by play of every turn he made, having almost as much fun in the retelling as he did in the Gator.

"I did see, honey! You did so *well*," I correct out of habit, but he doesn't even hear it.

"Coach B is the coolest, isn't he, Mom?" Cooper asks, looking up at me. His cheeks are bright pink from the little bit of wind whipping him as they drove around. As I scan his blue eyes, so clear and bright, I search for any doubts, any nerves, any fears, but find none. He is the happy, healthy, innocent boy I wanted him to be.

"He is, Cooper," I agree, looking back out to the OHV spinning mud into the air. But I don't see the messy, dirty craziness. I see the future—one with excitement and safety, love and security. A future with Bruce.

CHAPTER 25

BRUCE

I smell Mama Louise coming before I see her, or rather, I smell the stacks of freshly cooked burgers she's bringing on a big tray. "I've got hamburgers and cheeseburgers, or if you'd rather have a hot dog, line up with Katelyn."

Once everyone's settled with their burger or hot dog, a bag of chips, and a big plastic cup of Shay's juice, we get down to the real reason for this campout. "Guys, I want to tell you how proud I am of all your hard work. It's only been a few weeks, but you have become a true team. It hasn't been easy, and I know there've been some hiccups. But we've really come together, and I'm excited to see how the season goes because no matter what that scoreboard says, we're already winners. We're Wildcats."

I'm channeling some of my great coaches over the years. It feels both weird and completely natural to be on the other side of the pep talk now, the coach instead of the player, even if my brothers are looking at me like I've sprouted a second head on my right shoulder. Or just become someone new, but maybe that part's a little bit true.

I look at Brody and Bobby, telling them with my eyes to 'shut the fuck up'. They look back, eyes virtually identical to mine, except theirs are laughing at me.

Allyson chimes in her agreement. "Thanks for welcoming me to the team as a coach. I might not know a lot about football." She pauses as the kids chatter, some saying 'it's ok' and some saying 'no kidding', and she laughs along with them good-naturedly, all drama forgotten from their issue before. "But I know heart, and each of you have so much of that. Together, nothing can stop us. We're going into the season as Wildcats, we're going to play every game with our whole hearts as a team, and most of all, we're going to have fun. Let's make those home runs!" She blinks innocently and then grins hugely as laughter bursts forth at the silly joke.

"Good one, Coach Allyson! You had us going for a second!" Johnathan says through laughter of his own. Cooper rolls his eyes but smiles too.

After everyone's done with burgers, we get a bucket full of sticks and stab marshmallows on the ends as Brody stokes up the fire. The flames lick up, orange and yellow brightness against the darkening sky. Stars twinkle overhead and everyone is full and relaxed. Sticky, messy faces covered in melted chocolate and ooey-gooey marshmallow are smiling, and I even see a few yawns.

It's perfect, everything a team campout should be. Not that I've ever been on one before, but I can't imagine anything better.

Looking around the circle, my eyes land on Allyson and Cooper. I can't help but imagine nights like this out here with them, just the three of us cozied up after a football game. Like a family.

Bobby was right. Allyson is offering everything I ever dreamed of in one insta-family moment, but it doesn't scare me. Not in the least. In fact, I want it desperately. That woman, that boy, this land. I feel like someone hit pause on my life years ago and the play button has finally been pushed so I can get on with what I should've been doing all along.

I've seen the way she's been looking at me all day, hungry but also thoughtful. The hamster in her head has been running himself ragged, even as she goofed off with the kids. Those blue eyes of hers haven't missed a thing, not the joy of the kids and not the happiness in my heart. She sees it, she knows, and after what she said to Mama Louise, I know she feels it too.

It feels like possibility and hope. It feels like a future.

It's one I want desperately and will fight tooth and nail to possess, just like Allyson. I will have her—her body, her heart, and her future. I won't stop until she is so tangled up in me and I am so lost in her that there's no way to have one without the other and we are simply one.

I move to sit beside Allyson, me and Cooper bookending our girl. He looks over at me, and I expect a friendly smile. Instead, he offers a me narrow-eyed look of examination. "My mom's pretty awesome, yeah?"

His voice is flat, nothing how the sweet statement should sound.

I dip my chin in agreement as Allyson admonishes him in surprise. "Cooper! Be nice." Even she heard the adversarial tone in her son's voice which seems wholly at odds with the good time we've had today.

He looks down like he's ashamed, but I see him swallow as he eyeballs my hand holding Allyson's. We did this at their kitchen table not too long ago, and then it'd been Allyson I thought was going to freak out. Seems like it's Cooper's turn now. Guess he's caught on to the seriousness of my feelings toward his mom, way beyond more than just dating, and is feeling a bit protective.

I like it. I lay my arm over Al's shoulders and offer Cooper a handshake, looking him in the eye. "I couldn't agree more. She's the absolute best. You too."

I must pass some test because he smiles easily after shaking my hand. It's a good, firm shake just like we practiced on that first day of practice, which makes me proud.

The tension passes, and we all relax into each other. Cooper leans on Allyson and she leans on me, both of her guys holding one of her hands. With the parents and kids around us, it feels like our first official family outing.

A while later, when yawns have gotten more frequent and longer, we set up a big tarp with sleeping bags. We'd thought individual tents would be time-consuming, and honestly, part of the attraction of sleeping outside is the beauty of the sky above you, the night stars, and sunrise.

The kids fall asleep quickly, the parents taking a while longer even after the long day. Way off in the distance, I hear the Gator's engine and wonder who's driving around this late at night. I scan the group, seeing my brothers and the Bennett boys. Their women went home for the night, Katelyn to sleep in her bed and Sophie to care for Cindy Lou, and Mama Louise said her old bones wouldn't pull ground-sleeping duty anymore.

That leaves . . . Shayanne?

The engine dies still some way away, but when I listen closely, I can hear footsteps walking through the tall grass toward us.

Shayanne comes into view, a worried look on her face, which sets off my alarm bells. I raise my hand, waving it around so she can see me in the fading light of the fire. She comes over, squatting down to whisper, "Hey, I need you up in the barn for something. Come on."

"What's wrong?" I ask, hopping up. My brain roars with what could cause her to drag me out of here in the middle of the night. Okay, it's not even midnight, but still. If there were an animal issue, she'd get Sophie, and for just about anything else, she'd get Brody or Mark. I'm the big fucker she'd get if there were an intruder or if . . . the boys did something. Well, shit.

She doesn't answer me. Instead, Shay leans forward, looking around me at Allyson. "You too."

There's definitely something wrong. Her brows are pulled together and her jaw is tight, but today's been great as far as I'm aware, so I'm not sure what's happened. I do a quick headcount to make sure no one has snuck off to see Baaarbara again without supervision, but everyone's present and accounted for and mostly snoring away.

"Oh, uh . . .okay?" Allyson looks at Cooper uncertainly.

From a few feet away, Michelle lifts her head to whisper, "Go ahead. I've got him, and Mike's here as stand-in coach. We're good. Go handle Shayanne's barn emergency." She hums quietly. "Would that make it a barnmergency?"

I blink in confusion and grab Allyson's hand instead of figuring Michelle's brain out. We walk back through the grass, fighting to keep up with Shayanne's pace, and that's saying something because one of my strides is roughly equal to two of hers. "Shay, what's wrong?"

"Shh. Just come with me," she whispers over her shoulder, never missing a step. Once we reach the Gator, she climbs in the driver's seat, still silent as a church mouse, which is making me antsy. Shay ain't quiet, ever. She's mouthy as a rule, just like the sun rises in the east and sets in the west.

The engine roar is loud as fuck in the quiet night, and I realize why she parked so far away. She would've woken up the whole camp if she'd come any closer. But she takes off into the dark with ease, knowing the land like the back of her hand and making a direct beeline for our barn.

"Goats okay?" I ask, and she cuts her eyes to me as she nibbles on her bottom lip. Is she worried? Scared? Trying not to say something? I'm not sure, which I don't like. Shay's not just an open book. She usually shouts her thoughts and feelings from the nearest rooftop at rock concert levels. And yet, she's giving me nothing.

She pulls up with the slightest slide on the dry grass and then looks at me, not moving. I've already got one leg out of the Gator, ready to run at whatever she needs me to handle. Her hand on my arm stops me. "Bruce?"

"Yeah?" I say, scanning the night and then visually checking in with Shay and Allyson in the back seat. Nothing seems amiss, which adds to my confusion.

"You've been real busy this week planning the campout for those kids."

"Uh-huh," I grunt as a semi-answer, getting out and standing so I can get a better view of the black land around us.

"I know you two ain't had but a minute alone all week."

I face Shayanne fully, turning and putting my hands on my hips. "You keeping tabs on me now?"

She smirks, the first sign that she's up to something. "I can see that itchiness on you. Felt it myself when Luke and I were sneaking around and I missed him. You looked out for me then, and I thought it seemed like a fine time to return the favor. So get out." She says the last part of that to Allyson.

Allyson balks, interrupting the conversation for the first time. "What? I thought something was wrong?"

Shayanne's smile is sweet as pie, innocent as an angel. I know she's neither. "What's wrong is that my brother is head over fucking heels for you and needs a little alone time with his woman. Now, I'm driving the Gator to my house. I'd suggest you two head on into the barn, or up to the main house, or wherever it is you like to do whatever it is you like to do." Shay looks at me thoughtfully, one brow raised. "And then you can walk back to the campout having handled whatever it is you need to handle. Talk, fuck, I don't care."

With that, she shrugs and revs the engine.

I'm surprised, but then again, I'm not. This is exactly something Shay would do, a little crazy but nice at the same time. I guess I'm mostly surprised she knew I was itching to sweep Allyson away. Am I that transparent? My brother's earlier assurances that I am come back to mind.

I take Al's hand, helping her out. As soon as she's barely clear, Shay throws up a two-fingered wave. "Later, lovebirds. Don't do anything I wouldn't do. 'Course with Luke, that ain't much."

"That doesn't leave much off the table, does it?" I growl. I know Luke ain't responsible for all of it, but Shay's giving me details I do *not* want to know.

She laughs, taking off into the night.

Allyson sighs, a blissfully happy sound, and then laughs. "Your sister is something else. I remember her being young and a bit of a tomboy. But I get the feeling she's grown up a lot since then."

I squeeze the bridge of my nose between my thumb and index finger. "You have no idea. But she's not wrong."

I peek over at Al. She looks beautiful in the moonlight. Hair in a messy ponytail, not a stitch of makeup on, and wearing the sweats and a baggy T-shirt she planned to sleep in. I've seen her dressed to impress for work, I've seen her in workout gear ready to do drills along with the boys, but this? This dressed-down version of her feels like a private look at the woman beneath the face she presents the rest of the world. It feels like walls crumbling and fronts falling, and it's just us, here in the night.

"Want to go in the barn or to the house?" Allyson says quietly, almost like she's going shy on me. I know she feels my intention, the promise of what I'm going to do to her in the air between us. Because fuck, do I need her.

I consider the options and weigh the advantages and disadvantages. "Can I tell you a secret?" I don't want to, but if I'm demanding that she let me in, I've got to do the same. Lead by example, just like with the kids. She nods, and I will my stomach to stop turning. "When we were kids, I dreamed about having you in my room, in my bed. I wanted you in my space, like you were mine."

"And now?" She already heard the 'but' coming.

"But now, I guess I'm kinda ashamed that I'm a grown-ass man still sleeping in the same bed I had as a teenager. I barely fit in the damn thing diagonally." My laugh is sardonic and hard. I never really considered that I live at home because I never considered bringing anyone here. It's home, but it's mostly just a place to crash between days working. The few women I've been with have been at their place so I could make an exit when I needed to. I never wanted to bring anyone here but Allyson, and now that I have the chance, I don't want to.

I want her, I just don't want her to see me that way. How stuck I've been, how meaningless it's all been.

She's thoughtful for a moment. "You said before that it's a bit bachelor pad-like. Are there posters of half-naked women on the walls or anything like that? I didn't see any when we FaceTimed, but maybe you were choosing your angles?" She dips her chin, but I saw that grin.

I scoop her up into my arms. "Are you giving me shit, woman? I'm being all honest with you about some embarrassing stuff and you tease me about it?" I'm teasing her back, glad she's not mad at my reluctance.

Her head falls back. "Just take me in the barn, for fuck's sake. Like old times."

ctream..................

It's the best idea I've heard since Shay pulled away, and I damn near run for the barn. Inside, I turn on the bare minimum of lights so the sleeping animals aren't disturbed, giving the barn a soft glow. I let Allyson slide down my body until her feet hit the floor, but I keep her tight against me, dancing her back toward the ladder. "Hay loft. Now."

We've been here before, but this feels new and different. I like it.

Allyson smiles, just the corners of her mouth tilting up a bit, and then bolts for the ladder. I give chase, her laughter bright in the quiet. From a stall, I hear a rustling and shush her. "Don't wake up the goats or they'll start bleating for food and never shut up. Hungry little monsters."

"You talking about them or us?"

"Tou-fucking-ché. Up." I gesture at the ladder with my chin and she starts to climb. I stay below her, enjoying the view and sampling it by popping the right globe of her ass with a quick smack. It bounces back nicely, making climbing the ladder a bit more difficult as my cock thickens in my jeans.

"Oh!" Al exclaims at the spank, but when she looks down at me, ready to give me hell, I can see the heat in her eyes. "Don't make me fall!"

She's joking, but I'm dead-serious as I answer truthfully, meaning so much more than her footing on the ladder. "That's the plan, Al."

That shuts her right up and she turns back around, hustling the rest of the way up. I follow, and once in the hayloft, I search her expression. There's a longing there, but uncertainty too. She blinks, and the view to the depths of her mind clouds over with lust. I want all of her, even those scary thoughts, but I'll let her hide a bit longer.

I'm getting to her, more and more, bit by bit. And she's getting to me too. Just like I want. I want to weave myself into her and never let go.

"Come here." She hooks her finger, bidding me closer, and I stalk toward her, trapping her in the back corner by a stack of bales.

"Whatcha gonna do now that you got me where ya want me?" It's a dare and we both know it. I'm also giving her a chance to lead for a minute because we both know that once we're naked, things will change.

But if she wants to talk instead, I'm down for that. I want every bit of her—mind, body, and soul. And I'll get them all in due time.

Her eyes drift off, taking in the hayloft like it's a new space even though nothing much has changed since the last time she was up here, and then they return to me. She used the pause to devise a plan. I can see it in the subtle flicker in her baby blues.

She ducks past me, expecting me to grab her again, but I'm intrigued and want to let this play out to see what she's got in mind. She stands on her tippy toes, reaching into a small crate screwed into the wooden wall, and pulls out an old quilt.

It's not the same one from ten years ago. That one gave in to the passage of time and the effects of the elements years ago. But there's always a new one to take the last one's place. She smiles, fingering it lightly. "It's soft."

I grunt, never having noticed one way or another. She flicks her wrist, letting the blanket bubble in the air before floating to the floor, and then sits down on it looking prim and proper. Suddenly, I want this quilt to be soft as butterfly wings because she's going to need the contrast of the soft cocoon with how I want to fuck her. Rough, dirty, hard . . . till she's begging to stop coming on my cock.

I drop down next to her, knowing she can see all that in my eyes. I don't even try to hide it from her. I want her to not only know but to want it too. To want *me* too.

I'll have her love me again by filling her sweet pussy, writing my name on her silken walls with my cum, and working my way into her heart with as much patience as she needs. I've waited ten years. I can wait a little longer. But not to fuck her, not to make love to her.

I'm not sure where to start. I want to do everything, touch her everywhere all at once. But I begin with a kiss. Such a simple word for a decidedly not-simple thing. I taste her, sipping at her lips until she opens willingly for me, her lips parting on a sigh.

It's my entry point. I shove my tongue into her mouth, cupping her jaw and trailing down to gently squeeze at her neck, not hurting but letting her know that playtime's over as she falls back to the blanket, spreading out like a goddess. Her moan of agreement is dark and heady. "Take your clothes off, Al. Show me those pretty tits and that gorgeous pussy."

She rips her shirt and bra off first, and I can't wait. I dive for her, sucking one and then the other into my mouth, my tongue tracing circles on her skin. One of her hands pulls my hair, holding me to her, and the other works feverishly between us on the button of her jeans. Impatient for more, I help her by ripping her pants and panties down her legs as she toes off her shoes.

She's blissfully naked, bare before me, and I'm fully dressed. It's symbolically the exact opposite of our emotions. She'll give me her body freely, but she's cautious with her heart. I'll give her everything I am, yet I'm still in my clothes, a barrier between us. It's for her benefit, though, because I need to lick her, and if I strip, I'm going to slam into her without a proper taste.

Pushing her knees open, I can see the slick shine of her arousal coating her lips. I lie down between her thighs, settling in to eat her out until she's begging for my cock. I lap at her, teasing us both for a moment before devouring her.

I can feel her legs trembling, her thighs trying to close around my ears and her hips bucking even as she tries to stay still. I wrap my arms under her thighs, locking my fingers together over her belly like I'm prone at her altar. But I'm no good boy praying for mercy or forgiveness right now. No, I'm the filthy fucker who already possesses Allyson. She just needs a little reminding of that fact. A reminder I'm more than happy to give her.

I use the strength in my forearms to force her to my mouth and hold her immobile. "I'm gonna lick you, suck you, fuck you with my tongue until you come for me, baby." The words are sweet purrs against her soft lips.

"Yes . . ." she sighs out, hunger in the bit of growl beneath the breath.

I do as promised, knowing exactly what will get her to the edge quickly, but then I back off to let the orgasm slip away. She whines and I do it again. And again.

By the third time she's teetering on that knife-sharp edge, she's begging as she scratches at my arms. She's not trying to get free. She's using me for leverage to shove her pussy to my mouth. "Make me come, Bruce. Please."

I love that demanding tone, the backbone when she tells me what she wants so clearly. I suck her clit into my mouth, battering it with my tongue in rhythm with the suction. Her pussy drenches me as she cries out my name, and while a part of me celebrates my name on her lips, I don't lose focus as I coax her through the orgasm and tease her with the promise of another.

"Damn it, Allyson. I need to fuck you now." I sound like a monster, my voice gone even deeper and barely even forming human words. I yank at my clothes, focusing on my jeans as she pulls at my shirt. As soon as my cock is free, I slam into her.

Home. Bliss. Heaven.

She is all those to me and more. She is mine, and just as importantly, I'm hers. I always have been.

She cries out at the sharp invasion, her walls clamping down on me tightly at the shock. But I talk her through it, crashing into her to punctuate every word. "Too tight, God, you feel too good. Relax, baby, or you're gonna make me come already."

Her walls relax for a moment, a fresh gush of her juices letting me know that she's okay as she digs her nails into my back and squeezes my hips with her knees, pulling me against her even as she takes me deeper.

Soon, she starts fucking me back. It's a match to a stick of dynamite, and we explode in a mass of writhing need. It's messy, it's loud, it's wild. It's everything.

Even in the chaos of fucking like animals, there's more to it. An undercurrent flows through us, surrounding us. This is more than we had when we were young, more than I dreamed I'd ever have now, with Allyson or anyone. Even when we're rough and filthy, it's with love.

I love her. I know I do, and I always have.

The words are on the tip of my tongue, dying to be spoken into existence—shouted from rooftops and whispered in her ear, roared into the night and murmured on her skin—but not like this. I don't want her to think I said it because we're in the middle of having sex, and there's still a real chance she'll freak out on me, so I grit my teeth, clenching my jaw so hard I can feel the strain in the muscles of my neck.

"Come with me, please," I beg her. I'm not ashamed of it. I want her to come on my cock, squeeze me with her velvet sugar walls as she coats me with cum at the same time I paint my name inside her with mine.

Her breath hitches, and I'm done for. I fly and fall all at the same time—into her, into bliss, into black nothingness. I fight to keep my eyes open even as they want to roll back in my head, closing in pleasure. But I need to see her, know that this is real and that she is mine. I can't say the three words I want to yet, but with my dark eyes locked on her bright blue ones, I grunt out one word. "Allyson."

It's just her name, but there's a deeper meaning and she knows it.

This is us. Only her and me.

I don't know what happened with her ex, nor do I need to, to know that she didn't have this with him. And I certainly haven't felt anything remotely resembling how I feel for her.

I love her.

CHAPTER 26

ALLYSON

"*M*ove! Move! Move! Clock's a'ticking, mister!" I might as well be trying to hurry up a snail, or a sloth, with epic slow-mo skills.

"I am!" Cooper says back weakly. But he's not moving. He's got his head propped against his hand and the milk dribbling from his spoon back into his cereal bowl. He's taking so long to eat that the cereal is probably mushy and soggy.

"First day of school! So exciting!" I'm trying here. I might as well be Mary Poppins mixed with Dora the Explorer with all the energy and singing I'm giving this boy.

He's fine, really, ready for the next grade and in class with Liam, but it's so early for him and he's tired even though I bumped his bedtime back super early last night. Why does elementary school start at 7:30, anyway? I don't even have to be at work that early.

"Checklist . . . hair brushed? Face and hands washed? Teeth brushed? Dressed to the shoes? Lunch in your backpack?" Cooper nods along with my questions, used to our morning routine even if it's a little earlier than usual. "Okay, hop up and let's do your first day of school picture by the front door."

He gets up, and I sweep his bowl into the sink, filling it with water, which makes the soggy colorful circles float and bounce crazily. I'll wash it later, I promise myself.

Cooper stands by the door, a fake smile on his mouth and his eyes looking vaguely similar to the vacant zombie gaze he had at the campout a few days ago. I clap and smile, so proud of how big he's gotten even if he's a grumpasaurus right now.

I hold my phone up, praying for an actual, real smile. *"Knock, knock."*

Cooper rolls his eyes and sighs heavily. *"Mom."*

"Knock. Knock." I try again, finger at the ready.

"Who's there?"

"Gladys."

"That's an old lady name. Do people even name their kids Gladys anymore? Glaaaaadiiiiiis." He draws the name out, making it sound even weirder than the repetition.

I lift one brow, working my mom 'check yourself' look.

"Fine. Gladys who?"

"Aren't you Gladys the first day of school?" I grin stupidly big at the bad joke and giggle a bit.

Cooper rolls his eyes again. That's really getting to be a bad habit I'll have to watch, but when I bounce my shoulders up and down a bit, playing the goofball a bit more, he caves and laughs.

Click. Click. And a burst of shots just to be sure I got both the smile and open eyes.

"Gotcha!" I give him a finger-gun point, though only with one hand since I'm still holding my phone. It's still new and I'm a little overprotective. "Now let's get you on the bus or I'm going to tell another joke."

"No!" he cries, running to grab his backpack.

Mission accomplished. He's in a better mood, awake and moving, and if I know my son, he'll get some decent mileage in sharing the 'lame joke my mom told this morning'.

Practice tonight is a scrimmage with another team. It's the first time my utter lack of football knowledge really sinks in.

I mean, I know I don't have much of a clue, but I've been reading up a little on my too-short lunch breaks and Cooper talks football pretty non-stop, so I thought I'd do okay. Practices have been good, at least.

But from the coin toss, there are rules and plays I'm clueless about. At first, I think the kids are just running around like feral cats chasing a laser light and they're as confused as I am. But slowly, patterns emerge and I can see the kids' eyes on one another.

They're actually playing, and they know what they're doing. Luckily, we have Bruce, and he's a natural, both with the football aspect and with the boys too. He has really whipped them into a team and it shows. There's no showboating or ball hogging, and they're actually holding their positions and running the plays we've been practicing.

I'm a little in awe of the whole thing if I'm honest. I'm a lot in awe of Bruce.

I glance over at him, standing right beside me with his full attention locked on the field. He's watching every step, reading every kid out there and guiding them from the sideline in a way that makes them hear the direction and act accordingly. There's no yelling, no insults, no anger, just a good man doing a good thing.

He has no idea how much I appreciate that and even less of an idea of how special he truly is.

After a long line of high-fives from both teams and a coach handshake, we circle up for the team cheer.

"All right, guys, next meeting is our first game. We're ready. You've worked so hard for this, and as far as I'm concerned, we're already winners because we're a team. We're the Wildcats. The game is just a chance to pull together even more and maybe show off a bit." Bruce smirks at the boys, and they start flexing their little boy biceps like the Incredible Hulk. Bruce joins in, his muscles popping out in a way that makes my entire body flush.

And that's *before* I start imagining his sexy body with no clothes on, muscles rippling as he holds himself above me. And okay, I know this is a weird one, but my favorite thing about Bruce's muscles is when he wraps his arms around me and puts his chin on my head. It makes me feel safe and protected, my smaller body cocooned by his much larger one. I swear I could suffocate against his chest and die a happy woman.

His eyes jump over to me, checking to make sure I'm watching and gauging my reaction. I almost look away quickly, embarrassed at being busted so obviously, but instead, I stick my tongue out at him and join in with their 'gun show'. Granted, my stick arms aren't all that strong compared to Bruce's, but my biceps are bigger than several of the boys'.

That's not really a rousing endorsement of your muscle-y goodness.

Even my inner monologue is in a good mood today, teasing me with a healthy dose of silliness.

After the team cheer and a quick conversational recap of the first game expectations with the parents, we head home. Well, to mine and Cooper's house.

But it does feel more like our home as we sit down and have dinner. I listen dreamily as Bruce and Cooper replay practice, move by move and play by play. It all washes over me, buoying me like fizzy champagne.

I'm going to tell him tonight.

I love him, but also that I need his patience because while I'm swimming pretty well right now, drowning in him seems pretty possible too. I think he'd like that, though, and honestly, I might too.

The thought rolls in my head all evening, and when I come back down the hall from tucking Cooper in, the house is empty. It doesn't even occur to me that Bruce left because I know he wouldn't. My trust is that deep with him.

I look on the back porch to find him sipping on a beer, a second one with rivers running down the bottle sitting at his feet. *He got one for me too*, I think with a smile.

I open the door slowly so it doesn't creak in the dark evening. Bruce doesn't so much as move a muscle, eyes focused on the moon far out on the horizon. But he's aware of my every move, every expression, every thought. He's always attuned to me that way, and while not as skilled at it as he is, I can read him well enough to know that he's preparing for something. His shields are fortified, his walls ready for war.

"Been kinda quiet tonight. Everything okay?" he says finally.

I'm still frozen by the back door, but his quiet concern pulls me to his side. He's sitting back on a lounge chair, one leg stretched out in front of him and one foot on the deck. Like he's deciding whether he's going to stay or go.

Funny thing is, I don't think he wants to go anywhere. I think he's got that boot on the wood deck so he can be ready to chase me if I run again. I don't want to run anymore, but the idea that he wouldn't give up on me so easily is reassuring.

Especially with the leap of faith I'm about to take.

"I love you." I blurt it out with no preamble, no warning. Just an honest confession that forced its way free, from my heart to my mouth to the air.

"What?" Bruce says, his eyes finally locking on me. He looks shocked, his eyes wide and his brows high. A heartbeat later, his face relaxes into bliss as my words sink in, and a soft, happy smile appears on his face. "What?"

"I love you." It's easier to say this time, my voice clearer even as my heart races. Somewhere inside my head, there's a broken-winged bird who thought she'd never fly again fluttering like a madwoman at the too-small cage I've shoved her in. With a breath, I mentally release her, and she soars the same way my heart does.

But there's no anxiety, no fear, no finger tapping to focus. Because I am solidly here in this moment with Bruce and thrilled to have every single second with him I can get. If I could go back and get the last ten years, I would. As long as I could keep Cooper.

"Fuck, Allyson," Bruce groans, setting the beer down haphazardly as he grabs at me. He pulls me to the chair and into his lap, settling me between his spread legs as he cups my cheeks, forcing my eyes to his. "I love you too. I always have, always will."

I can see the honesty in his eyes, feel the intention in his body. He means always. He wants forever and so do I. He kisses me, deep and dark and slow like bitter chocolate melting deliciously on your tongue. And I want to get lost in him because I've found myself in him.

But there's more I need to say.

"Bruce—" I say, trying to break our kiss. He's not having it and smacks at me a couple more times, moaning like I'm too tasty to give up. "There's something else . . ."

He pauses at that, just barely. But then he's kissing down my neck, at least letting me speak. Or I would be able to if my whole body wasn't chanting *Bruce, Bruce, Bruce* right now.

I push at his chest, just the barest resistance, and he straightens to look me in the eye. "What is it?"

He's waiting for the other shoe to drop, so to speak, waiting for me to go flight-er, as he calls it, as he watches me carefully.

"I still need to go slow. I'm a mom, I've been a wife, we're starting something new, and I just . . . I've got scars, Bruce. Jeremy really fucked me up."

It's all the reasons I pushed him away, all the excuses I gave him and myself, all the objections I'm letting go of now with this leap of faith. I feel Bruce flinch beneath me, can taste his desire to understand exactly what I'm talking about, and know he'd be beyond livid. But I've moved past that. Anger, betrayal, hurt, and fear have no place in my life now. "I've done the work to be better, but I need to go slow."

It's a bare-boned confession that costs me a lot to say, mostly because it's to Bruce.

But I don't need to get back in that pit. I've dealt with it all, and Bruce is nothing like Jeremy. Literally nothing like each other. Jeremy was weak, playing at being strong, and I let him walk all over me to prove it. Bruce is strong but will tap into his softer side when needed, and neither side would hurt me.

Most importantly, Bruce wants me strong. After Jeremy, I've been building myself back up, brick by brick from the dirt up, and my greatest fear was that any man I dated would be like Jeremy and want me weak again. It's one of the reasons I'd sworn off men. But Bruce is not just any man. He never was, and he never will be. He's shown me that over the past weeks, and even over the years together so long ago.

Tears burn my eyes at the realization of what I almost lost, not just this chance with Bruce, but myself. I'd gone so astray that I lost me, but I'm better than back. I've grown up, learned from my mistakes, and molded myself into something greater than I was. So much of the past rears up inside me in this moment, and I fearlessly beat the demons into their boxes, shoving them away dismissively. It's an exercise in imagination, but powerful nonetheless, to see how weak they are and how strong I am.

The tears spill over, freely running down my face in relief and even happiness, and Bruce sweetly shushes me as he wipes at them reassuringly, for once not understanding the emotional journey the tears represent. "Hey, hey . . . what's wrong, baby? We can go slow. That's fine. As long as you're mine, everything else will work itself out."

Why doesn't that set off alarm bells? It should. His possessiveness, his demanding bossiness, his rough brand of love should scare the absolute bejesus out of me. I should fall in love with a nice accountant who likes puzzles and board games and missionary sex once a week with the lights off. That's the smart thing to do.

But that's not what I want. I want Bruce.

"I love you," I repeat again.

He snuggles me into his chest, patting my back soothingly. "I love you too, Allyson."

It's not the roses and rainbows most people get when they profess their love. It's not even the hot sex that often follows the declaration.

It's quietly profound, it's gut-deep, it's soul-baring. It's us in love. Again, or maybe still.

CHAPTER 27

BRUCE

*T*his first game is not going well. I meant it when I told the boys that we're winners before we even step foot on the field. But I think we all expected the actual game to be a little more evenly matched.

The other team is the same size but experienced, having been together for the past two years in the younger division. At this stage, that makes all the difference.

We're two touchdowns down, which for pee-wee ain't a big deal, but it's the level of mastery on the field that's most drastically different. Both teams are running plays, but the Wildcats look sloppy compared to the Bulldogs' crisp cleanliness on the field.

I'll admit to myself that I wanted a better showing for them. They've worked so damn hard, and I want them to feel the joy of success from that. And selfishly, I wanted to show off my own coaching prowess a bit too. The Tannens and Bennetts, each and every one of the loud and crazies, are standing on the sidelines, cheering for my guys. They're cheering for me.

Even Bobby. We might not have our shit straightened out about Allyson, but he supports my coaching, at least.

"Go, Derek, go!" I yell from the sidelines. Derek's giving it his all, legs pumping and elbows flying high as he beelines toward the endzone. At the five, though, he's tackled hard, going down in a tumble of limbs. I know a moment of real fear, one I never felt when it was me on the field getting beat up, but the knot releases in relief an instant later when Derek pops up. He even fist-bumps the player who tackled him.

He's showing good sportsmanship and will be a great player one day if he wants to be. He's got the skills, even at this early age, and most importantly, he's willing to take coaching and work hard.

We reset, and Anthony looks up and down the line. I can't read his face from this angle, but he's up to something. I scan too, and it hits me.

It's so fast I don't think anyone else even realizes what's happening until it's over. Anthony just ran in a quarterback sneak, rushing across the line into the end zone himself. Everyone cheers loudly, more for the boldness than anything else. A sneak is rare and virtually unheard of at this level. Hell, I don't even know if it's legal, but I don't give a fuck. That was some solid football playing.

"Woo-hoo! Way to go, Anthony!" Allyson cheers. When I look over, her cheeks are flushed pink and she's waving her fists around like she's got pompoms. Old habits die hard, I guess. "We get to kick now, right?"

I nod in answer, and she looks over to the teenaged scorekeeper on the sideline. "One more touchdown and we'll tie."

She's getting better. I imagine us sitting around watching Monday night football, the three of us with mouths full of burgers as we cheer the teams on television. Or maybe I'll take Allyson and Cooper to a game? We could start with the local high school game, then progress up to the state college level, and if we want, try a pro game. I like the idea of it being 'our thing'.

We make the extra point, and there's a renewed energy on the field. Anthony's ballsy move makes him a fresh target, and he gets hit a couple of times, barely tossing the ball away before he hits grass.

"Uh! C'mon, kid." I hear a male voice from the stands behind me call out in exasperation. I turn to see who's mouthing off at my team, scanning the tiny foldable bleachers for the culprit.

But I can't tell for sure. There are a couple of dads I haven't met, and all eyes are on the field, watching the next play.

I hear a couple more comments from the peanut gallery over the next three plays. When the kids set, I turn my back to the field, scanning the group of parents and watching for the offender. I even questioningly glance at Brody to see if he can point me in the right direction. From here, I can see that his jaw's clenched, but that's about it. No help from him or any of the other Bennetts or Tannens. They look as pissed as everyone else, but I can't tell who's smack talking.

"Throw to Killian! He's open! Killian's open!" It's loud and aggressive, threaded with anger. I don't have to turn around to know Anthony didn't throw to Killian because I can suddenly see Kyle Bloomdale as he steps almost onto the field. He's still mouthing but not yelling at least as he says, "Fucking useless QB. He should've thrown to Killer Killian. We would've gotten a TD if my kid had the ball. Yank number three and put in a quarterback who knows what the hell he's doing."

Parental eyes snap to me, silently asking me what I'm going to do.

I call a timeout and step closer to Kyle, my voice deep and scary. "Mr. Bloomdale."

He looks to me, a smile growing on his too-skinny face. "Hey, Brutal! Get my kid some action, a'ight?" He makes it sound like we're buddies and I'd be doing him a solid.

I don't return the too-casual, friendly tone. "Cheer or shut up. No insulting my players."

His brows knit together, but he holds up his hands in something resembling an apology.

I turn back around to see Allyson talking to the boys, who are all smiling. I tune in, listening to her tell them what a good job they're doing. "Keep it up, guys. Post-game pizza if we win."

It's an incentive we'd decided on as a team, and she's dangling it like a tantalizing carrot to keep them working hard. I rejoin the group. "Awesome work so far. That yardage was on point, Derek. All of you have been playing your hearts out. Make sure your moms save those videos for your varsity play reel." I wink at them and they laugh at the compliment. "Keep it up, Wildcats."

The kids hustle back out and play resumes.

We're doing pretty well, even make that other touchdown we need to tie up the game. But there's a cloud hanging over the excitement. The cloud's name is Kyle Bloomdale.

He's still mouthing, though quieter and not as obnoxiously. But now that I'm tuned in to him, I can't *not* hear him. The other parents are rolling their eyes, and I even hear a few tell him to hush. To their credit, my family doesn't interfere, letting me handle my own shit for a change. I know how hard that must be for them.

Kyle disappears for several minutes, missing a chunk of the third quarter, and a relieved sigh runs through the entire group. I try to stay focused on the team and the good effort they're putting forth. I'm damn proud of these boys and how far they've come.

Even with their hard work, the other team makes headway, scoring a touchdown and then, on a messed-up play, we basically hand them another. That puts the Bulldogs solidly in the lead.

Which is when Kyle returns, hot and red-faced. "What the fuck?" he yells. "I leave for five minutes and they're just giving the game away." He's gesturing wildly toward the scorekeeper's plastic number display.

I turn to head over there again, but Allyson puts a staying hand on my arm. "Let me," she says quietly. The absolute last fucking thing I want is her anywhere near this asshole, but there's something in the set of her shoulders that says she needs to do this. I don't understand it, but I dip my chin, letting her do what she thinks is best.

Still, my attention is torn between the boys on the field I've make a commitment to and Allyson going over to the stupid redneck who's still mouthing. His parents, Killian's grandparents who are so kind and caring, look embarrassed but unable to do anything about their son's ridiculous behavior.

I can hear Allyson, her voice calm and steady like she's talking to a rabid dog. She sounds submissive, non-threatening, which is definitely not the tact I would've taken with the asshole.

It's her professional voice, I realize. I can almost hear her mental reminders, the ones she told me play on repeat in her head at work. Mediate, mitigate, deescalate. None of those are my specialty. I'm more in the fuck shit up and figure it out later camp, but maybe she's got a point given the audience we have now.

"Mr. Bloomdale, please lower your voice. There are rules, and we really need to remember that they're kids and it's just a game. The point is for them to have fun and learn, not the numbers on the board." She's reasonable, rational, and I can hear her hope that this can all be settled easily. My thudding heart isn't so sure.

He scoffs at her. "Whatever. Just get the ball to Killer Killian." It's dismissive but still an order, one that makes my hackles rise.

"Every player will get a chance to play," she reassures him and returns to my side. The boys riding the bench look at her with concern, and I'm looking at her with barely-restrained fury. I'm not mad at her, but it's ridiculous that we're having to deal with this at a fucking pee-wee game. These boys are still scared of monsters under their beds and believe in Santa Claus. We're not talking NFL contracts here. And even if we were, Kyle Bloomdale's yelled 'advice' from the bleachers wouldn't help matters.

Allyson's smile is meant to reassure the boys, but as soon as their attention is back on the play, she talks quietly out of the side of her mouth. "I think he's drunk."

Her expression doesn't change, but I can see the tension in the faint lines around her eyes.

"Are you serious?" I ask softly. I'm shocked, but maybe I shouldn't be. I'm putting some puzzle pieces together that this might be why Killian lives with his sweet grandparents and not his shit stain of a father. Twice I've seen him, and twice, he's been under the influence. "It's eleven AM. Guess we know where he was during the third quarter."

I shake my head, glancing over my shoulder and gritting my teeth to keep from calling the bastard out.

Kyle looks back, his eyes hard as he mouths his son's name and points Killian's way. Like I need a fucking reminder.

We've only got a few minutes left in the fourth, but they seem to

take forever. The rest of the parents seem to unanimously decide
that the best way to deal with Kyle is to drown him out, and they
cheer loudly and encouragingly for every single action on the field. I
do the same, making sure that the boys only hear positive feedback
about their gameplay.

But I can still hear that nasally voice cutting through the air, the
current of his ugliness undermining the experience we're trying to
give these kids. When the scorekeeper blows her whistle, signaling
the end of the game, we lose by six. So close but yet so far.

We do the line-up of high-fives between the teams and shake the
other coach's hand. Lastly, the referee comes over. "Coach Meyers?"
The boy can't be more than sixteen, but he refereed the game fairly,
cleanly. Allyson turns to offer him a handshake too, but he hands
her a piece of paper. "I'm sorry to have to do this, Coach, but I'm
required to review the league's rules with you as a complaint was
lodged."

He goes on to say that a parent from the Bulldogs complained
about one of our spectators not following the positive-only rule. I'm
not surprised, and the boys do deserve that type of support. I just
wish there'd been a way for me to get fucking Kyle off the sideline
from the start of the game. But my way of handling it would've
resulted in someone calling the cops.

I inhale deeply, blinking slowly as I listen to the kid. I'm trying
my damnedest to not be intimidating, curling my shoulders in and
hunching down to listen. He's just doing his job and is honestly
doing it very well. He's a damn fine referee who made some tough
calls today.

When he's done with his spiel, I offer a hand. "Good job, man.
Reffing is a hard gig and you did great today. You a player yourself?" I scan his body, used to sizing up opponents. "Wide receiver?"

"Yes, sir." He nods, still shaking my hand. "Max Womack. It's an
honor to meet you, Brutal. I mean, Mr. Tannen." I laugh at how the
kid went from all self-assured confidence to bumbling over his own
tongue. "Uh, if it's not too much trouble, would you sign a ball for
me? Well, actually, it's for my coach at school. Maybe you know
him? Coach Wilson?"

"Coach Wilson is still at the high school?" I ask in shock. "What's he, like seventy now?" I take the ball and marker he hands me.

"Oh, if you don't mind, can you sign it Brutal Tannen? You're kind of a legend, an inspiration to us guys, I guess." I chuckle. I'm nothing special, just a guy who used to be good at being an immovable force. *My talent? Being a wall,* I think wryly.

I hand the ball back, and he blows on the drying ink, saying between breaths, "It's not the same Coach Wilson. It's his son. Father-son legacy thing, you know?"

"Wow. I didn't know that. Pretty cool, though. Maybe I'll come by a game and watch you play, catch up with Coach."

The kid looks like I offered him a winning lottery ticket.

The quick exchange ends abruptly when Kyle interrupts the conversation, pulling on my bicep to turn me around. "What the fuck, Brutal? Killian barely got any ball time. That's why we fucking lost." He points back at the bench where the boys have stopped eating their post-game snack of Mama Louise's zucchini bread and are instead watching with dropped jaws as Kyle curses loudly.

I reverse my posture from the unintimidating curve I adopted to not scare the ref, broadening my shoulders and bowing my chest out. "Mr. Bloomdale," I say quietly, my voice more of a harsh hiss than anything else.

To his credit, the referee steps forward, obviously quoting from the referee handbook. "Sir, as the referee for this game, I have to ask you to refrain from using vulgar language and also to lower your voice. As I was just explaining to Coach Meyers, a complaint was filed against the Wildcats because of your behavior. Further actions that go against the code of conduct will resort in a game suspension for the entire team. Also, spectators are not allowed on the field so I will have to ask you to step back."

Ballsy kid. I like him already, but I don't want him getting hurt. I turn, blocking the kid and putting myself in the line of fire. I'm who he wants, anyway.

"Kyle."

His eyes are slow to leave Max, Kyle's head turning before his eyes follow, but when he locks on me, they narrow. "Killian played.

Everyone played. It was a good game, but you need to shut the fuck up."

I never said I was good with words. In fact, I'm pretty sure I've loudly and somewhat proudly said that I suck with words. But I'm trying. I don't want to punch this asshole out in front of his kid, but the jump to fists over words is habitual.

The threat of impending violence must be coming through loud and clear, though, because Allyson bravely steps forward, thwarting the staredown Kyle and I are locked in. For my part, I'm clear-eyed and thoughtful. He's red-eyed and blustery, smelling like cheap whiskey and trying to playing tough. I don't need to play at it. I can simply send him to the hospital without flinching.

"Mr. Bloomdale, please calm down." Allyson holds up a hand, palm toward Kyle, imploring him. In the history of histories, I don't think anyone has ever calmed down from being told to do so and today is not an exception to that rule. "There are children watching."

I can hear her reaching into her professional bag of tricks again, but Kyle's not having it.

Somewhere in his brain, a switch is flipped and he turns redder. His voice gets louder and his arm movements more erratic. "Stop telling me to calm down! You did my son wrong and I won't stand for it. Killian's the best fucking football player you've got, and if you can't see that, then fuck you." He points at Max first, then me. "And fuck you." Before sticking his finger in Allyson's face. "And fuck you, bitch."

It happens so quickly and subtly, but her façade crumbles and she flinches as Kyle's finger gets too close. Her eyes slip shut and she turns away from his touch, like she's preparing . . .

Red. I see actual, literal red in my vision.

Allyson said Jeremy didn't treat her 'nice', but I see it now. See the instinctive reflex to protect herself in Allyson's movements. My heart breaks at the same time hot fury rushes through me, bitter and acidic, making me want to rage that someone could treat anyone that way. But most of all, disbelieving that anyone would treat *her* that way. My Allyson is special, a sweet angel who deserves the best of everything life can offer.

This is what she's holding back, the shadows that haunted her and weighed her down, making her question her own judgement and not trust anyone. I know it as sure as I know that I love her and she loves me.

But I can't deal with it right now. I have to protect her from the actual threat right in front of us, not the one that lurks in her past.

"Get the fuck away from her," I boom, stepping between Allyson and Kyle and slapping his hand out of the air. Yeah, I'm cussing in front of the kids too because they definitely heard that, but I can't even care. Not when it's Allyson at risk.

"You need to leave, go home or wherever the hell it is you hide. Rethink how you're treating people with a sober head because you're a loser and Killian deserves better. Thank God for his grand-parents."

I chance the quickest glance across the field to see them standing halfway across the field. It looks like they tried walking over but had to stop. Mr. Bloomdale is helping prop Mrs. Bloomdale up and she's crying softly.

The split-second look away is a mistake on my part, a poor judgement when I'm known for being observant and aware. Kyle takes advantage of my quick distraction, throwing a messy right hook my way.

Instinctively, I duck and throw up a block. He's untrained and drunk, which make him unpredictable and sloppy, and as his right arm moves away from me, he tries to come back with a left hook. It's a wide swing, wild and uncontrolled, and instead of hitting the intended target of my jaw, it connects with Allyson's cheek.

I see it happen in slow-motion, hear her cry of surprised shock and pain, and even feel her bump into me from the force of the hit.

My fist connects with Kyle's gut before I even think to do it, the reflexive movement primal and instinctual. He grunts, grinning like a fucking maniac, like we're goofing off as he flails back, his punches bouncing off my arms like raindrops. I follow up the first gut shot with one to his jaw, dropping him like a sack of potatoes.

The crazy drunk fuck is somehow still conscious, laughing mani-acally. "Good one, Brutal." He seems okay. Alcohol can do that to you, dull the pain enough that you think everything's fine until the buzz wears off and you feel the damage.

I spin to check on Allyson, scared to see the damage Kyle's punch did to her. She's soft and sober, and I'm afraid the violence will have done more than fuck up her face.

But she's not behind me. Max, the kid's eyes wide with shock, holds up his hands like I'm about to punch him too.

"Al?" I grunt.

Max points, and I follow the direction he's indicating. Allyson is full-on sprinting across the field toward the boys. I have a moment of hope that her Mama Bear instincts are kicked in and she's just protecting the team from the ugliness. "Allyson?" I call.

She looks over her shoulder, her face gone pale white and blank. It's the blankness that scares me. There's no fear, no surprise, just utter vacancy as she grabs Cooper's hand and drags him toward the parking lot.

"Allyson!" I holler again, louder this time.

She doesn't turn around even though I see her shoulders creep an inch higher, so I know she heard me.

Michelle runs after her, telling Liam to come on. "I'll get her. Handle that." She points at Kyle, who's laid on the grass curled into the fetal position with his hands folded together under his cheek. He looks like an angel except for the blood on his busted lip and the fact that it's not even lunch time and he's passed out drunk on a kids' football field.

I don't give a single flying fuck about Kyle. He can choke on his own goddamn vomit for all I care. My every cell is telling me to chase Allyson. She's a flight-er, but maybe now I know why. Maybe running is her way of fighting, not a retreat but a move for preservation. A smart strategy, but it kills me that she had to learn that.

Motherfucker! Not my Allyson.

Along with the urge to follow her is a desire to find this Jeremy asswipe and teach him a lesson or two on how to be 'nice' to women. He fucking deserves it. I take two steps, following Allyson's tracks, when I hear a noise behind me.

Max clears his throat, louder this time. "Want me to call the police? He totally threw the first punch so I've got your back, Brutal."

I look to Mr. and Mrs. Bloomdale, both of whom are sobbing openly and holding Killian against them as they do their best to plead with me through their watery eyes. They're their own little dysfunctional family in the middle of the chaos Kyle has created, trying to find something resembling normalcy for their grandson in the mess their son left behind.

"No, that's okay. Thanks for keeping your shit together though. Speaks volumes about the man you are." Some of the shock of the situation seems to have worn off, and he nods politely like this is just a normal post-game wrap-up.

"He's obviously banned." Max tilts his head to the snoring fucker on the ground. "If he shows up, the Wildcats will forfeit."

"Understood." I walk to the Bloomdales with my head held high, ready for their harsh words and judgment. But instead of contempt, I find sadness.

"Thanks for not calling the cops on him. He used to be such a good boy, but we lost him along the way. We'll get him back to rehab again and pray this time it sticks." Mrs. Bloomdale rubs Killian's shoulder soothingly.

"Come on, Killian. We've got a team meeting real quick, 'kay?" I look to his grandparents, who nod understandingly. When Killian lifts his head, there's a healthy dose of fear there. I offer my hand anyway, feeling a real doubt about whether he's going to take it. He just watched me beat the shit out of his dad, so I'm probably the monster in his eyes.

But he looks behind me at his dad on the ground and then takes my hand. I can't imagine what strength that requires. He's got a core of good in him, this kid. His grandparents should be so proud because they're the ones doing a damn fine job of instilling that in him.

I take a knee when I get close to the boys. "Guys, I am so sorry you saw that. First and foremost, let me say that fighting is very rarely the right thing to do. Almost *never*, which is something that took me a long time to learn. I want you to learn from my mistakes and not have to make them on your own because they hurt . . . you and other people." I hold up my hand, knuckles red from the punches, and look back at Kyle in the grass.

"On the other hand, you look out for each other—for the team-mate beside you, for the person beside you, for what's right. You support and protect people when they need it and always do the right thing. I know it might look ugly and even scary, but Kyle was being mean to Coach Allyson and I had to protect her."

'Mean' is putting what Kyle did so very lightly. I'm worried about Al, not just her emotions and reaction to the fight but her cheek, too. Did Kyle break a bone, hurt her eye, loosen teeth?

Fuck, I have to get to her. Now.

I need to hold her, check her over, and soothe whatever freakout she's in the midst of. And I have some questions I'm going to need answered because I think it's time to lay it all out. I've been patient. Fuck, have I been patient. But no longer.

Today might've made her scurry back into her shell to hide away from me, but if I have to, I'll follow her into the depths of her mind and drag her kicking and screaming back into the sunshine and into my arms. She deserves that. I want to give that to her.

A bright future for the three of us.

I signal Mike, glad he could make the first game even if it's all gone to hell in a handbasket. I point back at Kyle. "Help me with him, will ya?"

"Nah, we got him." He points between himself and Bobby, who's standing at the ready. Actually, with the snarl of wrinkles at the neck of his shirt, he looks like someone might've been holding him back from getting all up in my not-even-a-fair-fight with Kyle.

Bobby's dark eyes meet mine, filled with emotion. I don't need his apology. I can see straight into that guy's mind, and half the time, predict what he's gonna say.

"Go after Allyson and make sure she's okay," he growls. His message is clear—she's one of us now. He might not get it, he might not trust her fully, and hell if I even know what made her run out of here looking like she'd seen a ghost. But he's got my back when the shit hits the fan, no matter what.

"Thanks, man."

And I'm off to get my woman. Because she might be a fleer-slash-fighter, but whatever she is, she's mine. And I'm hers. And we're gonna figure this shit out right now. Together.

CHAPTER 28

ALLYSON

One second I'm trying to calm down Kyle Bloomdale, and the next his finger's in my face and he's calling me a bitch. It's not the first time I've been called names. Hell, it's not even the first time that's happened this month. I'm a mediator, after all, and my job is helping angry people on two sides of an issue come to some sort of resolution. It's sometimes an ugly process.

But I reflexively flinch. I feel the too-familiar electric jolt as my muscles tense, and it sends a wash of shame through me. I don't do this anymore. I worked too hard to not be this person ever again. Scared and shrinking is not me. I am bold and bright. I just lost that for a minute when I was with Jeremy.

So why is this happening now? Maybe it's because I've been thinking about the past a bit more the last few days, analyzing the differences between my relationship with Bruce and my marriage with Jeremy and revisiting my slow crumble under Jeremy's influence.

I know that eventually, I'll have to tell Bruce more about my marriage and divorce, but I've been putting it off, not wanting him to see me as the broken woman I was for too long.

Bruce steps between Kyle and me, and for the briefest of

seconds, I feel relieved that he's going to handle this. The tension amps up, and I step back, needing to get away.

It's not far enough, though, and I don't see the punch coming before my face explodes in pain. It's hot and fiery, bright and deep all at once. I stumble backward, almost falling to my ass, but the teenage referee steadies me with a firm hand on my elbow.

In slow motion, I see Bruce's face twist in rage as he bares his teeth. His fist lifts, connecting with Kyle's belly with a thud. Kyle throws wild punches back, barely any landing, and even the ones that do, Bruce doesn't show any sign of even feeling them. Bruce punches Kyle once more and he goes down.

It's over in a flash, but my blood is thundering through my body, a roar in my ears blocking out everything and everyone.

No, no, no, no. I can't do this. He hit me. I have to get out of here.

Cooper! Where's Cooper?

I hear Bruce calling my name, but I grab Cooper's hand. "Let's go, Cooper. Now." He starts to say something, but when he looks at my face, he quiets and lets me drag him to the car. "Buckle up, honey."

The drive is fast, my back ramrod straight as I check the rearview mirror for the tenth time. Nothing is behind us but open road.

"What's wrong, Mom? Why were Coach B and that guy fighting?" His voice is hesitant, but as I meet his eyes in the rearview mirror, the blue so similar to mine, he looks worried.

"It's fine, honey. It's fine." My voice trails off, not answering him because I'm mostly trying to reassure myself.

Cooper's quiet after that, and my brain whirls, replaying the scene at the football field but overlapping the way I felt with Kyle's pointing finger in my face with Jeremy's accusations and insults.

It's hitting me hard, flashbacks of arguments and sneered insults that made me feel small, accusations that made me doubt myself. I haven't had a panic attack like this in years. I didn't think it would ever happen again, but here I am.

My breathing quickens, trying to force oxygen into my too-tight chest, and my whole body gets tingly as adrenalin floods my veins.

Rationally, I know there's nothing to be scared of here in my car. I left the threat behind at the football field. But my brain doesn't care about rational and reasonable logic.

Bitch. His finger in my face. He hit me. Jeremy. Kyle. Bruce. People watching.

Run. Save Cooper. Run.

They're not complete thoughts, just words floating across my mind like a scrolling marquee, the red LED lights flashing in warning.

My fingers tap on the steering wheel, but I can't find a rhythm and it's more drumming than the anxiety-alleviating pattern I usually employ.

I pull into the driveway at home, a fleeting thankfulness at the closeness of my house trying to take root, but my brain swats the positive thought away like an annoying mosquito. "Inside. Let's go."

Cooper unbuckles his seatbelt and rushes inside with me, fear etched on his face.

Fuck. Fuck. Fuck. He doesn't need to see this. He shouldn't have seen that at the field. Is he scared of me? Bruce? Kyle?

The small bit of control and awareness I have takes hold for a moment. I squat down, eyes meeting Cooper's, and I promise him, "Everything's fine. Mom just got a bit nervous at the field so I thought we should come home." I can hear the false robotic note to my voice, but I can't change it. It's taking all I have to speak this calmly and not scare him further.

"Okay, Mom." I hug him to me, letting the sweaty boy smell of him ground me, feeling him solidly and safely in my arms. Tears prick at the corners of my eyes, hot and painful, but I blink them away so he doesn't see.

"Go to your room for a little bit for me, okay?" He nods and scurries down the hallway.

It's the last bit of restraint I have. Even as I know it's ridiculous, I'm in survival mode, and I can't help but check the lock on the front door and then the windows. I peek through the blinds, looking at the driveway that's empty except for my car.

He's not coming.

I'm not sure who 'he' even is . . . Kyle, Jeremy, Bruce? All of them? The image of the three of them converging on my lawn is ridiculous but not enough to stop the panic.

I'm glad . . . about Kyle and about Jeremy, who's not a threat, anyway, since I don't even know where he is now. I'm sad that Bruce isn't here to hold me and soothe this panic away.

I don't need him. I can do this on my own.

I sit down in the living room floor, crossing my legs in front of me and laying my hands on my knees. I close my eyes, inhaling as I count in my head, holding the too-deep breath until it stretches my chest, then exhaling. I repeat it several times, so many times that I lose count and drift into my subconsciousness, feeling dissociated from my body as if I'm floating.

Knock, knock, knock.

The firm knock on the door startles me. But I'm slightly calmer now and able to get up and peek through the peephole. It's Michelle.

Relief, cool and cleansing, washes over me.

"Open the door, Allyson. Now." She's doing that mom voice thing again, which under any other circumstances would make me smile. Now, I just do as she says, slowly cracking the door.

She busts through anyway. "Where's Cooper?"

"In his room."

Michelle looks at Liam. "Hey, can you go play with Cooper for a bit? We need some Grown-up Talk Time." I can hear the capitals, like she's naming a game we're going to play or a show we're gonna watch. I think I'm the show, though.

Once Liam is behind Cooper's closed door, Michelle narrows her eyes, all cursory lightness dissipating. "First things first, come sit down and let me look at that cheek."

Her nursing no-shit-allowed attitude shines as she shoves me toward the kitchen and plops me into a chair. She presses on the bone, causing me to wince, but she seems satisfied.

"Not broken, eye looks reactive to light, so all good. But you're going to have a hell of a shiner tomorrow." Her exam done, she leans back and glares at me, so many questions in the set of her lips as they press together like she doesn't know where to start with me.

"That was crazy, huh?" I try, starting slow.

"Yes, you were. Wanna tell me about it?" she answers.

I shake my head. "What? Not me! That dad, Kyle, and Bruce. They were fighting, like actual punches, for fuck's sake." The image is burned onto my retinas, and I close my eyes to consciously choose another image to see on my lids.

Michelle's hands cover mine. "Honey, I'm a nurse. I know what a panic attack looks like. And I know they're not always triggered by something that makes sense. But sometimes, they rear up for exactly the reasons you'd think. Talk to me, Allyson."

I pause, swallowing. I've talked about it. It's not like I haven't dealt with shit. But today is proof that even after all these years, deep down inside, there's still a little demon just waiting to get out of his box and fuck my life up.

I take back my control, telling him to fuck off as bits and pieces pour out of my mouth. I don't get too deep into it with Michelle now, not when it's feeling especially fresh, but it helps to be more transparent with her. I pace but ultimately sit back down, crossing my legs and putting my hands back on my knees to re-center myself.

She gasps and cusses and asks if she can hunt Jeremy down as I fill her in on what happened so many years ago. A tiny blip of time in the big scheme of my life but formative in a way I hate. And in a way I love . . . because that hell also made me into a mom.

It's quiet as Michelle processes, so the knock on the door sounds especially ominous.

"Allyson!" Bruce sounds scared. My big beast of a man, and I've scared the shit out of him.

CHAPTER 29

BRUCE

I mean to knock, I swear I do, but even to my ears, it sounds like a pounding. "Allyson!" I call out, wanting her to know it's me and hoping it makes a difference.

The door cracks open, and I see Michelle's dark eyes peek out. I don't let her say a word, too afraid she'll tell me to leave, so I push right in. "Where is she? Allyson?"

It's then I see her.

Al's sitting on the living room floor, her skin pale, but there's a high flush to her cheeks making her look like a porcelain doll. But she's not that fragile, and the tense set of her jaw, her ramrod-straight back, and the ice in her blue eyes tell me that she's *furious*.

At me? Fuck, I hope not, but whatever I did, I'll apologize and promise to never do it again. Unless it's to protect her, love her . . . because that shit's happening no matter what.

All of my urges to demand answers evaporate in the face of the possibility of losing her, and I'm ready to beg and plead with no shame.

For her, I'll do anything.

I drop to my knees beside her, reaching out hesitantly. I'm waiting for her rage to unleash on me, for her to have danced so far back that I can't reach her, but she sits frozen, not recoiling away from my touch, but not leaning into it, either. The distance is mere inches, but it feels like a chasm has opened its gaping mouth between us. So slowly, I get closer, my breath frozen in my chest in anticipation of her reaction. She watches blankly as I get closer, and only when my fingers touch her face does she crumble.

The stiff line of her back collapses and her soft cheek melts into my hand. Needing more and thankfully sensing she does too, I pull her into my lap, rearranging us so that she's cradled sideways with her head against my chest. I hold her tightly, wishing I could crawl inside her to know what she's thinking and feeling or maybe let her crawl into my heart so she can feel surrounded by my love. We rock naturally, my hand running down the length of her unrestrained hair as I soothe her and the reassure the monster inside me that she's okay.

Michelle clears her throat and says gently, "I'm going to take the boys for the night. Holler if you need anything. And Allyson?"

Allyson raises her head from my chest to look at her friend. They have a silent conversation I'm not privy to, but I can tell there's something deep being said between them. Michelle's next statement confirms that. "You need to tell him."

My gut drops at the confirmation that there is something to tell. I mean, I know that something's wrong, but I guess on some level, I was hoping I might have misread everything. I'd rather that than what I think Allyson's about to say.

That I've lost her, that even as she's wrapped in my arms, she's already decided that I'm not enough or maybe that I'm too much of a bad thing. Fuck, that hurts.

Michelle calls down the hall, and Cooper and Liam show up. Their lips are pulled down in matching frowns, and they both eye Allyson's position in my lap.

I offer Liam a fist and he bumps it. Behind him, I meet Cooper's eyes and hold my fist out for him. He didn't hear my explanation at the field, and there's a chance he's terrified of me after seeing me go after Kyle like that. I speak slow and low, with intention I hope he can feel. "I've got our girl, Cooper."

It sounds like the simplest truth in the world, but with Allyson, nothing is simple. Other than the fact that I'm not going any fucking where without her. She can fight me, she can refuse to let me in, but I'm tough enough to withstand it and rough enough to dance with her again if that's where this is going. I got her back once, and I'll get her back again.

Cooper bumps my fist with a nod like he understands the adult shit that's going on. If he does, I wish he'd explain it to me.

Then they're gone and I'm alone with my girl.

The words tumble out too fast, but I pray she can understand. "I am so sorry, baby. I know I shouldn't have fought like that, especially not in front of the boys, but when he hit you, I . . ." My voice chokes in my throat, dying as I growl instead, "I need to see, please."

She lets me lift her chin gently with one finger, and I peer into her eyes as much as check over her cheekbone. The blue depths are empty. Whatever she's feeling is hidden behind walls again. So many walls, so many defenses.

"Michelle checked it, said there's nothing broken, but it'll bruise." She says it easily, like she's not talking about some asshole leaving fucking marks on her perfect skin.

"Goddamn it. I'm so sorry if all that scared you—*if I scared you*. I know I'm a monster who fights more than I should, but I couldn't let him . . . he hit you, Allyson." My voice is a dark rumble that promises retribution, the pain of that connection between her pretty face and Kyle's ugly fist echoing in my head again. It's a sound I won't ever unhear.

I swallow thickly, holding her too tightly, but I can't let go. I won't let go. Not even as she wiggles against me, trying to put space between us that I don't want.

"You're not a monster. What are you talking about?"

Allyson's confusion is bordering on alarm, and I need to settle down again. I don't want her cowering in my arms.

"It's okay, I know. I'm so sorry. I won't fight anymore, ever again, if that's what you need me to do. Anything for you, Al. Anything." The begging plea to not leave me pierces the air.

"Bruce." Allyson pushes against me, putting space between our upper bodies even as she stays in my lap. "I think you're confused."

"Hell yes, I am," I huff miserably. "But I love you. That's the one thing I'm not fucking confused about at all." I pin her in place with my eyes and hold her hips, not letting her get away. Not that she's trying to, but just in case.

She grips my cheeks this time, pulling my beard sharply to get my attention. "I don't think you're a monster." Her brows knit together and she shakes her head. "I had a panic attack."

I was all ready to argue my case, but that stops me in my tracks. "A panic attack?"

Her hands lower to her lap, clasping together as her head falls to look at them. "Yes, I used to have them . . . when I was married . . . and for a while after. But I haven't had one in years until today."

She sounds ashamed, which I don't understand. It's not like she chose to have a panic attack or something. Her body just overreacted? I think that's what a panic attack is, anyway, but I'm no expert.

"What made it happen today, Al? Tell me so I can make sure I don't do it again."

She looks up, the tiniest light peeking through her walls. "Cocky much? It wasn't because of you—well, not *entirely* because of you." She tilts her head, angling it as her brows bounce up and then back down into a frown.

It's the first spark of my girl I've seen, and I want to swing from the fucking rafters in celebration. "Can you just tell me what happened then?"

"That's not an easy thing to do. I'm embarrassed and mad, and I don't want this to change how you see me. I'm better than this now, so much better than this, but today was like a perfect storm aimed right at my weakest parts."

Her shoulders curl in, and my first instinct is to tell her that she never has to be embarrassed, not with me. But she's entitled to feel whatever she's feeling, so I keep my mouth shut and simply press my lips to her forehead, letting her know I'm here and to take her time.

LAUREN LANDISH

She starts slowly, her words halting and soft. "I've been doing a lot of thinking lately, about us and about Jeremy. Not because I miss him or anything." She huffs like that's ridiculous, easing a fear I didn't even know I had.

I remember the slick and fancy guy I saw her with at college that day. Maybe I'm wrong about my suspicions, and if so, I could understand her missing her ex. It's hard to shut love off, even when things go wrong and it's been a long time. We're proof of that.

"But with him fresh on my mind, Kyle's finger in my face and calling me a bitch dredged up some ugly memories I'd rather stay buried. And the punch . . ." She chews on her lip worriedly, her eyes darting left and right unseeingly. I think she's lost to the past.

My hunch isn't wrong. I can feel it in my gut. I saw her flinch and shrink like she wanted to be a smaller target. I force my voice to be neutral even though my insides are on the verge of an angry eruption. "Did Jeremy hit you, Allyson?"

She nods absently. "Yes."

I'm furious and on the edge of spinning out and hunting this fucker down, but he's not my priority. Allyson is. So I say nothing, burying my face in her neck, her hair strangling me, but I burrow in deeper and hold her tight, my fingers digging into her skin but I can't stop. I don't want it to be true. Not her, not my Allyson.

She wraps her arms around my neck, scratching at my scalp and cooing platitudes. I should be comforting her, but I let her soothe me too, praying it's a sign that we're both in this together.

"It was only once," she rationalizes.

"One time too many," I state unequivocally. "I've hurt a lot of people, Al, mostly on the field, but I would . . . *could* never hurt you."

Her arms fall, and she pushes against me to get up. I can't let her go, but one look in her eyes tells me she's getting antsy, maybe even flighty, so I let her stand, staying at the ready to chase if she runs. She paces back and forth across the living room, from the front door to the kitchen, nibbling on her lip with her arms crossed tightly over her middle.

"The slap wasn't the bad part, honestly. It was everything

leading up to it, the years of little comments cutting me down inch by inch and isolating me from everything and everyone I knew, including my parents." She stops pacing and looks at me, her eyes shockingly blue in her pale face. "Do you know what gaslighting is?"

I don't bother racking my brain for the unfamiliar word. I just shake my head in answer.

She resumes her walk. "I didn't either. I just thought I was crazy until my therapist gave it a name. It's a kind of manipulation, little things that sound stupid but accumulate and change your perceptions of everything, even yourself. He made me doubt everything to the point I was confused all the time. I felt like I was losing my mind and didn't trust anything, especially myself because I was obviously so stupid. I only trusted him because he loved me in spite of my shortcomings."

"What the hell? I don't know what to say. There are *so* many things wrong with that. Who'd do something like that? Why would someone do that?" I am so far out of my element here, but if this is where Allyson's been in our years apart, I need to understand. I want to understand her.

"It started out small, even funny at first. I'd set my glasses down by the computer where I was working and go get a drink. I'd come back and they'd be moved. He'd laugh at how forgetful I was, like 'Ha-ha, you can't even keep up with glasses, silly girl,' and it was a little enough thing that I believed him. We've all done things on auto-pilot like put the remote control in the fridge or something, so it seemed plausible and I didn't realize for a long time that he was moving them."

I nod. "I can see that, I guess. Then what?"

She swallows. "It wasn't silly games anymore. But he didn't jump from hiding my glasses straight to the bad. It was incremental. Things got worse so slowly that I didn't even realize it was happening until it was too late."

She sits on the couch, and I turn, sitting at her feet as she delves into her past, offering up a story. "One time, there was this super-fancy Italian restaurant coming to town, and as soon as he saw the sign in the window, he wanted to go. I tried to tell him that it was too expensive and out of our budget. I mean, I was working and he was in his last semester of law school and we had a baby. Five-hundred-dollar Michelin-star food wasn't happening. But I wanted to do something nice for him, so I made lasagna. It was almost half the weekly grocery budget for all that meat and cheese, but he raved over it so it seemed worth it. I was so happy to have done something right."

A small smile lifts her lips, but there's a wry twist to the smile, not happiness like she's saying. "The weekend the restaurant opened, I made it again as sort of an apology that we couldn't go. He called it disgusting, dumped the whole 9x13 pan of it in the trash and spat on it. That was bad enough, but then he started ranting that if I loved him, I'd know that he doesn't even like lasagna, that his favorite Italian food was fettuccine alfredo. Two weeks later, he'd bugged his dad enough that he invited him to try out the fancy restaurant. Jeremy told his parents I couldn't come because I wouldn't leave Cooper, not even for an hour to have dinner. So he went alone and came back with a to-go box. I thought he'd brought me dinner after all, to be nice or something." She shakes her head. "I should've known better. He opened it, showed me the lasagna inside, saying it was his favorite and that the restaurant's was so good, he got one for his dinner the next night. He was baiting me, eager to get a rise out of me. This was early on, so I questioned him, and he told me he'd always loved lasagna, hated fettuccine alfredo, and had never told me otherwise. He laughed out loud when I tried to remind him that he'd thrown an entire pan of lasagna away, telling me that he would never do that because one, it's his favorite, and two, it's so expensive to make and we don't have the money to squander on things like that."

"He sounds like a prick," I spit out bitterly. A memory of her lasagna and her sweet smile at my complimenting how good it was runs through my mind. It'd seemed like such a little thing to me, but I can see now that it was major to her.

She sighs. "Yeah, but it was more than that. It was his being a prick in a sneaky, underhanded way that made me doubt myself and question reality. It wasn't that he threw the food away but that he said he never did it. And after a while, when he did things like that, I started to believe him over my own eyes, my own memories, my own thoughts. And like the narcissist he is, he basked in my needing him for everything even as he called me names for it."

I'm still not sure I get exactly what she's saying. I'm a simple guy, and this gaslighting sounds complicated and nuanced. But I can grasp that he was an asshole and she got away and divorced his sorry ass. I'd love to think that's all that matters, but whatever damage he did to her, it's still written in the scars on her heart. Today's proof of that.

"He tried to make you weak, but you were so strong you got out, baby," I say reassuringly, though I'm not sure it's the right thing to say.

Her frown is deep. "Not because he hit me. He didn't physically lay a hand on me except for that once, but he was too rough sometimes." I don't realize I'm growling, thinking she means he was hard on her in the bedroom in a way she didn't want, until she sets her palm on my chest. "Not like that. Sex with him was bland. He wanted the whole good girl, missionary, once a week, in the dark. And I figured it was just different because it was someone different." Her eyes meet mine, so much heartache and pain right there on the surface. She's not even hiding it from me, and I gladly take it in, carrying the weight of it with her.

"Again, it started little . . . bumping into me in the hallway or squeezing my fingers too hard when we were holding hands. He made it seem like I was bumbling and high-strung. The slap, though . . ."

She interrupts her own train of thought. "I don't even remember what brought the whole thing on, what drove him to that point that time. Was it work? Me? Cooper? Just a natural progression of our fucked-up relationship? I don't know. But I was standing in the kitchen, Cooper on my hip with my arm wrapped around him to keep him steady and a spoon in the other hand. I was making soup. I can remember that but not what triggered Jeremy."

Her eyes go vacant for a second and then she shrugs like it's inconsequential.

"He was yelling, and I was numbly tuning him out, only listening for the tone changes that signaled things were going to get better or worse but not hearing the words. He knew somehow, even though my back was to him. He grabbed my arm and spun me around, pointing in my face. I can see his face twisted in rage, white spittle gathered at the corners of his mouth, but I can't hear the words, not in my memories. I guess I wasn't reacting the way he wanted because he reared back and slapped me across the face. That woke me up, the hot burn of my skin, the pain in the muscle below, the stars dotting the black in my vision." She blinks, lost to the memory.

"So you left?"

She blinks again, coming back to the present time. "No, not at first. In the moment, he seemed horrified and apologized, said work was stressing him out and he promised it'd never happen again. It wasn't like some instantaneous wake-up call like in the movies because it almost wasn't a surprise. We'd been slowly getting closer to that for years at that point. It was the next morning. I was barely awake, just rolled out of bed and went into the kitchen to get a cup of coffee. He was sitting there at the table, reading the paper as usual. He told me good morning like everything was fine, just a normal day like any other, and I thought we'd gotten past it. Until I turned around and he screamed in shock, jumping in his chair. 'What happened to your face?' he asked me, pointing at what I later realized was a pretty ugly bruise along my cheekbone."

She delicately fingers her cheek, and I make the connection of why today's events set her off so badly. The yelling, the finger pointing, the hit . . . all unfortunately so familiar, the perfect storm, as she called it.

"I was so confused and tried to tell him that I accepted his apology for slapping me. He accused me of doing it to myself, even saying that I was going to try to use it against him. But I knew, and I think he realized his hold on me was tenuous, in this at least. He switched to telling me that I must've just slept funny and that it wasn't a bruise, just that I'd laid funny. He even said I'd tossed and turned all night. 'Maybe you bumped the nightstand,' he said."

She lifts her brow at the ridiculousness of that. "The moment I lay in bed that night, forcing myself to lie on my back and propping up with an extra pillow, with him telling me that I'd sleep better that way and not do any more damage to my face, was it. I listened to him snore and felt the bruise on my face. I knew how it got there. What's more, I knew I knew. I wanted to ignore it, but every time I opened my mouth, I felt that tenderness as a reminder of what had really happened."

"I did some soul searching lying there in bed that night. I'd been holding Cooper, just a tiny toddler, when Jeremy hit me. All I could think was that if Jeremy could do this to me, what would he do to Cooper? How fucked up would my little boy be? I went into the relationship strong and healthy, and yet, I was cringing at loud noises, praying Jeremy would be in a good mood, and didn't trust myself to do anything right. If he'd destroyed me, Cooper wouldn't stand a chance growing up like that. I knew if I stayed, Jeremy would destroy my son too."

I embrace her, needing to touch her. "You're not destroyed, Al. Neither is Cooper."

She hugs me back but pulls away. "Not anymore, thanks to a whole hell of a lot of intensive therapy. I had to rewrite my inner voice back to being my own, and my therapist gave me some tools and tricks to help when I get nervous or anxious."

"The finger tapping patterns?" I hold my hand up, mimicking what I've seen her do, and she looks shocked.

"You noticed that?" Her eyes are wide with the slightest pink to her cheeks.

"I notice everything about you, Allyson," I say honestly.

She doesn't respond to that, which worries me, but rather continues with her awful tale. "The next day, after Jeremy went to work and I took Cooper to the babysitter's, I went into my boss's office. He was the first person I told what was happening to me, and he definitely wasn't ready for that particular bout of verbal diarrhea at nine in the morning, but he had a lawyer friend at the office before lunch. That lawyer was an absolute shark, a beast in the mediation room. He inspired me to do mediations by helping me with my divorce." She glances over to her work bag, hanging on a hook by the door. But I'm not sure she's back in the present moment yet.

"I pressed charges, had to get pictures taken of the bruising and write out pages of history. But I got an emergency restraining order that day, and Jeremy couldn't come home. He went to his parents'. There's no telling what he told them because he was their golden child. I packed up what Cooper and I needed, and we were gone forty-eight hours later, first to a domestic violence placement facility where I got some help, then to my own apartment, and a few years ago, back to Great Falls. I came back because . . . I wanted a fresh restart, I guess. And Great Falls was the last place that was a hundred percent good."

"That took so much courage, Al. More than I know." I mean it. I can't imagine making that decision after something awful happened. Truly, just changing your whole life on a dime takes big brass ones, and my girl's got them, which makes me so fucking proud of her.

She smiles in thanks at the compliment. "Divorce was done by mail so I never had to sit in the room with him. But my lawyer got Jeremy to terminate his parental rights so he can never come after Cooper. In return, there's no child support, but I don't want his money and Cooper's better off without him. He asked for the divorce to be sealed because it'd affect him at work, and I honestly didn't care because I didn't want people knowing either, but my lawyer used that to our advantage. It worked, I guess. I am strong again, Cooper is strong, and he has the life he deserves. I won't do anything to mess that up."

There's a hint of something resembling an accusation in that last bit, whether she realizes it or not. "You think I'm like your ex?" She balks, but I rush to continue, not sure I want that answer. "Look, I'm an asshole, a possessive one at that, and rough around the edges for sure. I've been in more fights than I probably should've been, but I would never hit a woman or a man who didn't deserve it. I was defending you today."

She sags. "I know, but I freaked. I can't handle that, obviously."

"Look at me, Al." She slowly lifts her eyes, meeting mine hesitantly. I can see that hamster running in her head, her eyes tormented with thoughts of kicking me out or letting me stay in her heart. Because I'm there. I know that because she's already told me she loves me. But she's scared. "Everything you want is on the other side of this fear. I'm here, waiting to give you everything, but you have to want it enough to go after it. You have to want me enough to risk it. If it helps, I swear to God, I'm a sure thing."

She snorts a tiny laugh, and it feels like the scales are weighing in my favor so I keep going. "Jeremy wanted you small and scared." Even his name on my tongue pisses me off and makes me want to rage, but I push that thought away like the mature motherfucker I am. "I never want you to be those things. I like you proud and sassy, leading me around by my dick and putting me in my place."

Her smile is bigger now, little white teeth flashing between puffy lips I want to taste. "Your place? Where's that?"

This minx is flirting with me. After all the shit she just poured out, she's flirting. I guess she's had a few years to process and make some semblance of peace with it, but it's all painfully fresh to me. But if she's flirting, I'm damn sure flirting back. "Well, in private . . . with my head between your thighs. But in public, right next to you and Cooper."

CHAPTER 30

ALLYSON

*H*is answer shocks me if I'm honest. No, that's not it.

Bruce is a good man despite the roughness, as he calls it, and I knew he wouldn't bolt on me. Even though everything I just told him . . . it's a lot. To process, to carry, to understand, to accept. I don't have any choice because it's the reality I lived through. But Bruce could walk away.

I can see that thought never enters his mind, though. The vehemence with which he says that he belongs with Cooper and me makes that crystal clear, like he believes it with his whole being.

My heart soars, my chest filling with a heated happiness. But I have to be careful. For Bruce, for me, and most of all, for Cooper. This isn't a decision to take lightly for either of us. The minute stretches with pregnant possibilities.

"Are you sure?" I steady my nerves, tapping my thigh with my fingers softly so maybe he won't notice. "If it's too much, I'd understand. I swear it."

All my walls are down, and I don't know if I can handle losing Bruce again. Before, we were stupid kids, too inexperienced to have a hard conversation, and we lost each other and so many years, so much opportunity. Now, we're adults, and this conversation is heavy but not as weighed down as my heart is. If I lose him now, I won't ever be the same. I know that with certainty. This will change me more than any of the stuff with Jeremy ever did.

Losing Bruce would break me.

I love him. I love him so much I exposed my most ugly, vulnerable parts trusting that he wouldn't look away in disappointment even while expecting him to do just that.

Bruce tilts his head, his dark eyes boring into me. I feel so . . . seen. Not that I'm invisible most of the time. I'm not exactly a shrinking violet anymore, but Bruce sees more of me than anyone ever has. And I just shone a big old spotlight on my damage and invited him to weigh in on it.

He stands up, looming over me, and from my seat on the couch I feel so tiny. Common sense for self-preservation should tell me to run, but whatever inner alarm system I have is blissfully silent. He bends down slowly, reaching for my hand to pull me to my feet too.

There's more than a foot between us, but I can feel him. A magnetic pull draws us closer to one another, the promise of contact powerful as I stare at his chest. I measure his width, I count the small threads in his T-shirt, anything to avoid his eyes.

"Allyson, I can see that hamster in your mind running so fast he's about to destroy that wheel. Listen to me." He cups my jaw firmly, forcing my chin up and my eyes to his.

This is not a lover's touch but a power move. He's not letting me hide. In my mind, I'm sitting on the scattered and empty boxes of my demons, small and broken, with my knees cradled to my chest and my face tracked with tears I haven't cried in years. But here in reality, my hands are at my sides, my eyes hopeful and begging.

"I love you. There isn't a goddamn thing you could say or do that would change that. I've loved you since I was a kid, I loved you even when you were gone from me, and I love you now. I'll always love you, Al. And when I die, I'll still love you then, so you'd better get your fine ass in the fucking dirt with me because I lost so many days with you that I don't want to miss a single one again. Ever. I love you."

Doubts, like chains, release me. Hope, like wings, lift me. I'm where I was supposed to be all along, with Bruce. There are no walls between us, no questions, no more what-ifs.

I have to believe that the past happened so we could get to where we are right now, as who we are right now. It's a different path than either of us ever plotted, but it got us to the same place, nevertheless. Together.

I lift up to my toes, keeping my eyes open as I get incrementally closer to him. He bends forward, reading my intention, and we meet in the middle. Our lips touch softly, gently writing promises to each other with every caress.

Bruce releases my jaw, his hands tracing heat down my sides before wrapping around my back. I squeeze at his biceps, digging my nails in to make sure he's real and not some figment my imagination has drummed up. But he's remarkably solid and hard under my hands and groans into my mouth at the sharp bite of my trimmed nails. "Fuck, Allyson."

He sounds as emotionally wrung out as I am, but thankful, so thankful that I'm here in his arms finally as he holds me tight, my cheek pressed to his chest. The rumble of his words vibrates against me as he murmurs into my hair. "You are so goddamn beautiful, woman. Outside," I feel his fingers toying with the loose ends of my hair, "and inside."

He squeezes me again, the smallest shudder going through him. "So strong, so brave," he whispers, and then quiets. After a silent breath, he continues, "You turned your pain into power and wear it like a crown. Don't shrink yourself for me or anyone. Be this big hearted, loud, proud, amazing woman that you are. Because she is fucking stunning. I want it all, the full spectrum of whatever you're feeling, thinking - whatever it is, I can take it, always. Just share it with me, share your heart with me…"

He's still pleading his case, doesn't believe that he's had my heart all along too. "I love you," I say into his chest. "I always have."

"Fuck, baby." The words are choked out, a sense of completeness surrounding us. There's a finality to the moment, but also an exciting fresh start at the same time.

Yes, that's what I want. I'm naked emotionally, so bare and open that it spills over to my adrenalin-filled body. I let go of Bruce's arms to pull at my own shirt, wiggling to get it up in the tight space between us.

"Al?" Bruce questions delicately, though his voice is pure gravel.

"Fuck me, Bruce. No more defenses, no more secrets, no more 'before'. Everything changes right here, right now. It's just us, and I love you." I've never been surer of anything in my life. This is the moment everything begins.

"I love you too, but we don't have to right now. I know you're raw." His words are ones of tenderness, of sweetness, and I appreciate that. But it's not what I want, it's not what we need.

I find myself, the bold and brash girl who lived life wide open with no fear. She hid for so long, but I've got her back now and she's dancing on top of those demon boxes like she's a fucking queen. I get my shirt off, tossing it mindlessly behind me. Bruce's eyes lock on my breasts. They're heavy with need, my nipples hard against my thin bra.

"Bruce." I wait for his eyes to drift up, which takes a flatteringly long second like he can't look his fill of me. When he does meet my gaze, I can see the fiery, smoldering heat there in his dark eyes and also the warm depth of love.

"I want to start over right now with you buried so deep inside me that we're one, finally. Always. Like we were meant to be. I want you to take me to the bedroom and fuck me. Hard, rough. Show me that you know I can take it, that I can handle you at your best. Don't treat me like I'm damaged. Fuck me, Bruce." My voice is steady, no doubt that I mean every word.

His jaw is hard, his words fierce. "You're not fucking damaged, Al. You're perfect, and you're *mine*. Just like you were always meant to be."

He pushes at me, leaving no doubt about where we're going or who's in charge here. We're dancing, but it's not like before. This isn't me unsure of anything. This is him stepping me back toward my bedroom to take me, both of us knowing it's exactly what I want.

When he shuts the door behind us, it's like all the air gets sucked out of the room and I can only breathe him. Sweat and earth and the underlying musk that is all Bruce surrounds me.

He reaches behind his neck, pulling his shirt over his head without his eyes ever leaving mine. "Get naked, baby." The gruff order washes over me, bringing goosebumps out along my flesh. "I don't want anything between us ever again. Not even a fucking pair of panties."

I swear to God, I almost come right then and there. A shudder of pleasure shoots down my spine as I reach behind my back to undo my bra.

Bruce is faster, dropping his shorts and toeing off his tennis shoes at the same time. I freeze, my fingers in the waistband of my own shorts, when I see his thick cock bared before me. I don't think. I just do exactly what I want.

I drop to my knees in front of him.

"Allyson?" he grits out. He wants this from me, but he's still holding back, being careful with me as he watches my every reaction.

I glare up at him in challenge and lick a long line along the underside of his cock, from his balls to his crown. I lay a chaste kiss there, letting the bead of precum paint my lips. "Do you want me to kiss you sweetly and softly?"

I do it again, the barest flutter of teasing contact that I know won't get him where we're going, as I watch his abs jump in response.

He growls, and I reward him with a suck along the very tip, a promise of more. "Or do you want me to suck you off deep in my throat?"

His hand fists his cock, tightly staving off the pleasure even my slight words brought. His other hand works into my hair, tilting my head up to force my eyes to his. He searches my face, wanting to be sure. I nod slightly, the movement pulling my hair ever so faintly in his hand, and open my lips in invitation.

"Fuck, baby."

I know that tone. I've got him. My Bruce, the dirty-talking, rough-fucking god who brings out a side of me that only he can—the boldly free, wanton woman who can unblushingly do anything. I smile in triumph, over my past, over my fears, over the loss of what Bruce and I had.

Because we have it back, deeper and rawer, with a newfound appreciation for our special uniqueness.

Bruce rubs the crown of his cock along my lips, and I stick my tongue out hungrily, wanting to taste him. "Suck me, Allyson. Take me in your mouth, work me into your throat. But don't make me come. I'm not coming until I'm inside that sweet pussy."

He releases his hold on my hair, cradling me instead so that I have control. I take advantage, not going easy on him. I bob my head, letting him in my mouth first to coat my tongue with the salty taste of his skin before going deeper. I hum against him, knowing the vibration drives him wild, slurping messily along his length.

I own him, though I'm the one kneeling before him, greedily sucking his every thick, hard inch. I feel strong and sexy as he loses control, fucking my mouth. He tests me with a few careful thrusts, but I grip his thighs. As my nails dig in and I moan for more, he gives me what I'm demanding and what he wants, going deeper and harder as he roughly enters my throat.

My eyes water, not with tears but with joy. I am still me.

A tiny little seed of doubt still lived in my core, afraid that even if I were free, there would be a line I couldn't breach. A boundary that would send me spiraling. But as Bruce uses my face for his pleasure, I feel nothing but blessed relief at the fierce lust that consumes me as I devour him.

He pulls out sharply, breathing raggedly. "I need to be inside you."

A small smile teases at my lips as I wipe them messily. I raise a brow and he growls.

"Not in your mouth. I'm coming inside your pussy, Al. Get on the bed." He lifts me as he speaks, tossing me back. I love him like this, unapologetically starving for me and in a rush to get me underneath him.

He pulls my shorts off carelessly, my legs going askew. "Turn over," he instructs me. I flip to my stomach, and he pulls me back by my ankles, guiding me to bend my knees underneath me. Face down and ass up, I should feel submissive. Instead, I feel cherished as his eyes and his fingertips trace along my skin. I feel powerful as I hypnotize him with the sway of my hips.

I look over my shoulder, watching him fist himself as he lines up with me. "Fuck me, Bruce. Please," I beg, not wanting to wait a second longer.

To be his. For him to be mine. To be us again.

His hands go around my waist, pulling me back as he impales me deeply. Finally, it's everything I need and want.

Nothing between us, no secrets or doubts, no defensive walls or painful history. Just us, bare and primal.

It's a gut-wrenchingly simple movement, him moving fiercely in and out of my body, but it's more than the motion. It's a claiming, a taking mixed with a promise for the future.

He leans forward, covering me with his body, and I feel him everywhere . . . over me, in me. His arms go underneath me, criss-crossing over my chest to hold my shoulders, using the leverage to go harder and rougher as he slams into me, and I cry out at the beautiful invasion. "That's it, baby. Take me, tell me how much you want it."

He's always been better at dirty talk than I am, but this one I can do with no problem.

"Bruce, I want you so much. I love you . . . I love you!" It's sweeter than the filthy sex we're having, and the contrast is perfect, sending him over the edge.

I feel the heat of his cum filling me in spurts and spasms as he holds himself overwhelmingly deep inside me. He grits out my name, adding his own vow. "I love you, baby. Now fucking come for me, milk me with that sweet pussy."

I fly, freely soaring through space even as he holds me down. The waves shoot through me in a blissful shock of current as I shake and quiver against him.

It's perfect. It's everything.

As we float back to Earth, I feel wonderfully fulfilled. Not just physically, but emotionally. He moves us to lie down behind me, the big spoon cradling me as the little spoon, with his arms wrapped around my chest to hold me tight. The cocoon of him makes me feel so safe and secure, not that I need him to protect me, but rather that I can be me and he'll support that every step of the way, no matter which direction I want to go.

But all I want is him.

"I love you, Bruce," I say quietly, biting my lip to stop from grinning like a loon even though he can't see my face from behind. He'd know somehow. I know he would.

"I love you too, Allyson," he murmurs happily against my neck, sealing the words with a sucking open-mouthed kiss to the delicate skin.

And for the first time in a long time, I feel like I'm right where I'm supposed to be, in his arms.

CHAPTER 31

BRUCE

"Yeah, it's fine. We're good," I tell Brody. Through my phone, he grunts, and I take from that the approval he meant for me to hear.

"I believe you, but the Bennetts are like vultures, man. They're picking at me . . . pick, pick, pick with questions, and Mama Louise is listening to every word. She's like a damn spy, popping up where you least expect her with that knowing look. Reminds me of Mom when we'd fucked up but hadn't been caught . . . yet. And the worst of it is our own damn sister. Shayanne won't quit asking me shit."

He sounds every bit the beleaguered older brother that he is. He's been a good one, taking care of all of us for a long time, even when Dad was still alive. I'm glad he's got less on his shoulders now. *Maybe he won't be such an ass*, I think with a slight grin, imagining a nicer version of my older brother.

Nope, can't do it. He is what he is, a grunty bastard who's almost as bad as me. Or as bad as I was.

He's still talking while I've zoned out, listing questions that apparently everyone is asking. I tune back in as he growls in a voice pretty similar to my own, "Questions that are your fucking job to answer, not mine."

"Fine, fine. I'll be home later and have a damn family meeting or whatever the Bennetts do to handle stuff like this. Because you know they've got a tradition or something. They always do. We'll probably have to sit under the tree and sing *Kumbaya* or some shit."

I'm not as grumpy about the situation as I sound. Really, the family stuff the Bennetts do reminds me of the bonds they have. We used to do family stuff when Mom was alive, but those traditions are all but gone save a few, like birthday pancake breakfast with whipped cream and sprinkles. I look down at the plate in front of me, imagining covering it with ooey-gooey sweetness and serving it up to Allyson with an off-key song. The idea has merit, and I bet Cooper would get a kick out of it.

Brody chuckles darkly. "Negative, brother. You, your girl, and the kid are expected at dinner tonight. If you're a smart man, you won't show up without them. Shayanne has Mama Louise, Katelyn, and Sophie whipped up into a frenzy. Luke did you a solid and shut Shayanne up for a bit . . . *we won't discuss how* . . . but the man's got limits." He throws his voice high, mimicking our drawling sister, "How did I never even know about Allyson if she was this important to Bruce?" In his own deep timbre, he says, "I tried telling her she was a kid, even told her I didn't know much about the details from back then, but she's not having it. I'm afraid she's about to be all up in your business, with the rest of the crew as backup, so you'd best get ready."

I'm man enough to admit that I flinch a bit. Shayanne is intense and bull-headed, downright ornery when she wants to be. Mama Louise is that sweet but silent type you simply can't disappoint. The rest of them, the Bennett boys and their women and my brothers, I can handle just fine.

"We'll be there." I hang up with my brother, chuckling to myself.

"What?" Allyson asks suspiciously, one brow raised in curiosity. She didn't get much from my side of the conversation since the usually succinct Brody was feeling all Chatty Cathy for a change.

"Apparently, you're coming to dinner with the family tonight." The look on her face is one I wish I could frame—shock and surprise, fear and horror, delight and hope all blended together, but I can see each emotion as it treks across her face. I know her last dinner with the whole gang wasn't the best, so hopefully, this one will be better. "Mama Louise saw the whole thing yesterday, along with the whole family who was there for the first game. Brody's been running interference for me, especially with Shayanne, but if I don't show for dinner tonight, along with you and Cooper, he won't be able to stop her."

Allyson laughs lightly. "You sound scared. Of Mama Louise? I mean, she's this tiny little thing. I've seen her mom glare, and it's on-point, but I don't know if I'd go so far as to say she's scary. Or are you terrified of your baby sister?"

I take a slug of orange juice and talk around my mouthful of pancakes. "You'd be surprised by how scary both of them can be."

I'm saved by having to confess to any more male ego-crushing facts by a knock on the door.

"That'll be Michelle with Cooper," Allyson says as she passes me. Well, as she tries to. I grab her arm and spin her into my lap as she hoots, but when I cup her cheek, the surprise turns sweet with her smile. "What?"

"Just wanted one more kiss before Cooper comes in because I get the feeling he's a cockblocker." She laughs, and I swallow the sound as I meld my lips over hers.

She presses lightly at my chest and I let her go. She heads to the door looking a bit flushed and a lot happy. That's my girl.

Cooper comes in like a whirlwind with Michelle following behind, looking curious. I think her plan is to read the room and go from there, either eviscerating me or celebrating that we've got our shit straight. I'm glad it's the latter.

"Coach B, are you still gonna coach us?" Cooper looks mad as hell, so much fury in his tiny fists, and the words are his little-boy version of a growl. It's fucking adorable. I make a note to remind myself of how cute I find it now because I suspect it won't be nearly as endearing when he's a pissy teenager. Hopefully, he'll still be into football. I know how to steer that aggression from personal experience.

Allyson jumps in to answer her son. "Of course he is." But she pauses at the anger she sees in his eyes. "Uh, do you want him to?"

I give her credit for not asking in a leading fashion but rather in a way that says she's open to whatever he thinks and feels. She's a damn good mom.

Cooper walks over to me, meeting my eyes man to man. "Liam and Ms. Michelle told me what happened after Mom and me left. Did you really beat up Killian's dad?" His little lips are puffed out, but he doesn't seem to be pouting, more like he's got so many words in his mouth, he doesn't know how to get them all out.

I lay a hand on his shoulder, careful to be gentle with the kid. "I did. I'm not proud of it, and fighting should never be the first resort. It's the last resort after using your words. Killian's dad . . ."

I pause, trying to figure out how to say he's a drunk with an asshole streak in a kid-friendly way. "Well, he wasn't thinking very clearly so he said some mean things. I tried to talk to him, your mom tried to talk to him, the referee tried to talk to him, but he wasn't listening. He threw the first punch . . . which sounds like a stupid excuse but is important. You don't start shit, but you can finish it, especially if someone's in danger."

I realize a beat too late that while I censored myself about Kyle, I cursed in front of the kid. *Not cool, asshole,* I tell myself. But no one even reacts. I still need to be more careful in front of Cooper, though. Mama Louise will be proud, probably a bit shocked, too, if I can clean up my foul mouth, and it's definitely the better choice if I'm going to be hanging out with pipsqueaks all the time.

He nods sagely like my fucked-up wisdom means something to him. "Like my mom." He turns to look at her and I mirror the action. Her cheeks are pink from watching the interaction between us. One side is just slightly redder, but there's no purple hint, no bruise coloring. "He hit you."

Allyson nods. "He did. Killian's dad didn't mean to hit me. He was aiming for Bruce and it was an accident. But it was wrong. I'm okay, though, unless you wanna kiss it better? I'll totally take a boo-boo fixer kiss." She smiles over-exaggeratingly as she points at the affected cheek.

Cooper rolls his eyes but goes over to kiss Allyson's cheek. "There. All better, Mom. But coaches can't fight. It's in the code of conduct rulebook. So are they gonna fire you, Coach B?" Of course, he's read the rulebook. Like mother, like son.

"Honestly, Cooper, I don't know. If they let me coach, I'll be right there on the sidelines, doing my best to help the Wildcats do their best. If they won't, then I'll be in the bleachers cheering like a maniac." I hold my big fists up in the air, waving invisible pompoms around and sing-songing, "*Go Team!*"

His eyes drop, and in his shoes, I can see his toes wiggling. "You'd still come? Even if you weren't the coach?"

"Absolutely. Wild horses couldn't keep me away. If it's okay with you for me to come?" I don't know if I've ever been on a hook this hard before. My entire future with Allyson rests on this kid wanting me to come around. If he's scared from the fight or just flat doesn't like me, she'll never be with me and I won't get the chance to be here with her and Cooper.

Insta-fucking-family, just like Bobby said. And damn, do I want it.

Cooper looks confused over why I'd even ask. "Of course I want you to come watch. You gotta see me make my first touchdown." He throws his arms up over his head, cheering for himself for the imaginary score.

Michelle, who's been watching the whole exchange with a careful smile, finally grins. "All right, you guys, I'm out. I told the sitter I'd only be a minute." She holds up both hands, waving 'bye to us all.

But she sends a whole conversation's worth of eyes to Allyson. Even though I'm not fluent in their silent language, I can read the 'tell me everything later' and 'I'm happy for you.'

Once she's gone, the three of us settle in for pancakes. Allyson has to pop them in the microwave, but none of us mind. It feels quaint, which is a word I wouldn't even know if I hadn't had to get a tutor for English in high school.

Such a small thing from so long ago, but it set everything so off course. As I look around the table now, though, I can feel the course correction, that everything is finally as it should be.

"So, what's the plan for today?" I say, already knowing the answer but happy to set Cooper up for the answer.

"Bless this house!" he hollers with more excited celebration than dusting should ever get.

I smile, stuffing a forkful of pancakes into my mouth. "I remember where the vacuum is, so we'll get to it after breakfast."

FROM MY VANTAGE POINT OF THE DOORWAY, I CAN SEE THE WHOLE kitchen. Allyson is with Mama Louise and Shayanne, dipping chicken into egg wash and flour, and Sophie is feeding Cindy Lou some green mush while supervising Cooper. He's very carefully cutting tomatoes in half for the salad.

He's doing a great job, so maybe I was being a bit overly protective when I told Mama Louise that she could not give an eight-year-old a knife. She'd smiled sweet as she could be while showing me the special knife she'd bought just for Cooper. It's kid-friendly, blunt-tipped, and bright neon yellow like a highlighter. She'd been ready. She'd known he was gonna be here.

There's a real chance that she might be psychic. Brody and Bobby disagree with me on that, but the Bennett boys just smile like they know something I don't. Fuckers.

Speaking of, not that I said that part out loud in Mama Louise's kitchen, James comes up behind me. He's the craziest of his brothers, always ready with a kind smile and more often than not, a dirty joke. "There's my girls," he says happily.

I look at Sophie and Cindy Lou, who's currently green-faced, but at least Sophie's not wearing any of it, so that's progress.

"Oh, shit," James says quietly, smacking my arm with the back of his hand.

I glare down at him. Not much, he's tall too, but nothing like me. "What?"

He's looking at Allyson, Mama Louise, and Shayanne like he's seeing ghosts. "Are they making fried chicken?"

"Duh," I say, not getting why it's a big deal when we have fried chicken at least two or three times a month. It's not even his favorite, which I know from seeing how much roast he takes every time Mama Louise makes one.

James flashes me the biggest shit-eating grin I've ever seen on his face, and that's saying something. "You don't know, do you?"

I lift my brows sardonically. There's a lot of shit around this house I don't know, but it's usually not anything that warrants this.

Mark and Katelyn come in the back door, interrupting whatever James was about to say. Instead, he looks to them and whispers, "Mama's making fried chicken with Allyson."

Katelyn's eyes go as big as saucers, and Mark's lips twitch like he's fighting off a grin. He says softly, "Did you tell him yet?"

I'm done with this shit and growl, "Tell me what?"

The brothers don't speak, enjoying letting me twist on the hook too much, but Katelyn takes pity on me. "Mama Louise doesn't make fried chicken with just *anybody*. There are only three people in the whole wide world she will do that with, actually. Though I guess there's four now, each of us standing in this room."

They watch the realization dawn on my face with glee, and I look over to see Mama Louise inspecting me carefully. She waits a long beat, during which I feel judged, analyzed, and evaluated, before she gives me a small flour-coated thumbs-up.

I'm honestly not sure if it's approval that I've chosen Allyson or that Allyson has chosen me. But it's a stamp of approval, one I realize I hold in high regard. Mama Louise is a smart woman, maybe too smart for our own good, but she's made something special here with our motley ragtag crew.

I meet her eyes, telling her what I can silently, and dip my chin in appreciation. She smiles sweetly and goes right back to helping dip another chicken leg in egg wash like nothing happened.

But something did happen.

We just became a family in my eyes. All of us—Bennetts, Tannens, and Meyerses. Though I wonder how long it'll be before I can change Allyson and Cooper's names? Or hell, I'm progressive enough that if Allyson wants me to change my name to match hers, I could do that.

She's got work stuff to think about, and Cooper might not want to change his name. But we can talk about that, the three of us, and decide for our family.

Because that's what we are. Our little family of three inside this large mishmash of a clan.

CHAPTER 32

BRUCE

I raise a glass of lemonade, and a sea of drinks lifts around me. As an unofficial team sponsor, Hank let us borrow a big section off to the back for our team lunch to celebrate the end of the season, and we're all gathered around the mismatched tables that have been shoved together. I wouldn't bring kids in here at night when things get a little rowdy, but for a daytime lunch, it's fine.

Hell, I think Hank's even enjoying having the kids here. He hasn't come out from behind the bar on his bum leg, but he's sitting at the end closest to our table eavesdropping with a smile big enough to wrinkle his face. Well, he's got wrinkles all the time since he's an old guy, but the lines are deeper as his teeth flash with laughter.

"To a great season, a great team, and a great experience. I never thought that pulling over to yell at some unruly kids . . ." I pause, glancing at Cooper and Johnathan, who bump each other's shoulder good-naturedly.

"I never thought that would change the entire course of my life, but you boys did that and I'll be forever grateful. I might've taught you a bit about the game of football, but I hope that in a bigger way, you learned something about life. It ain't always pretty and perfect, or even what you'd planned, but it can be *good* anyway, especially if you work for it. And when you've got a team . . . because a team is like a family. I'm proud of each and every one of you."

They're not platitudes and every kid here knows that. I've made an honest investment in them, and they've returned the favor by trusting me to do right by them. Just like a team should be.

We've had a hard season, winning a few and losing several, but these boys played their hearts out, no matter what the scoreboard said. Or who the roster listed as coach.

Yeah, after the incident with Kyle, the association wouldn't let me be a coach anymore. It sucked ass and pissed me off, but I understood. They've got rules that are black and white for a good reason, and even if it's in self-defense, they can't have coaches punching people out.

But practices are held at a public park, and with the boys' parents' permission, I happen to wander by on Tuesdays and Thursdays around seven to set up a delivery point for Shayanne's smashed pumpkin and offer a bit of advice.

But it isn't 'coaching' per se, I think with the smallest smirk.

It was totally coaching, but we kept it quiet and unofficial. After studying the code of conduct, Allyson had deemed that 'legal' in her professional opinion. Legal or not, I wasn't going to abandon my guys.

The games were harder, though, because I had to be a spectator and sit in the bleachers, but I was glad the association at least allowed me that because they did uphold Max's ruling and ban Kyle.

Killian's grandparents were remarkably understanding about the whole thing. Mrs. Bloomdale even brought me chocolate chip cookies as a way of apologizing for her son, who disappeared again before they could get him into rehab. But while I'd thanked her and shared the delicious treats with the team, I assured her that wasn't necessary and checked in with Killian to make sure he wasn't upset about his dad's absence. Like the resilient kid he is, he'd just looked at his grandparents and said he was 'just fine.' Damn near brought a tear to my eye, but I'd offered him a handshake and coughed it off like the tough fucker I am.

With me in the stands and not able to coach, Allyson had to really step it up. And she did great, leading the Wildcats into each week with confidence after studying playbooks and watching games with me and Cooper as research.

She's such a smart woman, just like I always knew she was, but I can see now that any insecurities I had back when we were kids were strictly my own. She never thought of me as a dumb jock with no real future. That was all my fear, not her judgment.

I wonder what would've happened to us if I'd never had those doubts, never gotten a tutor, and she'd never had a concern about my faithfulness. Where would we be now? Would we have made it through the test of time? There's no way to know for sure.

We got so off course, but we're back on track now, just like we should be. Well, almost like we should be.

I meet Cooper's eyes, and he's basically bouncing off the walls with excitement. I swear it looks like he's vibrating inside his skin. "Be chill, man," I tell him quietly as the celebration lunch goes on around us.

The kids talk about the season, dissecting each game with braggy memories of great catches they made and touchdowns they ran for.

Somewhere along the way, their chatter turns to video games, and I'm mostly out of my element there, but I try to interject so they can laugh at the old guy a bit. Cooper's teaching me, but he says I'm still a level-one noob. I tried to give him an excuse, telling him that my fingers are just too big to push the tiny buttons, but he'd laughed and said we all had to work with what we're given.

Smart little shit had turned my own words around on me because I'd told him the same thing about his small stature on the field. No, he's probably never going to be a linebacker, but each position has special requirements and he'll be a damn good defensive back if he keeps working at it. Allyson stands up, tapping her glass of tea with a spoon. The room quiets and all eyes turn to her, captivated.

"I just want to say thank you to each and every one of you. Thank you for letting me be your coach even though I definitely wasn't anyone's first choice for the role." She looks at Mike, who shrugs like he had nothing to do with it. He's made it to a few games and told me he was glad Allyson and I worked our shit out because he could see from a mile away that we had a spark. I think he fancies himself the Cupid of our little reunion.

"Thank you for working hard and playing your hearts out. Thank you for teaching a cheerleader about actual football." She winks at Johnathan, who's had some pretty significant growth this season. He's gotten better at impulse control, both with his hands and his mouth, and is the first one to say 'yes, ma'am' when Allyson orders them to do another drill. He's a natural leader and is using his powers for good these days. He and Cooper have even made peace and are decent buddies now.

"And most of all, thank you for a great season! On three . . . one, two, three . . . GO WILDCATS!" Everyone joins in with the cheer, and the few non-team folks in Hank's look our way in surprise. Cooper lets out a growl that I'm pretty sure is supposed to be a tiger, and everyone laughs, copying him.

Before it gets too wild and Hank kicks us out, I stand up. "One last drill, fellas."

They groan, but it's over-exaggerated and so fake-sounding that I can't believe Allyson doesn't immediately suspect something's up. But she's cluelessly whining along with them. "Seriously, Bruce? No more drills. The season's over." She feigns lying back in her chair, one hand draped across her forehead dramatically.

I take her hand and the boys all get loud once again. "*Ooh*" echoes around us.

"Shut it," I say with a snap of my fingers and a mean mugging glare, but a second later, I'm grinning and laughing along with them so they know I'm kidding. "Line up, three kids per side of the floor. Parents, you too. Just space out with the boys."

The boys hop to it, dragging their parents to stand near them. The Bloomdales stand to the side, off the dance floor but with ready smiles. I pull Allyson to the floor too, situating us in the middle of the misshapen circle.

I signal Bobby, and he gives me a chin lift of acknowledgement before he struts over to the jukebox, slipping money in the slot and pressing the numbers for the song I requested. J12 is about to be epic at Hank's. I hope.

Electronic violins whine out through the surround sound speakers and Allyson's brows jump together in confusion. "What is this?"

"Cotton Eye Joe. It's a classic, great for footwork for the boys." I say it casually, praying she doesn't question me too much. It's true, after all, even if it is a ploy.

There's also the little fact that none of these kids actually knew the dance until recently. Cooper and I had a heart-to-heart about the future a few weeks ago, and he helped me come up with this idea to surprise Allyson. I taught him and Liam the fancy footwork when they came out to the farm to help with Shayanne's pumpkin harvest, and they taught the rest of the team at recess at school.

It's all coming together.

The lyrics start, and a thread of anticipation weaves through the kids. We all start with the cross-kick and shuffle movements the line dance is known for, everyone grinning and laughing as the circle moves forward.

I keep Allyson in the middle so she can see the whole effect, every player and most of the parents plus the Bennett-Tannen crowd surrounding us.

The tempo gets faster, the shuffles wilder, and the laughs louder as we all succumb to the sillies. I grab Allyson's hand, spinning her around and then pressing her front to mine. Two-stepping to this song is basically sacrilegious, but she goes along with me, following my lead and smiling brightly.

I look at her in this moment, seeing the girl she once was and the woman she's become, both mine in every way, owning my entire heart.

As the song ends, I lean back, roaring to the ceiling, "*Gooo* Wild-cats!" Allyson laughs, and out of the corner of my eyes, I can see the boys following the plan. I spin Allyson around, catching her with her back pressed to my chest.

I angle her toward one side of the floor. Johnathan, Joshua, and Derek hold up a poster board that says *Will*. Slowly, I rotate her to see Marcus, Trey, and Killian holding up *You*, then Evan, Anthony, and Julio with *Marry*.

Allyson's jaw drops, and she lets out this soft little sound that brings a smile to my face. I turn her to the last side, where Cooper, Liam, and Christopher hold up *Me?* to complete the question.

As Allyson whirls around to face me, I drop to one knee and hold up the ring Cooper helped me pick out. Her hands cover her mouth, but I hear the 'ohmygod, ohmygod, ohmygod' from behind her palms.

I reach up to take one of her hands in mine, locking eyes with her. She's already tearing up, but I can see that it's in surprise and happiness. "Allyson, I lost you once and it was like the sunshine left my sky. I lived without you, but honestly, I was just going through the motions. When you came back into my life, full of sass and fire, I thought the sun had finally returned."

Her other hand drops to cup my cheek, my beard scratching at her palm. "Bruce . . ."

I lean into her touch, but I'm not done. Bobby helped me write this speech since he's so good with words. I've practiced at least a million times, by myself in front of a mirror and even a few times with Bobby so he could tell me what a starry-eyed fucker I am. He's firmly on Team Allyson-Bruce-Cooper now, calling us the ABCs, so I took his insults along with the help on my speech.

I steel my nerves, trying to remember the words perfectly. "We've been through a lot—together, apart, and together again, and I want to spend the rest of my life with you. Not behind you or in front of you but right beside you, sharing our days and our nights and our forever. I love you, Allyson Meyers. Will you marry me?"

I can see the yes on the tip of her tongue, the light in her eyes, and feel the way her hand trembles against my cheek. I turn my head, laying a kiss to her palm.

It breaks the spell and she blinks rapidly. Her eyes leave mine and find Cooper.

"I asked him already, Al. He helped me plan all this and pick out the ring," I explain.

Cooper runs over to us, his voice loud. "Mom, say yes. Bruce said he'll be my dad if you get married."

It's the first time he's called me Bruce and not Coach B, and my heart stops and then hammers out of my chest with joy.

Allyson looks at Cooper, his face open and happy, and then at me. I'm a rough farm guy with only my love to offer her, but I know she can see it, feel it. I pray it's enough.

"Yes," she says with a nod. "Oh, my God, yes!"

I slip the ring on her finger and stand up, scooping her into my arms to kiss her deeply. Cheers erupt around us, reminding me that the kids are watching. It's the only thing that prevents me from shoving her to the floor and getting inside her. She's in my heart so deep, and the urge to be inside her just as deeply is strong.

But her hoot of joy makes me so fucking happy. I spin her around, yelling out, "She said yes!" I set her down, picking up Cooper next and spinning him around too. "She said yes!"

EPILOGUE

ALLYSON

"*T*hanks, Rick. Have a Merry Christmas!" I call out, my bag already on my shoulder.

"You too, Allyson. And thank you again for the pie. I can't wait to dig in." I look over to see him ready to leave too, briefcase in one hand and an apple pie carefully held in the other. He's eyeing the pie like he might eat it in the car on the way home rather than save it for Christmas dinner like he's supposed to.

"Don't forget that Carol is expecting that pie. She ordered it from Shayanne so that she didn't have to bake one. And I can't bring you another one because Shay has sold out, one hundred percent."

The warning is clear, and his face falls, but it's the truth. Shayanne has been slammed, rolling from smashed pumpkin season into her holiday busy time. She's been making soap and apple pies like a madwoman. But it's been fun, too, a way for Cooper and me to hop right into the family and help out. We've been picking apples, stirring cinnamon-y apple goodness on the stove, and putting ribbons on blocks of soap right alongside the Bennetts and Tannens.

"Fine. I won't eat it . . . yet. But I'm having a slice for Christmas breakfast," he declares. "It's fruit, so it counts."

I laugh, holding up my hands. "That's between you and Carol.

Negotiate your own deal with your wife." He tilts his head considering that, but I pop his bubble. "You know she can out-deal you. Don't get greedy or you won't even get a slice."

He laughs and nods, knowing I'm right. Carol is a pistol, but she'd win mostly because Rick would let her win any negotiation they had.

We pull out of the parking lot at the same time, heading to our respective homes for the long break until New Year's.

The drive from town to the country doesn't seem so long now that I've been doing it every day. It's turned into my chance to decompress, and on days when there's school, it's my talk time with Cooper. Today, he's already home at the farm on winter break.

At our home.

Almost as soon as I said yes to his proposal, Bruce offered to move into the city and commute to the farm to work, but it made more sense for Cooper and me to move to the farm. Cooper loves the wide-open space of the country, and having family around all the time was a powerful decision maker for me.

That's been another big change for us. After some awkward and stuttered phone calls with my parents, I introduced them to Bruce and Cooper over brunch two weeks ago. They'd welcomed me back with open arms after I explained what I'd gone through that led me to cut them out of my life in the first place. My mom had cried, and we'd mourned the time lost, but we're committed to making up for it. With their planning to come to Christmas dinner tomorrow, it'll be one last thing Jeremy took from me that I've gotten back.

My courage, my happiness, my family, myself, and my soon-to-be husband. It's all mine again, and I won't let go of any of it for anything.

My tires crunch over the snow and ice along the drive, and I roll slowly up to park in my new space in front of the Tannen house. There's a warm glow coming from several of the windows.

I bundle up and make a run for the front door. Inside, I pet Murphy behind the ears, even though the old dog doesn't so much as lift his head. "Where is everyone?" I ask him, and his wrinkly brows raise but that's it. "You're the worst, but cutest, guard dog ever," I tell him quietly as he rolls over, giving me his belly for scratches.

"In here," Bruce calls out from the kitchen.

I walk in to find Bruce, Bobby, Brody, and Cooper sitting around the kitchen table with dominoes spread out in front of them.

I walk in as Brody lays down a domino I can't see with a hum of self-satisfaction and Bobby and Cooper instantly cry out in disappointment. Bruce's eyes are all for me though. Heat flows between us, just like it always does and I'm drawn to his side for a hello kiss.

His lips against mine feel like coming home.

I lean against him comfortably, my hip against his shoulder and his arm around my waist as I survey the table. "Are you guys corrupting my kid?"

Brody scowls at me, not the least bit scary to me now. It's just his face. "No, we're teaching him an important life skill."

"Yeah, Mom. Dominoes are life," Cooper mimics, and I shake my head, not buying it for a second.

But I'm glad Brody and Bobby have been so accepting of Cooper and me. Bruce might've willingly taken us as a package deal, but his family didn't make that choice. They have accepted us with open arms, though, even going so far as to redo Shayanne's old room so that it's a bit more boyish for Cooper. We've done a little updating to Bruce's bachelor pad room too so it was more 'us', and Bruce doesn't even complain about the ten smooshy pillows that now reside on his bed.

But Bruce's brothers have helped our move out here be easier, and while being surrounded by this much testosterone is a bit jarring at times, I'm used to them now too. We might be an unusual family, but we are one.

"I'm gonna fold, fellas. You mind finishing the game without me? I've got something to show Allyson," Bruce says, standing up from the table. His tone belies nothing, but I can read the set of his jaw. He's nervous, which makes me nervous.

Bobby teases his brother, "I bet you've got something to show her." His brows waggle with not-subtle meaning. Luckily, Cooper is young enough that he doesn't pick up on Bobby's meaning yet.

"Shh, Bobby! Don't ruin the surprise!" Cooper blurts out, then his eyes go wide as he looks at me in horror. "Oops," he says sadly.

I grin. "Surprise? For me? It wouldn't be a Christmas present, would it?" I snuggle up to Bruce's chest, blinking up at him with innocent eyes.

He smiles, but it's full of dark promise. "Guess the cat's outta the bag." He dips his chin at his brothers and Cooper. "You guys good for dinner?"

I love that he's stepped right in with Cooper, treating him like one of the guys. Treating him like his son.

They all nod in answer, and Bruce takes my hand, pulling me toward the back door. "We're out then."

In surprise, my feet stutter underneath me and Bruce steadies me. "Out? Where are we going?" It's the night before Christmas Eve and my plans included exciting things like Hallmark movies, mass quantities of wrapping paper, and adding Bailey's to my decaf coffee.

Bruce leans in and whispers hotly in my ear, "It's a surprise, Al. Come on."

Well, all right then. That's enough for me, and I let him lead me out the door and to his truck. He helps me in and then hops in himself, turning the heater up high to ward off the chill of the night.

I don't ask where we're going, trusting him implicitly. Even so, my hand reaches up to grip the handle over the door as he bumps along over the land, eschewing the driveway and the road we usually use to go anywhere. But he doesn't go far, just a few acres away from the Tannen homestead.

He stops in the middle of a clearing, but I'm not sure where we are or why we're here. "What am I looking at?" I ask, pointing at the orange spray paint lines in the snow and looking at Bruce.

The truck's headlights reflect on the snow and in the dim light, I swear I see him blush. But that can't be. I mean . . . he's *him*.

"The paint's just symbolic, but I talked to Mama Louise and Mark. This is the site where we can build. It's where our home will be—you, Cooper and me. Merry Christmas, Allyson." There's the slightest tremble in his voice as it goes deep.

"Our home?" I repeat, his meaning hitting me. "Oh, my gosh, I love it!" I lean over the console, needing to kiss him.

He kisses me back hard and messy, tasting like cinnamon and instantly lighting a fire inside me. "Come here, baby," he growls.

Awkwardly, I climb over the console as he pushes his seat back. I straddle him, my professional work skirt riding up my thighs to make room for him between my legs.

"Fuck, I love you, Allyson. I can't wait . . . for any of it. For the wedding, for our house, for our family, for our life."

The simple but meaningful words surround us.

He shakes his head like he can't believe it, like he's getting everything he ever wanted. So am I.

"I love you too. I feel like we should celebrate." I'm flirting with him, hungry for him the way I'm hungry for the picture he's painting.

His hands knead at my thighs, working higher as his eyes bore into me, reading my every reaction. I grind against him, feeling his cock thicken beneath me. "Kinda like old times, isn't it? In your truck. Seems like we've been here a time or two before."

That's an understatement. But as much as I loved him then, it's nothing compared to now.

"You like these tights?" he asks with wicked promise.

I bite my lip, shaking my head, but my eyes are locked on his. "Not particularly." I know why he's asking, but I still gasp when his fingers dig in, tearing a hole in the tights I wore to work today. I'll happily get another pair.

My fingers drop between us, working at his zipper to free his cock. I have to lift up a little bit to give him room to move his jeans and underwear out of the way, but then I feel him against my slick core.

He's satin over steel, rock hard for me. "Give me that pussy, baby. Ride me." It's barely a whisper, but I feel the words on my skin like tattoos.

I move my hips, my lips kissing at his crown. He grips my ass hard, his fingers digging into the flesh there to still me. "Slow or fast, Al?"

Oh, God, so many memories assail me. Us, just like this, in his truck and the barn. He used to always ask me that right before entering me. He never does anymore, knowing the answer. But it's a hot reminder of just how far we've come. "Fast, Bruce . . . fast."

He pulls me down, slamming me onto his thick cock and trusting that I'll stretch around him.

I cry out, filled and fulfilled in ways I never imagined. No, that's not true—in ways I used to dream of and then gave up on. But I will never give up on Bruce again. Or myself.

He holds me still, hammering up into me. I press against the roof of the truck for leverage, wanting to keep him . . .

In my body, in my heart . . . forever.

"I love you."

"I love you too," he grits out through clenched teeth.

It might've been a rough road to get here, but we're finally exactly where we're supposed to be. Together.

Thank you for reading! I hope you enjoyed the book! **Want to see where Bruce and Allyson are in the future? Grab the extended epilogue here. If the link doesn't work, just visit www. laurenlandish.com and click on Rough Love and you'll be directed to it.**

Continue reading for a preview of Buck Wild, Bennett Boys Book 1 (the Tannens are supporting characters)! And don't forget to preorder Rough Edge, Tannen Boys book 2!

EXCERPT: BUCK WILD

JAMES

*W*ith a squeeze of the snips and a twist of my pliers, I finish one more section of fence. Gazing left, then right, I can see just how much I've done and just how far I have left to go. The answer is the same as the last time I checked. Not enough and too much.

We need this pasture secure before we move the herd over, and that's happening one way or another by the end of the week. Unfortunately, this fence was totally wrecked last winter, and with everything that's happened to the family, it's been put off until the last minute. And it seems that last minute is my new middle name.

I know I need to hurry, but my back needs a break more. This isn't a sprint, the eight seconds of exhilaration and adrenaline that I'm used to. This is still hours of work left, and if I'm not careful, I'll end up useless with miles of fence to go. I stand tall to stretch, raising my arms high above me and lifting my face to the bright sun of the June day.

Taking a deep breath, I can feel the sweat rolling down my face, so I pull my hat off to mop a rag across my brow. It's strange, but in the barely blowing breeze, I can feel my dad's presence, proud that I'm back here, home on the ranch, doing what he always wanted me to do. In the sound of the creek that's just on the other side of this

313

rise I'm working on fencing, it almost sounds like he's chuckling in that way he used to when he knew something would happen even if my brothers and I swore it never would.

His passing is still so new that it sometimes doesn't feel real. Speaking to the refreshing wind at my back, I tuck my rag in my back pocket and adjust my Stetson on my head. "So, you're watching, are you? I know exactly what you're gonna say, Pops. *Fence ain't gonna fix itself, boy. Back to work, only way to get done what needs to be done.* I know, and I'm gonna get it done."

Taking one last deep breath, I let the air current guide me back to the next section, ready to roll for another few hours. It's been hours already, Or maybe minutes. Shit, it's hard to tell when the work is this repetitive. All I know is that I'm in that eternity between my quickly eaten lunch and sunset when I hear hoofbeats coming.

I don't even have to look to know it's my older brother. Especially since both my brothers are older than me and have never let me forget that I'm the baby. But right now, I know it's my oldest brother, coming to check on me like he always does.

Turning to face Mark, I tug the brim of my hat down to shield my eyes from the sun, which is hanging pretty low in the sky. Ah, hours then, not the minutes I'd feared. I've kept up a good pace, the end must be in sight.

"Hey, Mark." I greet with a single lift of my chin.

He reins in his horse Sugarpea, his favorite gelding that he's had since he was a teenager. "Have you been napping out here or something, James? This as far as you've made it? Gonna be some early mornings and late nights to get this pasture prepped in time. Guess it's a good thing you brought the ATV, it'll let you work after dark with those floodlamps."

He makes a *tsking* sound that both irritates me and makes me laugh. I take a closer look around, I've got less than a half mile to go before I reach the corner and today's goal. "Fuck you, man. I'm working my ass off out here while you've been pushing papers around in the barn office. I bet I've earned more sweat in the past half hour than your big ass has sitting in that old swivel chair all day. But don't you worry, I'll be in for dinner."

He smirks at me, leaning onto the horn of his saddle to look down at me with a knowing grin. "Of course you will. I might be a scary fella, but none of us want Mama chasing after us. She's the scariest son of a gun I know."

I twist my face into a fictitious mask of fear, staring behind him with wide eyes. "Oh, you done bought it now!"

Mark spins to look behind him, just as I'd planned, but there's nothing there besides the wide-open acres of golden-green land. "Shit, you had me thinking Mama was right behind me. You been taking acting lessons or something when you're on that rodeo tour?"

I laugh, the gentle shake of my body and lightness in my head feeling good. It's been foreign lately and maybe just what I need. Mark, never being one to laugh, merely smiles, but for him, that's basically the same as laughter, so I'm calling it a win. "You've always been easy to fool. Remember when we were kids and I jumped from the hayloft and faked breaking my leg? You were so scared you damn near pissed your Levis. It don't take being Daniel Day-Lewis to get you."

Mark's mouth thins, but he nods and gives me an evil grin. "Well, I planned to help you with a length of fence, but after that stunt, I'm thinking maybe I'll go on in and have a shower before dinner. Might even prop my feet up and watch some of Mama's shows with her while she gets dinner ready."

My jaw drops; he's so serious that when he plays it straight, it's hard to tell if he's joking or not. "The fuck you will! Get your ass off your high horse and help. Just because the corner's just up ahead don't mean the whole damn fence is done! We've got miles to go and not enough time to do it."

Mark shakes his head, looking a lot older than he really is. Sure, I'm the baby of the group, but Mark isn't that much older. But in the afternoon light, the weight of responsibility hangs on his face so much that he looks like he's pushing forty instead of still two stepping with thirty. "There's never enough time. Hasn't been for a while now."

The silence stretches for a moment, both of us lost in thought of missing Pops. He loved this land, the land he bought on faith, back in the time when everyone was saying old-fashioned family farming and ranching was going the way of bell bottoms and the Marlboro man. He'd been the one who saw what this land could be, a harsh mistress that still loved us back and provided for a man who was willing to use his brains as well as his body and heart to tend it.

He loved us boys, all three of us. He spent every day teaching us how to be men and how to be ranchers. He'd taught me to ride almost as soon as I could walk, to respect the value of a man's hard work, and that sweat was sometimes more valuable than gold. And he taught us to love.

The best example of that was how Pops loved Mama. He would often tell us about how once he saw his Louise, he knew right then and there that he was going to marry that girl. He'd been eighteen at the time.

His passing hit us hard, especially Mark. It was Mark who found Pops, lying just beyond the big elm tree we've got in the front yard, a peaceful look on his face and his hat somehow placed respectfully over his eyes like he was taking a nap.

By everyone's guess, he realized what was coming, the years of hard work and workman's breakfasts catching up to him, and had laid down and sent his horse back to the barn. As soon as Duster nickered at the back door riderless, Mark said he knew something was wrong. It took him awhile to find Pops, but it didn't matter. He could have been faster than the Flash and he would've been too late. When the reaper comes for you, there's never enough time.

Mark found our father lying next to the same tree that he proposed to Mama under thirty-two years ago. We didn't have the years with him we thought we would. I'm back home for now, but only for the long summer. When the fall circuit starts up again, my ass needs to be on the back of a fifteen-hundred-pound pissed-off bull if I want to get my sponsorship checks. I'm not sure how Pops managed to time his unexpected passing with the rodeo schedule he always hated, but since he did, I've got a long stretch of months to stay here, settle in with Mama and my brothers to make the ranch work somehow without Pops' fiercely loving hand guiding us all.

My eyes meet Mark's and he growls, swinging off Sugarpea and tying her off on the back gate of my ATV trailer before bumping my shoulder as he passes by me in a sign of brotherly love that also means "shut the fuck up." Saying nothing, he roots around in the back of the trailer and comes out with another pair of snips. "Okay, James, let's see if we can get all the sections from here to the corner and a few beyond done before dinner. Deal?"

I eye the length of fence, not seeing too much that needs repair. This part of the pasture is in the lee of the rise, and because of that, didn't catch the driving winds that some of the other areas did. "Hell, if it's mostly just inspection, I bet we can do five or six. Let's hit it."

We get to work, side by side, the same way we did for years, words not even needed as we dance around each other, checking each level of wire and all the barbs, careful to scan and fix any weak spots.

We complete our goal, loading up our tools in the back of the ATV just as we hear the ringing of the bell out across the flat land. Mark grins and unties the lead on Sugarpea, swinging up into the saddle easily. "Nice job."

I smile, hopping behind the handlebars of the ATV. "Told you we'd make it. How about I race you to the house. If I win, I get your roll. If you win, you get…"

He interrupts me, already wheeling Sugarpea around. "I get your whole plate."

Before I can even register what he said, he's off and running, Sugarpea tearing up great hunks of turf with every step like Mark's racing him in the Kentucky Derby. I twist the throttle on my ATV, but I'm held back some as I can't just floor it, or else I'd flip the small trailer and send my tools flying everywhere.

Still, it's a race of one horsepower versus twenty-eight, and I'm close on Mark's heels as we get to the barn. He unsaddles and stalls Sugarpea while I unload my tools before we both wash our hands and splash our faces with the cool water from the old-fashioned pump, then go bursting in the back door, still jockeying for position. The race is more about bragging rights than dinner, but make no mistake, Mark will totally take my plate if he wins, and I'll damn sure enjoy that extra roll with lots of moans at how delicious it is to stir the shit if I win.

Our roughhousing catches Mama's attention though, and she turns from the stove, a big wooden spoon in her hand, the same kind that she's threatened to break over my ass if I didn't behave myself. "What the hell are you two doing? Behave yourself in my house, or you'll be eating on the back porch with the dogs. And they don't get dessert."

We sober up, knowing that she's dead serious, but the competitive spirit we've always had doesn't just stop so we discreetly rib each other, daring the other to make a sound and be the loser. Neither of us will ever give in though, and ultimately, we sit at our respective spots at the table. Pops' spot is empty, Mark's is at his left as the eldest son, while Mom will sit at the other end of the table, nearest me. Luke used to sit on Pops' right, but he's adjusted, he'll sit next to Mama.

Mark glances over, removing his hat and hanging it off the back of his chair. "I'm getting your plate tomorrow." He swings two fingers between his eyes and mine, indicating that he's watching me. I grin, and give him the finger. Like hell he will.

Mama turns around in a huff, thankfully slow enough that I can hide my hand. "Mark Thompson Bennett, did you just say you were gonna eat your brother's dinner? You know how hard he works, how hard you all work, and he needs his dinner. You'll do no such thing."

Being the baby in the family is sometimes the most annoying thing in my life, but other times, like this, it's a blessing.

Deciding to needle Mark just a little bit, I rub my stomach, moaning a little. "I'm so fucking hungry. I worked damn hard, I'm almost halfway around the back pasture and didn't have enough lunch because it was too far to come back to the house for a nibble. Is that my favorite pot roast?"

Yeah, I'm laying it on thick, but the hard expression on Mark's face is worth it. He spent most of my life eating the grisly end of pot roasts while I was getting the nice, juicy cuts. No wonder he prefers steak or hamburgers over roast.

Apparently, I overplayed though, as Mama turns around, pointing her spoon at me. "Boy, do I look like a fool? I packed your lunch and you had two big sandwiches in there, so quit needling your brother and just eat. And don't you dare cuss at my dinner table. You might be a grown man, but you're not too big for me to bend you over my knee and remind you of those proper manners I taught you growing up."

Mark smirks at me, the image of our petite mother, who's barely five-foot-two and maybe a buck fifteen soaking wet after Thanksgiving dinner, bending my six-foot-three-inch, two-hundred-pound frame over her knee to deliver a whoopin' quite comical.

I duck my head, putting my hands in my lap. "Sorry ma'am."

Thinking to do what she said and "just eat", I reach for a serving dish of potatoes before feeling eyes on me. Looking up, Mama's eyes are boring into me, and I snatch my hand back so fast my knuckles rap on the edge of the table. "I think those rodeo folks aren't doing you any favors, James. Bunch of wild heathens. You don't start until everyone's at the table."

I sigh, knowing that Mama's right. There are advantages to being a professional rodeo rider, and not waiting on big brothers is one of them. "Where is Luke anyways? He's late."

Mama swats me in the back of the head before I can reach for the potatoes again, clucking her tongue. "He'll be just a minute. He's checking on Briarbelle."

Suitably chastised, I glance up as the backdoor swings open and slams against the frame.

I lean back as Luke, all lanky six-foot-two of him, comes in, his face still streaked with dirt from the barn. "Well, speak of the devil and he shall appear."

He doesn't respond, just turns to the big industrial sink by the back door to wash up, but I see him sneak me a middle finger so I know he heard me. Once he sits, Mama brings the roast over and prays quickly so we can dig in, passing dishes back and forth and filling up our plates.

Dinner is a rowdy affair, full of fast eating, belly pats, and moans of delight when Mama brings out chocolate pudding for dessert. "Now boys, I appreciate all the hard work you're doing... so there's a little bit extra in here tonight for all three of you."

I don't know how she does it, never really thought about it I guess, but she's been feeding the three of us and Pops for decades, every meal delicious and filling and worth all the hard work to earn a place at her table.

It's odd to have the head of the table be empty now, but for the most part, our conversations about the ranch take up enough space to make it feel like Pops is still ghosting about in his vacated chair.

"Make some headway on the fence today, James?" Luke asks.

"If you can imagine it, Mark actually helped a little," I admit. "We got around the far corner and six sections back the other way. It'll be ready."

As we take our empty plates to the sink and rinse them off for the dishwasher just like we were taught, Luke fills us in on Briarbelle, his favorite mare. She's old for a first-time mother, and it's been tough on her.

"Briarbelle is ready to foal, but she's not handling it too well. She's been pacing and sweating all day, and she's already leaking milk. I'll watch her tonight, but I already told Doc to be on alert. He plans to come out bright and early in the morning. I just don't have a good feeling."

Luke is the best of any of us with the horses. There's something about his manner, his mellow presence setting them at ease usually, so him having a bad feeling is tantamount to a prophesy of something being wrong and we know better than to squash it.

Mark dries off his hands, and leans against the big counter in the kitchen, his eyes dark with concern. "Shi... sorry to hear that," he says, still aware of Mama's presence as she scrubs at the roasting pan. Just because dinner is done is no reason to curse in Louise Bennett's kitchen. Clearing his throat, Mark continues. "Need a hand tonight? I can take a shift to watch over her."

Never one to be outshined by my brothers, I speak up. "Me too. Whatever you need."

Luke shakes his head, smiling a little. He's always been the one of us to be sort of solo, not really antisocial but just... private. "Naw, I've got it. She's comfortable with me, and I already got my cot set up so I can rest when I can. But come on out in the morning, nice and easy. Hopefully, we'll have a new foal and both momma and baby will be healthy."

SOPHIE

I can't help it, bouncing side to side as excitement courses through my body. It's either bounce or fidget, and I know if I fidget I'm going to end up looking like I need to pee. Actually, I probably look like I need to pee now, but I can't stop.

Who'd have thought a few years ago that a summer internship with a crusty old seen-it-all vet way out in the country would cause this degree of joy in my heart, especially when the sun's not even up yet?

Definitely not me. I'd grown up a city slicker, the sort of girl who was wealthy and never had to worry much because my brother, Jake, always took care of me... and everything. He was a little over-bearing at times, but I didn't fault him for it too much.

After all, he didn't ask to be both brother and caretaker. When our parents died and I was barely out of elementary school, he didn't have much choice. But he stepped up and was the best fill-in parent an orphan could have, and I know he worked his ass off to make sure I had a happy life, even when I went through a rough patch in my teen years and gave him more than a fair ration of hell.

But Jake never wavered, never questioned taking me in. It was just the two of us against the world for a lot of years, but he'd met and married the love of his life, Roxy, several years ago and in her, I'd found a friend and sister before going off to college.

My original plan had been to follow Jake's footsteps, attending the same private university he had and getting my business degree before staying on track for my MBA. I figured I could join Jake in business and make oodles of money just like him. And that plan worked through my freshman year, when I took the same old boring

English and Math that everyone has to do. But a mess-up in my schedule my sophomore year changed everything for me.

I'd filled out my course request for basic biology, an easy A class that would let me check the box before moving on to my business courses. But one typo in the computer, and I found myself in Animal Studies, and no matter what I tried with the counselor, it was just too late to switch.

So, I resigned myself to studying dogs and cats and rabbits for a semester. Considering I'd never even had a pet, the experience was eye-opening and... amazing. Somehow, in the sixteen weeks of that intro class, my whole life changed. Getting to see the wonderful tapestry that is life on this planet up close, it touched me in a way that all of the money Jake had in the bank just... didn't.

I changed my major from business to pre-veterinary studies and never looked back, spending the next three years learning all about animals, big and small. My semester with large farm animals was my absolute favorite, following our John Wayne-esque mentor around on his ranch, checking on his cattle, administering vaccines, and doing wellness checks before they went to market.

I did a summer internship with him to prolong my learning, and that's when he taught me to ride horses. I loved the freedom of riding, feeling the wind in my face and a powerful beast beneath me, willing to cede control and go where I led.

It was exhilarating and I felt honored to experience it. It was then that I knew my specialty as a vet would be large ranch animals. The more time I can spend on wide-open land, keeping the herds and horses healthy, the happier I'll be. Not that I don't mind deworming a dog or spaying a cat, but there's something about the large animals that call to me.

Jake and Roxy have been supportive, if a little confused by the drastic change I've gone through in the last few years. I think Jake is wondering if I've had a brain transplant. For the most part, they're still living a jetsetter, urban trend-setter life and as happy as I am for them, I want something different.

Which is why I'm bouncing around on my toes now, looking more like I'm getting ready to fight Ronda Rousey than go to work. I

officially graduated two weeks ago, my bachelor's degree in hand
and my invitation to vet school is pinned to the refrigerator in the
small house I rented for the summer.

Sure, I could sit on my ass and take a couple of breather months
before jumping into my vet courses, but I'm too much like Jake. I
want to *do*. So I found a summer job in an area where I can be close-
ish to my support people, but far enough away that I can stand on
my own two feet.

I was lucky enough, and damn well qualified, to snag a summer
internship working with a local vet named Doc Jones. It's a perfect
fit, really. He's well-versed in everything animal related, having
likely seen it all and done it all at least once, while I bring what he
calls "fresh air" to the office. Better than that, he's actually a really
great teacher, willing to share his knowledge and help me be ready
for a career with big animals.

Like today, the reason I'm bouncing. Doc got a call last night,
and this morning we're doing a wellness check on a foaling horse at
a ranch way outside of town. A lot better than what I'd expected,
which was preparing two thousand doses of vaccine for a local
sheep rancher. I'm sure I'll be sticking sheep in the ass at some point
this week, but seeing a live birth? That'll get me standing here on
the curb outside my tiny house in town, two insulated cups of coffee
in hand and a thermos of caffeine nectar in my bag at my feet.

It's nice and crisp right now, but it's supposed to be hot as balls
today. Even so, I need my morning coffee fix, and Doc Jones *definitely* does. I hear him coming long before I actually see him, his
old as hell GMC pickup squealing to a stop in front of me. He looks
like he always does, sort of a cross between Sam Elliot and
DeForest Kelley, which I guess is appropriate. "Hop in," he says,
reaching over and pulling up the old-fashioned lock on his
passenger door. "I just talked to the boy at the ranch and Briarbelle's foal still isn't here. If we hustle, we'll get to see her deliver.
You seen that yet?"

I nod, sliding in and handing Doc his coffee. "Oh yeah. Actually,
I've seen four deliveries. But they were pretty by the book, only one
needed a minor assist."

"Well, I'm thinking this might not be as textbook. Hope you don't mind some funk."

I shake my head, sipping at my coffee. "I don't mind. It's always amazing to see, it's such a miracle every time."

I know my eyes are sparkling with anticipation because I'm not just blowing smoke, I really do love to see the miracle and make sure mom and baby are okay.

Doc looks over at me, studying me. "Eager, aren't ya?"

"Come on Doc," I complain a little. "Aren't you just as excited?"

He laughs and pushes the gas on his old truck a little harder. He could afford a new one, but I think he's determined to run this thing to the half million mile mark before he'll feel like he's gotten his money's worth. "Well, I've done this a few more than four times, but I reckon it's always a sight to see."

As we drive out, Doc quizzes me on what I'm likely to see, what I need to be concerned about, procedures if this happens, what about if that happens, and more. I nail every single one of them, and as he turns down the last road, he gives me a satisfied grunt. "That'll do, Miss Sophie. That'll do just fine."

I can feel the blush on my cheeks at his praise, pleased to have answered his questions correctly. This might be just a summer job, but I want to be the best at it.

Doc gives me a half smile and makes another little grunt, patting the dashboard.

SOPHIE

The air is still and cool as we get out of Doc's truck, and I spare a moment to look around. The setting is idyllic, a huge ranch style house that looks surprisingly balanced—old-fashioned and modern blended together—with two big barns dominating the space behind me before the fields start, rolling in the hills with the mountains that Great Falls is famous for rising off to my right in the north. "Wow."

Doc quietly grabs his bag. "Sort of looks like a little slice of paradise, don't it? Come on."

We enter the barn soft and slow, not wanting to disturb the

laboring mare who I can hear panting, obviously uncomfortable in her stall. There's not much light, just what filters in from the sun rising behind me, and a single fluorescent track near the stall. As my eyes adjust, I can see a man sitting still as a statue, leaned back and almost disappearing into his surroundings.

Doc said he talked to the "the boy at the ranch", but who I see is definitely no boy. The man is tall, judging by his legs. He's lean, his waist much trimmer than his shoulders and his t-shirt is tight across his back but loose where it disappears into the waistband of his jeans.

I can't see his face; his hat is tipped down too low and the angle of his head makes me think he's side-eyeing the moaning mare in the stall. He notices us though, and brings a hand up slowly as we approach, touching the rim of his baseball cap in a sort of salute. "Good morning, Doc."

Doc returns the salute with a nod before he kneels down, spry even though he's constantly making jokes about being an old man. "Hey Luke, how's Briarbelle doing?"

Doc's voice is quiet and calm and Luke responds in kind, sounding almost country-Zen in his softly drawling reply. "She's been up and down, pacing and lying, but no real progress. She might need some assistance, Doc."

"That's what we're here for, don't worry. We'll help her."

Luke looks up, a little bit of pride flaring in his eyes. "I'm happy to help. Just tell me where you need me."

Doc smiles and points back at me. It's one of those things I've not quite gotten used to, not being introduced to people until it feels about five seconds too late. "Thanks, Luke, and I'm gonna need your help too, but I meant me and Sophie. She's working with me this summer."

He nods at Doc, then meets my eyes and gives me a chin lift of greeting. "Assistant, huh?"

I give him a smile and nod my head. "I got my degree a few weeks back, going to vet school next year. I work hard and will do Briarbelle right."

Luke nods, and I think I see him crack a smile. Guess I handled that right, confident without coming off as some book-learning city girl. Doc gestures me towards the door of the stall, keeping his voice soft but unmistakably commanding. "Okay, slow and steady, let's get in here, give soon-to-be Mama Briarbelle an exam and see what seems to be the problem."

Luke doesn't move out of our way, so we gingerly step over him and into the stall, moving slowly so as not to startle the mare. I can see that she's in pain, her eyes are wide but not glassy yet. Still, we bend down carefully to stay out of range of her potential kicks, knowing that an animal in pain can sometimes strike out. And a horse, even one that's pregnant and weakened with birthing pains, could do serious damage if I'm not careful.

Doc starts to ask me questions, "What do you see, Sophie?"

I scan the mare from nose to tail, taking in everything as I slowly circle, still aware of her hind legs. "She's struggling, you can see the foam on her where she's been sweating, her breathing is ragged. I'd say she's getting close to exhaustion, but she's still got fight in her."

He asks a few more questions, some of me and some of Luke. I kneel down, gently rubbing her flank, trying to comfort her through the pain she's feeling, when I hear another voice. "Luke, how's she doing?"

I look up and my eyes lock on another man, again definitely not a "boy" as Doc described, although this one appears a little younger, and has a wildness in his mysterious, dark eyes. He's dressed for work in jeans and a faded denim work shirt, although he's not wearing a hat so I can see he's got dirty blonde hair.

He's taller than his brother, and a little more muscular, wiry muscles corded along his forearms where his shirt-sleeves are rolled up. He's looking at Luke, running his fingers through his hair as he waits for an answer.

Luke, who's still sitting in his chair with infinite patience, looks up. "They're checking on her now. James... this is Doc's assistant, Sophie. Sophie, this is my brother, James."

I nod at him, never stopping my gentle soothing of Briarbelle, but my attention is lock, stock, and barrel on James.

Holy fuck, he's hot.

I could lose myself in those eyes, so dark blue they're nearly navy, mysterious like a summer's night where magic and mayhem run hand in hand with warm breezes and explorations of things that you don't tell your overprotective older brother about. I want to run my fingers through his hair just like he's doing, and I'd give my left pinkie toe for him to turn around so I can see his ass in those tight jeans that look to be sculpted over his muscular thighs. The faded, ripped look was popular on campus this past year, but James' jeans got theirs the old-fashioned way... he *earned* them.

Mmm, maybe my summer gig just got even better.

James seems to be smiling back at me, but his mouth never moves, it's all in a slight crinkling around his eyes and I swear he knows what I'm thinking.

He goes to open his mouth to say something, but before he can, Doc swears and it draws my attention back to him and Briarbelle. "Sophie, it's a red bag delivery. Tell me what that means."

I don't even have to think, the textbook answers rolling off my tongue like I've engraved them on my brain during multiple study sessions, which I did. I'm not the kind to just cram facts in for a test and then forget them an hour later. "The placenta is coming first due to premature separation from the womb wall. It's urgent to deliver foal immediately before hypoxia sets in. Rare and associated with placental infection. Commonly, both mare and foal need antibiotics post-delivery."

Doc grunts. "Good enough. C'mere, ain't got time to glove up."

I move to where he indicates, surprised when he hands me a pair of scissors. "Quick and easy, watch the foal. Just let off the pressure and we'll get it out quickly afterwards."

I look at him, shocked. This is something I've studied about, but not actually done. Technically, you're not supposed to even try this until you have your DVM. "You want *me* to do it?"

Doc nods, no humor at all in his voice. "Clock's ticking. Can you do this?"

There's no judgment in his question, he just genuinely wants to know if I can or not. If I say no, he'll take care of it. But he's giving me a chance to excel, to show that I'm ready. I take a big breath and calm myself.

"Let's do this." I lean down, bringing the sharp edge of the scissor to the sac, releasing a gush of amniotic fluid that covers the hay of the stall, the dirt, and a good amount getting onto my jeans. No time to worry about that right now.

Behind me, I can hear James talking to Luke. "What the hell? Why isn't Doc doing that? Is she even qualified?"

Luke seems to be shushing James, but it's not enough and it distracts me. Looking over my shoulder, I glare at James, my voice steely without raising the volume and startling Briarbelle. "Shut up or get out. Your choice."

James sputters, obviously not used to being talked to like that and I decide that my earlier thoughts of him were off-base. Screw him and his doubt that I can handle this. Still, I see Luke grin a little, glad to see his brother get scolded.

Fuck it, I've got this.

I reach deep inside myself, seizing hold of my guts and my knowledge, and with an ease I'm surprised to demonstrate, I deliver the foal successfully.

She lies in the hay, breathing and alive, and Briarbelle lets out an exhausted whinny, calling to her baby. The foal whinnies back, and I finally feel like I can breathe again. Doc takes care of injections for both of them while I put the tools away.

After a moment, Briarbelle moves, nosing and nudging her foal, and we step back and out to let them bond without interruption.

Doc smiles at me, nodding his pleasure at the good job I did. It makes me feel warm inside, but really all the reward I need is lying in the hay in the stall.

My buzz is thwarted when James interrupts the moment, his voice near outrage. "Doc, what was that? Why'd you let her do the delivery? That could've cost us a good foal."

Doc clears his throat, but before he can answer, I jump in, pointing a finger towards the middle of James' muscular chest. "He let me do it because he knew I could. Briarbelle is fine, the foal is fine and I'm fine. The only person not fine is… you. You were the one out of control, raising your voice and scaring her while I was trying to save the foal's life."

His eyes flash fire, and I wonder what's about to come out of his mouth. I'm sure it'll be a doozy. But I'm almost disappointed with what he comes up with. "You've got a real bitch streak in you, you know that?"

I laugh, dismissing him from my mind even as he stands in front of me. "As if I haven't been called that before. Try for some originality next time, why don't ya?"

Doc tries to break the tension, yanking back on an invisible halter. "Okay, let's rein it in. Get it… rein? It's a horse joke."

Not getting the laughs he was hoping for, he gives up and focuses his attention on Luke. "I was keeping watch the whole time. Briarbelle and her babe are fine. I want them to have antibiotics for a little bit just in case. They'll both need daily checks for the next week, and maybe even some follow up after that. You don't mind, do you?"

Luke nods like a bobblehead, seemingly on board. I feel Doc's eyes on me and glance back at him, as he looks over to James.

Doc nods and continues. "I think checking in will be part of your daily duties, Sophie. You can leave the office early and head out here to check on them as your last duty of the day before heading home."

My stomach churns and my heart stops. Is he serious, come back out here every day for the next week?

Shit.

Well, I guess if I have to deal with Luke, it'll be fine. I'll just cross my fingers and toes that I don't have another run-in with James. Besides, I think Doc's teaching me a lesson here too. You don't have to like your customers, you just have to treat your patients with care and your customers with a bit of respect.

"Sure thing, Doc. Guess I'll be here tomorrow afternoon then."

I nod at Luke, pointedly ignoring James and turn to blow a kiss to Briarbelle, before heading to the sink to wash up as best I can, glad that I wore old jeans.

JAMES

Luke's quietly laughing his ass off at me as Sophie struts out to Doc's truck. I still can't help but watch her go, her dark hair swishing back and forth right above the heart shape of her ass in tight jeans. Total bitch... but she's hotter than the noontime sun, there's no doubt about that.

I'm for sure gonna hate seeing her every day for the next week, but I can handle it as long as I get to watch her leave like that.

Luke leans against one of the barn support beams as Doc and Sophie pull away, giving them a wave while he talks to me out of the side of his mouth. "Damn James, you show off those skills with all the ladies when you're on the circuit? Why, I bet you must take home a woman once a year with game like that."

I jab him on his shoulder, laughing. "Fuck you, my game is just fine. I could take a different woman back to my hotel in every city if I wanted. I wasn't trying to put the moves on that one, just trying to save the foal. Which is supposed to be your job, I might add."

He doesn't take the admonishment like I intended, laughing instead of getting pissed off. "Oh, I was doing my job just fine. Doc wouldn't have allowed her to do that if he wasn't confident. You've been away from the farm too long, James. Besides, Doc's getting old. This ain't the pro tour, where organizers have nothing but top-flight docs on call all the time. That pretty girl needed to learn. Also, I was rather enjoying watching my famous little brother go down in flames of his own making."

My face screws up, slightly pissed. I've been hearing it from Mark for years now, I don't need this shit from Luke, too. "Goddammit Luke, I ain't famous. What the hell are you talking about? I just ride bulls, not like I'm a movie star or some shit."

Luke brushes off his hands on his jeans and heads back into the barn to fetch his hat. Jamming it on his head, he turns and points towards the house. "You keep saying that. We've watched every ride you make that's televised. I saw the signs in the audience in Vegas, what those women were holding up. 'Ride me, James' ... 'Bennett's Bitch'. Oh, and just a little FYI... Mom was pissed as a hornet about that one especially. You wanna say you're not famous, that's fine. You can lie to yourself, you can lie to me about it. Next time you really start thinking it though, I'll make sure to bring up those signs and remind Mom. You can see what she has to say about the matter. Spoiler alert; it ain't gonna be pleasant."

He flashes a wide toothy grin at me, and I know he'll damn well do it just to rile Mama up and aim her my direction.

"Kiss my ass, Luke," I growl, knowing I can't win this argument. "I guess I'll head out to the back pasture and see how many more sections of fence I can get done before dinner again. I'll leave you here with your horses."

I give him a middle finger salute after surreptitiously making sure Mama isn't on the porch, and head out, his laughter ringing behind me.

While I drive the ATV with its cart of supplies out, I fume about Luke and his bullshit. Yeah, I make more money than most farmboys and a few people might know of me. But it's only for a few years. Bull riding isn't an old man's game and I'm by no means getting rich.

So fuck them. I'm riding bulls because of me. Getting out to the fence, I work my ass off all day again, my thoughts mainly focused on the fence, the ranch, and how we're gonna keep it running. I'm not totally selfish, I'll do what I can even if it means missing some of the smaller events on the circuit. But I have to be my own man too, not third fiddle in some fucked up version of *King Lear* or something.

Unbidden, Sophie keeps slashing into the pictures moving across my brain, feisty and sassy, self-assured and not taking any shit, especially from me. I thought she was going to slap me when she got in my face, her eyes fiery and her lips wet and juicy... yeah, she's got a face as pretty as the rest of her.

In the moment, it pissed me off. But in hindsight, it makes me smile a bit. That touch of wild fire is intriguing, and so similar to the one in my core. That spark is what ignites inside me every time I climb on the back of a bull. I've been riding bulls since I was a boy, growing up in the ranks of small-time amateur rodeos, even when travel was difficult. Pops had always gone to bat for me, telling Mama that I just had a little more of a wild side to me than most folks and riding bulls was a damn fine way to let it out. "Better than a lot of kids, Louise," Pops said the one time Mama protested really hard. "Too many of them going out, gettin' drunk and starting fights in bars. At least James has a chance to *buy* a big house instead of *go* to the big house."

I smile at the memory, still hearing his voice in my mind as he would call me his "Wild Child" and tell Mama that's why I was last. Because if they'd had me first, I'd have been an only child.

But I haven't been on a bull in months, not since Pops passed, and I told Mark I'd spend the whole summer on the ranch instead of blowing in and out like usual. Nope, I've been too busy busting my ass getting things straightened out before finals in November.

Of course, busting my ass means a lot of doing the same thing, day in and day out… fence, cattle check, eat, sleep, repeat. I hate to sound bitter, even to my own ears, because I know Pops worked so hard to buy and keep this land. And he raised us right on this ranch too. But Mark was always Pops' right-hand man, the firstborn golden child to carry on the family legacy. I don't fault Pops for that, or even Mark for being a bit bossy.

I'd have never been right for running this whole place anyway. There's a piece of me already on the lookout for an escape, back to the rodeo, a new town every weekend, the adrenaline rush of strapping myself to a bucking bull and hanging on for dear life and eight seconds.

Riding a bull is like nothing else. You can prep, you can rosin up your glove and cinch that rope in tight, but when the bull just decides to say fuck you and do something you never could have prepared for, nothing matters.

The argument with Sophie this morning was kinda like that, an unexpected ride of excitement in what I thought would be the same old day. My mind swept back to her sneering at my "unoriginality" as though she was disappointed I didn't insult her better.

After watching how she handled the situation with Briarbelle, and honestly, the situation with me, I realize I don't really want to insult her again.

Hell, maybe I owe her an apology when she comes out here tomorrow.

Maybe.

The dinner bell rings across the pasture and I finish the last tie on this section, realizing that my fingers have been damn productive while my mind wandered. One more solid day of work and I think we'll be able to move the cattle over.

That thought makes me feel good as I bring in the ATV, putting it away before topping off the tank with the gas can just like Pops taught us. Mark and Luke come in around the same time, and after washing up, we all stumble in and sit down around the table, passing around a casserole dish of noodles and veggies.

Before I can eat a single bite, Mama can't wait any longer. "So how's Briarbelle doing?"

Luke grins around a big spoonful of casserole, nodding. "She's doing just fine, her foal too. Little mare with paint spots like her momma. Doc came out with his new assistant, Sophie. She did the delivery, even with the complications."

"Oh, I didn't know he had someone working with him now," Mama says, very interested. "It's about time. That man runs all over the county and he's not much older than I am."

Mark interrupts, gruffly correcting her while I keep my mouth shut, not wanting to step anywhere near this conversation. "He's near seventy years old and should be retired, Mama. You're in your fifties and still move like a woman ten years younger. That's nowhere near the same thing."

Mama just nods, patting Mark's hand comfortingly like his grumpy ass is normal, although I guess it mostly is, especially these days.

"You're too sweet, honey. I think I'll have to go out to the barn and see her tonight after dinner. By the way Luke, what kind of complications? Anything we need to be worried about?"

Luke shakes his head, sipping at his glass of iced tea. "Nope. Just needed some help delivering, but all is well now. Doc said that

Sophie would come by and make daily checks for about a week just to make sure though. Isn't that right, James?"

I look up, feigning ignorance. "Huh? Oh yeah, right... she's coming out tomorrow to check on them and bring the antibiotic dose."

Mama eyeballs me, and I can feel her piercing gaze delving into the deepest parts of my brain like the lie detector she's always been. "What are you not telling me?"

I shrug, seriously wishing we could move on. I smell lemon pie, and while it's not my favorite, it's a damn sight better than talking about this. "Nothing really. I might not have been gracious about her doing the delivery instead of Doc."

Luke's mouth drops open, and I know what he's going to say even before he says it. "That's what you call it? Not gracious? She had to tell you to shut up or get out so she could do the delivery and then you called her a bitch."

Mama screeches, slamming her fork down on the table. "You did *what*?!"

"Mama I—"

That's all I'm able to get out before she continues her scolding. "I didn't raise a son of mine to call a lady a name like that, especially when she was just helping. What were you thinking?"

I'm silent, knowing that I not only crossed a line, but hopped way over into no-man's land when I said that as far as Mama is concerned.

Luke helps me out, and I consider just yelling at him later instead of taking a pitchfork to his ass. "The best part was after he called her... that... " he waffles. "She tells him to try for some originality next time! She swatted him away like a mosquito in the spring."

He laughs, unable to control it until Mark gives him an evil eye. Never mind, the pitchfork's too good for Luke... I think the chainsaw sounds about right.

Mark sees nothing humorous in any of it, though for him, that's just normal. "That's enough. Guys... really? She's gonna be out here again tomorrow? Sounds like you owe her an apology, James."

I know he's right, hell I'd already come to the same conclusion myself, but it chafes to have your bossy big brother tell you what to do, even if that's what he's always done. Maybe moreso *because* that's what he's always done. Bossy Big Brother. "Yeah, thanks genius. Like I didn't come up with that before lunch."

Mama heads off the argument at the pass, sounding pleased for some reason. I guess she has been pretty devoid of female company recently. "She's coming in the afternoon? Sounds like you should apologize and invite her to dinner too. If she's new in town, she probably needs some friends, not some grumpy old boys too stupid to do the right thing when it smacks them in the face."

I grimace, but say nothing. I'll apologize, but I'm not asking her to dinner.

It must show on my face, because Mama turns hard eyes on me, picking up her fork again in that way that says she's about to lay down the law, and the Lord above won't change what she's about to say. "Apology *and* dinner. You won't eat at my table until she gets both."

I sigh, knowing her threat is real. One time she even made Pops eat outside when he was being stubborn about something the Pastor said, and Pops went off on him. Pops ate outside on the porch steps for a week until he became the better man and apologized. "Yes ma'am."

"That's my boy," Mama says sweetly. "Now, who'd like some lemon pie?"

Read the full book here!

ABOUT THE AUTHOR

Bennett Boys Ranch:
Buck Wild | | Riding Hard | | Racing Hearts

Dirty Fairy Tales:
Beauty and the Billionaire | | Not So Prince Charming | | Happily
Never After

Get Dirty:
Dirty Talk | | Dirty Laundry | | Dirty Deeds | | Dirty Secrets

Irresistible Bachelors:
Anaconda | | Mr. Fiance | | Heartstopper
Stud Muffin | | Mr. Fixit | | Matchmaker
Motorhead | | Baby Daddy | | Untamed

Connect with Lauren Landish
www.laurenlandish.com
admin@laurenlandish.com
www.facebook.com / lauren.landish